Blink of her Eye
By Adrian Cousins

Copyright © 2024 Adrian Cousins

All rights reserved. This book or any portion thereof may not be reproduced or used in any manner whatsoever without the author's express written permission except for the use of brief quotations in a book review.

This book is a work of fiction. Names, characters, businesses, schools, places, locales, and incidents are either products of the author's imagination or used in a fictitious manner. Any resemblance to actual persons, living or dead, or actual events is purely coincidental.

...

www.adriancousins.co.uk

Also by Adrian Cousins

The Jason Apsley Series
Jason Apsley's Second Chance
Ahead of his Time
Force of Time
Calling Time
Beyond his Time

Deana Demon or Diva Series
It's Payback Time
Death Becomes Them
Dead Goode
Deana – Demon or Diva Series Boxset

The Frank Stone Series
Eye of Time
Blink of her Eye

Before you dive in ... have you read Eye of Time?

Hello, and thanks for purchasing this book. Blink of her Eye, my tenth novel, is the second book in the Frank Stone series. If you haven't already, you may want to (and I heartily recommend you do) read Eye of Time before turning the page or swiping left on your eReader.

You have ... great, thank you!

Okay, you're up to speed with Frank's previous adventures, so please don't let me hold you back ... dive in and join Jayne and Frank as they face the fiendish plans Hartland, The Hooded Claw, has in store for them.

Oh, how remiss of me, I haven't mentioned Alf. Well, read on and meet a very special pooch ... he's quite something.

Prologue

Present Day

Love is in The Air

"That'll be eight-fifty."

Craig threw a tenner on the bar, not once averting his eyes from the widescreen TV broadcasting the live game. Being a lifelong Gooner, and the fact his team were about to take a penalty kick at the business end of the second half during the North London derby, attempting to secure a much-needed point, he wasn't too fussed about whether he received the change.

In a similar fashion to the other fifty-or-so punters peering up at the screen, he held his breath, preparing to celebrate the certain goal.

"Oi, you're not see-through, Sonny Jim. You're blocking my view."

"Do what?" Craig swivelled around to come face to face with an elderly gent perched on a bar stool beside him. "Naff off, gramps. Shouldn't you be pissing your pants in some care home or rinsing your dentures?"

Whilst demonstrating surprising agility, the elderly gent slid off his stool and, at an inch taller and a couple of stones heavier than Craig, nudged his forehead towards the younger man's nose.

"D'you wanna try saying that again, Sonny Jim? Hear me right, laddie, you're liable to find that pretty face of yours rearranged by my knuckles."

Craig raised a placating hand. Although he knew the vast majority of the local headcases, drug lords, and their associated enforcers, this was a new face. And despite being of an age that warranted a free bus pass and senior concession to most attractions and sporting venues, something about his demeanour suggested he might be connected to the sort of characters whose radar Craig wished to avoid landing on. Craig could handle himself against the best of them but, something nagging, that self-defence voice in his subconscious suggested the old git wasn't one to be messed with.

Without another word exchanged, the elderly gent retook his seat. Craig swivelled around and plucked up his pint, ensuring he leaned sideways so he and the old git behind him could watch the penalty kick.

"Jeeesus! You frigging knob," Craig bellowed when witnessing the ball hurtling over the crossbar towards row Z in The Clock End of the Emirates Stadium.

A comment that probably ranked as the politest when compared to the cacophony of vociferations of disgust offered up by the disgruntled patrons of the Star and Garter. The backstreet, Neolithic boozer, a throwback to the days when the local *'firm'* frequented the back rooms as their headquarters, had witnessed its fair share of the North London borough's bar brawls. Tonight, there appeared to be all the signs that another one was about to ensue.

However, as the hundred-million-so-called-super-star held his head in his hands, seemingly shocked that a man of his quality could miss the target from twelve yards, Dazza, the landlord, wielded his weapon of choice. Two hefty raps on the bar with his extensively dented, skull-crushing baseball bat effectively halted a few punters who appeared ready to hurl their half-drunk pints at the seventy-two-inch screen.

Dazza, or 'Hairpin' as he was often referred to due to the switchback form of his large, previously broken hooter – a byproduct of days when an enforcer for the *firm* – jabbed the bat towards a lad with his arm aloft, ready to launch his pint.

"Oi, knobhead."

The youth, a well-known hoodlum from the local estate, wearing a retro Arsenal shirt, still with the glass poised, primed and ready to hurl as if posing for one of Banksy's more famous pieces, shifted his focus towards the bar and away from the live pictures of Arsenal's latest inept record signing.

"Not in my boozer. Put the glass down and naff off."

Although Dazza held a certain reputation, which his heavyweight frame, collection of amateurish tattoos and cauliflower ears supported, he wasn't the person most punters feared. Carol, the petite landlady, a woman of advancing years, despite her hankering for youth by insisting on wearing animal-print miniskirts, ensured all patrons abided by the house rules. Her viperous tongue, ghoulish bulging eyes, and a pair of four-inch stilettoes were all the martinet required to enforce order.

In one well-practised swift movement, Carol scooted through the standing-room-only bar, relieved the lad of his half-consumed beverage, and rapped her ring-festooned fist across the back of his head whilst simultaneously forcing the point of her heel into the lad's metatarsals. Despite her diminutive stature, her heel applied at least two thousand PSI on the delicate foot bone. The cracking of which could be heard above the football commentator politely verbalising what most punters thought about Arsenal's latest signing.

Craig tutted. "Useless, git. My grannie could have scored that," he muttered before taking a swig of his pint.

Dazza slapped the one-fifty change on the bar and nodded to the back room. "Tommo and Jolene are waiting. I'll be through in a minute when this bunch of scrotes calm down." Dazza, now with his bat tucked under his arm, presumably satisfied his vicious missus had control of the situation, leaned in close to whisper. "Jolene reckons we're good to go. D-day's next Thursday."

Craig nodded. "Cool. After watching that shower of shite, I'm about ready to blow up the bloody world."

"Shush," he hissed. "Jesus, Craig, if Jolene hears you mouthing off, she'll rip you a good'un, mate."

Craig nodded as he raised his pint to his lips. "Yeah, whatever." He paused before taking a sip. "She's getting too gobby, that one."

"You gonna tell her?" chuckled Dazza.

Craig puffed out his cheeks. "I'm not that frigging stupid."

"I know what you mean. There's no geezer I won't take on, but that Jolene and my Carol are a different bleedin' league."

"Need your missus to sort out that shower of shite." Craig nodded to the TV screen, showing pictures of the Arsenal players with their heads in their hands and the Tottenham team performing a lap of honour after a famous win at the Emirates. A victory that had all but ruined the chances of the Gooners securing the Premier League title.

Dazza snorted a laugh. "Overpaid prissy knobs wouldn't know what hit them. Long gone are the days of Donkey Adams and the like. You wouldn't see him prancing around like a bleedin' fairy, concerned about his hairdo and wearing pink boots."

Dazza laid the bat on the back of the bar and nodded to the far corner where broken-metatarsal-boy and his mates huddled into a bench seat, cowering from the five-foot Carol. Whether they were shitting themselves about further threats of violence or trying to gain some distance from the vision of her rising skirt hemline, who could tell? However, Dazza's bug-eyed missus looked set for the kill.

Craig necked his pint before waving the empty glass. "Give us another. If Jolene's on one, I'm gonna need something to dull the pain."

Dazza plucked up his glass and gestured towards the back room. "Go on, I'll bring it through. Carol can sort these tossers out. On the subject of tossers, I can't watch any more of that shite with those prima donnas prancing around the pitch in Barbie-coloured boots. I mean, what kind of bloke would wear pink frigging football boots, eh?"

Craig snorted an agreement regarding the unacceptable colour of boots that many professional footballers seemed to prefer. He stepped away from the bar, weaved his way through the throng of disgruntled punters, and pushed through the door to the back room.

The faded '70s-styled flock wallpaper, tassel-fringed shades adorning the wall lamps, and the threadbare Axminster carpet were a throwback to the days when the Dempsey boys used the facilities as the headquarters for their racketeering and intimidation business.

Craig's grandfather, when not ensconced in his frequently-visited cell in Belmarsh Prison, worked as hired muscle for 'Slasher' Dempsey, the younger of the brothers who ruled the manor back when the cigarette-stained wallpaper could be considered fashionable. Craig never knew his father, but had inherited his grandfather's penchant for violence and a deep mistrust of authority.

"Tommo," muttered Craig before slumping onto the MFI well-worn black leather sofa whilst keeping a wary eye on the mad blonde woman who made Carol appear angelic.

"You're late, knobhead," snarled Jolene, not once taking her eyes off the screen of her laptop.

As he rocked back on his chair with his feet propped up on the table, Tommo, Jolene's man, smirked at Craig when clocking his discomfort.

Jolene, despite her slight stature, assumed the lead role in the extreme left-wing, loosely-termed terrorist organisation, *Fight Against Right-Wing Tyranny*, or *FART*, for short. With her all too regular displays of her bellicose attitude, she put the fear of God in most who had the misfortune to cross her, which included those arriving late for planned meetings.

Jolene harboured the ideology that only violence on an industrial scale would deliver real and sustained change.

The tyrannical ex-junkie blonde miscreant, sporting a string of petty convictions, an Oxbridge degree, a generous stipend from her stepfather, and a pathological hatred for authority, had recently recruited the other three members to her organisation. A significantly more radical splinter group from other popular extreme left-wing organisations, with the sole purpose of causing chaos.

"I said, you're effin' late," she barked, slamming the lid on her laptop before pinning Craig to the sofa with her well-practised hate stare.

Craig sniffed and shifted nervously in his seat. "I'm here now, ain't I?"

Dazza, the fourth member of the organisation's quartet, kicked open the door whilst clasping two pints of lager before handing one to Craig and taking the seat opposite Jolene.

"Thursday ... this Thursday is when we hit them." Jolene folded her arms and waited for a nod from each man as she glared at them in turn.

"Sure thing." Dazza sipped his pint before offering an agreeing nod as he placed his glass on the plastic tablecloth. "You can get into your father's briefcase? He ain't gonna suspect anything?"

"Stepfather! The git has nothing to do with me. He's just the waster my mother decided to hook up with, alright?"

Tommo snorted a chuckle as Dazza shrunk a few inches in his chair.

"I get it ... stepfather." Dazza held up a placating palm. "But there ain't gonna be no hitches like last time? I'm all for the cause, but I ain't getting my bleedin' head blown off like Rocco."

A month ago, Rocco, the man who shared Jolene's bed before Tommo found himself promoted to that position, had unfortunately miscalculated the chemical ratios, thus blowing himself into a plethora of unidentifiable lumps of flesh. The resulting fireball, which engulfed his rented flat situated in the affluent Cromwell Road, took six fire crews and all night to extinguish. Fortunately, Rocco wasn't known to the authorities. Thus, their newly formed terrorist organisation wasn't connected to the incident which hogged the local news headlines that evening.

"This time, there ain't gonna be no cock-ups. Rocco was a tit and didn't know what he was doing."

"What, you done an online course on how to build a bomb? Watched a YouTube video, have you?" scoffed Dazza, instantly regretting his tone when detecting Jolene's upper lip curl.

"Don't ... be ... a ... dick."

"Alright, I'm just saying, that's all."

"Evening all, as Dixon of Dock Green used to say."

All eyes swivelled to the now-opened door and the man filling the space, holding a salute and sporting a smirk.

"Jolene, Jolene ..." the man sang, dropping his salute and stepping in before closing the door. "Looking as gorgeous and ravishing as ever, I see."

"Who the frig's this old git?" blurted Tommo.

"Shit," hissed Craig.

"Hello again, Sonny Jim." The elderly gent smirked at Craig. "Me and the lad here met earlier, isn't that so? I had to teach the boy some manners."

Jolene shot a look at Craig, who shrugged.

"What the frig—"

"Shut it, Tommo." Jolene barked.

Dazza shot a look at Craig before bug-eyeing Jolene. "Does he know?" he hissed. "Who the frig is he?"

"I, Landlord, is the man who's gonna ensure your little operation doesn't go south. Like I have no desire to know your name, none of you need to know mine. However, my knowledge of explosives is what's going to ensure you don't end up like your compatriot, the unfortunate, dismembered and over-barbecued Rocco."

Craig pointed his pint at the newcomer. "Can we trust him?"

"We can. Anyone want to question my decision?" snarled Jolene.

The three male members of *FART* exchanged glances, all taking turns to shake their heads.

"Alright, lad?" The newcomer smirked as he sank into the sofa beside Craig, tapping the younger man's knee on the way down. "Don't worry, I can't stay long. I need to get back to my care home and flush me dentures through."

"Good. So, with the proper kit, this guy will build for us, it'll be a piece of piss." Jolene shook her head and smirked. "As I said, that knob jockey of a stepfather of mine thinks I've turned over a new leaf. He's agreed to meet me for a coffee in Starbucks on Thursday morning on his way to Westminster." She paused to nod at her man. "Tommo and Craig will be there and cause a disturbance. The Right Honourable Giles Horsley might come across all confident on TV, but I know my stepfather will shit himself when Tommo and Craig start swinging at each other. All I need is a few seconds of distraction to get the gear in his briefcase, and we're set."

Tommo clenched his fist at Craig and smirked. "Gonna break your nose, mate."

Jolene shot Tommo a look.

"Joking, alright? We gotta make it look real, though, yeah?" Tommo shot back, appearing hurt by his woman's glower.

"I couldn't give a shit what you do to each other. Just keep it going long enough to cause a distraction so I can do what I gotta do."

"In your dreams," scoffed Craig, pointing his glass at Tommo before taking a slug of beer.

"Oi!" Jolene jabbed a bony finger at the slouching Craig whilst slapping a hand on her man's chest. "Save it for Thursday." Again, she glanced back and forth between the two men, waiting for their nods.

"You're certain your stepfather will get it into the room? Y'know, won't there be sniffer dogs and shit like that?" Dazza questioned, breaking the silence as the two younger men continued to give each other the eye.

Out of Jolene's eyeline, Tommo shot a couple of 'see you' gestures at Craig.

"Yeah, it'll be cool. He's the frigging Home Secretary, so the security team are hardly gonna think he's got a briefcase full of … you know."

"And you're sure he's only got one protection officer?"

"Yeah. I've told Giles I don't want his bodyguard standing beside us while we chat. He's agreed to make him stand outside."

"That's where I come in?" chimed in Dazza.

"Yup. As soon as Craig and Tommo start throwing punches, you flatten the bodyguard and do a runner."

Dazza nodded.

"Right, any questions?" When no one replied, Jolene slapped her hands on the plastic tablecloth and eased herself upright. "Thursday, we change the world. Where Catesby failed, the *Fight Against Right-Wing Tyranny* will succeed."

"Who's Catesby?" muttered Tommo.

Jolene offered her man an exaggerated eye roll before shooting an acerbic glare at Craig in response to his snorted laugh aimed at Tommo.

"What?" Craig feigned innocence before taking a sip of beer to hide his smirk.

"Oi!" Jolene barked when jabbing her finger at Craig. "If you value your bollocks, I suggest you reel it in."

"You taking the piss?" Tommo flipped his boots off the table but remained in position when his woman slapped her free hand on his shoulder, indicating he should stay seated.

"You two, save it for Thursday." She kept her eyes on Craig, who nodded, and her palm on Tommo's shoulder for a few seconds until she detected his tension dissipate.

"Who's this Catesby geezer, then?"

"Jeeesus," muttered Craig. "Tommo, you are such a thick tosser."

Part 1

1

New Year's Eve 1999

Timekeepers of the Millennium

"Oh, Stephen, haven't you done enough for today? Everyone will be here soon. For one night, can't they leave you alone?" Barbara asked, or more instructed, her husband to come off the phone and out of his study where the senior Whitehall official had been holed up for the best part of the day whilst dealing with one potential disaster after another.

Stephen held up a 'hang on' finger to Barbara as he continued his conversation. "I need an update on the situation immediately. Has the PM been made aware?" He momentarily paused before interrupting. "Yes, man, listen! I'm acutely bloody aware he's attending the New Year's Eve bash at the damn Millennium Dome with the Queen, but the ruddy shit will not only splatter the air conditioning but render it inoperable if this turns out to be a bigger issue than we suspected. Get hold of Cook, the ruddy Foreign Secretary, and confirm that he's aware." A flustered, haggard-looking Stephen Denton slammed the receiver down, then offered his wife, who still clasped the doorframe, his well-practised sorry-it's-work-apologetic smile.

Barbara, dressed in her evening gown, a long glittering number her nineteen-year-old daughter, Phillipa, had persuaded her to pick up in Harrods when enjoying a trip up to 'Town' together a few months back, sashayed into her husband's office.

"Well, you scrub up alright for an old girl," he smirked, poking his tongue into his cheek as he rocked back in his leather-studded swivel chair.

Barbara snorted as she fanned her fingers and placed the tips on her husband's desk. The Georgian window framing her Civil Servant husband would usually offer stunning views of the lawns of their 'modest' six-bedroom Oxfordshire home. However, now early evening and the dark vista obscuring the view, the light from the banker's desk lamp threw back her reflection from the window, causing her to turn her nose up.

Barbara Denton, a rotund woman blessed with an ample frame that any haute couture-designed fashion would struggle to flatter, harboured no desire for evening wear or associated dinner parties.

"I'll take that as a compliment coming from you." She pulled at the sequined material that clung to what the fashion industry would term as her fuller figure. "It's a bit too figure-hugging for my liking, but Philli was insistent we all get dressed up for this special night."

"Well, if you ask me, our daughter could benefit from a few extra pounds. It's a damn pity she hasn't taken after you."

"Fat, you mean?"

"Barbara, have I ever called you fat?"

"No, true, you haven't. But I am."

Stephen tutted. "There's nothing attractive about these waif-like super-models. They're all willowy and underfed. And I can assure you, from this man's perspective, there's nothing womanly about them whatsoever." Stephen added a pronounced nod to force home his point. A mannerism he usually employed when putting a government minister firmly in their place.

"If you say so. But Lord knows why I let Philli talk me into buying it. As you know, I'm a jeans and wellies type of woman."

"Well, you look fabulous. A welcome distraction from all this damn bother."

"What's happened now?"

"Yes, a right ruddy shit storm, I can tell you. Not only have we got the issue that Boris Yeltsin has thrown in the towel and handed power to that loony Putin, which is bound to cause all sorts of instability, but we're also trying to ascertain confirmation that a volley of Scud missiles launched at Chechnya was an intended strike and not some computer malfunction caused by the millennium bug. And now I've been informed that the Ishikawa Nuclear plant is reporting a fault."

"Japan?"

"Yes. Suggestions are being bandied about that the fault may have something to do with the bug."

"Oh, what's actually happened?"

"We don't know. I've just spoken with Tomkins—"

"That man with that debilitating lisp whose wife's now a lesbian?"

"That's him," he chuckled. "Can't blame the girl, can you? I mean, whether she's always preferred the fairer sex or not, after marrying that twit, it's enough to turn her off men for life."

"Stephen, it's not an affliction. I would imagine his wife was probably browbeaten into conforming and married the man to appease everyone but herself. I think it's courageous of her to push against society and follow her heart."

"Yes, of course," Stephen grumbled under his breath, an involuntary action he would perform when knowing his wife was correct. "Anyway, he was saying that it's become apparent that just after midnight there, about three hours ago, the Japanese have reported a fault and a concerning electrical malfunction, which they're frantically trying to investigate."

"Oh dear."

"Let's just hope it's got nothing to do with this bug, and we're not, God forbid, heading for round two of Chernobyl. Christ, and we still have nearly six hours to go until bloody midnight here. God knows what will happen here when Big Ben strikes twelve."

"We'll raise a glass to the new millennium. That's what will happen. You, me, along with all our guests. Oh, did I mention Philli and Tom are bringing a plus one?"

"Plus one?" asked Stephen, furrowing his brow, showing his disapproval.

"Philli has a new man. Apparently, he's a leading light at the Conservative Club and is tipped to run at the next election."

"Who is this leading light bloke that's got my girl all gooey-eyed, then?"

"Giles Horsley."

"Never heard of him."

"He comes from the Horsley family, who own Hallows Hall."

"Oh ... plenty of money, then."

"Yes, buckets of the stuff. Although I must say, I'm a little concerned because Giles is in his early thirties. Phillipa's very mature, but that's a big age gap."

"Oh, don't fuss. I expect our girl will bin him off when the next eligible bachelor waves around his significantly larger wallet."

Barbara offered her husband one of her famous glowers.

"Oh, don't give me that look. Philli's always been materialistic. Spoilt is the word. Anyway, he's got to be better than that hippy bloke she hooked up with last year."

"Yes, well, we'll see. Just be nice, and don't bully the man. You can be a frightening beast at the best of times."

"Hmmm."

"Tom's bringing Suzie."

"Suzie Marchant?" he enquired in a significantly improved lilt.

"Yes."

"Ah, I like Suzie. He could do a lot worse than that girl, could our Tommy."

"I agree. Anyway, you've only got half an hour before they arrive, so I suggest you get your skates on." She dismissively waved her hand at the phone. "Japan's nuclear problems and the Russian transition of power issues will still be there in the morning. Let your team worry about that and give your attention to our guests and our children for one night. I'm sure Mr Blair won't be concerning himself with those problems tonight, so neither should you."

Stephen grunted and nodded as he hauled his considerable bulk from his chair. "Come on, let's have a small G an' T before I change."

Not in her usual stride, her legs now pinned into the wide-gait-restricting gown, Barbara led the way into the kitchen diner. Going by the Georgian façade, the house appeared to be the traditional abode of a successful upper-middle-class family. However, from the inside, the Denton's home could be an advert for open-plan modern living. The sort of minimalist style everyone clambered for and lifestyle magazines promoted.

Barbara had come from humble beginnings. However, now the wife of a man who held real power, accompanied with a befitting salary, unlike the elected politicians who came and went at the whims of the electorate, she'd developed an eye for expensive interior design that quickly became the envy of all her friends.

Without acknowledging his wife, Stephen accepted the drink on offer. His furrowed brow formed deep trenches as he studied the television broadcasting the early evening news.

"That's Frank Stone, isn't it?"

Barbara, who busied herself with the final checks to ensure her dinner preparations were all on track, shot a look at the TV. The fifty-something-year-old man being interviewed, who appeared to be standing somewhere in central London with a backdrop of a long line of rough sleepers, was indeed her old friend, Frank Stone.

Although they'd lost touch many years ago, Frank, who now managed an influential charitable organisation, had become a bit of a celebrity. Frank had always had a personable way about him, a certain magnetism that drew people in, a trait he used to great effect when banging his drum about those less fortunate.

Stephen turned and raised an eyebrow at his wife. "That's him, isn't it?"

"Yes, that's Frank."

"You heard from him lately? I know you used to be close."

Barbara glowered at her husband.

"Sorry ... I didn't mean to ... well, you know."

"I know." She flashed him a tight smile. "Come on, hurry up. Everyone will be here soon."

Stephen nodded before upending his glass. "What about Sarah? Did that airhead daughter of ours ever let you know if she's going to grace us with her presence tonight?"

Barbara lifted a saucepan lid and peered inside, careful not to allow the steam to spoil her makeup. "No, not a peep."

Stephen placed his glass down before cupping a hand on the small of her back. "I'll go and change. We did our best with her. You know that, don't you?"

Barbara nodded but couldn't look up at her husband for fear that tears would come. She's spent far too long putting her face on for it to be spoilt by tears for her daughter.

"It wasn't your fault."

"It was! Everything that's happened is because of what I did."

"Babs. Barbara, look at me." When she failed to comply, Stephen reached out and gently lifted his wife's chin. "Babs, it wasn't your fault."

Barbara huffed and nodded. "I know, but that doesn't stop the guilt."

Hovering by her side, not knowing what to do, Stephen continued to rub her back comfortingly.

"Go! You need to change. I'm fine. Sarah, or talking about her, is not going to spoil tonight, alright?"

"Alright," he nodded and smirked. "You look ravishing, by the way."

Barbara shot him a teary smile. "Oh, go on, you old fool." She playfully slapped his arm, sending him on his way.

Although twenty-one years had passed since those traumatic few months at the latter end of 1979, time hadn't fully healed her emotional wounds. A few months before the dawn of the 'decade of decadence', as the 1980s would become known, David Bolton's body, Barbara's first husband, had been discovered in a layby near Fairfield Woods.

A few weeks prior to that event, Barbara had booted her husband out of the marital home after discovering his infidelity – well, chest fondling another woman at work. Her husband's murder, along with that of an army veteran, remained an unsolved case to this day. Both men had suffered a single execution-style shot to the head, and the police alluded that both murders heralded a 'contract killing' look about them.

Despite their marital difficulties, for Barbara and their five-year-old daughter, Sarah, as expected, these events had blown their world apart. If her husband, a supermarket manager, had died as the police suggested, it served to confirm she never really knew the man.

Just at the point when Barbara believed her life couldn't get any worse – and probably because of her lack of concentration when wallowing in a whirlpool of depression – a month later, she caused a multiple pile up on the M1 motorway. Seven cars, two articulated lorries and a white van ended up in a crumpled heap, resulting in the closure of England's main artery for over seven hours. Three deaths, five hospitalisations, and a charge of death by dangerous driving were levied at Barbara.

However, the driver of the car which Barbara rear-ended just happened to be a rising star in the civil service who also enjoyed influential connections in the Justice Department. Stephen Denton had not only saved Barbara's and Sarah's lives when administering roadside first aid, but he'd engineered the right team to ensure she avoided a custodial sentence. Then – and although twelve years her senior – eight months later, he married her.

In the space of twelve months, Barbara had experienced what most wouldn't in a lifetime: a marriage separation, her husband murdered, her daughter critically ill after the accident, causing the death of three other road users, being arrested and facing prison, meeting and marrying a man of influence, and becoming pregnant with twins to boot.

For Sarah Bolton, the events of that year negatively shaped her life. At the tender age of five, she'd lost her daddy, then spent the years in and out of hospital as surgeons attempted to repair her broken spine, the direct result of her mother's careless driving. It's fair to say the mother-and-daughter relationship took a bit of a nose dive over the following years and remained tense ever since. Now, a twenty-five-year-old drifter, Sarah hadn't spoken with her mother or stepfather for nigh on a year.

Barbara dabbed the corners of her eyes with a tissue as she watched Frank Stone through the steam rising from the simmering vegetables. Frank had been David Bolton's closest friend. Although she'd always liked Frank, his rising fame, exacerbated by his constant TV appearances and feature articles in the Sunday broadsheets, only served to haul back memories Barbara wished to forget.

Movement in her peripheral vision hauled Barbara from her wool-gathering gaze. Her mouth gaped as she shot her head around to look through to the hallway.

"Hello, Mum."

Fixated by the sight of her daughter and incapable of closing her parted lips as she bug-eyed the markedly altered frame of her eldest child, Barbara didn't offer a greeting.

"I let myself in ... I still have a key."

"Why ... what—"

"You invited me," Sarah interrupted her mother. "You said as much on my Christmas card."

"I know ... but—"

"This?" she interrupted again, smirking when glancing down and rubbing her hand over her swollen tummy. "I'm due in three weeks."

"Oh ... who, who's the father?"

Still rubbing her hand back and forth, Sarah lifted her head and shrugged. "I don't know ... it doesn't matter."

"Oh."

"All that matters is for me and my daughter to love each other. A *proper* mother and daughter relationship."

Barbara winced, almost feeling the blade of her daughter's verbal knife sinking between her shoulders.

"It's a girl, then?" she croaked.

"Yup," Sarah emphasised the 'p' as she nodded vigorously. "I'll shower her with love ... no one needs material things; just love."

Barbara knew that to be a dig at Stephen. Her husband had not only saved Sarah's life when kneeling in his Saville-Row suit on the rain-soaked M1 in December 1979, but he'd then brought her up as his own and showered her with gifts. Stephen had provided her with a privileged upbringing, spoilt if you like, but Sarah had made every effort to reject him.

Barbara could feel that knife twisting.

"She's gonna be the best thing that ever happened to me. My baby girl will radiate positive energy, be at one with nature, and shine light into the world."

Barbara raised an eyebrow whilst arching her back in an attempt to halt that metaphorical twisting knife. Her husband recently used the term 'airhead' when Sarah came into the conversation. Her daughter's last statement served to confirm Stephen's description.

Since her latter teenage years, Sarah had strolled through a succession of beliefs, all of which were apparently her calling at the time. Now her daughter, pregnant daughter, she corrected herself, sounded like that elastic woman who ran those regularly missed yoga classes.

During the last class Barbara dragged herself to, *Ms Elastic* introduced a 'get to know your womb' session, which involved sitting cross-legged, no mean feat for Barbara, whilst humming rhythmically to the sound of piped panpipe music and chanting 'hello womb'. Apart from being excruciatingly embarrassing, after giving birth to three children, two of whom popped out within a minute of each other, she'd recently informed her gynaecologist that she and her womb weren't getting on too well. So, despite *Ms Elastic's* best intentions, the 'getting to know your womb' session just about put the kibosh on her Thursday evening sessions at the local gym.

Ms Elastic was that sort who packed her kids' lunchboxes with hummus and berries instead of Cheestrings and Monster Munch, baked flourless raw chocolate avocado brownies, and banished all recognisable furniture in favour of Moroccan rugs and patchwork beanbags. Anyway, Sarah was now starting to sound like *Ms Elastic*.

"Look, Mum, for your granddaughter's wellbeing, we need to bury the hatchet. I want her to know you and Stephen, but she can't be exposed to negative energy. My daughter must be surrounded by positive vibes that provide her with the environment conducive to soaking up and sharing love."

"Yes, well, I'm all for burying the hatchet. You know there's nothing I'd like more. And, of course, Stephen and I will help you financially—"

"No." Sarah raised her palm to interrupt her mother. "I can't have her tainted by materialism. She's special. She's going to bring light into a world that's full of darkness."

Barbara, somewhat bemused by her daughter's statement, focused on the thought of becoming a grandmother. However, as the two women hovered awkwardly, neither knowing what to say next, little did they know the 'light' that child would orchestrate in the future.

2

2015

Kiss Me Hardy

After ducking under the royal-blue canopy, Frank shook his umbrella before bounding up the stone steps into the foyer of the Barrington Club. Although a Knight of the Realm, an honour bestowed upon him by Queen Elizabeth a few years back, his title did not afford Frank Stone the right to enter the prestigious gentlemen's club situated in an offensively opulent part of Knightsbridge. The Barrington Club existed for gentlemen who came from old money, not self-made millionaires, such as Frank.

If the truth be known, rather than enter this establishment for the privileged, Frank would prefer a pint and a pickled egg in the Lord Nelson Pub near his hometown of Sheringham.

During his regular Friday evening jaunts to his favoured drinking hole, which sported stunning views across the cruel North Sea and far enough away from those plaguey day-trippers, Frank would chew the cud with the locals. Usually, a variety of topics, from disrespectful tourists who plundered the seaside town from spring through autumn, the abject performance of the government, to the disturbing relaxation of planning laws. The latter of the three having given rise to an ever-increasing emergence of construction sites for second homes for the wealthy, which he and the regulars who held up the bar believed blighted the picturesque if not largely unblemished, North Norfolk coastline.

Of course, as many commentators and trolls on social media pointed out with some regularity, Frank was on dangerously thin ice when publicly voicing his concerns about the nouveau riche. However, little did they know, or could ever know, of Frank's previous existence.

An existence expunged thirty-six years ago.

After building a globally successful firm of architects sporting a turnover that ran into the millions, Frank, his wife Jayne, their four daughters, and their families enjoyed all the trappings of luxury of the very people he openly criticised.

However, those trolls couldn't deny that Frank's charity, which had just celebrated twenty-five years of existence and to which he personally donated a significant portion of his wealth, had become a force to be reckoned with in changing government policy regarding support for the homeless.

Two miles as the crow flies, in an easterly direction from where he now stood, sits the South Bank, the London Eye and Jubilee Park. For Frank, this area holds a particular significance because that's where he spent many years as a rough sleeper and the very location he'd time-travelled from 2015 to 1979.

Thirty-six years after that event, and now in 2015 again, his life had taken on a significantly different trajectory from how his first one had panned out. In this version of the new millennium, he wasn't 'smelly Frank', the hobo, but Sir Frank Stone, a successful entrepreneur, charity mogul, and general pain in the backside for the government and the elite. Frank Stone had made a career of calling out society's unfairness.

"Good afternoon, Sir Frank," stated the concierge, offering a kowtowing bow as the man, a few years younger than Frank's sixty-six years, encouraged Frank to step forward with a welcoming wave of his arm.

"Please, it's Frank. I don't use my title."

Although Frank assumed he'd never been acquainted with the acquiescent doorman, he was aware his face was well known, often interviewed on television. Also, his ageing mug would be regularly splashed across the newspapers and Sunday supplements. Last summer, and against his better judgment, he and Jayne, with their daughters, appeared on the cover of one of those dreadful lifestyle magazines.

Yes, Frank Stone was a celebrity.

"Very good, sir. May I?" the affable doorman questioned with a raised eyebrow, offering to take Frank's umbrella. After stowing the dripping item in the stand, he reached behind the counter before presenting a cellophane-wrapped package to Frank. "House rules, I'm afraid, sir. All gentlemen must be appropriately dressed."

Frank curled his lip as he glanced down at the royal-blue tie now on offer, held by the doorman in a similar fashion that a sommelier might when offering up a bottle from the cellar. Frank reluctantly nodded as the assiduous concierge unwrapped the item.

Not that he'd purposefully bowled up to the meeting without what he suspected to be the required attire, but Frank had been in London for a couple of days to attend to charity business and, as Chairman, he set the dress code for his organisation.

As Phil Collins had stated. *No Jacket Required.* As Frank Stone stipulated, neither was a tie.

Whilst Frank expertly spun the blue silk into a Windsor knot, the doorman made a call to announce his arrival to the man Frank had agreed to meet after a chance encounter on Cromer Pier not a fortnight ago and that telephone call the following day.

With his gifted tie hanging loosely below his open collar, Frank tucked his thumbs into the front pockets of his jeans and took in the foyer's décor whilst the doorman attended to a motorcycle courier delivering a padded envelope.

Frank chuckled as he watched the doorman, sporting an open palm, force the courier to retreat down the stone steps to the pavement. His demeanour made it abundantly clear that no leather-clad biker could enter the dark-wooden-panelled, marble-floored foyer. A floor that threw up echoes of an unseen man's gait that reverberated off the polished marble arches.

Akin to Hitchcock-esque styled rising tension, and with ever-increasing trepidation, Frank listened to the sonance produced by those clanging shoe-segs, or Blakey's as they were sometimes referred to, as they, and the man wearing them, ominously approached. Eventually, those echoes gave way to the clunk of a door handle before the approaching man entered the foyer and flashed his vampiric grin.

What stood before Frank could be described as a beacon of sartorial elegance. His attire an ode to timeless style and attention to detail. From the polished Oxfords, the pristine double-breasted suit, the glint of his gold cufflinks, and the perfectly positioned, presidential folded pocket square, which added flair without shouting attention, all confirmed the man to be well groomed and of significant substance – Douglas Hartland – The Hooded Claw.

"Sir Frank. Marvellous to see you again, old chap."

"Maybe for you. Not for me."

"No," he guffawed. "You've always had the ability to make me chuckle, you know, Frank?" The Hooded Claw thrust out his hand, allowing his hooded eyelids to narrow as his grey eyes pierced Frank's skull.

"You know I'm not coming back to help you, don't you? I have no intention of ever stepping into that nut-house organisation ever again." Frank authoritatively stated whilst taking the offer of Hartland's proffered right hand. Frank squeezed and held on tightly as The Hooded Claw attempted to pull away. "Let's be clear. I'm done with time-travel."

Hartland torpidly blinked like a sleepy owl whilst battling for supremacy on the hand-crushing technique.

"As I said a few weeks ago, we'd appreciate some of your time on a consultancy basis, nothing more," he affirmed with a languid reveal of his teeth and a barely audible murmur. When his mouth eventually formed a grin, his grey owlish eyes conveyed the opposite.

Frank opened his palm and nodded, still holding The Hooded Claw's glare.

"I'm not guaranteeing that either."

"But you're here, are you not?"

"I am." Frank nodded and paused. "Only because you mentioned my son."

"Ah, yes, the Right Honourable Andrew Barrington-Scott. A name that has some significance to our club, of course."

Douglas nodded to the great crest positioned above the concierge's desk. "Your son's forbearers created our club over two hundred years ago, you know."

"Andrew is *my* flesh and blood. My ex-wife married a Barrington-Scott, so technically, those ancestors have nothing to do with Andrew. Also, my boy wouldn't step foot in this place." Frank's acerbic tone when uttering the word 'place' wasn't lost on Douglas.

"You don't believe in such establishments?"

"Not really ... boys' clubs for the privileged few."

"Agreed, but necessary. The ruling elite require these sorts of establishments. In the lounges and restaurants of places like this is where the important decisions are made. Westminster is just the public face of governance. Here is where the action's at."

Frank offered a wry smile.

Douglas slapped Frank's shoulder.

"Listen to me, prattling on," he chuckled, which morphed into a whine as he pointedly assessed Frank's inappropriate attire. Douglas considered, apart from complying with the club's rules, the application of a silk tie achieved little in improving the man's appearance. "Hmmm, oh dear, old chap. We'll probably have to step through to the Morning Lounge." He paused as he leaned forward. "Denim is not really acceptable in here. So, rather than upset a few of the more conservative members and avoid them raising a bushy eyebrow at me, we'll enjoy a drink and a catch-up through here."

Frank snorted a chuckle.

"This way, old chap." Douglas waved to a heavy oak door sporting the nameplate stating, 'William Lounge'. "Us chaps call it the Morning Lounge, but it's named after William Pitt the Younger," Douglas added when clocking Frank's bemused look. He jauntily hopped forward to grab the door handle before, in a similar manner to the doorman, waving at the open doorway for Frank to step through.

Although Frank hadn't frequented a gentlemen's club, the décor was as he expected, as in a throwback to an era that had long since faded in history, which now only existed in these four walls and others alike. Churchill, Disraeli, and William Pitt himself could be imagined nestled into wingback Queen Anne chairs, sipping single malts whilst discussing politics and enjoying the comfort of a warming hearth. Of course, that couldn't have happened despite Disraeli's life just spanning the years when the former and latter Prime Ministers of our green and pleasant land existed.

With a wave of his hand, Douglas offered Frank a chair. Then, in one well-practised swift movement, he flicked back the seat of his jacket, tugged up his trousers at the knees, gracefully guided his posterior into the seat opposite, and waved at the steward to gain his attention.

"Nice place."

"It is, isn't it? You know, in this very room, in fact this very chair, that back in 1996, I had a word in the right ear with an old acquaintance of mine and pretty much ensured the Millennium Wheel secured the winning bid in the British Landmark competition."

"The London Eye, which you bunch of ... well, whoever you are, send people back in time."

"Correct, Frank, we do. If you remember that little chat we enjoyed all those years ago, that large Ferris Wheel on the South Bank holds in place a wormhole to the past. A portal which enables us at The Correction Years Association to change history and thus prevent future disasters. Before that, it was a touch hit and miss, to say the least. God knows how many travellers we lost before the millennium. Still, I certainly wouldn't have fancied travelling with the odds of surviving not much better than winning the lottery."

"Not something I'm likely to forget, is it?" Frank raised a questioning eyebrow.

"No," Hartland chortled. "And look at you now." He raised an appraising hand. "No longer a stinking old tramp, but a Knight of the Realm, no less, a successful businessman and a bit of a celebrity, I'm told."

Frank gurned as he loosened his tie another inch lower before shifting forward in his seat.

"Look, I know you can send people through time, but how come you still seem the same? You haven't changed. How can that be?"

"I don't follow, old chap."

"Thirty-six years ago, when I was living on the streets, your crack team of SAS types scraped me off the pavement and plonked me in your office—"

"Ah, no, that wasn't thirty-six years ago," interrupted The Hooded Claw. "That was about three months in the future in this year ... 2015 ... the year we are living in."

"Yes, okay. I get that. But how come I've lived thirty-six years in the past since meeting you, and now here I am again ... but you haven't changed?"

"Time-travel, old boy."

"But—"

Douglas held his palm aloft to halt Frank's questioning as the steward placed two monogrammed paper coasters and two large single malts on the ornate marquetry surface of the coffee table. A piece of antique furniture that appeared to have originated from an era before Disraeli occupied Number Ten. Frank pondered if furniture could listen, the tales it could recite. Douglas nodded a thanks to the steward before lowering his hand.

"Can't be too careful who overhears our conversation. Walls have ears." He tapped the side of his nose, allowing his hooded eyelids to drop to half-mast.

"They said that during the war."

"Correct." Douglas plucked up his cut-glass tumbler, using it as a pointer as he lowered his voice a couple of octaves. "That was a particularly tricky period for our organisation. Bloody difficult to run ops when Jerry was pounding the capital with bombs and those blasted doodlebugs."

"And why didn't your organisation stop that war before it happened? If you can see the future, then surely that would have been a high priority?"

"That's precisely what I argued for at the time. I was overruled because data suggested Chamberlain's Appeasement talks in '38 would achieve what the man himself claimed ... peace for our time. We got that one rather wrong, I'm afraid."

"Err ... how old are you?"

"Oh, that's rather an impertinent question. Now, I would call you a friend, but it's not good form to ask a chap's age, old boy."

"Well, whatever, good form or not, I'm assuming we are of a similar age?" Frank paused whilst Hartland swallowed the double measure in one swift movement. "I was born in '49 ... and even if you're ten years my senior, that could only make you a glint in your father's eye in '38."

Hartland's jovial demeanour switched to his trademark vampiric glower. An expression Frank had never forgotten despite the passage of time. Douglas Hartland, The Hooded Claw, with his permafrost lour, harboured the ability to freeze the fiery river of Phlegethon.

"Frank ... how old I am or how *my* organisation operates is of no concern to you. As I told you all those years ago, before *we* provided you the opportunity to live your life for a second time, we operate outside the boundaries of time. Which, I might add, mere mortals, such as your good self, do not need to concern yourself with."

Frank huffed and slumped in his chair after snatching up his glass, the ice cubes clinking as he sniffed its content. A pint of the local Norfolk fare would have been his preferred tipple. The landlord at The Lord Nelson always offered a monthly special, some local cottage industry banging out a new ale with an incredulous name. *Clergy's Prayer* being last month's offering. But, hey, when in Rome, as they say. He sipped the whisky, allowing The Hooded Claw to continue.

"The Correction Years Association is essential in ensuring the world order is maintained and future disasters are averted. Without my organisation, we'd be in a right old pickle."

"The China issue you mentioned when you collared me on Cromer Pier."

"Yes, Frank. The *China Fault* ... a particularly nasty event that, unless we stop it, will affect the entire world. A pandemic the likes of which we haven't seen since the Spanish Flu of a hundred years ago, my good chap."

"So, you predict—"

"Data, Frank. We have accurate data about the future."

"Okay, data. So, what do you need me for regarding this *China Fault*, as you call it?"

"Oh, not that nasty event. We have other irons in the fire regarding that one. No, Frank, we need you to assist us with a future event that's a touch closer to home. In fact, just a stone's throw from where we sit enjoying these Babylonian surroundings." Douglas paused as he glanced around, nodding to an elderly gent peering over the top of a copy of The Times. He cleared his throat, shifted forward in his seat, and lowered his voice. "*The Monteagle Fault*, we're calling this one. Now, although not on the scale of the *China Fault*, if not resolved, it has the potential to cause all sorts of unnecessary bother."

"*The Monteagle Fault?*"

"Correct."

"Where's Monteagle? I've never heard of it. You say that's in London?"

"Who, not where, old chap."

Frank shook his head, conveying he was none the wiser, before sipping his whisky.

"Lord Monteagle alerted the authorities of Catesby's plot to blow up the Houses of Parliament."

"Oh … when does this take place?"

"1605 … November the 5th, to be precise."

3

Thank You for the Music

"Taxi," I hollered before sticking my fingers in my mouth to whistle.

The resulting shrill emanating from my lips caused the woman beside me to jump back from the kerb, appearing to be in a state of shock whilst wincing and holding her palm to her ear.

I ignored her glower and proceeded to wave my handbag around above my head, frantically attempting to flag down one of the black cabs that weaved and bobbed through the throng of afternoon traffic along Brompton Road in Knightsbridge.

The woman with the perforated eardrum, along with a few other rubberneckers darting along the pavement outside Harrods, probably thought my actions were that of a demented bag lady. My dishevelled appearance resulted from an ungainly slip in a puddle, not due to a week of sleeping rough. Now in my mid-sixties, dolled up to the nines in a summer dress and rarely-worn compound-fracture-high stilettoes, one of which the heel snapped off when performing my slapstick upending, I guess I could be classed as too old to be wolf-whistling like a hairy-bummed builder from the '80s.

In my defence, with a torn, sodden dress and broken shoes, I heralded a keen sense of urgency to return to my hotel and enjoy a long soak in the bath before changing into something more casual that hadn't been soaked in what appeared to be unmentionable slurry.

As the procession of cabs whizzed past, leaving me stranded and facing the possibility of hobbling up to Sloane Square tube station, that's when I spotted an innocuous event which would become the catalyst to altering my life to such an extent I'd end up questioning my sanity.

The sight of my husband, Frank Stone, standing not a hundred yards away with his arm aloft, hailing a cab, triggered something within me to suggest something wasn't quite right. Frank should be attending a board meeting at his charity and wouldn't be leaving his office for hours.

We'd already celebrated our coral wedding anniversary and, during that lifetime of love and companionship, my husband had never given me any cause to be suspicious of him. However, I harboured a feeling in the pit of my stomach, which suggested all was not well. And, I was pretty sure it had nothing to do with the plate of out-of-season Whitstable oysters I'd just slugged back with the aid of three glasses of Veuve Clicquot Champagne.

"Hiya, you gettin' in?"

The black-cab driver's bellowed question hauled me from my reverie. After watching Frank hop into a cab on the other side of the road, I nodded a reply before grabbing the door handle. With my handbag and broken shoes lobbed on the seat beside me, I swivelled around in my seat just in time to spot Frank's cab whizz past.

"Where to?"

"Follow that cab!"

"Do what?" the cabbie, appearing to be a forty-something love child of Max Headroom and Daenerys Targaryen, sporting to-die-for natural platinum locks styled in a mixture of spikes and braids, barked in reply as she shot a surprised glance at the rear-view mirror.

"Just follow that cab," I repeated, shifting forward on the seat and jabbing my arm towards the dividing security screen.

"You got it, sweetheart. Buckle up," she hollered before pulling out into the traffic, receiving a couple of hoots from other road users forced to take evasive action. "JKO, that cab?" she waved her finger at the windscreen.

"Sorry?" I replied, attempting to comply with her request to clip in the seatbelt.

"Black cab. Reg plate JKO. That one trying to turn into Montpellier Street?" she bellowed before muting the radio just at the point when Agnetha Fältskog vocalised about how lucky she was to be the girl with golden hair.

Despite my locks being brunette with hints of grey, like the Swedish icon, I, Jayne Stone, had been lucky. A privileged lifestyle, four daughters and a doting husband. After Frank split from his first wife in 1979, when declaring his undying love for me, life had been pretty idyllic. I had a lot to be thankful for. However, apart from a broken pair of Jimmy Choo's and a torn, slurry-stained sleeveless number from Louis Vuitton, I just knew something wasn't right.

Frank Stone had always been a man of habit, a man of integrity. To demonstrate my point, my husband visited the lavatory at precisely the same time each morning, always putting the seat down after completing his clockwork-like ablutions. When up in town visiting his charity, a monthly event now he'd taken a backseat from directing the day-to-day affairs, my husband would always take lunch at work, mixing with the employees ... not shooting off in a taxi to God knows where.

"Oh, yes. Please, don't lose sight of it. I'll pay double," I replied, when leaning forward as far as the seatbelt would allow.

"I got it. Don't worry, sweetheart. What's going down then?" the Dragon Queen quizzed when pulling up behind Frank's cab as it waited for an opening in the oncoming traffic to turn right. "You don't look like the James Bond or Emma Peel type. No offence."

"Oh ... erm—"

"Don't tell me, you reckon your old man's been playing away, and you're keen to see what he's up to. That it? Am I right, or am I right?"

"Oh, well, um—"

"Binned my husband off years ago, I did. What d'you reckon is wrong with 'em, eh? I know I'm not exactly Beyoncé, but I gave him twenty years, y'know. My mate, Cindy, finks they reach forty and then this switch goes off in their 'ead. Cindy said, Pink, that's what she calls me on account that I apparently look like the pop star," she glanced in the rear-view mirror before continuing. "She said, and I quote ... Pink, blokes have an inbuilt self-destruct button that causes them to go running around like some randy dog looking to knob any tart with a pulse as long as they're half their age." Pink paused as we continued to wait for a break in the traffic, again glancing up at me in the rear-view mirror.

On second glance, I had her pegged to be slightly younger than I'd first thought. Perhaps a good thirty years my junior, blessed with impossibly high cheekbones, giving her that striking shield-maiden Scandinavian look.

"You alright, sweetheart? Not in trouble, are ya? You want me to call the Old Bill?"

"No, it's not like ..." my voice trailed away, unsure what to say or if I should utter anything at all. I was probably shaken up from my fall and now jumping to silly conclusions. As we waited to turn, I considered aborting the chase and redirecting Pink to head for my hotel.

Pink nodded at the rearview mirror, watching as I finger-combed my hair and attempted to improve my bedraggled appearance whilst contemplating my next move. When turning the steering wheel, preparing to sneak through a tight gap, Pink continued her cabbie-styled questioning.

"Where d'you reckon he's hightailing off to, then? You old man got some floozy up in Kensington, has he? Am I right, or am I right?" Pink shot me a fleeting glance as she floored the accelerator whilst maintaining a Rizla-paper distance between both cabs. When performing the right turn, she held up an apologetic hand to the driver of a BMW, who'd braked hard to let both cabs cut across. "You know, I caught my hubby, Paul, with his pants down. Literally. There he was, up the Duck and Feathers, doing some dozy tart in the lav. God knows what the silly cow saw in him. My ex isn't exactly George Clooney, and he's as fat as they come."

"Oh, does he have a condition?"

"Paul?" Pink glanced at the rear-view mirror. "Yeah, he's got a condition, alright. Overactive knife and fork, I think they call it."

"Oh."

"Yeah, fat lump couldn't keep it in his trousers."

"Oh, I'm sorry—"

"Don't be. No loss. Look, sweetheart, sorry, none of my business. I don't mean to poke me nose in."

I offered a tight smile in reply. After deciding not to provide a verbal response, I hoped Pink would focus on keeping Frank's cab in her sights and refrain from recounting what may or may not have taken place beside the urinals in the Duck and Feathers.

"What's made you suspicious, then? Your old man got a second phone? Been working late at the office, has he? You got kids? Always tough on kids, ain't it? My two haven't spoken to their father for years. Blames me, he does. He has the gall to say I've turned them against him. I mean, the bleedin' cheek of it. How the frig can it be my fault? Am I right, or am I right?"

My chatty cabbie shot me another look in the mirror. We momentarily made eye contact as I flicked my eyes from the back of the black cab not more than a few feet ahead.

"Turning left. Deffo heading up Kensington, I reckon." Once more, Pink glanced up again and held my stare for a fraction longer than I considered to be normal, as if taking a moment to scrutinise my features.

Since the summer of last year, when Frank and I, along with the girls and their families, had agreed to a photo shoot for a society magazine, there'd been a few occasions when we'd been recognised. Not the full-on celeb status, but the knowing nod in a restaurant or an occasional rant at Frank by someone who disagreed with his standpoint regarding homelessness.

Usually, due to Frank being the one who often appeared on TV, I avoided these cringeworthy encounters when not enjoying my husband's company. However, something in Pink's expression suggested she was an avid reader of society publications or had flicked through a dog-eared back copy when bored in a doctor's waiting room.

Pink maintained the gap to her compatriot ahead as we careered left into the throng of traffic along Knightsbridge, thus causing me to grab the handrail to avoid a second inelegant slip to the floor in the space of an hour. As we picked up pace when heading west, glimpses of Hyde Park became visible through the gaps between the buildings on my right. I managed to squirm into an upright position and no longer felt I was experiencing the undulating, spinning sensation of the Waltzer fairground ride.

"You look familiar. You on TV or somefink?" Pink asked as she expertly swung the cab away from a wayward takeaway delivery man weaving his way along on an electric scooter. "Should ban those damn fings. I tell you, when one of us lot knocks them off, it'll be us who lose our licence. Am I right, or am I right?" Pink glanced up again into the rear-view mirror, either looking for confirmation regarding her views on the latest mode of transport or grabbing another look when trying to guess my celeb status, which I didn't own.

I replied with a pained grimace and a shake of my head to the TV star question, and an 'I'm sure you're right' mumbled response to her electric scooter statement.

My husband could probably claim D-list celeb status, that category which afforded you the 'right' to scream *'Do you know who I am?'* at a crew member of a fast-food restaurant who steadfastly refused to serve the breakfast offer post 11am.

However, as Mr D-List's wife, and apart from those few airbrushed shots in that glossy mag which transformed me from a curvy size twelve with a hint of bingo wings down to a death-warmed-up, waif-like size eight, I couldn't claim any celeb status regardless of how far the categories sunk through the alphabet.

"Another left. Going down Rutland Gate. Posh down 'ere, I can tell ya," Pink announced as she maintained our dangerously close position to the rear of Frank's cab.

There was none of this stealth-like tailing depicted in the movies; Pink was on it. Whilst I held on to the grab rail, attempting to keep my soaked backside on the slippery bench seat, my cabbie continued her commentary.

"I reckon he's doing a loop around to avoid the road works on Brompton. We're going back to Belgravia. Whichever, if your old man's up to no good, his floozy's got some dosh. Course, it could be a fella. You see it on the news last night? That actor in that soap. Oh, what's it called? That whatchamacallit with that old thingamajig geezer in it. Anyway, it was on the news. They caught him up Hampstead Heath doing some rent boy. Now, I'm not here to judge, course not. But it's his wife I feel sorry for. You should have heard the poor woman when they interviewed her …"

Due to having no idea what she was on about, not being an avid watcher of soaps, I allowed Pink to drivel on about said actor's apparent claims that he'd made a silly mistake when doing whatever he was doing when caught. Instead I focused on the rear of Frank's cab and wondered what I planned to do when we reached our final destination.

Of course, I fully expected Frank's jaunt would be perfectly innocent. If he spotted me tailing him, that would only lead to a difficult conversation. Frank and I were what was classed in the modern day as an unusual couple. We were open and honest with each other and harboured no secrets. However, as his cab pulled up to the kerb and Pink slowly cruised past, I wondered if I was about to suffer a similar shock to what Pink had just alluded that actor's wife had stated when interviewed on her doorstep.

Pink trundled on for another fifty yards before pulling in. As I swivelled around to watch Frank alight, my cabbie adjusted her wing mirror to see back up the street.

"Where are we?" I quizzed, holding my position so I could just spot through the car window behind us when Frank turned away from the taxi and strode up the steps into what appeared to be a posh London townhouse.

"Still on Rutland place. Bottom end back near Brompton Road."

I felt sick. And again, although they probably didn't help, I very much doubted the oysters could be blamed for the queasy feeling.

"What now, sweetheart? You gonna follow him? Course, they won't let you in, but we can wait. Meters running, but I'm all yours."

"Sorry?" I swivelled back to look at Pink, who'd shimmied around to face me. "Who won't let me go in where?"

"There," she nodded. "The Barrington Club. Your old man a member?"

I shook my head and pulled a face, conveying I was floundering to keep up.

"Well, he's kept that a secret. It's one of those gentlemen's clubs ... women aren't allowed in."

"Oh ... really?"

"Old boys' sort of place. No offence. I've had a few jobs ferrying city types back and forth over the years. Loose Women!"

"Sorry?"

"Loose Women."

"Oh ... good God! It's a knocking shop?"

"No," she chuckled. "Well, it could be. Who knows what they get up to in there? Nah, I mean, that's where I recognise you from. You're on that show, Loose Women. Course, I only see it on me days off. But that's you, ain't it?"

"No," I shook my head and wafted away her suggestion with a dismissive wave of my hand. I'd seen the show a few times and now momentarily wondered which one of the presenters I might be.

"Oh, you sure?"

"Quite sure. What d'you think I should do now?" As soon as I said it, I realised asking a London black cab driver for advice in this situation was probably not my best move. However, Pink seemed to have an opinion on most things.

"Up to you, sweetheart. I'm happy to sit here and wait. No skin off my nose. If it was my old man, and I thought he was up to no good, I'd confront the git. Just like I did when I found Paul boffing that bit of strumpet in the Duck and Feathers."

Whilst she held a heavily pencilled-in eyebrow aloft, I chewed my lip and weighed up options.

"Thanks for the advice."

"All part of the service, sweetheart. Talking of which, that's twelve quid."

4

The Monteagle Warning

"Christ!" Frank paused as he swallowed his whisky, Douglas style. "You're sending some poor sod back to 1605? Heavens above, I never realised you sent people that far back in history," Frank blurted before wincing when the mouthful of whisky he'd just hoofed down his neck burnt his throat.

"No, Frank, not at all. We're sending a volunteer back to 1979." Douglas provided air quotes on the word 'volunteer'.

"How will sending someone to 1979 help prevent the Gunpowder Plot? Oh, but that was prevented, so why—"

"Frank," interrupted Hartland whilst waving his hand to gain the steward's attention. "Where Robert Catesby and his band of mercenaries and Jesuit conspirators failed, in a few years from now, a renegade group of halfwit terrorists succeed."

"Blow up the Houses of Parliament?"

"Hmmm, not quite. Number Ten, old boy. To be precise, the Cabinet rooms along with the PM, his band of lunatic ministers, two private secretaries, a tea lady, two footmen, and Bubbles."

"Bubbles?"

"Ten-year-old tabby. Sort of an adopted mascot. I'm led to believe he's the son of the current moggie, who's known as the Chief Mouser to the Cabinet Office."

"A cat?"

"Correct. From what we can ascertain from our data, only Bubbles and the tea lady, Maureen Hawksworth, are afforded a memorial statue. A garish lump of modern art placed at the entrance to Downing Street. The precise spot where that Tory MP did, or didn't, depending on who you believe, call a policeman a pleb."

"David Cameron and his whole Cabinet are murdered?"

"Oh, no, Cameron is long gone by that time. But yes, Frank, the whole ruddy Cabinet. Now, the name of the incumbent PM at that time is irrelevant. To be honest with you, Churchill and Atlee aside, none of them, past or present, pass muster or managed to achieve much. However, although woefully flawed, our political system is integral in maintaining some semblance of order. We can't have any old rabble thinking they can change what we in the ruling classes have spent centuries putting in place."

Frank raised an eyebrow but chose not to interrupt The Hooded Claw's hissed rant.

"Our data suggests that event, the killing of our government leaders—"

"And Bubbles."

"Yes ..." Hartland sneered at the interruption, flaring his nostrils and holding a rictus grin before continuing. "That event results in political chaos. From what we can ascertain, the whole political system will be ripped to shreds: the House of Lords abolished, proportional representation introduced, the seat of government relocated to some dreadful modern purpose-built monstrosity in Milton Keynes, that dreadful town full of roundabouts and houses made of ticky-tacky. The Palace of Westminster will be turned into some Harry-Potter-styled theme park, and the bloody working class ruling the damn country. That, my friend, cannot and bloody well will not be allowed to happen."

Frank smirked.

"Frank, this is serious. Although I like you, I really do, and despite the fact that you dedicate an inordinate amount of your time publicly ripping government policy to pieces, I suspect even you would be averse to wholesale changes to our political system. Our data suggests the impact has far-reaching consequences which we must avoid."

"Douglas, of course, I don't condone terrorist acts." Frank nodded and held his palm aloft. "I will agree that our political system requires wholesale changes. However, killing our elected leaders is not the way to go about it."

"Quite. Good of you to recognise the pathos of the situation."

"But why 1979 ... why send someone back to 1979 to prevent what will happen in the future?"

"When we sent you back in time, 1979 was the year your wife was murdered. So, of course, 1979 was the obvious time to send you back to expunge that piece of history."

"Which I did."

"Correct, you did. However, as you know, although you were successful, that change unfortunately didn't have the desired effect, which we at the CYA had hoped for." Douglas batted away that statement with a dismissive wave of his hand. "No matter, we dealt with that future little issue in another way."

"Douglas, that doesn't explain—"

"Hang on, Frank. Let me enlighten you ..." Douglas paused, awaiting Frank to nod and allow him to continue. "Okay, without diving down into too much detail, we are not able to send travellers through time to just any old point in history or the future that takes our fancy. There are only certain years at our disposal when we can send time-travellers. All, I might add, with a nine as the hindmost. 1919, 1939, 1959, 1979 ... and a new one we've discovered, 2029."

"Oh."

"We're not sure about the significance of each year ending in nine, though some have suggested it's because that number is associated with spiritual awakenings. Personally, that sounds like a load of mumbo jumbo bollocks to me," he chuckled.

"Like time-travel?" quipped Frank.

"Yes, but you now know that's possible."

"I do. Although, as the years have rolled on by, I sometimes wonder if my first life was some vivid dream."

"I can imagine. However, Frank, my friend, you *did* time-travel."

"So, that's why you chose me for time-travel. 1979 was a year you could send time-travellers to and in my first life Jemma was murdered that year."

"Correct. If you remember, we believed keeping Jemma alive would alter history. Now, as we said, that didn't quite pan out how we imagined."

"I saved her life, though."

"Hmmm, well, to be honest with you, Frank, I'm not sure you did."

"Sorry?"

"We had to send some assistance, if you remember."

"Oh, the eliminators."

"Yes, Collinson. Our man killed your best mate, David Bolton, who, it appeared, had murdered your lovely wife the first time around, did he not?"

"He did. I thought Jemma was lovely, but when I returned to 1979, she wasn't the woman I remembered."

"No, by all accounts, a bit of a good-time girl."

"Well, whatever you want to call her, she wasn't the woman I remembered."

"And you married Jayne and have a rather delightful family, to boot."

"I do."

"I take it you've never confided in Jayne?"

"Time-travel?"

Douglas nodded.

Frank blew a raspberry. "No! I'm never going to do that, am I? My wife will have me bundled off to some padded cell if I suddenly decide to inform her I've returned from the future. Also, you made it quite clear if I ever divulged to a living soul that I was a time-traveller, you'd have me eliminated."

"Correct, Frank. A wise decision on your part. Unfortunately, we have had cause to dispose of quite a few who just couldn't keep their damn mouths shut. You'd think being afforded a second chance at life would be enough for most people, wouldn't you? But, alas, no. Some of the bloody idiots we've sent back just weren't able to help themselves."

As the attentive steward refreshed their glasses, Frank slumped in his chair and offered a shudder at that thought of elimination. While both he and Douglas paused their conversation, Frank thought about his old, long-departed mate, Dave. Throughout his first life, especially when as a street dweller, Frank had often pondered about who'd murdered his wife. Despite the extensive police investigation, with hundreds of detectives delving into the details and possibilities of who had murdered the local MP, Jemma's murder had remained an unsolved case.

Of course, When Hartland and his bunch of nutters at the CYA pinged Frank back in time, he travelled with the knowledge of the date of her murder and thus was able to investigate possible suspects before the event. That said, although it became clear that Dave wasn't his wife's number one fan, why, in Frank's second life, he'd attempted to kill her still remained a mystery.

"So, Frank. As I said, we require your assistance."

"Douglas, I understand why you need to prevent this terrorist group from blowing up Number Ten, but how on earth can I have any bearing on it?"

"Frank, hear me out. There are two years we can use to change this particular unsavoury future event. 1959 and 1979. However, for 1959, we're struggling to locate a suitable change agent."

"Change agent?"

"You were our change agent in 1979."

"Ah, I see. You can't locate anyone who's alive now or healthy enough to send back to the '50s? I presume whoever you identify to send back to 1959 would either be dead or elderly."

"That's correct. Obviously, whoever we send back has to be an adult in the year they land in and, crucially, also have a connection to the future issue that requires altering. Unfortunately, our operations are suffering due to time moving forward. Although we have pretty much secured 2029 as a year we can use, in reality, we only have 1979 as a usable year. I have a crack team of analysts working on trying to bring 1999 into the fore, but that's some way off at the moment."

"I take it you've identified some poor sod who you want to send back to the '70s, then? This person can change something which will prevent this terrorist group in the future?"

"Yes, Frank. Fortunately, we have. Our chosen change agent is the grandmother of one of the terrorists."

"Okay, so you need me to help your change agent, as you call them, understand what life is like in 1979 and how to live in the past again?"

"Sort of ... it's a bit more complicated than that."

"Oh ... how so? Not that I've agreed to this, but hypothetically, what exactly do you require from me if I were to assist?"

"So, as you suggest, we have identified a change agent, and they are currently undergoing their preparation for travel. However, they're, how shall I put it—"

"They don't believe you can send them back in time."

"Spot on. Let's just say our change agent is a smidge sceptical."

"You can hardly blame them, can you? I mean, it wasn't until I woke in 1979 that I believed it would happen. I was convinced you scraped me off the pavement along Queen's Walk for some sick upper-class fun." Frank shifted forward and lowered his voice. "You know, I thought you were preparing to use me as the 'fox' in some sicko twisted human hunt."

"Really, Frank? You do have a vivid imagination," chuckled Hartland.

Frank shrugged. "Come on, then, why should I help you? Apart from the fact that I agree with preventing future acts of terror, why would I want to get involved?"

"Your son, old boy."

"Sorry. What's Andrew got to do with this?"

"Frank, your son is a member of Parliament. And from what I hear, a bit of a rising star."

"Well, he's done well for himself, that's correct."

"He has. I imagine your constant bashing of government policy must cause some tension between the two of you."

"We don't discuss politics. But, sorry, what's Andrew's connection to this issue?"

Hartland shifted further forward, conspiratorially glancing around before continuing.

"This might focus the mind, my good friend. Andrew, as you said, is doing rather well. In a few years, he will rise up the greasy pole of politics and hold the post of Secretary of State for Work and Pensions. Your son will be part of the Cabinet."

Frank swallowed hard; the penny had dropped.

"Frank, unless we can prepare and successfully send our change agent back to 1979 and alter history, your son will meet his untimely death with the efficient tea lady and Bubbles."

5

Casino Royale

"The meter's up to fifty quid."

Pink's announcement regarding the meter hitting fifty broke the silence cloaking the inside of her cab for the last fifteen minutes of the forty we'd been stationary on Rutland Place, positioned just a few yards along from The Barrington Club.

At some point during the last quarter of an hour, when maintaining my half-turned pose to keep a beady eye on the entrance to the club, Pink must have stopped talking when I offered no response to her constant *'Am I right, or am I right'* questions along with her preferred *'no offence'* comments when voicing her opinions. Of which she held many.

To fill the void, my cabbie flicked the radio on. I assumed she'd tuned into a station that dedicated the majority of airtime to the Swedish phenomenon of my twenties. The poignant change from the song playing when I hopped into Pink's cab to this one wasn't lost on me. Whilst Anni-Frid Lyngstad soulfully sang about memories of past happiness, I thought of my husband. Like so many of our friends, had we now reached the natural conclusion of our marriage?

My mind was on overdrive.

What was Frank doing in a gentlemen's club when he should be at his office? Was he a member? Had he been keeping this secret for years? The man I knew would never set foot in such a place.

As I craned my neck, now suffering shooting pains along my shoulders as a result of holding this uncomfortable position for far too long, I'd rolled around two courses of action, plumping for neither as I procrastinated my decision.

Of course, the sensible thing would be to return to our hotel, wait for Frank, and see if he mentions where he'd been today. We would always download the events of each other's day over dinner, whether at home in North Norfolk or on our monthly trips to London. I would know something was afoot if Frank failed to mention his little jaunt. Or I could barefoot bowl up to the entrance and demand to see my husband and ask him what he was doing.

As my mind flitted from one thought to the other, time, along with the meter, ticked on.

Assuming my husband wasn't being entertained by 'loose women', the only other possibility I'd considered was that his visit here had something to do with his ex-wife. Just before Frank and I got together, Jemma Stone had an affair, then married the Tory toff, Rupert Barrington-Scott. The first part of Jemma's husband's compound surname just happened to be the same as this gentlemen's club's name. Was that a coincidence? And would Frank have planned a meeting with Rupert?

Surprisingly, considering the circumstances, the four of us had remained friends. I'd known Jemma longer than I'd known Frank. And for Frank and Jemma's son's sake, the four of us regularly kept in touch. That said, I wasn't aware that Rupert was a member of a gentlemen's club, and even if he was, why would Frank be meeting him without telling me?

"What d'you want to do, sweetheart? I've got no problem hanging on, but you did want to know when the meter hit fifty quid."

I swivelled around, feeling an uncomfortable twinge in my stiff neck. Also, despite now being ruined, my figure-hugging Louis Vuitton summer number was quite restricting, the material cutting into the side of my boobs as I held that twisted pose. My designer outfit was a perfect choice for my luncheon date with a couple of girlfriends but wasn't designed to be worn on stakeouts in the back of a black cab.

"Oh, hang on. I think we have bandits at five o'clock. That looks like your old man coming out. Am I right, or am I right?" she announced as she focused on her wing mirror.

I swivelled back to peer up the street. There he was, my husband and another dapper-looking gent. A man sporting a top hat, presumably the doorman, strode past them into the street to hail a taxi. Fortunately, he was looking in the other direction up Rutland Place and thus didn't spot Pink's cab positioned just further along, idling by the kerb. If he had, he might have trotted down to enquire if Pink had a fare, and that may have brought Frank and the mystery man along with him. Although I wanted to know what my husband was up to, I'd decided confronting him here wasn't a sensible option.

"You want me to follow them?" Pink enquired as a taxi pulled up, blocking the centre of the street.

To be fair to the cabbie, unless he intended to plough straight over the top of the club's doorman, he had little choice but to stop. As Frank and the other gent, who appeared somewhat familiar, bundled into their cab, I grabbed hold of my seat belt.

"Yes. Follow that cab."

Pink flicked off the radio just at the point the two girls duetted something about being the best they could do. Yes, I'm an ABBA superfan. That said, I don't know all the lyrics and, at this point in time, I harboured concerns regarding my husband's antics rather than humming along to one of my favourite tunes.

"This don't happen as much as people might think, y'know."

"Sorry?" I shouted back, grabbing the handrail as Pink lurched the cab out from our parking space into the slipstream of Frank's cab.

"Following other cars. You see it in films all the time, but it don't happen that often. Most of the time, it's just boring trips back and forth from one station or another, dropping off shoppers up Oxford Street or theatre goers up West. Not a full-on chase across town."

"Oh, yes, I see."

"A couple of years back … woah, hold on, sweetheart. I'm gonna have to gun it across here," Pink announced as she careered into the chaos of Hyde Park Corner and around to Piccadilly. Her actions invited a cacophony of horn blasts. As we swung left onto Constitution Hill, narrowly avoiding killing a cyclist who verbally vented his spleen accompanied by various unpleasant hand gestures regarding Pink's driving technique, we fell back to a more sedate drive with Frank's cab three cars ahead.

"Yeah, as I was saying. Couple of years back, this geezer had me following his missus all over, like. He reckoned she said she was gonna take him for everyfink he had when she upped sticks and left him. I felt sorry for him, poor sod. He said his lawyer reckoned if he could gain evidence of her dallying, it would help his case. He had me charging all over town. That cab fare was over two 'undred nicker, can you believe?"

"Yes, I can imagine," I replied, still white-knuckle gripping the door handle as I prepared myself for whatever rally-driving technique Pink had planned to deal with the curve around The Victoria Memorial that loomed ever closer.

"I tell you when that was. The day of Maggie's funeral. She wasn't my cup of tea. No offence. Anyway, the City was gridlocked 'cos of the funeral procession, so I had to dodge in and out of side roads. It was bleedin' chaos."

"Did he catch his wife up to no good?" Why I felt the need to ask, I had no idea. Perhaps this was a similar scenario, and I just felt the need to know the outcome.

"Did he ever," she chuckled, glancing up at me before continuing. "There she was, bold as brass, sucking the face off this bloke outside The Savoy. I mean, posh place, not the sort of hotel you drop into for a quickie when paying for a suite by the hour, is it? Am I right, or am I right?"

"I'm sure."

"You a royalist?" she asked, seamlessly changing tack and hardly coming up for breath as we almost two-wheel careered around the gilded bronze Winged Victory memorial statue. "You know it's two weeks from today that our Queen becomes the longest-serving monarch? That'll be sixty-three years, two-'undred and seventeen days."

"I didn't know that."

"Love the monarchy. You know, the Queen's the best thing about this country. Am I right—"

"Yes, you're right," I interrupted.

"Yeah, sorry, sweetheart, I say that a lot, I know."

I didn't confirm her statement. Instead, focused on the back of Frank's cab, which was now only two cars in front, as we left Buckingham Palace behind us and scooted along the side of St. James's Park.

"Elegant lady, ain't she? Well, your old man's not off to a garden party on the lawns with Lizzy. We're heading for Westminster, The South Bank and the London Eye."

"Oh, right."

"You been on the Eye? My brother took me on there last year for a birthday treat. Scared the bejesus out of me. There I was, holding onto the rail ..."

The London Eye.

I let Pink recount her story regarding her fear of heights, throwing in the odd 'Uh-huh' whilst allowing my mind to drift. Frank had an obsession with that landmark. Although I'd often questioned what the fascination was, my husband never elaborated. And on the subject of birthday surprises, I'd arranged a trip for the whole family for his sixtieth. We all enjoyed a weekend at the Ritz, culminating with a ride on the Wheel.

And what happened?

Well, Frank refused to get on, preferring to watch from Queen's Walk as I, the girls, their partners, and our grandchildren enjoyed the thirty-minute excursion. After the ride, when back at our hotel, we had one of our extremely rare full-on rows.

Of course, knowing his obsession with the giant Ferris wheel, it was reasonable for me to assume that a trip with all our family in a privately hired pod would be something Frank would have enjoyed. But, no, he steadfastly refused and pretty much ruined the day.

As we pulled up at the lights in Parliament Square, Pink gave up on her story to shout across to another cab driver who'd pulled up alongside. Fortunately, even though Frank's cab was still a couple of cars ahead, their cab had also been caught at the red light.

"Alright, Fonzy, how's it going?" Pink hollered.

Whether the other cabbie was actually called Fonzy or not, the receding quiff and leather jacket suited his name.

"Alright, Treacle? Loving the new Barnet," Fonzy replied, pointing to Pink's blonde spikey look.

"Cheers. Had it done a couple of weeks back." She twizzled one of the long braids that snaked down her back. "Bleedin' extensions cost me an arm and a leg, I can tell you."

"I've just seen Skidder. He's a couple of motors up at the front of the lights." Fonzy paused to shoot me a look before continuing. If Frank's cabbie was called Skidder, then I hoped for my husband's safety his name wasn't applied due to his driving techniques. "I recognise one of the geezers in the back. It's that Frank Stone bloke. Y'know, that one that's always on the TV down on the embankment talking about the 'omeless."

"Oh, yeah, I know who you mean." Pink shot me a look in the rearview mirror whilst Fonzy gave her a wave before pulling forward when the lights changed.

"That your old man? You Frank Stone's missus? Top bloke, your hubby. Well, that's as long as he ain't up to no good, course. Now Fonzy said it, I can see it was him." Pink glanced up again when I didn't respond, only offering a pained grimace in reply. "Hey, don't worry. Us cabbies have a code of conduct.

If he's dipping his wick where he shouldn't, no tabloid's gonna hear that story from me, sweetheart. The press in this country are gutter sludge. The lot of them should be strung up. No offence."

I glanced up at the twelve-foot-high bronze Sir Winston Churchill. "When you're going through hell, keep going," I muttered. Although I wasn't sure that quote could be attributed to the man, it sounded Churchillian.

Also, that statement for my current predicament might be a smidge dramatic. Yes, I had a ruined pair of Jimmy Choo's by my side, and I was unsure what my husband was up to. However, I admonished myself for such thoughts when considering all the poor souls who relied on Frank's charity to provide one of life's simple staples, such as a bed to sleep in. That said, everything is relative. Today was rapidly turning into a living hell and, now they'd started to repeat, those bloody oysters weren't helping much.

Pink took my lack of confirmation that I was Mrs Stone as a cue to give her tongue a rest. As we kept close to Frank's cab along the Victoria Embankment, I focused on the Eye and the early September warm sunshine that glinted from the indolently rotating pods. Wherever my husband and his familiar-looking dapper companion were heading, it wasn't for a spin on the Eye. As the wheel drifted out of sight on my right, Pink swung a left and pulled into the kerb, causing me to refocus on the events of the here and now.

"Looks like your hubby is heading for the Old War Office."

I unclipped my seatbelt and shifted forward to watch Frank and the man I now recognised alight their cab before hot-footing across towards the ornate Edwardian Baroque trapezoidal building.

"The Old War office?" I questioned, whilst remembering that trip down to Cromer pier not two weeks ago.

When the girls and I, along with the rest of my family, left Frank dozing in a deck chair to grab some ice creams, that man now crossing the street approached my husband and chatted for a few minutes. When I later questioned who he was, Frank had replied somewhat cryptically. If my memory serves me correctly, he'd called him Sylvester Sneekly, The Hooded Claw. I'd left it at that, assuming that was Frank's name for the man, who was some crooked lawyer as per the cartoon character.

"Yes, sweetheart. It used to be the War Office. Loads of James Bond films have been made there, and Ian Fleming actually worked in that building during the Second World War."

"Wow, you are a fount of knowledge," I vacantly muttered as my eyes followed Frank's progress down the side of the building.

"Us London cabbies have to know everyfink. It's our job, sweetheart."

"Yes, I'm sure you're right. What is it now?"

"Well, I heard the government were selling it off. Rumours floating about say that part of it will become an 'otel."

"Oh … so, is it, what … derelict?"

"No idea." Pink wagged a finger through the open driver's window as it glided down. "Whatever it is, looks like your old fella is going in there. You reckon he's looking to purchase the place and then turn it into some hostel for the 'omeless?"

"Good, God, I shouldn't think so," I scoffed, shifting further forward in my seat whilst tugging the damp hem of my dress to cover my knees. "It's huge. I'd imagine a building like that here in Whitehall would be worth hundreds of millions of pounds."

"What now, then? We wait again?"

I glanced at my Jimmy Choo's. "What size shoe d'you take?"

Pink swivelled around and raised that thick, pencilled eyebrow at me. "You what, sweetheart?"

"What shoe size are you?" I repeated, plucking up the shoe with the flapping heel and waving it in her direction. Pink's eyes followed the swinging heel like a hypnotist's pocket watch.

"Nice pumps. Are they Jimmy's?"

"They are. I bought them in Harrods when we came up to town in June. Unfortunately, I slipped over after luncheon this afternoon and bent the heel back."

"Shame, they're beauties. You could get them mended, though. I'm a thirty-eight."

"Five?"

"Yeah."

"Same as me. I don't suppose we could do a swap? I know the heel needs repairing, and they're not really designed for driving in, but I can't very well chase after Frank in these, can I?"

Pink glanced at my dress and smirked. "I reckon that outfit cost more than the pumps and probably a shade more than I make in a month."

I raised a questioning eyebrow, wondering where she was going with this conversation. Although I wasn't of a mind to divulge the cost of my outfit, I think her assumption wasn't far off the mark. Designer clothes weren't my usual day-to-day attire. Still, lunch had been a special occasion, celebrating the birthday of a girlfriend from way back.

Frank always encouraged me to spend big when clothes shopping. In fact, I think he chose this particular dress and purchased it, despite my protestation that it cost somewhere north of two grand. My sodden, ripped frock came from a limited collection sold exclusively by Harrods.

"I'm wearing me old Doc Martens, so I ain't sure they really go with the look," she chuckled.

"I'll risk it. How about I give you two hundred for the fare, and we swap shoes? I paid nearly seventeen hundred for the pumps only a couple of months ago."

"Yeah, go on then. I fancy a pair of pink Jimmy Choo's. I reckon a squirt of Super Glue, they'll be as good as new."

With her boots now on my feet and Pink left wearing only a pair of what appeared to be Christmas Homer Simpson novelty socks, and because of the restricted movement afforded by my dress, my accommodating cabbie stooped to tie the laces of my newly acquired footwear.

I looked ridiculous.

Also, although I wasn't in a position to complain, Pink clearly suffered from sweaty feet. The experience reminded me of those ten-pin bowling shoes, which always afforded that rather unpleasant warm feeling when you slipped them on despite the attendant spraying the insides.

Fortunately, the warm late afternoon sunshine had dried the pavement after the flash showers from earlier. Otherwise, Pink would be driving the rest of the day in sodden socks.

London, New York, and Paris, like most fashionable cities around the world, are home to an eclectic and diverse collection of individuals. How the population dressed in the big city was markedly different from the more conservative countryside. As I hot-footed across the road towards the side entrance of the Old War Office, dressed in my eight-hole psychedelic-patterned Doc Martens, with the torn hem of my dress flapping against the back of my knee, no one gave me a second look.

When hovering by the closed double wooden doors where my husband had disappeared through a few minutes ago, I noticed a small brass plaque screwed to the stonework depicting just three letters.

CYA

After a furtive scan of the street, procrastinating my decision when hoping those letters stood for something like the Christian Youth Association and not some debauched seedy men's club where God knows what happens, I pushed against the heavy door. A door that yielded with ease, revealing an entrance I wasn't expecting.

6

Green Card

Whilst harbouring an uneasy feeling and concern about returning to this building, Frank surveyed the views of the London skyline from the very same balcony where he'd stood thirty-six years ago. Due to the complexities of time-travel, although that event being over three decades in the past, both excursions onto the rooftop terrace took place in the same year.

In 2015, the first time around, the CYA's extraction team had just scraped him off the streets as part of the operation to send him back to 1979. Now, here again in 2015, the same age as the last time he stood here, Frank waited for Douglas Hartland to escort through and introduce their latest Change Agent, whom the CYA planned to ping back through time.

Although he would be forever grateful for his second life, that could only be considered to be a vast improvement on his first, which, considering he spent nearly twenty years sleeping rough, wouldn't be difficult, Frank wasn't wild about returning to the headquarters of the Correction Years Association. An organisation, along with its employees, which appeared to defy the laws of time.

When he'd earlier nipped out of the office, this excursion from the Barrington Club wasn't part of the plan. After

Douglas had made contact a few weeks back, he'd agreed to meet him at his club the next time he and Jayne were up in town. However, Frank had fully intended to make it crystal clear that he had no intention of being involved in their time-travel games, even on a consultancy basis.

Of course, the news that Andrew, his and Jemma's son, would lose his life at the hands of some dissident terrorist group, obviously had the effect of focusing his mind and thus quickly arriving at the decision to accompany The Hooded Claw back to the CYA's HQ. Whoever they had lined up to send, Frank needed to ensure they were fully prepared for what was about to happen and thus successfully prevent their grandchild from becoming a terrorist in the future.

Unable to tear his eyes away from the vision of the London Eye as the September sun glistened off the brilliant white, languidly rotating pods, Frank raised his arm and flicked his eyes to check his watch. By now, he expected that Jayne, his wife, would have finished her luncheon date – a birthday celebration for a close friend, Jenny Apsley – and presumably be enjoying some retail therapy before returning to their hotel. If he was going to keep his little jaunt a secret, this meeting with whoever would have to be done and dusted within the hour.

Of course, Frank should be at his office chairing the quarterly board meeting. However, after throwing his son-in-law, Denzil, now the CEO, an excuse about needing to pop out of the office, he'd been missing in action for far longer than intended.

As Frank had confirmed to Douglas earlier, apart from Jemma, he kept his time-travelling credentials under wraps. For obvious reasons, he couldn't tell Jayne. And despite the events of September 1979, Jemma still struggled to believe his fantastic story. Fair enough, it was a bit of a stretch for anyone to believe in time-travel. That said, his ex-wife had steadfastly honoured her commitment never to tell a living soul what Frank claimed happened to him on the London Eye.

"Frank."

Hearing his name being called hauled Frank from his reverie – namely pod thirteen of the London Eye, discovering his best mate had murdered Jemma in his first life, the guilt about not letting on to Jayne about time-travel, and a whole host of other crazy thoughts – he swivelled around to find Douglas and a woman of similar age to himself enter the preparation suite, as he knew these rooms to be called.

"Hello, Frank, it's been a long time." The woman, sporting a haggard, gaunt appearance, death warmed up if not to be overly uncharitable about it, offered a familiar smile.

Frank padded back to the open French doors, in those few seconds racking his brain in an attempt to recall where he'd previously met the woman who now stood before him with her hand held out to greet him.

"D'you remember me? I know it's years since we last saw each other. And look at you, you've become a bit of a celebrity," she chuckled.

Although grinning, still holding out her hand, Frank detected sadness in the woman's eyes. Her forced smile belied her true feelings either about meeting him or her situation. Whoever she was, he felt sure her demeanour was a marked difference to the woman he couldn't place from his past.

"I'm so sorry … I think you have me at a disadvantage. I can't—"

"You were my first husband's best man," she interrupted.

"Babs?" quizzed Frank, his voice involuntarily elevating a few octaves due to the shock. Sporting a gaping mouth, he took her proffered hand before pulling his old friend into a tight hug.

A few moments passed before The Hooded Claw cleared his throat, causing Frank and Babs to break their embrace.

"Frank, you know what I need you to do. Barbara travels tonight. Get her head in the right place because your son's life depends on it."

Frank nodded.

Babs tutted at Douglas before offering Frank an exaggerated eye roll. Hartland scooted to the door, purposefully yanking it open before glancing back.

"Frank, I'll be back in half an hour. I'll get one of our chaps to run you back to your hotel, so your lovely wife is none the wiser to where you've been."

"Frank, what the hell are you doing here?" Babs hissed when Hartland disappeared.

"More to the point, what are *you* doing here?"

Babs puffed out those gaunt cheeks and closed her eyes.

The woman in front of him was clearly his murderous old mate's ex-wife. However, recent years hadn't been kind to her. As far as Frank could recall, Babs had always been an attractive lady with what you might describe as the fuller, 'jolly farmer's wife' figure. Now, the poor woman appeared almost skeletal.

"Babs?" Frank shook her arm, encouraging her to answer.

"Oh, Jesus, I have no idea. This has got to be some joke, hasn't it?"

Frank raised an eyebrow.

"Frank?"

"Babs, if you think it's a joke, why are you here?"

"Long story—"

"Well, we don't have long, so you'd better enlighten me."

Babs nodded before flopping onto a leather sofa and expelling an elongated, frustrated sigh. Although decades had passed, Frank thought it to be the same piece of furniture he'd used when enduring his six weeks of preparation thirty-six years ago, a couple of months in the future. He obviously knew he'd time-travelled. However, that statement in his head always sounded like some impossible conundrum.

"Well?" Frank asked with open palms as he perched on the edge of the armrest of the chair opposite.

"Oh, hell, where do I start?"

Frank held his questioning pose, just adding a raised eyebrow to encourage his old friend to start talking.

"Okay, to cut a long story short. The last few years have been pretty awful. Dreadful if the truth be known, and even that's putting it rather mildly. Ha, all my life, I've lurched from one ruddy diet to the next and even took up yoga some years ago, but the pounds just continued to pile on." She paused to wave her hand down her torso. "The best diet on the planet is to have your life ripped from underneath you, and voilà ... skinny as a rake."

"Babs, what's happened?" Frank quizzed, checking his watch.

"Did you ever meet my second husband, Stephen?"

"No, I don't think so," Frank shook his head. "I can't remember the last time we spoke. To be honest with you, I don't think I've seen you since a month or so after Dave died." He winced at the memory of Dave Bolton's dead body splayed out on the muddy ground after one of the CYA's eliminators had sent a nine-millimetre slug through his brain. Just at the point Dave chose to throttle Jemma. Of course, circumstances that he presumed Babs was still blissfully unaware of.

"Christ, I had no idea who David was. And what the hell was he up to in those woods? I still can't believe the police never discovered who killed him. And here I am in this place with Douglas and his cronies saying all sorts of silly things. They reckon you were there in Fairfield Woods that evening Dave was murdered. They also said Dave was trying to strangle Jemma and that I'm going to time-travel. Why on earth would they claim such an absurd thing?"

"Babs ... I know—"

"And, they're trotting out a line about some mercenaries. Who, according to Douglas, they had to send back to clean up an operation, claiming the man who died with Dave was a time-traveller."

"Sinclair."

"That's it, I'd forgotten his name. It feels like a lifetime ago, doesn't it?"

"It was." Frank pursed his lips and nodded as he thought about his two lives.

"D'you know why they're saying about you supposedly being up at the woods? And that ridiculous story about Dave trying to kill Jemma?"

"Yes, I probably do. But let's come back to that in a moment. You were saying about your husband."

Babs removed a scrunched-up tissue from her sleeve and wiped the end of her nose before continuing. "Stephen used to be a civil servant, operating in high office in Whitehall. Of course, we enjoyed all the trappings of a privileged lifestyle, with a lovely house in the country, money, friends in high places ... a life of luxury—"

"You're talking in the past tense," Frank interrupted.

Babs nodded before wiping her nose again. Whilst keeping her head bowed and fiddling with the tissue, she continued. "A year ago, Stephen made a ludicrous investment. Bitcoin, or something like that. Without boring you with the details, we lost everything. The house, his pension, the bloody lot, right down to our last farthing. The shame of his mistake killed him." Babs made eye contact. "Heart attack. Mercifully, it was quick. Stephen was dead before the paramedics arrived ten minutes after I called the emergency services."

"Oh, I'm so sorry."

Babs batted away Frank's condolences with a waft of her tissue. "That's not all. Stephen and I were blessed with twins, Phillipa and Tom ..." Bab's voice faltered, appearing to be in the early throes of hyperventilating. She paused and attempted to control her breathing.

Frank shifted forward, perching on the edge of the armrest before grabbing the distressed woman's hand, offering it a comforting squeeze while waiting for his old friend to compose herself.

Babs sucked in a long, ragged breath before continuing. "There's no way to palliate what I have to say, so I'll just say it. Ten years ago, the twins came into town to meet Stephen and I for his birthday. We attended a show up West and enjoyed dinner together. It was a chance for the four of us to be together before Philli moved to the States, where she'd secured a swish job on Wall Street. We had a lovely evening ... I shall ... I will never forgive ..." Babs paused again, squeezing her eyes shut as her chin trembled.

"Babs?" Frank wiggled her hand after she fell silent.

"The following morning, Philli and Tom caught the same tube, heading back to Paddington Station. Stephen's birthday was the 6th of July."

"Ten years ago?"

Babs nodded before dabbing the corner of her eyes.

"Oh, my God, 7/7 ... the terrorist attack?"

"Yes," Babs nodded before lifting her head. "We lost them both."

Frank puffed out his cheeks. "Jesus, I don't know what to say."

"Stephen and I, although destroyed, had each other." She shrugged one shoulder, attempting to offer a resigned smile. "He left the Civil Service soon after, and we muddled through. However, after what happened with his investment, we lost all our friends. As you can probably imagine, it was all rather embarrassing, and pretty much everyone chose to distance themselves. I've spent the last five months living alone in a crummy B&B."

"But how did you—"

"End up here?"

Frank nodded.

"Stephen was a bit older than me and quite the traditionalist. He was a member of a gentlemen's club over in Knightsbridge—"

"The Barrington Club?"

"Err ... yes—"

"Stephen knew Douglas Hartland."

"Yes ... you've joined the dots. To be honest with you, I came here because the owners of the B&B were turfing me out. It was the streets or here. Not much of a choice, really."

"Do you believe what Douglas is telling you?"

"No! It's ruddy ridiculous. I have no idea what the man's on about. My worry, because clearly I'm not going to time-travel on the London Eye back to 1979, is where I will go when I leave here tonight. Frank, I'm destitute."

Frank leaned back and puffed out his cheeks. To be fair, when in her position, he'd considered the CYA's claim of time-travel via the Millennium Wheel as some sort of silly joke. Unless you were a few sandwiches short of a picnic, anyone in their right mind would find their suggestion ludicrous.

"Frank—"

"Hang on," he interrupted, releasing his comforting grip on her hand when recalling Douglas alluding that the Change Agent's grandchild became a terrorist. "Babs, d'you have any grandchildren?"

"Yes. Sarah has—"

"Oh, of course. What's happened to Sarah? I'm so sorry, I'd forgotten about her."

Despite Babs relaying the most horrific story, the mention of her and Dave's daughter seemed to elevate the sadness in his old friend's eyes.

"As you know, Sarah was only five when Dave died. Stephen raised her as his own. He doted on her, even when the twins came along. Unfortunately, Sarah was difficult and rejected Stephen as her father. She left home at seventeen and became quite wayward, I'm afraid."

"And now?"

"I've had almost no contact with her for years. When the twins died, Sarah drifted back into our lives for a period of time. For a few months, it was as if the difficult times of before had never happened. She soon showed her true colours, though. You see, Sarah was a single mother, and I'm convinced she only made contact when needing financial support. Which, of course, Stephen and I were happy to supply."

"Oh, Babs, you really have gone through the wringer, haven't you?"

"I won't deny it's been tough."

"And where is Sarah now?"

"D'you know an MP called Giles Horsley."

"Err ... name sort of rings a bell."

"He's a junior minister. He and Philli were an item some years ago. Anyway, at the twin's funeral, Giles met Sarah, and the rest is history, as they say. I thought it was just circumstances that brought them together. You know, grief has a funny way of manifesting itself. And I certainly never expected the relationship to last. I mean, Philli and Sarah couldn't be more different. I suppose, what with Giles getting on a bit and probably needing a wife to be accepted in certain circles, the general public like their politicians to conform to society, don't they? And Sarah needing stability and a father for her daughter. I always considered it a marriage of convenience, but they've been together ever since."

"Oh, right. But you and Sarah don't have much to do with each other?"

"No ..." Babs shook her head and paused, appearing to choose her words carefully. "Look, I won't go into detail, but Sarah suffered some pretty horrific health issues as a child, which were my fault. Safe to say, my daughter has never forgiven me."

"Health issues? How can that be your fault—"

"Please, don't ask." She held her palm aloft. "I really can't talk about it. In short, a car accident which *was* my fault. Sarah broke her spine and underwent years of painful treatment. She recovered. Not fully, but enough to lead a relatively normal life up until a few years ago. These days, I'm led to believe she's confined to a wheelchair."

Frank winced, struggling to find the appropriate words.

"I know," Babs nodded. "With one thing and another, I think I've had my fill of disasters."

"You have. But you have a grandchild?"

"Since the twins died, I've only met her a few times. She's fifteen now. I send cards and money on birthdays and Christmas. Well, I did, but I've had no contact for years."

Frank stood and padded across towards the floor-to-ceiling window, rubbing his lower back and groaning when feeling an uncomfortable twinge.

"Frank, these people in this damn place are saying some frightening things about her. Ridiculous claims about what happens in the future."

Frank rammed his hands into his jeans pockets and swivelled around. "Your granddaughter becomes a leading light in a terrorist organisation."

"That's what they claim. I mean, how ludicrous is that?" she scoffed.

Frank pursed his lips, taking a moment to consider his response.

"Anyway, how d'you know Douglas Hartland? And, although I have to say it's really wonderful to see you again, why are you here?"

"Babs, you *are* going to time-travel tonight. Just as I did thirty-six years ago."

7

Too Fast To Live, Too Young To Die

Other than a plethora of nameless brass buttons regimentally lined in two rows of six protruding from a polished panel positioned to the left of a locked inner entrance door, the Portakabin-sized foyer offered nothing other than stark white walls, a marble floor and that dead-air stench. As the heavy outer door clunked back into its frame, I jumped and shivered despite the temperature maintaining a pleasant degree.

"What the hell is this place?" I muttered when glancing up at the high ceilings, the bare, single iridescent bulb, which cast Halloween-esque shadows from the decade-long collection of cobwebs, and the flaking, greying paint precariously sagging akin to flaps of flesh from a decaying zombie.

Although there'd been a bit of a faff when Pink and I exchanged footwear, so it's possible they could have left the building without me spotting them, I felt sure Frank and that man he'd called Sylvester Sneekly must have entered through the second door.

I plumped for the button on the top right, depressing it with my thumb and holding it in position as I waited to hear the chime or buzzer. After thirty seconds of further silence, I moved to the button below. Five minutes later, after attacking each button with ever-increasing fervour and accompanying escalation of frustration, I remained in position with no doorman forthcoming.

Similar to when holed up in the back of Pink's cab, I weighed up my options. Assuming this would be the only entrance, I could wait until Frank had concluded whatever he was up to and opened the door to leave. Or I could give up, scoot back to my hotel, and save my feet from the innards of these sweaty boots.

Despite my vexations regarding what my husband was playing at, concerns about my feet and specifically the disturbing dampness squelching between my toes inside these boots, option two swiftly won the argument. However, when grabbing the doorhandle of the outer door to enact my escape, my plans were thwarted when discovering it to be steadfastly locked in position. When a few hearty yanks on the brass handle achieved nothing, I applied both hands and tugged, gaining purchase on the marble floor with Pink's Doc Martens. Despite my frenzied approach, I only managed to rattle the solid oak door in its frame, strain my biceps, and cause my bra-strap-length hair to fly forward and cover my eyes.

"Oh, that's just peachy!" I announced, before puffing my hair away from my eyes.

After scraping back my mane and tucking the loose ponytail inside the neckline at the back of my frock, I rattled the door again.

"Come on, open!" I hissed.

However, I halted my desperate efforts when spotting through the gap in the doorjamb the lock had engaged. Unless that inner door opened, I was incarcerated in a grim, soulless Edwardian tomb.

"Oh, Jesus, now what?" I mumbled, crossing my arms to rub my bare skin when detecting my body horripilate caused by the rising panic of the thought of being locked in. Although not someone who could be classed as claustrophobic, per se, the memory of an unfortunate experience in an elevator some years back resurfaced. "Come on, get a grip, girl," I muttered, attempting to counter my shivers.

After another round of button pushing, which yielded similar results to my first attempt to gain anyone's attention, and despite my valiant attempts to hold on to rational thoughts, full-blown panic took hold. When repeatedly slapping my palms on the inner door failed to raise the dead, I resorted to booting the door and screaming.

"Hello! Hello, anyone there? Hello. I'm stuck in here. Hello."

Of course, it didn't take long before I ran out of steam, also suffering from sore palms and a jarred right foot, and still no one appeared to be of a mind to come to my rescue. When taking a breather from rather unladylike larruping the sole of Pink's boots on the door, a minuscule, blinking red light positioned on the ceiling caught my attention.

During my earlier perfunctory glance around the tomb, what I'd assumed to be a smoke detector on close inspection appeared to be a CCTV camera.

Of course, now knowing the inner chamber may well be monitored, my spirits rose at the thought that, surely, someone would notice me at some point. In case the CCTV operative wasn't paying enough attention to the monitors, I proceeded to wave my hands at the camera. I hoped my exaggerated movement might haul the dozy gits from daydreaming or distract the idiots from scrolling through YouTube or whatever they were doing instead of monitoring the screens.

After building up a bit of a sweat, feeling like I'd just been put through my paces at the gym on a Wednesday morning when attempting to keep up with the younger ladies at my Zumba class, my efforts bore fruit when hearing the lock disengage on the inner door.

"Oh, well, about bloody time, too! D'you know how long I've been stuck in here? I should report you for this. What if I were a child who'd wandered in here and got trapped? Half a damn hour, I've been banging on that door and hollering to get someone's attention. What is this damn place, eh? Who are you?"

As I ran out of steam when venting my spleen at the two chaps who'd opened the inner door, something about their expressions and the way they looked me up and down sent a chill up my spine.

Although both dressed identically, wearing black jumpsuits, the hems tucked into socks above sturdy boots not too dissimilar to mine, albeit black and not decorated with psychedelic-coloured flowers, the older, thirty-something black guy with Captain Pryor printed on his army-styled fatigues took the lead.

With his thumb and forefinger on a continuous loop, he repeatedly smoothed his bushy moustache whilst assessing what stood before him. Namely, me, hands on hips, hair and head a mess, the crazy lady of pensionable age, dressed in a torn designer dress and colourful DMs sporting rainbow laces.

"Madam, what are you doing here? You shouldn't be in this building."

"I'm ... oh," I paused and twisted my lips. Although frustrated about being stuck in this God-forsaken chamber, I realised Captain Pryor made a good point and posed an impossible question. What was I doing here?

More to the point, what was Frank doing here?

"Madam?"

"Well, where is here? What is the CYA? And why have I been stuck down here, in this ... chamber of horrors?"

Pryor glanced at his scowling sidekick; a younger man devoid of a name tag. I presumed he could remember his own name and thus didn't need a reminder, or his mother had just plain forgotten to sew it onto his uniform. Going by his bemused expression, suggesting confusion regarding my simple question, the big lad who could easily have played John Candy's stunt double as long as he wasn't required to replicate the large man's larger-than-life humour continued to offer his rudimentary countenance.

With no answers forthcoming from the duo, I bashed on. "I've been pushing all those buttons for half an hour or more." I nodded at the panel of brass buttons rather than point because I believed my hands-on-hip pose gave off an air of superiority, and I didn't want to appear intimidated, even though I was. "It's quite rotten of you to leave me trapped in here. Unfortunately, I got stuck in a lift for over an hour when shopping for lingerie at Macy's in New York a few years back. It was quite frightening, and although this isn't a lift, I was still trapped." I chewed my lip, trying to figure out why I needed to have added the last statement and certainly not the bit about which department I'd been browsing.

"Madam, how did you get in here?"

"I came through there," I thumbed over my shoulder at the outer door. "I seem to somehow have gotten myself locked in."

"How did you get through that door?"

"It was open. I just pushed it."

The two men exchanged a glance. "Get that door secured and report there's a fault with the locks," Pryor instructed Candy, before addressing me again. "Madam, this is private property. As I asked you a moment ago, what are you doing here?"

"I was ... I was following my husband."

"And who might he be?"

"He's ... oh, err," I paused and scrunched my nose due to not wanting to divulge Frank's name. Whatever my husband was playing at, this wasn't the time to announce that the wife of Frank Stone, a D-List celebrity, was tailing her husband. "Bugger," I muttered.

Captain Pryor offered his moustache a couple of comforting strokes before nodding at his compatriot, who raised and spoke into a walkie-talkie.

"Control, we have a situation on level one. Some odd-looking woman wearing, err, ... well, hell knows, has gained access through door five."

I peered down at my attire as the young chap rather disparagingly ran his eyes up and down me. To be fair, despite that 'anything goes' attitude to fashion and the banishment of the requirement to conform to a certain style, I had to admit the addition of Pink's boots sufficiently altered my look to suggest I didn't cut the appearance of your average sixty-five-year-old. In fact, my attire probably was more suited to be paraded on the catwalk as part of a Vivienne Westwood collection.

In my defence, it had been a hell of a day.

"This is Control. I have escalated the situation. Secure door five, contain intruder and await instruction."

On hearing the response from *Control*, I shot my head up and backed up a pace. "Err … contain an intruder? I'm not an intruder. You can't detain me!"

"Madam, you are an intruder. If you think you can leave, be my guest." Captain Pryor waved his hand at the locked, seemingly unmovable, outer door.

I glanced at the door and pursed my lips before responding. Disappointingly, he'd made another good point.

"What happens now? And you didn't answer me about what this place is? My husband is in here somewhere. He came through that door with another gentleman … I saw them. I know he's here." I paused but continued when neither seemed forthcoming with an answer. "Can't you just open that door, and I'll go. I won't say anything to anyone … I promise," my last two words uttered in a whinging, pleading tone more akin to my granddaughter Alesha when begging not to be punished for misbehaving.

"This is Control. I've received instructions from the highest authority. This is to be treated as a collateral damage situation. Escort the intruder to the containment suite and await further instructions."

"Excuse me?" I barked, backing up to the outer door as the two men approached. "What the hell d'you mean, collateral damage?" I hysterically shrieked.

In what appeared to be a well-practised pincer movement, both men positioned themselves on either side of me and employed a synchronised arm-grabbing technique before forcibly dragging me through the door.

"Help! Somebody help me!"

8

The Penitent Man

"Have you completely lost your mind?" Babs asked when shifting on the sofa to peer up at Frank as he turned and leaned his back against the window.

"I agree; it does sound like it. But no, I haven't. I'm as sane as the next man."

"Well, if that's the case, the next man must be completely barmy!"

"Babs, how long have you been here?" Frank waved his hand around the room. "I don't mean in this room, but here in this building."

"Three weeks, six days, and a few hours."

"Okay. So, if Douglas and the rest of them are as barmy as me, why are you still here?"

Babs dropped her eyes and picked at a loose thread from the stitching on the top of the sofa.

"I'm in trouble, Frank. When I said I'm destitute, I meant it." She glanced up, still maintaining her thread-picking routine. "Douglas said to trust him. As he pointed out, the worst that could happen is I'd have a roof over my head. But," she paused, appearing to formulate in her mind how to articulate the 'but' sentence. "Frank, you, of all people, can't believe this claptrap drivel. And why would you say such a daft thing about time-travel?"

Frank scooted around the sofa and, with cracking knees, crouched down to take her hands in his.

"I know, that's a ridiculous statement. But what Douglas has stated *is* going to happen. Tonight, you *will* time-travel back to 1979."

"Oh, please, Frank, don't be ridiculous." She yanked her hand from his grip. "After all I've just told you, why would you say such a thing? You're as cruel as this lot claiming I can go back, start again, remarry Stephen, stop Philli and Tom—"

"Babs, listen. Listen to me. I'm not spinning you a line. I've time-travelled. Thirty-six years ago, I time-travelled on the London Eye back to 1979."

"Christ, almighty, Frank, apart from being cruel, you're forgetting that the London Eye didn't exist thirty-six years ago."

"Babs ..." Frank made a grab for her hands.

"Get off!" she barked, shuffling along the sofa to put distance between them.

"Alright ... alright." He raised his hands placatingly before kneeling when detecting a blood flow loss to his feet. "Just hear me out. It's not as if you've got anywhere to be, so you might as well listen."

Although Babs didn't respond or offer any sign that she was prepared to hear him out, she didn't protest any further. Frank took this as a cue to bash on with a story he'd only told Jemma the night his old mate had tried, and in that timeline failed, to strangle her.

"In 2015, thirty-six years ago, I was a rough sleeper. In 1979, in my first life, Jemma *was* murdered the night Dave, in my second life, died."

Babs tutted, shook her head and offered a disparaging lip curl.

"Okay, this is complicated. Look, after Jemma was murdered, without going into too much detail, my life fell apart and I ended up homeless for many years. Douglas and his organisation scraped me off the streets and claimed they needed me to go back in time and stop Jemma's murder. They believed that one change in history would alter a more significant tragedy in the future. Douglas is telling you the truth. I was there that night Dave died up in Fairfield Woods. He was about to strangle Jemma when a time-traveller sent by this lot stepped in and shot Dave and another time-traveller who'd been sent to assist me."

"My good God. What the hell has happened to you?"

Frank huffed before shuffling forward on his knees, clasping his hands in a praying position. "Babs, I know how this sounds—"

"How are we getting on?" boomed The Hooded Claw. As he barrelled through the door, his vampiric grin emerged when taking in the scene of Frank praying and Babs almost backing into the sofa as if her old friend had morphed into a vision of evil. "Oh, all is not well, I presume?"

Accompanying a frustrated sigh, Frank thumped his hands down, one on the coffee table and the other on the sofa beside Babs before glancing up at Hartland.

"You can't blame her, can you? I mean, I accused you of all sorts when you spun out the same story to me."

"Hmmm. Disappointing. Talking of disappointing, we have a situation."

"Oh."

"Unfortunately, we've suffered a security breach."

"A cyber-attack?"

"No, physical. It appears the locking mechanism on the door by which we entered the building earlier has developed a fault. Someone followed us in."

"Right," Frank nodded, glancing at Babs, who remained wide-eyed and pinned back to the sofa, sporting an expression that suggested she faced some hideous demon. "Sorry to hear of your troubles, but I must get going. I've done my best with Babs but, unsurprisingly, she's not going to swallow this until she actually travels back." Using the coffee table as leverage, Frank hauled himself up to a standing position. "Before I go, I'm assuming that Babs is returning to 1979 at a point after her husband Dave is dead?"

Hartland allowed his eyelids to dip to half-mast as he gestured with an outstretched arm for Frank to sit, nodding to the vacant chair when Frank didn't move.

"Frank," he paused and waved his hand as he conjured up his next line, uncharacteristically appearing a wee bit sheepish.

"Oh, no. No, for the love of God," Frank muttered whilst easing himself into the armchair.

"I'm sorry, Frank, but I'm sure you understand. We really don't have much choice, old chap."

"No choice about what?" Babs whispered.

Frank buried his head in his hands and groaned, leaving Hartland to address Babs.

"As you will soon discover, when we drop you back in 1979, your mission is to prevent David Bolton from dying on the 28th of September 1979."

"Yes, I know that," Babs rolled her eyes. "You've drummed that drivel into me. But what's that got to do with Frank?"

"Everything, I'm afraid. Now, run with me on this one for Frank's benefit. As we have briefed you, you must prevent your husband's death. You can divorce him, go on and marry Stephen Denton, but David Bolton must stay alive."

"Why?" Frank mumbled through his fingers.

"Because, my good fellow, our data tells us that by the simple fact her father is alive, Sarah Bolton's life changes dramatically. She no longer produces a child in the year 2000, and that now unconceived child never goes on to form a terrorist organisation. Thus, the event that we call the *Monteagle Fault* never occurs."

"Shit!" hissed Frank when dragging his hands down his face. "What about Jemma? If my old murdering mate, Dave Bolton, stays alive, how will Babs prevent him from straggling Jemma?"

"Yes, I see your point. We, the board and my directors, have discussed this side issue at great length. However, it's a chance we're prepared to take."

"Sorry, what are you talking about? Dave never murdered anyone. I have no idea what the hell he was doing in those woods that night, but he's the one who was murdered."

Hartland offered an exaggerated sigh. "This never gets any easier, does it?" he muttered to the ceiling before addressing Barbara. "My team have taken you through the events of that night and have explained why and how your first husband met his demise. The only information we didn't divulge is that Frank time-travelled to prevent Jemma's murder. I thought, wrongly, it now seems, seeing Frank today and letting him explain would help you understand, believe if you like, and thus set you up in a better frame of mind for tonight's little jaunt on the Wheel."

"Christ," Frank mumbled, shaking his head in disbelief.

"Oh, so, *now* you're agreeing with Frank and rather conveniently claiming he's a time-traveller, is that right? You expect me to believe that in some 'first life' of Frank's," Babs produced air quotes and an eye roll as she paused. "Whatever, or whenever, my husband murdered Jemma Stone? Then, in this supposed 'second life', someone kills Dave just before he murders Jemma and kills him instead? Is that the drivel you're trying to convey?"

"Yes, spot on. Although, not drivel, fact."

Babs blew a raspberry, dismissively waving her arm as she turned to look at the window.

"Hang on," blurted Frank, pointing at Hartland. "Your lot sent an eliminator through time to kill Dave Bolton. The CYA ordered his death, and now you want to reverse that."

"We did and, at the time, for very good reasons. However, circumstances have changed. Back then, we didn't know Barbara's and David's granddaughter would grow up to become a terrorist."

"Jesus, are you saying that if Dave strangles Jemma again, my life could revert back to my first life? I never meet Jayne ..." Frank's rant tailed off as he contemplated that thought.

"Technically, yes, it's possible, but highly improbable. The data boys have run that scenario, and, as I say, it's very unlikely. You're overthinking it, old chap," chuckled Hartland.

"Oh, well, it's bloody easy for you to say! In about six or seven hours from now, my whole life could be wiped, and I'll wake up huddled under a heap of damp cardboard along the Embankment."

"Frank, you weren't listening. I said that scenario is improbable. Our data boys have run the numbers, triple-checked the data, and all the intel suggests there will be absolutely no change to your existence. Also, my good chap, you're forgetting that inaction on our part means that your son, soon to be Secretary of State for Work and Pensions, and Barbara's son-in-law, soon to be Home Secretary, will have their DNA splattered across the rubble of Ten Downing Street along with a rather fine tabby called Bubbles."

"And what about me?" Barbara whispered.

"As we have told you. As long as you still rear-end Stephen Denton's car on the M1 in December '79, your life will continue on the same trajectory. And, my dear, you will have the opportunity to prevent your two children from embarking on their commute on the London Underground on the 7th of July 2005."

"But I will still cause Sarah great harm, and my actions kill those three people in that crash."

"Collateral damage that can't be avoided, I'm afraid. However, that's your choice. If you can't bring yourself to crash your car, our data suggests you will never meet and marry Stephen Denton." Hartland turned his attention to Frank, leaving Barbara shaking her head in disbelief. "Now, Frank, speaking of collateral damage. The only issue we can foresee if Barbara's mission goes pear-shaped, as in if Dave Bolton were to murder your wife again, would be your son, the Rt. Hon. Andrew Barrington-Scott, not existing. However, if Dave Bolton remains dead, your son will die anyway, along with Bubbles. So, as you see, if it all goes belly-up for Barbara, it'll be the same outcome for your boy in the long run."

"Sorry?" Frank quizzed, whilst squinting his eyes and rhythmically shaking his head as if to remove a fuzzy fog.

"Complicated business, time-travel. Frank, if nothing changes, your boy will either not be born or die when Bab's granddaughter obliterates our way of governance by way of a briefcase full of plastic explosives."

Frank and Babs shot each other a look. Whilst leaving his old friend gazing into the middle distance, presumably pondering the thought of a time-travel jaunt or where she might find a bed tonight if all the time-travel talk was claptrap, Frank turned to Hartland, who now sported a ruddy complexion following his frustrated rant.

"Douglas, can't this *Monteagle Fault* be stopped another way? A different time-traveller who's not connected to me?"

"Hmmm." Douglas adjusted his pocket square and flicked an invisible piece of lint from his sleeve before answering. "Frank, we run thousands of scenarios through our systems on ways to prevent the future by altering history. Most have a minute chance of success. Barbara's percentage calculation for success, in our terms, is huge. Our data indicates that if she were to be successful, her life will significantly improve, your life will be unaffected, and the Houses of Parliament will no longer become a Harry Potter-styled Theme Park."

"Frigging Hell." Again, for a few moments, Frank buried his head in his hands before glancing up at Hartland and nodding. "Okay, okay. So be it."

"Good man. Now, as I said earlier, we have that security breach to deal with."

"Oh, yes, good luck with that. Look, can I have a few moments with Babs to say goodbye? Then I really must get going. There's no need to get one of your chaps to run me back to the hotel. I'll just grab a cab."

"Oh, sorry, Frank, how remiss of me. I should have said. The security breach was your rather lovely wife. We have her in the containment suite, and she's kicking up a bit of a fuss, to say the least."

9

La Belle Époque – The Stripper Spy

"What *is* she wearing? What the hell has she got on her feet?"

"She's your wife, old boy," Hartland chuckled from his position behind Frank, who stood nose to glass at the one-way mirror that offered a full view of the containment suite.

"I'm sorry about this, Frank. We would have let her go, but she followed us in here, and we couldn't risk the exposure. As you know, we are a secret organisation, so turfing your wife out could have led to some difficult questions and situations I'd rather avoid."

Frank, somewhat mesmerised, continued to watch his wife as she repeatedly wellied her bizarre footwear on the door, interspersed with slapping her palms and yelling obscenities.

That evening back in 1979, when perched on a barstool in the Murderer's Pub in Fairfield, Frank had been instantly attracted to Jayne because of her stunning beauty. Holly Golightly, he remembered thinking as she playfully drew on her More cigarette. However, he quickly fell in love with her because of her vibrance, humour and zest for life. Jayne was then, and still is, a passionate, ebullient woman, bursting with energy from every pore of her petite frame. That effervescence, pizzazz if you like, now poured out of her as she continued to throw a tantrum similar to how his eldest granddaughter, his eldest daughter's child, could occasionally be guilty of. There was no doubt that grandmother Jayne Stone, daughter Sharon Warlow, née Stone, and granddaughter Alesha Warlow came from the same mould.

Frank turned to face The Hooded Claw, leaving the vision of his hysterical wife behind him.

"I have an idea."

~

"You can't hold me in here! This is kidnapping. Can anyone hear me? Let … me … out!" I boomed again, slapping my hands on the steel door before exhaustion took hold when resting my forehead on the cold, grey steel. A door that, for the best part of half an hour with the aid of Pink's boots, I'd been hammering on to try to gain someone's attention.

The suite of rooms those two goons had earlier forced me into, although sporting a steel door similar to something I imagine Fletch and Godber might face each night, could only be described as palatial. However, my situation, as in being locked in an opulent prison cell, harboured a Kafka-esque feel about it.

"This can't be happening," I feebly muttered when detecting my anger and frustration ebbing away and fear nudging in. I sniffed and wiped my nose with the back of my hand when my eyes began to water and blur my vision. "Frank, where the hell are you?"

As if my whisper became an answered prayer, the door lock disengaged. I hopped back as it opened outwards to reveal my husband and that man whom Frank called Sylvester Sneekly.

"Jesus, Frank, what the blue blazes is going on?" I screeched, reeling my arms around like a demented Catherine wheel.

"Jayne, I'm sorry," my husband calmly answered, stepping through the open door with the dapper gent following close behind.

Although tempted to rip into him, scream and holler about my rather unpleasant experience, something in his demeanour suggested there was far worse to come for both of us. Apart from wondering why he'd shot off for a late luncheon date in a gentlemen's club in Knightsbridge, I'd always trusted my husband. So, for that reason only, I attempted to stay calm. There had to be a rational explanation.

"Frank?"

Before he could answer, the dapper chap stepped forward and offered his hand.

"Mrs Stone, or as I should say, Lady Stone, delighted to make your acquaintance. I'm Douglas Hartland, head of this organisation. Please allow me to apologise for how we've treated you. I have refreshments on the way and, if you will allow, I would like to offer an explanation."

Although rude of me, I ignored his outstretched hand. Instead, I chewed my lip and allowed Frank to take my arm, lift my hand to his mouth and kiss it.

"Frank?" I repeated.

"Jayne, there's some information about what happened to me in 1979, which I need to discuss with you. I promise you, I haven't lied, broken the law, or been unfaithful. However, following events of this afternoon, what I've kept secret for the best part of forty years ... well, now is the time to ..." Frank paused, wincing as he appeared to try to think of the next line. "Err ... tell you the truth, I guess."

While my husband continued to hold my hand, a troop of waiters bustled past, laying out refreshments beautifully presented as if we'd nipped into the Palm Court for a spot of afternoon tea at The Ritz.

"Shall I be mother?" the dapper chap asked, holding up the teapot and offering what I considered a somewhat evil grin. Although his mouth performed the required facial movements to smile, his grey hooded eyes conveyed an altogether different story.

Despite wanting to rip my husband's head off and throttle him half to death as I tortured the truth out of him regarding what was actually occurring, after being locked in this suite and that chamber of horrors for the last hour, I seemed to have run out of steam. And to think, not two hours ago, there I was spreadeagled outside Harrods, thinking my day had just imploded when I snapped the heel on my favoured pair of Jimmy Choo's.

I'd spent my working career as a schoolteacher, mainly applying my pedagogy skills to the sciences at a once prestigious grammar school in the unremarkable Hertfordshire town of Fairfield. In fact, the very school Frank attended in the early sixties when the school operated as an all-boys affair. Although I also taught French and English Literature when required, usually when the poo hit the air conditioning after a bout of tummy bugs ravaged my colleagues who suffered from a delicate constitution, I'd always excelled at the sciences and mathematics.

Of course, when Frank's business became an international success, I'd had no financial reason to work. Also, I'd taken part-time hours and some supply-teacher work when raising our four girls through their primary school years. However, teaching was a calling, not a career and, as I said, the factual subjects being my preference.

So, when dealing with facts, black and white, no grey areas, hearing my husband and this Hartland bloke spout off about time-travel sent my mind scooting off in all sorts of tangents.

Had my husband succumbed to some strange cult? Perhaps a wacky organisation led by the man who could double up as a vampiric owl if such a thing existed. Or, although appearing entirely rational this morning, had Frank suddenly developed a rapid delusional disorder or even schizophrenia? I wasn't aware that condition could take over a brain at such speed, and he certainly didn't accuse the Cumberland sausage or black pudding of conspiring against him when he chased them around his plate when tucking into his full English at our hotel this morning.

However, one of us had to be suffering some sort of delusional disorder. As Frank drivelled on about his time-travelling escapade, I wondered if I'd hit my head on the flagstones when performing my clown-ish slapstick upending. Therefore, in reality, a team of eminent neurosurgeons had placed me in an induced coma up at the ICU of Guy's and St Thomas's. Perhaps that experience in Pink's cab, careering around the streets of Knightsbridge, Westminster and Whitehall, never happened. Could my brain be trying to recover whilst Frank and the girls hovered around my bedside, either wringing their hands or holding mine whilst praying the swelling on my brain would abate?

To be fair, although quite ridiculous, that possibility was far higher in the believable stakes than what my husband continued to spout.

"Jayne." Frank shook my hand to haul me from my reverie. "Jayne, I know how this all sounds. Douglas and I have agreed that we, that's you and me, will escort Babs to the Eye tonight so I can show you I'm telling the truth. In a few hours, Babs will disappear through time back to 1979."

"Hmmm," I cleared my throat, rubbed the back of his hand and peered into his ocean-blue eyes. "Frank, honey, are you alright? You are under a lot of stress, what with all your commitments. You should just let Denzil run the charity and not interfere so much. He's more than capable, and I'm sure he would rather you step back and let him get on with it. The same goes for the business. Now you've handed the reins to Rachel, I think it's high time to take a break and start looking after yourself. It's been on my mind for months ... you've been taking on far too much recently, what with all your media work, too."

"Jayne, this is serious—"

"I know. That's why we should grab a break and recuperate," I interrupted. "You're worn out, Frank, like an old warhorse, battle-weary and exhausted. Why don't we take that holiday we've talked about? Hmmm? We could go down to the cottage or abroad and soak up some sun. It'll do us both good." I peered into his eyes and somewhat patronisingly patted his hand like I might my granddaughter when comforting her about some tragedy that had occurred, like her bestie from school calling her names.

Despite not being totally convinced I wasn't in a coma, I thought perhaps Frank had burned himself out, and the stress of being chairman of his charity and his architect business was all too much for him. He wasn't getting any younger, and the media often deferred to Frank for quotes about the government's performance. Frank, at sixty-six, was what these days they called an influencer. He even had his own YouTube channel.

Over the past few years, to a certain extent, he'd let go of the stresses and strains of running two businesses. Denzil Warlow, married to our eldest, Sharon, now taking control of the charity, and Rachel, married to our second eldest, Helen, elevated to the CEO position at Stone Architects Ltd. That aside, it appeared with everything else happening, my poor husband's brain had raised the white flag. And, rather disturbingly, surrendered to whoever this man was relaxing in a crossed-leg position whilst boring his hooded eyes into my skull. The dapper man who called himself Hartland and who Frank had named The Hooded Claw.

Frank offered a comforting squeeze to my hand and nodded, presumably at my holiday suggestion, before turning to face the vampiric owl.

"This is a lot for Jayne to take in. I presume, like me, everyone you send back thinks you're all raving loonies?"

Hartland nodded at Frank as he shifted forward before leaning towards me.

"When we were searching for a Change Agent who we believed could successfully prevent Frank's first wife's murder, you, my dear, were on our short list of candidates. I recall my Services Director salivating over your university picture, saying you looked like Kate Bush—"

"Oh, per–lease," I tutted and rolled my eyes. "If I had a penny for every time someone said that, I'd be a millionaire."

"Yes, I'm sure." Hartland grinned at my response before chuckling when looking at Frank. "Mrs Stone, I believe you and your husband already hold that status many times over."

"Yes, okay, but—"

"Mrs Stone." Hartland interrupted. "If we'd have sent you back instead of Frank, there was a high probability that you too could have prevented Jemma from meeting a grisly end—"

"She's not dead! Jemma and I enjoyed lunch not three weeks ago."

Frank shot me a look. "Did you?"

"Oh ..." I winced, nervously clearing my throat. "Sorry, honey, I was going to tell you, but I know how Jemma can annoy you so. I thought it best not said."

"Why did you meet? Was it to do with Andrew?"

"Oh, no. Look, my love, Jemma and I go way back. We just enjoyed lunch and a chat about the old days."

"Oh ... I'm surprised you didn't say."

"Well, it appears we both enjoy lunch dates that we haven't told each other about," I sarcastically quipped, shooting a look at the smirking owl whom I had half a mind to slap and remove that grin he now sported.

"As I was saying, before you two become embroiled in a domestic—"

"We're not having a domestic," we both barked.

Hartland held up an accepting palm. "As I was saying, we couldn't choose you because of your connections. Extracting you from your home and placing you here for a month to complete preparations would have been nigh on impossible."

"What connections? And, if you were listening to me, I said, Jemma isn't dead."

"No, because Frank travelled back in time and prevented that unfortunate event from happening. Regarding your connections, although a spinster, you were a school governor and a leading light in the local Women's Institute, amongst a plethora of other social clubs and activities. A busybody type with your nose in everything," he chortled.

I pursed my lips and side-eyed my husband, who just shrugged his response.

"Look, we have a few hours before we take Barbara through to the Eye. I'll have a suite prepared for you both so you can freshen up. In the meantime, I'll get Johnson, my Data and Technical Director, to give you a brief tour. That's quite a privilege, you know. Not many 'normals', as we call them, are afforded that opportunity." Hartland produced air quotes on the word 'normals' before raising his hand and clicking his fingers.

"Normals?" I quizzed, shooting looks between Frank and the man who clicked his fingers again. His glower suggested he wasn't best pleased that he'd had to perform that action twice. Similarly dressed to Pryor and Candy, a man poked his head around the door.

"Sir?"

"Get Johnson," Hartland barked without looking at the poor, admonished fellow who instantly disappeared. "Mrs Stone. 'Normals' are what we call the vast, vast majority of the population and anyone not connected to our organisation. Frank, being one of our successful time-travellers, is what we refer to as an associate. You, my dear, are going to be one of a very rare kind indeed."

"Excuse me?"

"An associate who hasn't time-travelled. We have very few of you, and that role comes with great responsibility."

"Oh, give me strength—"

"Save it." He halted my bluster and prevented my planned wrath with a raised palm.

"Excuse me, how damn rude. I don't think—"

Frank squeezed my hand and shook his head, suggesting this wasn't the time to vent my spleen.

"All will come clear. Now, Johnson—"

"What happened to Morehouse?" Frank interjected.

"Ah, yes, you remember him?"

"Wasn't Morehouse your data chap? He seemed a nervous sort, if I recall correctly."

"Yes, he could be like that, I agree. Brilliant mind. However, there was a bit of bother after you travelled. Penelope organised a coup d'état and temporarily ousted me. I'm afraid Morehouse chose the wrong side. A Mata Hari and a turncoat if ever there was," he chuckled, which morphed into a whine when neither my husband nor I appeared to grasp the funny side. "It all worked out rather well in the end because I was able to outmanoeuvre her and the board, expose Morehouse's duplicity, and thus take over the entire organisation. I've streamlined the entire operation since then. Some may call it a dictatorship, but I prefer to say that our organisation now benefits from strong leadership. My directors and I run a collective governance, an oligarchy, if you like, with some being more equal than others … me, for example." Hartland concluded his speech, smirking and relaxing by way of leaning back in his chair and crossing his legs.

"And Johnson?" quizzed Frank.

"Ah, yes, Johnson. Now, talking of brilliant minds, the man is a walking computer. Funnily enough, I think you could say that you owe a great deal to that man."

"Oh?"

"Yes, your entire way of life, not to put too fine a point on it. The two of you having the opportunity to live the life of luxury that you have carved out for yourselves is down to that man."

"Frank and I have achieved our successes through hard work and dedication."

"Quite right, Mrs Stone. However, if it hadn't been for Johnson coming up with an inspired idea when Frank's mission appeared to be going pear-shaped, sending a second eliminator to dispose of the first and David Bolton, we may have been forced to dispense with and terminate Frank's services."

"What are you wittering on about?" I growled, before detecting Frank squeeze my hand again. That tiny act through years of being together conveying so much without words.

"Mrs Stone, I'm saying, without Johnson, we would have had to dispose of Frank back in 1979. Luckily for you both, his inspired suggestion saved your husband's life."

"Frank, I have no idea what is going on, but it's time we left."

"Mrs Stone, you leave here when I, head and Commander-in-Chief of this organisation, say you can, and not a moment before. Also, you wouldn't want to miss out on the little tour I have lined up for you, would you now?"

"You can't keep me here against my will! And another thing—"

"Mrs Stone." Hartland wagged a finger at me. "Be clear. I can do whatever I damn well choose."

10

None of the Above

"Who on earth does he think he is? I'm quite sure I've never been spoken to so rudely. It's an absolute outrage. Frank, as soon as we get out of here, we're going to the authorities. That man's a total lunatic; dangerous, I might suggest. I mean, how many others could be locked in rooms in this building? You hear of these things, don't you? Poor souls snatched from the streets and held in dungeons for decades."

"Jayne—"

"There was that man in Sweden who took women into his cellar and did all sorts of horrid things."

"Jayne, that was a story by Stieg Larsson, later made into a film."

"Oh, yes, well, what about that crazy woman who kidnapped that writer?

"Film."

"The boy kidnapped by his uncle and sold to slavery, then?"

"Book."

"Aargh!" I bellowed, stamping my boots on the plush, thick carpet.

"Jayne, look, in a few hours—"

"Terry Waite, then?"

"Okay, a hostage situation, as opposed to kidnapping. Also, this place isn't run by Jihadi militants."

"Who the hell are they, then?"

"I don't actually know. But, listen, when we send Babs off, you'll see that what I, Douglas, and Johnson have been telling you is all true."

"Aargh!" I gritted my teeth, just avoiding throwing a tantrum and stamping my boots again. Not that I would typically act in such a petulant manner, but cut me some slack here. Despite my now senior years and childish actions not being part of my usual persona, this was infuriating. I could now empathise with my granddaughter when her parents, as far as she was concerned, caused her life to implode when limiting her screen time.

My totally rational husband, for some bizarre reason best known to him, seemed to have been sucked into the clutches of a crazy organisation. Some clandestine agency that, without any doubt, appeared to benefit from an endless pot of money and wielded significant power. Considering our location and what Pink had mentioned about Ian Fleming, I momentarily pondered that the CYA could be aligned with a top-secret government department. Not that I believed these sorts of organisations actually existed outside of an Albert Broccoli film, but, hey, my husband and I were locked in a palatial concrete box run by a vampiric owl.

"Where did you get those boots? Apart from when we go hiking, I can't say I've ever seen you wear anything like them. And, for that matter, you haven't said how you ended up here."

"Two men dressed as commandoes manhandled me up a flight of stairs and locked me in that room. That's how I ended up in this damn place!"

"No, I mean in this building."

"Oh … hmm." I gritted my teeth and winced. Although clearly something was afoot, admitting I'd tailed my husband from Knightsbridge felt a smidge awkward.

"Jayne?" Frank asked, stepping towards me before placing his hand on my elbow.

"It's … well, a long story, shall we say?"

"We've got a few hours, so I'm all ears."

I puffed out my cheeks, raising my arms out before allowing them to flop by my side. "Oh, well, I followed you. I followed you, didn't I?"

"I gather that."

"Look, I spotted you getting into a taxi when I thought you should be at the office. It was a spur-of-the-moment thing."

"Why? What d'you mean a spur-of-the-moment thing?"

Despite the situation and setting to one side that Frank believed he had actually time-travelled, fully bought into the notion that Barbara Denton, the woman I met many years ago and knew as Babs Bolton, would soon time-travel back to the 1970s via a private pod on the London Eye during the middle of the night, I needed a cuddle. After wrapping my arms around his waist, I pulled him close and rested my head on his chest.

Frank stroked my hair as we held that position, standing in the ostentatious suite Hartland had provided. As I sucked in his scent, I took some comfort in the knowledge that my husband hadn't scooted up to that secret gentlemen's club for a spot of womanising. Also, unlike many of my friends, I hadn't caught my husband cheating on me. That said, If I'd hypothetically tabled these two scenarios to a group of girlfriends over a few glasses of something fruity and sparkling on one of our spa weekends, I'm not sure which one of these Hobson's choices they would plump for. A cheating husband or one who believes in time-travel, suggesting the man must have lost his mind, are equally objectionable alternatives.

During our tour with Johnson, a suave-looking man in his thirties and as clean-cut and well-presented as the vampiric owl, I'd tagged along, mostly keeping schtum whilst furtively scanning the corridors and rooms trying to spot an escape route. As expected, following my experience in that chamber of horrors before being manhandled by the cast of *Brewster's Millions* – a rather apt comparison considering my 'none of the above' preferences to what my husband was up to – I'd failed to spot any green-running-man exit signs or a single door that didn't require the waving of a swipe-card to pass. Whether this was because we were in this particular building or it was just how things were run around here, Johnson wasn't of the mind to enlighten me when I'd casually enquired. However, the Old War Office, now in the clutches of the CYA, appeared to be in lockdown.

Frank, on the other hand, appeared mesmerised by the continued string of BS the pleasant chap spouted, a cacophony of utter drivel about how they calculate the effects of future events. And that was nothing compared to my husband's fascination when Johnson offered an enthusiastic monologue regarding their organisation's back catalogue of historical successes.

Of course, all fanciful drivel that I doubt any publishing house would have shaken a shitty stick at if some budding historical fiction author had conjured up the plot and lobbed said completed manuscript their way. I suspect there would be many 'thanks, but no thanks' replies.

That said, if given the chance, I imagine some desperate movie director might grab the story Johnson claimed to be true about when they sent a time-traveller back to deal with the *Papal Fault*, as he called it.

According to him, they sent an Irish nun back to 1959 to prevent her brother, an eminent psychiatrist of that era, from giving evidence to suggest a troubled man, Patrick Haugh, was fit and safe to be released from a secure unit in 1971. Johnson claimed that through their data and ability to see the future, the CYA knew said troubled man would go on to gun down and kill Pope John Paul II during his visit to Ireland in 1979.

Poppycock, I'd exclaimed, which I think is a reasonable reply to that codswallop.

However, unfazed by my retort, Johnson went on to say that the death of the Pope became the catalyst for civil war on the island of Ireland. So, as I say, utter drivel, but I presume some film director would snap up the fanciful story.

Although not sucked into this charade, I had casually asked why, if they could see the future and how to prevent, shall we say, unsavoury events, had they not stopped Lee Harvey Oswald from firing his gun from the Texas Library? In his reply, Johnson stated that a future where Kennedy had not been shot would mean Jacqueline Kennedy wouldn't have met and married Aristotle Onassis. If that had played out, it would have resulted in far-reaching consequences, details of which he wasn't at liberty to disclose.

Apparently, one great man's misfortune was the wider society's gain. I'd suggested that it was not too dissimilar to the plot of a rather hefty novel by Stephen King. Of course, he offered no reply to my sarcastic quip, just that supercilious smirk he'd borrowed from Hartland.

"Frank?" I whispered, keeping my face buried in his flannel check shirt.

"Uh-huh."

"You really believe in the future Babs's granddaughter will blow up Ten Downing Street and the Cabinet, including Andrew?"

"I do."

"That man, Johnson, who apparently worked in this place when you supposedly came here thirty-six years ago, how come he's only in his thirties now?"

"I have absolutely no idea. Although, when I was last here, that was about a month from now in the future. I travelled through time, then lived my life again back to this time."

"Frank ..." I paused, deciding I really couldn't strike up this conversation again.

"What?"

"Nothing."

"Hartland said an odd thing to me earlier. He reckoned he worked here during the Second World War. I can't see how that could be possible."

"Yes, well, in case you haven't noticed, there's rather a lot of stuff being said that isn't possible." I rubbed my twitchy nose on his shirt before glancing up at him. "You remember when we had our first kiss on that street where I'd parked my little red VW Beetle? Y'know, after we'd had a drink together in the Murderer's Pub?"

"Not ever going to forget that, am I?"

"Hmmm, so you shouldn't. You're saying, at that point in time, you'd time-travelled a few days earlier and realised you didn't love Jemma anymore?"

"I am. Although I was a thirty-year-old man again, in my head, I was sixty-six. Not to mention the string of affairs, but Jemma was spoilt, childish, bitchy, and generally pretty unlikable back then."

"She was, wasn't she?" I quipped. "Still can be now."

Frank lowered his head and kissed me before slowly pulling away and placing his hands on either side of my cheeks.

"I know how mad this all is. But, please, trust me for a few more hours, and then we can go back to our hotel. Tomorrow, we'll book that holiday."

For over three decades, we'd been together as a couple. During that time, I could count on one hand how many nights we'd spent apart. I knew this man, trusted him, loved him. Despite the absurdity of what he was asking, it was a reasonable request.

I chewed my lip, then nodded to agree.

"Good. Now, tell me, how on earth did you end up with those on your feet?"

I glanced down at Pink's boots.

"Ah, talking of ridiculous stories. I met this platinum blonde, spikey-haired cabbie, who held strong opinions on most subjects, seemed to love a bit of ABBA, thought you were a complete superstar, took great delight when relaying the story about when she caught her husband cheating on her with a barmaid in the gents up at the Duck and Feathers, clearly a monarchist and said the Queen was the best thing about being

British, also claiming our monarch is the spit of her auntie Lil, plus ... she said that she's always fancied owning a pair of Pink Jimmy Choo's."

"Course, she did," he chuckled. "The Queen wanted a pair of pink shoes or the cabbie?"

"The cabbie. Of course, the Queen also might, but I'm not in a position to corroborate that."

"And where's the Duck and Feathers?"

"I have absolutely no idea."

11

The Fallen Madonna

"Frank," I hissed, clinging to his arm as we kept pace with two escorts dressed as per Pryor and Candy, who guided Babs under the London Eye and through a series of locked gates. "Is this illegal? Could this be deemed as breaking and entering?"

"Who knows?" Frank shrugged as he shot me a look. "They've got keys, though."

As we reached the landing stage, the number thirteen pod serenely glided to a halt. I knew from the excursion that Frank had refused to partake, and perhaps I now knew why, pods rarely came to a complete stop. Also, there wasn't a pod numbered thirteen due to the architects, or whoever, being ultra-superstitious.

We hovered outside in the dimly lit boarding area as Babs and one of her escorts entered the pod. The other swivelled on his heels to address Frank and me as we huddled close due to the rapidly dropping early-morning temperature.

"You've got precisely seven minutes," he announced, checking his watch before lifting his head and flicking his eyes back and forth between us. "We stick to a tight schedule, and Mrs Denton must travel at 1am sharp. Delays will not be tolerated." He jutted his head forward, chicken style, as if to force home his point.

I glanced up at Frank, who offered a tight smile in response to the escort's instructions.

Dressed in his black military-styled fatigues, I almost expected the escort to stamp his foot and salute. Instead, and somewhat out of character, he hopped sideways and theatrically waved a clear path for us to pass unhindered into the almost blacked-out pod.

"Babs, you okay?" Frank asked, causing the slight woman to turn around from where she'd been gazing across the river towards the Victoria Embankment.

She huffed and scraped back her hair with both hands before slowly shaking her head back and forth.

"This is ridiculous."

"Hear, hear," I chimed in.

My husband side-eyed me before encouraging me with his hand placed on the small of my back to step further into the pod.

"Babs, this is my wife, Jayne. I can't remember, but have you two met before?"

With Pink's boots seemingly glued to the floor, I leaned forward and offered my hand.

"Hello, Babs. We met a few times in the late seventies when Frank was married to Jemma. Wasn't there a dinner party, and you and … and, err, your husband, late husband … shit," I hissed the last word before continuing. "Well, I mean your first late husband, Dave. You and Dave were there, I seem to recall," I winced again at my rather awkward attempt at avoiding the delicate subject that the poor woman had buried two husbands.

A situation that some might call careless, others regard as fortunate.

Babs offered a thin smile. That tiny action exonerated any offence from my somewhat awkward introduction. The lantern-jawed, hollowed-out version of the robust woman I once knew limply took my hand.

"Of course. I would say it's nice to see you again," she shrugged. "Which it is, but not in this stupid thing."

"Oh, don't get me started," I chortled, which morphed into a braying hiccup laugh before shooting a look at Frank. "My husband, God love him, I fear, must have been on wacky-backy all day. I'm quite sure you and I are the only two sane beings left on the planet," I brayed again, instantly wishing I hadn't.

"You don't believe all this nonsense, then?"

I blew a raspberry. "Good God, no! I'm pretty sure that bloke … oh, what was his name? Anyway, the man from the telly is about to spring forward—"

"Jeremy Beadle."

"That's him! Although, I think he's dead. But anyway, any moment now, some prankster will leap through the door, and we'll have a jolly good laugh about it." I chuckled before allowing it to morph into a whine when realising no one else seemed amused. "Yes, well, something like that." I shot a glance at Frank, then back at a lamentable-looking Babs. "Although it's not funny, is it? Babs, I'm sorry. I didn't mean to make light of your predicament. Frank has told me all about what's happened. I can't imagine what you're going through. It must be truly dreadful. I can tell you, I really don't know how I'd cope if something like that happened to one of the girls, let alone losing two children as you have … and your husband.

That's both husbands. You've lost two of them ... how shocking." Although I could hear the drivel pouring from my mouth, rapidly digging a hole for myself, I seemed incapable of shoving a sock in it and thus bashed on in an attempt to recover the situation. "I don't mean it's your fault, you know, losing two husbands. I mean, it's deplorable, tragic, I mean."

Babs snorted a laugh and wiggled my hand. I guess to indicate she took no offence.

"Oh, hell, apologies for my prattle. I'm absolutely poo at these conversations." I glanced up at Frank. "Do you remember that woman who used to work for you? The one whose husband fell overboard when fishing and got chopped up by the propeller? Poor woman was devastated for months, and me and my big mouth just said that I'm sure her husband wouldn't want her to go to pieces over his death."

Frank raised an eyebrow.

"Jayne, thank you for your kind words. You're quite right. It's been truly dreadful."

I excitedly grabbed Frank's arm and peered up at him. "Frank, when this charade is done, can't we help Babs out? Get her set up somewhere whilst she gets back on her feet?"

"Oh, Jayne, that's so thoughtful, but I couldn't impose—"

"Nonsense," I interrupted. "I tell you what, why don't you take our little cottage in Cornwall? You could stay there over the winter, have a decent break, and escape all this." I glanced at Frank. "Babs could go there, couldn't she? I'm sure we don't have anyone booked in for months. Not until the spring, in fact. It's perfect."

"Hang on."

"No, Frank. We must help Babs in her time of crisis. It's settled." I turned my attention to Babs, laying my hand on her arm as I spoke. "No arguments; you take our cottage and recuperate."

"Ladies!" hissed Frank. "Look, I understand that both of you don't believe what's about to happen, but listen to me. Babs, in a minute or so, you need to be prepared. I'm quite sure Hartland and his team informed you that you won't know you've time-travelled until you hear someone state your name. Then, your memories from 1979 until now will come flooding back. You can't prepare yourself for that moment, but believe me, it's a lot to cope with."

"Oh, Frank. Please, please, can we stop this now?"

"Jayne, please," my husband hissed before grabbing the poor woman's shoulders. "Babs, this is it. For Andrew's sake, change the past so my son doesn't die in the future."

Babs clicked her tongue. "I've had enough," she barked, shaking off Frank's hands. "I really don't know what's the matter with me. I've been nothing but a credulous fool, sucked into the ridiculous possibility of seeing my children again. I'm vulnerable. I've lost everything, and you, Douglas, and everyone else think you can have a damn good laugh at my expense. I'm going to do what I should have done weeks ago," Babs came up for air as her voice faltered and her chin wobbled. Although her exasperated rant was clearly directed at my husband, I suspected she was berating herself.

"Babs?"

"Don't Babs me, Frank Stone. I'm going to give Douglas a piece of my mind, and I don't want to see or hear from you ever again." She jabbed a finger at Frank, then turned to me. "Jayne," she hawked, causing me to jolt my head back before continuing in a softer tone. "Jayne, it was nice to see you again, but I have to say, I think it's *your* situation that is truly tragic. At least my husband is dead and not a raving lunatic. I wish you well and hope you manage to sort him out." Rant delivered, she bustled past us and barrelled from the pod.

"Oh, great!" Frank announced, spinning on his heels.

"Frank?"

"Stay there. I'll go and get her," my husband threw over his shoulder as he hot-footed after her.

"Hang on," I called out, but he'd gone, only able to make out his silhouette trotting across the landing stage.

"What a day." I plonked my bottom on the central, oval wooden bench, huffed and rubbed my bare arms to abate the goosebumps. "Holiday, huh!" I muttered. As much as I fancied a short break somewhere sunny with a decent beach and perhaps a cocktail bar, instead, I considered that I'd probably need to wheel my husband along to the doctors as soon as surgery opened later this morning and get him checked out.

"No luck. She's shot off to God knows where," Frank panted as he scooted into the pod.

"Well, I don't blame the woman. What about all those commandos? They must be out there, aren't they?" I shifted my position on the bench seat to follow my husband's progress as he padded past me to gawp across the river.

"Where is everyone?" he muttered, before pointing to the Victoria Embankment on the other side of the Thames. "There isn't a single person or car moving over there. Look, it's deserted."

"So? It's one o'clock in the morning. Any right-minded folk are tucked up in bed, which is where we should be, old boy," I quipped, pushing off the seat and joining him at the far end of the pod. "Come on, you silly old fool," I linked my arm through his before resting my head on his shoulder, "I'm tired, Frank, and to be honest with you, I'm starting to stiffen up after my puddle-diving escapade. I think I need a good long soak in the bath." I peered up at his troubled expression. "Frank, come on, let's go. You can join me in the tub and scrub my back." I wiggled his arm to break his trance. "Don't you want to share a bath with your wife, sweetheart?" I playfully asked.

Whilst waiting for my husband to decide if he fancied bathing with his wife, something we would often do, even at our age, I felt a jolt, as if some giant's hand had nudged the pod.

When shifting around to glance at the entrance, to my horror, I realised the doors had swished closed and the pod had glided a few feet away from the landing platform.

"Frank!"

"Oh crap, no!" he blurted, after my shriek had the effect of hauling him out of his wool-gathering gaze across the Thames.

"Oh, you've got to be joking!" I hollered, bolting across the pod and slapping my palms on the glass before applying my previous, now perfected, action of putting the boot into the door with my newly acquired footwear.

"Hello! Anyone! Hello, can someone hear me? We're stuck in this damn pod." I glanced around the landing stage, trying to pick out one of those army types in their black fatigues. Although I couldn't spot anyone, I thought another round of demented slapping on the glass was in order and proceeded to give it my all.

When a good fifteen feet from the landing platform, I resigned myself to the fact that we would just have to sit it out and wait the thirty minutes until the Eye fully rotated before we could alight. One thing for sure, my patience with my husband's tomfoolery was shot. As Babs had so eloquently put it, I'd had enough; this charade had to stop.

Despite my love for the man, Frank Stone was about to receive a piece of my mind. When spinning around, preparing to rip him a good'un and suspecting my temper wouldn't abate throughout the half-hour free ride in the pitch-black around one of London's premier attractions, Frank stood stooped with his head in his hands.

"Frank? I whispered, his fate-resigning pose enough to evaporate my intended bluster.

"Jayne, I'm sorry. I'm so, so, sorry."

I marched across, dragged his hands down from his face and, as if guiding a frail old gent, motioned that we should take a seat. "Come on. Yes, I'm annoyed, but what is it? Thirty minutes, and then we can get off this silly thing. We'll sit it out, then we must return to the hotel. Now, don't get all tetchy with me, but it's a trip up to see Doctor Haider in the morning. I said earlier that you've been overdoing it of late, and it's time to rest. I'm thinking, perhaps you should see someone about these ... these delusions."

Frank took a deep breath, squeezing my hands together before raising them to his lips.

"Jayne, if in thirty minutes we arrive back at the landing stage, then, yes, we will go and see Doctor Haider, and I agree to seeing someone as you suggest—"

"Good—"

"Hang on. That's on one proviso."

"Go on."

"You hear me out and listen to what I've got to say."

"About what?"

"What I'm pretty sure is about to happen."

I huffed before offering him a disappointed shake of my head. "Okay! It's not as if I have anything else to do whilst stuck on this damn thing, is it?"

"Jayne, please, listen very carefully—"

"I shall say this only once?" I interrupted in my best French accent.

"Jayne! Be serious."

"Alright, I'm all ears," I patronisingly replied.

"From what I can remember, within the next ten minutes or so, we will both time-travel. We certainly won't make it through the full turn of the Wheel." When releasing his right hand from where he held mine, my deluded husband pointed through the glass. "As you can see, the Eye is rotating anti-clockwise, which it would normally only do on the night when British Summertime ends. Also, they increase the speed from point-six miles per hour up to one mile per hour so it engages with the wormhole that's situated in the acre that covers this part of the South Bank—"

"Course it does."

Frank paused at my interruption, squeezing my fingers before continuing.

"That means the Wheel will only take about eighteen minutes to fully rotate. So, we don't have much time."

"You should think about becoming a tour guide. Very informative."

Through the gloom of the dark pod, only partially illuminated by the perpetual light pollution thrown up during the witching hours, I detected the pain and worry of a madman in my husband's eyes. Whilst he continued, ignoring my witty suggestion about a little part-time job to see him through his retirement years, I considered I'd underestimated how far his mental health had declined.

"Within the next few minutes, we will both time-travel back to 1979. I don't know when, but if we land when Babs should have, then it's before Dave Bolton dies—"

"Frank, we're not—"

"Please don't interrupt. We really don't have much time."

I playfully mimed zipping my lips.

"That will mean I'm still married to Jemma. That will also mean our girls aren't yet born."

Although ridiculous, the mention of our daughters not existing hauled thoughts of Babs's tragedy to the fore.

"But look, don't worry. Here, now in 2015, the girls will still be here, as will you and I—"

"I thought you said we were going back to 1979?" My raised eyebrows blowing cannon-ball-sized holes in his delusions.

"Yes, we are. Time-travel, Jayne. We will exist in both times."

"Course, silly me."

"Look, you remember what I said to Babs a moment ago?"

I shrugged my shoulders and bulged my eyes at him.

"You'll wake up on whatever day in 1979, and you'll have no memory of this life until someone says your name. I'm assuming you were living with your mother at that time. She's bound to call your name fairly soon after waking, and then it will hit you like a dead weight," Frank paused, presumably expecting me to ask a question or throw in another quipped remark. However, I stayed schtum, allowing him to continue. "In that moment, all your memories from 1979 until now will return. Your mother will think you're having a seizure or something."

"Frank ... this isn't funny anymore."

"I know." He released his grip on me and scrubbed his hand over his face. "Christ, not again. I can't do this again."

"Come on, my love." I pulled his hands away from his face. "Come on," I whispered, attempting to pull him close, just as I would one of the girls when some catastrophe had sullied their lives like a boyfriend dumping them or a bestie bust up.

In that moment, I recalled when Helen, our second eldest daughter, presumably concerned about my reaction, informed me she was gay. After cuddling her forever, my daughter's angst evaporated when I told her that her father and I had known about her sexuality ever since she was in pigtails and wore white, knee-length socks. Mothers just know stuff. It's an inbuilt skill installed in us by our makers, providing the ability to understand our children better than they know themselves.

Before Frank relented and fell into my embrace, he peered up at me. "Jayne, meet me in the Murderer's Pub at seven. I'll go there every day until you show up."

"Alright. I promise." With his head on my bosom, I rolled my eyes before shooting worried looks around the city skyline when noticing the sky glow of London fading as if controlled by some giant dimmer switch.

"How odd," I muttered, still petting my husband's greying locks. "Time-travel, it's against reason," I whispered, remembering the line from H. G. Wells.

As I uttered those words, my pupils dilated to refocus due to the lack of light. At that point, little could I imagine I would no longer be inside when the Eye had completed one full turn and pod thirteen returned to the landing station.

Part 2

12

No More Heroes

"In all my years, I've never come across such a shit shower of useless, incompetent, good-for-nothing, worthless, half-witted morons like you bunch of bloody idiots!" Captain Pryor blustered as he walked the line of operatives who stood to attention in the CYA's foyer after being summoned back when reporting the unfortunate events that transpired at the Wheel not five minutes earlier.

Pryor halted, turned away from the line of men and offered a few strokes to his moustache as he attempted to calm himself after verbalising his fury regarding what was probably the worst operational cock-up in the CYA's history. Before resuming his back-and-forth pacing along the line of his terrified team, Brimley, the Transportation team leader assigned to escort Mrs Denton to the Wheel, tentatively raised a finger.

"Sir."

"Shut up!" Pryor, who stood a good six inches taller than the man who now appeared to be regretting raising a digit, spun around and bore down upon him with bulging eyes, giving the appearance that he'd developed a particular prevalent case of proptosis.

Brimley swallowed hard while trying to control his wobbling knees, keeping his eyes forward as his commanding officer stared him down.

"What in God's name have you got to say for yourself, you babbling, useless, imbecilic buffoon?"

Brimley blinked as globules of Pryor's spit fired into his eyes. Before attempting to swallow again, he bit the side of his mouth in an attempt to moisten his desiccated tongue. Akin to a circus act, when the tamer placed their head in a lion's mouth, Brimley held his breath and silently prayed he'd still be alive come breakfast time. Apart from not wanting to die, this being a Thursday, the cook always placed waffles, which were his favourites, on the menu as a weekly special. Whilst feeling Pryor's breath on his face and tightly squeezing his eyes shut, the terrified team leader mustered up the fortitude to speak.

"Sir … sir, there appears to have been a bit of a mix-up—"

"Sir, sir," parroted Pryor, employing a timid tone when interrupting the now heavily perspiring team leader. "Shut up, you bloody idiot," he screamed, his bluster causing the veins in his forehead to bulge as if some alien life form behold there and now battled to escape. Returning to the timid voice, the furious captain mocked the man further. "Err, sir, sir, there appears to have been a bit of a mix-up. Sorry, sir, sorry, sir."

"Sir?"

"You can shut up as well!" Pryor boomed at his sergeant behind him without turning from where he held his forehead millimetres from Brimley's quivering form. With clenched fists held behind his back, he raised his voice to a level never previously heard, causing all within the confined space, including the now admonished sergeant, to jump and the door to rattle in sympathy for the doomed men. "How the hell can this be classed as a bit of a mix-up? You and this bunch of delinquent imbeciles set the sodding Wheel in motion with the wrong sodding people in it, and the one we should have sent back through time is now sodding AWOL!"

"Sir, if you will allow me to speak?" his sergeant interjected when stepping forward into the captain's eyeline.

Without shifting from his intimidating pose, Pryor side-eyed his sergeant before shooting a glare back at Brimley when detecting the man had briefly dared to open his eyes.

"Sir, I can see how this has happened. Just at the point of travel, a woman and a man exited the pod. It's reasonable for the team to assume those were Mr and Mrs Stone and, due to time pushing on, they quite rightly set the wheels in motion." The sergeant cleared his throat, feeling the need to continue when the captain didn't respond. "Err, no pun intended, sir. I wasn't being flippant. You know, wheels in motion … Millennium Wheel, if you see?"

Pryor glowered at his sergeant. "I don't give a damn what is reasonable or what isn't. Cock ups of this magnitude cannot be tolerated!"

"I know, sir."

When glancing over his sergeant's shoulder and spotting the approaching figures, Pryor hopped back and saluted. "Attention!" he boomed.

Douglas Hartland and the Data Director, Johnson, entered the room. A couple of the men flicked their eyes to assess the threat level, all of them turning a somewhat disagreeable shade of green when realising the Commander-in-Chief himself stood before them.

"Sir," confidently stated Pryor before abruptly closing his mouth when receiving a death stare from Hartland, who then turned and faced the line of petrified men.

Uncharacteristically, Douglas unbuttoned his double-breasted suit jacket, rammed his hands in his trouser pockets and bowed his head as he walked the line, not dissimilar to how Pryer had not moments before. In that moment of silence, Pryor and Johnson exchanged a glance.

"Gentlemen, gentlemen, what shall we do? What ... shall ... we ... do?" Hartland threw out, not looking at anyone in particular, just throwing his calmly delivered question into the ether. "Against popular belief, I'm a reasonable man." He halted and squared up to a fresh-faced young man positioned in the centre of the line. "Isn't ... that ... so?" Hartland's measured cadence entirely at odds with the underlying threat and the vampiric grin he offered when positioning his face millimetres from the poor chap who appeared ready to faint.

Pryor and Johnson again exchanged a glance, Johnson nodding to convey he would try to intervene.

"Sir, perhaps—"

"Not now, Johnson. Not now, there's a good chap." Hartland calmly cut him off whilst maintaining his glare at the young lad who, going by the rather odd leg movement that didn't look too far from an Elvis 'rubber legs' dance, appeared to have lost control of his quadriceps and hamstrings. Hartland pulled back and continued to pace the line with his head bowed.

"So, as I'm quite sure Captain Pryor has informed you, tonight's debacle is the most catastrophic balls up in our long and successful history. Very soon, in say," he paused and glanced at his watch for effect. "Well, in about five minutes, we will know what disasters have occurred over the last thirty-odd years due to setting the Wheel in motion with Frank and his rather delightful wife, Jayne, inside." He halted and raised a finger, looking along the line. "Of course, that's not to mention that the *Monteagle Fault* is still unresolved, and we've carelessly misplaced Mrs Denton." He glanced at Johnson. "About five minutes, would you say?"

"Yes, sir. My team will have preliminary results ready at a quarter past the hour."

Hartland pursed his lips and nodded before halting his pacing to face the line of fifteen men.

"So, as I said, I'm a reasonable man. Now, we can go one of two ways with this. Either the man who made the imbecilic decision to set the Wheel in motion takes one pace forward, or all of you will fail to see the sunrise. Which would be a shame for two reasons. Firstly, recruiting and training replacements is time-consuming and damn costly, not to mention a right royal pain in the bloody arse. And secondly, I'm led to believe the forecast for today is a pleasant twenty degrees and sunny. It would be a shame to miss it."

When no man moved, Pryor cleared his throat.

"Sir, can I respectfully suggest—"

"No, Captain Pryor, you cannot respectfully suggest or unrespectfully suggest either," Hartland interrupted him, turning to face the Captain as he remained standing to attention, staring straight ahead, as did his men.

"Captain, I commend you for your unwavering loyalty to your men and the team ethic you have instilled. All very touching, this one for all, all for one attitude."

"Sir."

"However," Hartland paused and again pursed his lips. "Tell me, Captain, how long have you been with us now?"

Pryor flicked his eyes left, then back at Hartland. "Err ... joined in '85, sir. I've just received my thirty-year service medal and the catalogue from where to choose a gift, sir."

"Oh, how lovely. And have you decided which gift you would like? Not that I'm au fait with what HR offer for thirty-years service, but I imagine the gifts are quite something."

"Yes, sir. Very generous, sir. My wife is rather taken with the air-fryer machine, sir. Apparently, it offers the facility to fry chips without fat."

"Really? How lovely. I must mention that to my wife if I can ever be bothered to talk to her again," Hartland sarcastically offered before stepping closer. "Captain Pryor, if you wish to see the sunrise and enjoy a fat-free chips supper, I suggest you follow through with what's required following this debacle."

"Yes, sir."

Two men fainted; one chundered down his tunic, and Brimley involuntarily allowed his bowels to noisily open.

"Sir, it's nearly 1:15," Johnson interjected. "My team will have the preliminary data from the last thirty-six years by now. Shall I whizz up and grab the file and meet you in your office?"

"No, I want to hear what damn disasters are afoot directly from your team. So, God help them, I'll come with you," growled Hartland before waving a warning finger at Pryor, spinning on his heels and pushing past Johnson to then stride purposefully along the corridor, his open jacket fanning out as he made haste. "And get an eliminator ready to travel within the hour. If this monumental screw-up has caused any major changes, we'll have to send one of them back to clean up this mess," he threw over his shoulder.

Johnson nodded at Pryor, reaffirming that he must follow through with Hartland's instructions, before spinning on his heels and chasing after Douglas. Although discipline was important, and errors of this magnitude couldn't be tolerated, Johnson was always uncomfortable with the ultimate penalty being meted out to either his colleagues or time-travellers who'd made a pig's ear of things.

However, even though he was now a senior player in the organisation, he wasn't going to be the one to suggest a less radical attitude on how to deal with failure. No, he liked his head attached to his body far too much to suggest such a policy change.

Usually, within twelve to fifteen minutes after sending a traveller to the past, his team would have a provisional report detailing the changes their latest traveller had inflicted upon the world.

Of course, the most critical intel required would be regarding the data on whether the traveller had been successful and achieved their mission. In this case, that would be checking whether Dave Bolton didn't die on the 28th of September 1979, which their data suggested would be the catalyst to prevent his then five-year-old daughter from becoming pregnant in the year 2000 and ultimately mean that Jolene Horsley would never be born. If that had happened, the terrorist organisation *Freedom Against Right-wing Tyranny* would never be formed.

All good; mission accomplished; the *Monteagle Fault* averted.

After that, success or failure, a review of changes would need to be categorised. His team of analysts placed each alteration of history into a category depending on its severity. Categories one through four pretty much instantly triggered the immediate despatch through time of an eliminator to dispose of the aforementioned traveller, thus expunging any changes they caused. The CYA maintained a few ex-SAS types on a retainer for such an eventuality. Of course, these highly trained individuals were gagging for a time-traveller to make an error so they were afforded the chance to relive their life, just as Collinson had when Frank travelled thirty-six years ago.

Any changes in the five through seven categories would be a discussion point that Douglas and his team of directors would muse over whether it was deemed severe enough to eliminate the traveller. Categories eight, nine, and ten usually involved changes that could be tolerated, so no further action was required.

That all said, tonight would be a first because his team wouldn't be assessing the results of sending Barbara Denton as planned. What mayhem this error might have caused really didn't bear thinking about.

Johnson trotted along the corridor to catch up with his boss, a smidge concerned how Douglas might react if the news wasn't favourable. He was acutely aware that the act of Douglas entering the Data Office would result in his team resembling the residents of a hen house when said secure living space had been breached by a fox.

Many years ago, Johnson himself had been an analyst and could recall the sheer terror Douglas could evoke in him and his peers. Back then, when Hartland held the position of Operations Director, the organisation could be considered less autocratic. Although in a senior role in the organisation, Douglas had been answerable to the board, and thus the man was on a tight leash. Now, after the 'Great Purge' when Hartland organised a counter coup d'état, removing the board and most senior officials, he held supreme power and was answerable to no one.

Due to his iron grip, their supreme commander had earned the moniker 'Uncle Joe' because of his ruthlessness and similar handlebar-styled moustache sported by the tyrannical Soviet leader who ordered the removal of Leon Trotsky and a million or so others who didn't quite agree with his take on things.

When in close proximity to anyone affiliated with the CYA, Douglas Hartland harboured the ability to make the masses scatter, at the very least, look the other way and pray he didn't talk to them, akin to passengers on the Tube when the regulation nutter boarded the carriage.

Johnson, after putting a bit of a lick on, dived ahead of Hartland as they reached the open plan office area, which housed thirty analysts who beavered away on their banks of screens that flashed up data and metrics. To the untrained eye, the complex chains of information appeared to be hieroglyphics and muddled symbols more at home on a retro gaming machine or DOS operating system on speed.

Like an intrusion of cockroaches when illuminated in the beam of a flashlight, all thirty analysts, bar one, scuttled away and ducked low behind their screens at the sight of Uncle Joe. Whitman, Johnson's senior analyst, promoted to said position when he'd achieved his board appointment, confidently stood and raised her chin. Whilst clutching a leather-bound file, she marched into Johnson's office – a glass cube in the centre of the main room that afforded three-hundred-and-sixty-degree views of the open plan area – halted by the desk and held the file to her chest.

Whitman and Johnson exchanged a glance. The flaring of her nostrils conveyed, as expected, she wasn't about to present favourable news following the monumental cock up not more than twenty minutes ago. Johnson mused the champagne would have to stay on ice or, more likely, be returned to the cellar.

Hartland slumped into Johnson's chair, fished out his cigarette case and extracted one before snapping it shut and slotting it back into his jacket pocket. Using the paperweight lighter on the desk, he lit the cigarette, inhaled and blew a plume of smoke to the ceiling as he waited for the heavy glass door to slot back into a closed position. Standing near the slowly closing door, Johnson offered a silent prayer to whoever might be of a mind to listen that what Whitman was about to say wasn't too horrific.

Although safer than previous modes of travel, time-travel via the London Eye came with risks. A small percentage of travellers never made it, their bodies evaporating into the ether. For the greater good, the association and all those who worked within deemed the seven-point-four per cent of failures to arrive safely as an acceptable failure rate. Johnson prayed that tonight, that percentage would increase a notch.

In that moment of silence, Johnson shot Whitman another look. Despite hopes that tonight his senior analyst would report a failed mission and nothing more, Whitman's slow-blinked response confirmed what he feared. Hartland raised an eyebrow at Whitman as the glass door thunked into position, sealing out the noise of tapping keyboards in the open-plan office area.

"Well, what have you got, woman? I haven't got all bloody night. Was time-travel successful?"

"Yes. I'm afraid so, sir."

"Christ! Sod it!"

"That's not all, sir. The preliminary results are not favourable. *Your* failed mission has caused a catalogue of issues the likes of which we've never experienced. It's a shit storm, to say the least."

13

1979

Hit Me With Your Rhythm Stick

"Oh, botherations, I forgot to mention. Simon called for you yesterday afternoon. I said you'd ring him back, but it must have slipped clean out of my mind. Perhaps you should call him before you go to work? He's a lovely young man, and I know he's keen."

I side-eyed my mother whilst buttering my toast, knowing she was doing her level best to help me find a suitor and ultimately produce grandchildren. While she prattled on, I let my mind drift to thoughts about today's lessons. Disappointingly, the first hour would constitute a hellish experience in the company of thirty students from F Band. Whilst I attempted to instil a basic knowledge of mathematics and survive the whole encounter unscathed, the demonic offspring of the local area, most of whom crawled out of the Broxworth Estate, did their level best to turn the one-hour event into a maelstrom. It was fair to say, what F Band students lacked in enthusiasm for furthering their education, they more than compensated with their ability to riot.

"Did you hear me?" Mother asked, handing me my tea, thus hauling me from thoughts about riot shields and the myriad of projectiles that bunch of delinquents might have prepared for this week's showdown.

Compass points carefully secreted in the tips of paper aeroplanes were child's play when compared to the ingenuity devised by this year's form class to inflict pain.

"Oh, sorry, Mum, I was miles away."

"I said, if you'd been listening, I don't know what you're waiting for."

"Sorry? Waiting for what?"

"Simon! He's a lovely young man. He's got that steady job at the council, as you well know. His father has some swish job at the bus depot, and his mother is a leading light in the WI. I heard in the gossip in the queue at the Post Office last week they've purchased a new caravan, so they must be well off."

"Mum, I'm not going to date a man based on the fact his parents have joined the Caravan Club, and his mother takes charge of the judging of the annual Victoria sponge baking competition."

"Hmmm. Time's running out, and your clock is ticking. When I was your age, I'd been married to your father, God rest his soul, for ten years, and you were already in school."

I huffed before slurping my tea whilst glancing at Alf, who, for some reason, seemed to be acting strange this morning.

"He very kindly gave us ladies that wonderful talk at last week's meeting about traffic lights and street lamps with a very informative slide show on the different styles of car park lighting. Fascinating, it was. As I said, a lovely young man and I'm sure he'd make you very happy, my dear."

"What?" I asked, with a mouth full of toast, now wondering what relevance car park lighting had to do with a conversation regarding Simon's suitability as husband material.

"Simon! And it's pardon, not what, and please don't talk with your mouth full." Mother tutted and shook her head, a trait that appeared to be on the increase either due to becoming grumpy since she'd passed fifty or because of my lacklustre attitude and lack of desire to agree to any more riveting dates with Mr Traffic-Light. "You're in a trance this morning. I hope you buck your ideas up before you get to school. Otherwise, your poor students will learn nothing today."

Alf took a fleeting break to yawn and lick his lips before reapplying that rather odd snarl on his chops.

"Oh, I see. Simon gave a talk at the WI?"

"Yes! As I said, very informative it was too."

I raised an eyebrow before taking another bite of toast.

Alf dipped his head and offered a long, guttural growl. Whatever his problem, there appeared to be something not right with him today.

I'd endured, no suffered, to be more precise, a few dates with Simon over the summer months. There was nothing wrong with him, per se. Thirty-two, so only three years older than me, owned his own car, a yellow Austin 1100 with regularly polished hubcaps, well turned out in that drawstring blue anorak purchased from C&A, razor-sharp ironed creases in his jeans, courtesy of his mother, and there was no denying he could talk passionately for hours about traffic control systems in Fairfield.

So, for a girl like me, unattached, living at home with my mother, and the ability to only attract men who made Dylan from the Magic Roundabout appear positively outgoing, perhaps I should grab Simon before he wooed and bored to death some other poor unsuspecting woman.

However, as keen as Mother was that I didn't wait too long and end up on the shelf, as she put it, Simon wasn't the man for me. No, most certainly not. And anyway, a few years ago, one-thousand one-hundred and fifty-eight days to be precise, I'd fallen in love with someone else. Not that I was counting, as such. Well, okay, maybe I was.

Unfortunately, that someone just happened to be married to one of my closest friends. So, my long-held desire for Frank Stone, the husband of our local MP, Jemma Stone, meant that I was not only destined to be unhappy, but Simon or any other man really didn't measure up to the ocean-blue-eyed, blond-haired Frank.

For some months, I'd been doing pretty well on my mission to forget the man I loved. Well, there's no point pining over a man who couldn't be mine, is there? And anyway, if by some miracle Jemma suddenly decided that she didn't want him anymore, the chances that Frank would then bowl up to school and declare his love for me during lunchbreak were, I suspected, on the low side.

"The trouble with your generation is you want it all on a plate. Television is to blame, especially all that American rubbish filling our screens these days. In my day, I was just happy to meet a boy at a dance. If he came from a decent family and was prepared to work hard, then that's all a girl needed. You, your generation, think life's going to be all Bogart and Bergman."

"Oh, Mum, give it a rest. I'm friends with Simon, but that's it."

"Well, look." She tapped the newspaper that Alf had half mauled, something he performed most mornings when enjoying a tug of war with the paperboy, that depicted a picture of wretched Barbara Leach's parents on the front page. "Those poor people, losing their daughter like that. All I'm saying is there are some sick, depraved men in this world, and you could do a lot worse than Simon."

"Mum, not every man, bar Simon, is like this Ripper bloke."

"No, I'm not saying that. What if you bump into this monster and end up being his next victim? If you were with Simon, that won't happen, will it?"

"Mum! We live in Fairfield, and last time I checked, that's in Hertfordshire, not Yorkshire."

"Yes, well, I'm just saying."

"Well, please don't. And what's the matter with Alf this morning? He's been snarling at me ever since I came out of the bathroom."

Alf bared his teeth whilst keeping his eyes trained on me. If I didn't know better, our matted mongrel with the usually dopey persona rather uncharacteristically appeared primed and ready to tear my throat out. Apart from his regular morning workout with said paperboy, Alf would rarely muster up the energy to crawl out of his basket and usually considered growling far too energetic.

"Alf! Alf … basket!" Mother ordered in her acerbic tone, which she exclusively employed when ordering around my late father's dog.

I say a tone of voice exclusive to Alf, but with my love life, or lack of, becoming an all too frequent subject at mealtimes, I suspected Alf and I may become kindred spirits when avoiding my mother's wrath. Presumably, if I continued to poo-poo her suggestions regarding suitable boyfriends, I wouldn't be relegated to a dog basket. Still, perhaps it was time to move out and start living a life. To use Mother's analogy, at twenty-nine, I was running out of shelf life.

"Bad dog, bad dog. Get in your basket," Mother ordered, accompanying her growl with a forceful jab of her arm as she eyeballed Alf.

Alf, keeping a wary eye on me, backed up, slithering his bottom along the lino so as to be out of reach of Mother's raised hand.

"What on earth is the matter with him?"

"Lord knows! Your damn father's dog. If I'd have known he was going to have a heart attack and leave me with it, I'd have never agreed to having the blessed thing."

"Oh, Mum, it's not Alf's fault Dad died." I shot a frowned pout at Alf as he continued to snarl at me from a safe distance. "You don't think there's something wrong with him, do you? You hear about dogs that suddenly flip and turn on their owners."

"Oh, I don't know. Anyway, he seems fine with me."

Alf shot Mother a doggy smile as if to concur with her statement before inching towards me and again baring his teeth.

"Well, something's not right with him."

"Simon's got a dog. Very well behaved, if I recall. You know, at his talk, his golden retriever—"

"Mother! Please. I'm not going to marry Simon. I'm not even going to call him back, alright? So, for my sanity, please drop the subject." Apart from Alf not taking too kindly to my raised voice, I now felt guilty as my mother fussed with her apron, clearly disappointed with my outburst. When all was said and done, she was only looking out for me.

"You've got your father's temper, my girl."

"Mum, I'm sorry."

"Hmmm. Now, remember, I'm at bingo tonight, so you'll have to get your own tea."

"Oh, don't worry, I'm popping into town after school. I'm meeting Jason and Jenny for a drink."

"That's nice, dear. Will Jason be bringing a friend?"

"If you're meaning a blind date, no. Sorry to disappoint."

"Be careful and make sure they walk you back to your car." She tapped the paper before rising from her seat and grabbing the teapot. "As you can see, there are nasty men roaming the streets at night."

"Yes, Mum," I rolled my eyes behind her back, causing Alf to offer a disapproving growl.

"Make sure you do. I know you think I'm interfering, but it's just because I care," Mother threw over her shoulder as she rammed her hands in the washing-up bowl.

"Yes, Mother," I muttered.

"Perhaps later we can look at those holiday brochures I picked up at the travel agents last week. The lady said that Benidorm is getting booked up for half-term, so if we're going, we'd better decide which hotel."

I chose not to reply. Although going on a holiday was a lovely thought, accompanying Mother half-board in some crummy hotel really didn't float my boat. During the summer, when all my friends holidayed with their husbands and kids, I, the saddo, endured days out with Mother. The dread of a whole week in her company would probably bring me out in hives.

"Jayne, did you hear me?"

As if I'd hit fast forward on the Sky Box to zip through the adverts during my favourite programmes, my mind flashed through a billion images of my life up until I slumped on that oval wooden seat in that pod on the London Eye when my husband, Frank, tried to convince me about his ridiculous notion regarding time-travel. After sucking in air, when it suddenly occurred to me I'd stopped breathing, I clutched my chest, suspecting that my heart was about to split. Not in a similar way to how my father's had a few years back, but for the overwhelming sense of loss.

"Come on, you'll be late. Shouldn't you have left by now? Look, it's gone eight." When I failed to answer, Mother swivelled around, holding up her soapsuds-covered, pink-marigold-gloved hands. "Jayne, what on earth's the matter?"

"My girls," I barely audibly croaked. My eyes clouded as tears welled up, morphing the vision of Mother into that of a shimmering apparition. When sensing my chin uncontrollably wobble, I swivelled around to hide in the terror that must have surely oozed from my traumatised expression.

"Good grief, are you alright? You've gone as white as a sheet. You've probably picked up some bug that's doing the rounds. I heard Mrs Fotheringhay, who lives across the road, you know, number seven, the house with all those silly gnomes in the front garden. Well, she's been poorly for weeks. The doctor's been out twice already."

"Where's Frank? Where are the girls?" I muttered, before clamping my mouth shut and grinding my teeth to control my facial muscles, which felt as if they were all simultaneously in the throes of attempting to recover from being tasered. Although under different circumstances, I could now fully empathise with Barbara Denton. In the blink of an eye, I'd lost my four children.

"Jayne? Jayne, what on earth are you wittering on about? I said you look rather peaky, as if you've seen a ghost."

With my hand firmly planted on my chest, satisfied I could detect my thumping heart, I glanced around at Mother.

"I have," I whispered.

Apart from trying to cope with the realisation that not only had Frank, Sylvester Sneekly, and everyone else in that CYA place been telling the truth regarding time-travel, coupled with the crushing realisation that my four daughters didn't exist, my dead mother stood not a few feet from me. On the subject of ghosts, my mother should be dead, not staring at me, sporting a worried look and a pair of soapy pink marigold gloves.

Mother died in a care home in 2001. It had been a particularly torrid year. Clara, our youngest at fifteen, had reached that difficult stage of puberty. Unlike her three elder sisters, who pretty much managed to traverse their teenage years reasonably unscathed, avoiding drugs, sex and rock and roll, to paraphrase Mr Ian Dury, Clara had monumentally gone off the rails.

Apart from her schoolwork going by the wayside, she'd discovered boys. Clara quickly learned that if she copied Britney Spears' dress sense from her raunchy pop videos, boys would swarm around her like the paparazzi soon will a young, shy Lady Spencer if this was the year Frank had suggested it would be. As I said, to add to all that drama of our wayward daughter, after the millennium, I also had daily visits to my mother's deathbed to contend with.

Now, here she stood, large as life, glaring at me as if I'd grown a second head. Whilst Alf, who appeared to have undergone his second personality transplant within the space of as many minutes, nuzzled his head on my lap, shooting looks of endearment at me.

"Jayne, you're not making any sense. Come on, you'll be late for school," she ordered before turning back to face the window and delving her hands into the soapsuds. "Put Alf in the garden on your way out. I'm meeting Cheryl this morning, so I haven't got time to drag him around the park. If the annoying woman doesn't prattle on too much, I might make it back in time for the Jimmy Young Show and Pebble Mill at One."

Alf lifted his head and sprung up to place his paws on my lap before nudging the paper across the table towards me with his nose. Without moving I shot my eyes to the doggy-dribbled torn front page, which displayed a picture of the wretched couple depicted next to the article regarding the Ripper's twelfth victim, who was to be buried this week. My eyes flicked to the date at the top of the paper.

"Christ, they still don't know who he is," I vacantly muttered.

As if to convince myself that I was here in yesteryear, I rubbed my hand on the news sheet as if feeling the printed pages would confirm the impossible, the horrible, the ridiculous, the inexplicitly damn right daft.

Apart from the last half hour, I hadn't held a coherent conversation with Mother for over twenty years, primarily because she'd been dead for nearly fifteen of those twenty. Unfortunately, Mother had succumbed to dementia in her late sixties. Apart from not knowing what to say to her, now realising time-travel was a thing, I shuffled out to the hallway to grab my bag and jacket with Alf tagging along by my side.

Of course, I could be dreaming. After overindulging in oysters and champagne yesterday, maybe my mind was on one. I held onto those thoughts for a brief moment, praying I would wake up and my girls would be with me. However, when glancing at the full-length hall mirror, what reflected back suggested this was no hallucinating effect of swallowing copious amounts of contaminated shellfish.

"Was I really this tiny?" I whispered, peering at my features when leaning closer to inspect my, in comparison to yesterday, almost flawless skin. I glanced down at Alf as he patiently waited by my side. "You know, don't you?"

Alf licked his chops, furiously wagging his tail that rhythmically thumped against the stair newel post on every other swish.

"All that growling and snarling was to get me to realise what's happened?"

Alf panted and licked his chops.

"Christ, get a grip. You're talking to a dog. He's not going to answer, you daft cow," I muttered whilst Alf excitedly barked.

"Was that a yes?" I quizzed him.

Alf turned his head sideways and again licked his chops as if to confirm.

After grabbing my jacket, I reinspected myself in the mirror. Okay, the pleated skirt wasn't a total disaster, but the ruffled, high-necked blouse was ruddy awful. Had I really dressed like my mother at the age of twenty-nine? No wonder Drawstring-Anorak-Simon had the hots for me.

Whilst trying to see past my dowdy school wear, I jauntily placed my hand on my hip, slung my jacket over my shoulder and pouted at the mirror, Marilyn Monroe style, which, despite the crazy goings on, my reflection followed suit.

"Not bad, even if I do say so myself."

If that reflection was me, then my boobs had definitely ratcheted up a few notches, and my frame now resembled that air-brushed, photoshopped image of me in that society magazine. In an instant, I'd gone from a size twelve battling bingo wings down to a svelte-like size eight with pert boobs.

Keen to inspect further, somewhat mesmerised by my youthful appearance, I swished my long-wavy hair to one side and felt my earlobe. Due to not being into earrings, I hadn't had my ears pierced until reaching my mid-thirties when Frank offered to buy me a gorgeous pair of pear-drop pearl earrings for our wedding anniversary. As they were before that event, my earlobe appeared unpierced.

"Shit, what on earth …"

Alf nudged my leg, effectively hauling me out of my self-appreciation and back to … well, back to reality, if this is what it was and not a case of bad-shellfish hallucinations. Last night, when Frank was frantically trying to inform me about what was about to transpire as the Wheel slowly rotated backwards, I'd freaked about our girls. He promised me they'd be alright. History would repeat. We would still marry, the girls would be born, and in 2015, they were still there living their lives as were older me and Frank.

I took a couple of ragged breaths, holding my index fingers to my tear ducts. If today was the 20th of September 1979, as the chewed paper suggested, then within six weeks from now, I'd be pregnant with Frank's child and our firstborn, Sharon, would still enter this world in August next year.

The girls had grown up too quickly. Maybe, if I were to relive this life again, I could savour those years. Perhaps put the girls first and see those school plays I'd missed when attending functions to do with Frank's work or charity.

I sniffed and dabbed my eyes at the wretched memory of Helen's distraught face when I'd flatly refused to run in the parents' race on sports day. Although my frame suggested I should be reasonably proficient at athletics and gymnastics, I'd always been somewhat hapless in that department. With two left feet and the hand-eye coordination of a one-legged, blind alcoholic, sports and dancing had never been my forte.

Unfortunately, the day I refused to run, causing Helen to sob, just happened to be the same day Diana showed us all how it's done at Prince Harry's school event. As our nine-year-old daughter had tearily pointed out, if a princess could do it, then why couldn't her mother? Of course, as far as my daughter was concerned, her mother's unwillingness to partake was soon forgotten. However, I'd hung on to that image of her little teary face for many years. Now, this time, I would be first on the starting line.

"Oh, bugger," I announced at my reflection when remembering the labour. Twenty-one sodding hellish hours with Sharon. When our daughter finally decided to stick her head out and come into the world, Frank had hugged me and said, and I quote, 'Well done'.

"Well done!" I exclaimed in the mirror. Jesus, that's what you ask the waiter to do to a steak if you're a bit squeamish on the blood front and don't fancy your meat mooing back at you as you chase it around the plate, not what you say to your wife after she just spent the best part of a full day desperately trying to force a seven-pound alien through her fanny. "Frank Stone, you'd better come up with something better than 'well done' this time around."

Alf nudged my leg again.

"You're right, Alf, it's time to find my husband." However, the worrying thought, on the 20th of September 1979, he was still married to that gorgeous, somewhat bitchy, MP.

14

I'm a Stranger in Paradise

"No! You can't come with me, absolutely no way. Don't give me that look. Come on, get out!" I thumped my hands on my hips, turned my head to the clouds, and uttered a frustrated growl. "This can't be happening!" I hissed whilst hopping up and down as if urgently needing to pee, which I didn't.

However, despite that fleeting moment in front of the hall mirror when considering the opportunities to improve my life the second time around, as I stood by the open driver's door of my clapped-out VW Beetle, the realisation of how my life had turned out pretty perfectly gave rise to worry that it might not be the same this time.

Of course, that's assuming this was 1979, and the conversation I'd just held with my dead mother about the opportunity to marry Drawstring-Anorak-Simon and her plans for our trip to Benidorm wasn't a figment of my imagination.

Well, my mother did mention wanting to watch Pebble Mill, a daytime show that ended decades ago, and the newspaper as much confirmed the date. Now, if you'd asked me yesterday what I'd watched on telly in mid-September 1979, I wouldn't have the foggiest. Christ, I was barely able to remember what I watched last week, let alone thirty-odd years ago. Also, I didn't watch TV last night because I was with my husband in that palatial suite in the Old War Office when trying to determine if Frank had lost his marbles.

However, clear in my mind, apart from arguing with Frank about time-travel in 2015, last night after tea, Mother and I watched the news programme *Nationwide*. I can clearly recall the reports about Mrs Thatcher saying something about the trade unions and then Frank Bough reporting from Brighton whilst astride a Lambretta, for whatever reason best known to him, because I wasn't listening that intently. And after Mother had gone up to bed, I'd watched *The Old Grey Whistle Test*, presented by Annie Nightingale, with the Tourists playing a set. So, as much as I wanted to believe this wasn't 1979, last night's telly would suggest it was.

Also, on the subject of holiday brochures, Mother and I didn't whizz off to Benidorm because Frank and I enjoyed that holiday come the October half term. I allowed my mind to drift and reminisce about that holiday. The cheap, shitty hotel, that disco called Papa Whiskey's, and the two days with my head in the toilet after consuming a dodgy kebab that I presume contained rancid horse meat. That said, although Frank and I lived a privileged life, with many an exotic holiday, that week, without any measure of doubt, produced some of my fondest memories. Also, although it's hard to pinpoint the exact day, our Sharon was conceived during that week away in the sun.

Whilst we're on the subject of my children, despite that short-lived euphoria about being able to relive those years and again treasure the moments when watching my girls grow and develop, I missed them. Of course, now adults with their own families, I didn't enjoy their company every day. However, without fail, we either spoke or, at the very least, exchanged WhatsApps or texts. If that bat-shit, nutty bloke, Hartland, had somehow pinged Frank and me back to 1979, then I would have to wait a year before seeing Sharon again.

Even then, the conversation will be somewhat one-sided because I don't recall any of my girls developing much conversation before the age of two. And love my children as I do, at the tender age of two, their conversation wasn't exactly stimulating.

I can recall one particular hellish day just after Clara was born. At that point, probably 1987, we were blessed with four daughters under the age of seven. Now, even for the most even-tempered of mothers out there, that's a challenge. Clara had chosen to scream her head off all day, and Sharon, Helen, and Trudy systematically wrecked the house, turning it into something of a war zone that could rival any trench warfare nightmare. A situation that could most certainly not be described as all quiet on the Western front. At my wits' end, when Frank had arrived home late from the office, I bellowed at my husband that they were *his* daughters before grabbing a bottle of Riesling and retreating to the greenhouse to get royally shitfaced. That, along with the horse-meat kebab, were two days in my new life that I can confidently state I wasn't looking forward to repeating.

Taking a deep breath, I stooped and leaned forward to make a grab for Alf's collar. However, the little sod hopped around on the back seat, avoiding my flailing hand. When I'd left our mangy pooch in the back garden as instructed, he'd somewhat surprisingly demonstrated previously unseen agility and scrambled over the gate before bolting into my car when I'd opened the driver's door. The precise moment when I'd stood gawping at a rather basic dashboard compared to my under-used, albeit rather swish, Lexus, which presumably older me still owned in 2015.

"Alf, come on, get out of the car. You can't come with me."

Now backed into the far corner, Alf seated his bottom and grinned back at me.

"Oh, you infuriating dog. Have it your way, then. You'll have to stay in the car, though. God knows what Mother will think has happened to you … probably put the flags out because you've gone missing. And don't you dare poo on the seats," I belligerently moaned when slipping my pleated-skirt-clad backside onto the tatty velour seat.

After a difficult moment of crunching the gears before backing out onto the road, Alf, rather ungainly, scampered forward onto the passenger seat, offering me a close-up vision of his exposed bottom before getting comfortable.

"What?" I snapped, as he stared at me with his tongue hanging out the right side of his mouth. "You know you should be dead. Mother had you put down in 1982, or around that time because you were unwell. You got this skin condition where your fur became matted, and you were covered in some rather horrible weeping sores. I presume the vet cremated you."

Alf dipped his head, shooting me a doe-eyed look.

"Sorry, that was crass. I didn't mean to upset you." Alf offered his best doggy grin. "Oh, for heaven's sake, I'm talking to a damn dog!"

Alf glanced around me towards the driver's window, causing me to swivel my head. There, grinning and waving, was some bloke astride a racing bike.

"Shit, who the hell is this?" I muttered, looking for the button to glide the window down before realising said button didn't exist. Therefore, I would have to wind it down manually.

"Sorry! Sorry, I'm blocking the road, I've just—"

"Morning, Miss, err ... Jayne. No, it's not that." He bobbed his head down and peered past me. "You're taking Alf into school, I see," he chuckled.

"Oh, yes, something like that. It's 'take your pet to school' day. You know, like 'take your daughter to work' day, but pets instead."

Mystery man with his cycle clips snapped around the bottom of his suit trousers frowned at me, appearing confused. Hmmm ... I guess 'take your daughter to work' days weren't a thing yet, and take your mangy, annoying dog to school probably never would be.

"Right, okay. Well, that should be fun."

"Was there anything else besides enquiring where I was taking Alf?"

"Oh, yes. I thought I'd just catch you before you drove off and check that you're still okay for the cinema on Saturday?"

"Cinema?"

"Yeah."

"Saturday?"

"Yeah."

"Cinema. Saturday?"

"Yeah, we agreed last week. Have you forgotten?" He appeared crestfallen, which was worrying.

"Oh, err ... no, that's fine."

Christ, why did I say that? It's not bloody fine. I'm married.

"Great. Shall I pick you up at six? I thought we could grab a pizza at that new Pizzaland place that's opened on the High

Street. There was a coupon in the Fairfield Chronicle for a pound off."

"Really?"

"Yeah."

"A coupon?"

"Yeah, I know, cracking good saving that. Mum borrowed next door's copy, so I've got two. If we pay separately, we can both get a pound off."

"Oh, right. Sounds like a bargain." I crinkled up my nose.

Alf headbutted the dashboard.

Whether his paws had slipped on the seat, or his actions were in despair at what appeared to be me agreeing to a date with a man I didn't know, who also seemed even too young to date my youngest, Clara, who can tell? Apart from the ridiculous situation of appearing to time-travel back to my late twenties, Alf seemed to have developed the ability to understand the English language.

Presumably, sensing my facial expression suggested I wasn't too enamoured with the idea of cheap pizza, Cycle-Clip-Man attempted to recover the situation.

"Or, we could just grab popcorn, if you like?" he nervously grinned. "Anyway, I'd better get going. Can't be late for work. Have a think, and I'll see you Saturday."

As I watched him pedal away, the memory of that Saturday night in 1979 resurfaced in frightening, full technicolour detail.

If you'd have asked me yesterday what I got up to on any Saturday night in September 1979, I suspect I wouldn't have offered up much in response other than I didn't have a damn clue. If you asked me if I've ever seen the film *Alien*, again, I wouldn't have a clue. Maybe I had, perhaps I hadn't. Who knew, and who cared?

However, now I could remember very clearly. I winced at Alf, who disapprovingly shook his head at me.

"Alf, that's not very helpful, is it? What the hell am I going to do? I can't very well repeat that night, can I? I'm married to Frank. I'm sixty-five years old, with four daughters and three grandchildren, so scooting off to the cinema with a boy who's only twenty-two-ish and used to be a pupil of mine really isn't the done thing!"

Other than running his tongue around his chops, Alf offered little in the way of response.

"Oh, it's the 20th of September. What an idiot. How the hell could I have forgotten that?" I muttered, causing Alf to offer me that chop-licking routine.

"Alf, is licking your chops your way of saying yes?"

My father's scruffy mutt licked his chops and grinned.

I puffed out my cheeks and glanced away. As nutty as this all was, I knew I really must stop holding a conversation with a dog who should be dead.

Yesterday evening, when Frank and I discussed his ridiculous claims about time-travel, I'd mentioned our first kiss after enjoying a drink together in the Murderer's Pub. Remembering events from nearly forty years ago isn't easy. However, as I imagine most would, recalling the evening of your first kiss with the man you end up marrying isn't something you're likely to forget.

At the time, when stuck in that damn pod on the London Eye, I'd been concerned for my husband's mental health, therefore not taking too much notice about the finer points of his claims about time-travel. However, I do remember him saying something about our lives would repeat. Also, unless we attempt to change the past, what happened before will happen again. So tonight, after a drink with Jenny and Jason, I will again kiss Frank.

All good.

Also, this time, Frank and I will know we are time-travellers.

All good again. I think.

Not so good, will be Saturday night with Kevin.

Yes, Cycle-Clip-Kevin. We did go on the agreed date. Yes, we went Dutch and used our newspaper coupons in Pizzaland. And yes, we watched *Alien.* And yes, I freaked and grabbed Cycle-Clip-Kevin's knee at the John Hurt chest-bursting scene. Unfortunately, an action which my date took as a sign I was up for some back-row hanky-panky.

I winced at the memory whilst shooting Alf a look, hoping my father's dog could utter some pearl of wisdom whilst my mind tormented me with events I'd rather not remember.

After university and my teacher training, I'd taken a position at Eaton, City of Fairfield School. Not long after, a sixth former had asked me on a date. He was seventeen, and I was twenty-three. Apart from the age gap, I was a teacher and he a loved-up student. So, although flattered, I rebuffed his offer. However, five years later, that boy and his parents moved onto the same road as Mother and I, thus becoming near neighbours. Cycle-Clip-Kevin, now twenty-two-ish, was nothing if not persistent. When realising his old teacher, and I mean old as in twenty-nine, lived nearby and was still single, he grabbed the opportunity to ask me out again. Of course, that was before Frank kissed me and during the time when I was trying to forget

Frank due to believing I could never be with him because he was married to Jemma.

So, back then, I'd agreed to the date, and why not? He wasn't a pupil of mine anymore, and rather than sit and watch James Last in concert on a Saturday night with Mother, I'd thought I might as well go out.

"Christ, James Last," I mumbled. The vision of my mother tapping her slipper-clad feet and humming the tunes highjacked my thoughts. During the regular weekly shows, if the band played any of her favourites, such as *I'm a Stranger in Paradise* – a tune she insisted was played at her funeral, along with Matt Monroe, the singing bus conductor, belting out his rendition of Maria, my mother's name – I recall she would add sideways swaying to accompany her bobbing slippers. And if Richard Clayderman just happened to put in a guest appearance, then Mother would escalate her odd movements all the way up to seated sofa dancing.

At that time, when a single left-on-the-shelf schoolteacher, my choices were either Drawstring-Anorak-Simon or Cycle-Clip-Kevin. Presumably, I must have plumped for cycle clips over traffic lights in my continued attempts to forget Frank.

Of course, when that Saturday came around, Frank had kissed me two days earlier, sending me into a bit of a spin. I'd agonised for days whether Frank was just a cheating git, wooing other women when already married, or if he really felt something for me. However, I'd already agreed to the date with Kevin, and it would have been churlish to have let the boy down. Unfortunately, due to my fried emotions and desperately trying to get Frank out of my head, I'd consumed way too much alcohol, and I recall making a bit of a fool of myself after the knee-grabbing incident.

A week later, Frank came to school to inform me he and Jemma were splitting and the rather wonderful news that he was in love with me. That all sounds a smidge Mills and Boon, but it was romantic, sort of. I remember Kevin being very decent about it when I gave him the Spanish archer the very next day. However, I never told Frank about Cycle-Clip-Kevin and the knee-fondling incident.

The last thing my husband said to me on that Wheel was to meet him at the Murderer's Pub at seven. Rather spookily, that's precisely where I would be meeting Jenny and Jason tonight after work before having a drink with Frank.

The first time that event happened, Frank and I only knew each other through Jemma. Tonight, I would be meeting him again, but this time with thirty-five years of marriage under our belts.

I turned to look at Alf, feeling the need to run my options past someone else, albeit a dog, and one that seemed to have undergone a personality transplant. I'd read somewhere, maybe some inane post on Facebook or an article in a tatty magazine when visiting my gynaecologist, that dogs are blessed with special senses. They can detect seismic activity, changes to barometric pressure, and electromagnetic fields. Perhaps my father's tatty, daft pooch knew there to be something strange about me, as in detecting I was different today to how I acted yesterday.

"Alf, are you a time-traveller like me?"

Alf dipped his head.

"Oh, you're not. Course not. Silly me. Jesus, what the hell am I saying?"

Alf maintained his doe-eyed look.

"But, you are the same dog? Y'know, the same dog I always knew?"

Alf licked his chops and grinned. I took that as a nod.

"But, since I've time-travelled … well, you know what's happened to me?"

Alf maintained that grin after another round of chop-licking.

"Okay, Alf, listen up. I … well, we, that's you and me, have some decisions to make."

Alf licked his chops.

"Do I change history and go straight over to Frank's house, like right now?"

Alf dipped his head.

"No, you're right. Jemma will probably be there."

The thought of my Frank being in that house with her caused bile to rise in my throat. Although I knew, at this point in time, Jemma was indulging in many extramarital activities with Tobias and then Rupert, the latter of the two being the man she would marry, would she still expect Frank to perform in the bedroom?

"No, Frank wouldn't."

Alf licked his chops.

"Is that a yes he would, or are you agreeing with me?"

Alf tipped his head sideways.

"Oh, sorry, I need to ask yes or no questions, don't I?"

Alf licked his chops.

"Frank … Frank, err …Christ, how do I word this?" I threw my hands in the air before allowing them to slap back on the steering wheel. "Jesus, Jayne, stop talking to a dog!"

Alf nudged my arm, causing me to side-eye him.

"Alright." I shifted sideways to face him. "Frank will stay faithful to me?"

Alf licked his chops.

"Good doggy!" I ruffled the fur of his chest and tickled the back of his ears, causing Alf to thump his tail back and forth.

"Okay, next question. Do I shoot over to Frank's office?"

Alf dipped his head.

"Oh. So, I have to go to school, teach a bunch of marauding delinquents, and wait all day to meet my husband later at the pub?"

Alf licked his chops.

"Okay. No, you're probably right."

I rammed the gear stick in first, grinding the gearbox before remembering to engage the clutch, then kangarooed a few yards before getting into the rhythm.

Alf headbutted the dashboard again. This time, I wasn't sure if that was due to the jerky motion of the car or his way of showing he disapproved of my driving techniques.

Either way, it wouldn't bode well for me if I relied on a dog to hold my hand and guide me through this version of 'paradise'.

15

What's My Line

Of course, I fully expected to wake up either lying in a hospital bed with a plethora of tubes poking out of me whilst wired up to a bank of monitors with a myriad of flashing lights that could put an amusement arcade on the Golden Mile to shame and cause a photosensitive epileptic seizure, or in our hotel room whilst feeling just a wee bit sore after my pavement flip performance from the day before. However, so far, neither of those two situations appeared forthcoming. It seemed I was in 1979, either due to this disturbing new reality or because I now lay in an induced coma and experienced this 1970s-styled vivid dream.

During lunch break, I'd given Alf walkies along Eaton Road, just along from the school gates. Without a poop bag at my disposal, I'd had to leave his offerings where he'd deposited them on the grass verge. Although feeling a smidge guilty, I didn't overly concern myself due to Alf's hefty turnout appearing to be in good company. I guess if I'd attempted to pick it up, that might have courted a few strange looks.

Apart from breakfast with my dead mother discussing Drawstring-Anorak-Simon's suitability, that conversation with

Cycle-Clip-Kevin, and then Alf, I'd endured a bizarre morning culminating in arriving at school a tad on the late side.

In my defence, and leaving Alf's human antics to one side, the mesmerising drive through my largely unrecognisable home town had resulted in my stopping every hundred yards or so to soak up the visions of yesteryear.

For starters, the monolithic brutal grey concrete multistorey car park my husband designed and built didn't exist, the area still being the old cattle market. Perhaps I should persuade Frank to reconsider throwing up that monstrosity because it would become a commune for smackheads and crack addicts come the turn of the millennium.

Then, as I waited at the traffic lights at the top of the High Street, I was visually assaulted by a thirty-foot-high, semi-naked woman. Not as in the '50s film *Attack of the 50ft Woman,* but a seriously risqué billboard poster of said scantily clad beauty advertising Ratner's Jewellery with the slogan *'When did you last buy her something to wear?'.* Not that I minded, per se, but that suggested advertising agencies were still focused on the old mantra that *sex sells.* Confirming I was in the era when you could slap up a picture of a pouting model wearing a dental-floss bikini whilst writhing on a shag pile carpet, and you could sell anything to anyone as long as they were male and struggled to take their eyes from the naked female form. This was further confirmed by the billboard opposite, displaying what I can only describe as an image of a seductive pose of a woman whose red lips appeared seconds away from giving a blow-job to a chocolate bar.

Now, there's an odd thing. My mind talk said blow-job. Not that I could be labelled a prude, but I would probably never say that phrase out loud, and not even in my mind. But then, for the last few hours, I'd regressed back to being twenty-nine-year-old me again, and perhaps my mind from thirty-odd years ago may have harboured different thoughts than in my latter years. And, on the subject of ridiculous, which was crazier, a fifty-foot woman rampaging through an American town looking to take revenge on her husband or a sixty-five-year-old woman from 2015 time-travelling back to 1979?

Hmmm. Not an easy question to answer, I wager.

Anyway, missing concrete monstrosities, thirty-foot-tall semi-naked women, streets full of vintage cars, and not one bugger seen holding a mobile slapped to their ear aside, the showstoppers on my journey had to be the Timothy Whites and Woolworth's shop façades. The sight of which caused me to veer into the kerb, receive hoots from angry drivers, and poor Alf to perform his headbutting routine when I employed a near-perfect emergency stop manoeuvre.

After I'd recovered from the fact that, come lunchtime, I could nip into town and grab a quarter pound of Sherbert Bon-Bons, I'd attempted to strap Alf into the seat. However, apart from odd looks from passersby, Alf was having none of it.

Due to my tardiness, the deputy head, my good friend Jason Apsley, in my absence was forced to take register for my class. All somewhat embarrassing, leaving me flustered and affording me no time to prepare. Despite being a good fifteen years since teaching, and considerably longer than that from wielding a stick of chalk, I'd bashed on with the lesson, miraculously remembering the syllabus and somehow managing to make it through F Band's distraction tactics remarkably unscathed.

Now, with Alf secured in the car and a moment to myself, I hot-footed to the school office to hunt down a copy of the

Yellow Pages to dig out the number for my husband's workplace, Stone and Wilson Builders.

"Where's Alexa or bloody Siri when you need them," I muttered when scooping a handful of my hair and tucking it behind my ear before licking my fingers to gain purchase on the flimsy yellow pages as I frantically tore my way through the hefty book.

Despite Alf's chop-licking confirmation that I shouldn't bowl around to my husband's and ex-wife's house but wait until our agreed rendezvous later, I was somewhat surprised Frank hadn't arrived at school trying to hunt me down.

I now harboured disturbing concerns as to whether my husband had made it back to 1979 when remembering that nutter, The Hooded Claw, saying something about not all time-travellers successfully made it through with the odd unfortunate soul evaporating into the ether.

If Frank were to be in that small percentage of failed travellers, I fear my life would be about to implode. The thought that my girls may never be born caused the onslaught of hot flushes similar to when going through the menopause, something I'd experienced some years back. That said, I'd been the lucky one, displaying only mild symptoms. Whereas Susan, a close friend, had suffered the full suite of symptoms, including vaginal dryness, which she described in great detail all too regularly.

Too much detail? Yes, you're probably right, but it was a topic of many a lunch date for far too long, that much I can remember. What I learned about water-based lubricants over a glass of Chablis you wouldn't believe.

Also, whether elated to be twenty-nine and size eight again or not, I now had to face periods again, or as my mother referred to them, the woman's curse. On a positive note, like the menopause, I hadn't suffered too badly from that monthly ordeal.

"Are you alright, Miss Hart? You look a little flustered?"

Thirty-five years had elapsed since anyone had addressed me as Miss Hart, and the utterance of my maiden name caused me to shoot a look at my left hand. My bare fingers held my gaze, knowing that I never removed my engagement or wedding rings, and neither was there a mark to suggest they ever existed.

"Miss Hart?"

I peered up from the well-thumbed, hefty book to spot our dependable, super-nosy school secretary peering at me over the top of her glasses when taking a break from rhythmically thrashing the keys on her typewriter. Like my mother and Alf, she should be dead. I know that because I attended her funeral five years ago. Well, five years ago from the year my husband and I should be in.

"Erm ... yes, I'm fine, thank you."

"Give it here, my dear." Before I knew what had happened, Mrs Trosh had snatched the book. "Now, who is it you're looking for?"

"Oh, um, ha," I stretched my hair back with both hands and held that pose as Mrs Trosh looked up expectantly.

"Builders," I mumbled.

"Oh, are you having work done? My neighbour has just had a lovely conservatory built, and Mr Trosh and I were given the grand tour only last week. They're all the rage, you know. Harold, that's my neighbour, has erected a bar in the corner of their new conservatory, and it all looks rather swish. It's got a thatched roof, and I must say it felt like just being on holiday in Spain at one of those tikka masala bars."

"Tikka masala?"

"Yes, you know, cocktail bar. As I said, with a thatched roof."

"Tiki bar, perhaps?"

"That's what I said, dear."

Mrs Trosh conspiratorially shot a quick glance left and right before leaning forward and employing her well-favoured hushed tones when launching into gossip or an accusation.

"Far be it for me to say, but I do hope our neighbour used a reputable company. It was on *That's Life* only a few weeks ago. Did you see it?"

"See what?"

"That's Life."

"That's Life?"

"Yes, dear, with Esther Rantzen and Cyril Fletcher. Mr Trosh does enjoy Cyril's little odes. Pin back your lugholes," she chuckled.

I shook my head, bemused.

"Yes, as I was saying, they had a feature about these companies selling conservatories that aren't conservatories."

"How can a conservatory not be a conservatory?"

"Oh, I don't know, but that Esther Rantzen said something about these con men."

"Right."

"And did you see that episode with the Old English Sheepdog that's learnt to drive a car?"

"Did it happen to be a fifty-foot Old English Sheepdog that time-travelled too?" I muttered, thinking that the conversation I was holding with the dead school secretary appeared somewhat off-piste and morphing into a sketch more suited to *Monty Python*.

"Oh, don't be silly, dear. Dogs can't time-travel."

"But they can drive a car?"

"Yes, well, that one could. Of course, the owner had to change gear for him, but otherwise, the dog was able to control the steering and …"

Whilst Mrs Trosh rattled on about a driving dog, I glanced through the window to the car park. Considering the subject of the school secretary's prattle, I was somewhat surprised to spot Alf with his paws on the steering wheel, tongue wagging when hanging out the side of his mouth as he appeared to survey the comings and goings of pupils as they headed back to class.

"Anyway, here you are, dear. There're quite a few builders in the local area."

Turning away from thoughts about whether Alf could drive – although at least if he could, that would allow me to wallop a few glasses of wine after school, assuming Alf was prepared to take on the role of designated driver – I became distracted by a collection of framed photographs. One in particular caught my eye.

The office back wall sported the group shots of all students in their final school years, stretching back to 1946. The one that held my attention being the class of 1965, the year my husband had featured in. Of course, I'd seen the photo a million times, right up until the mid-nineties when the school underwent a bit of a revamp, and the collection of framed photographs were relocated to the new library wing.

"Miss Hart?"

Ignoring Mrs Trosh, and as if mesmerised, I padded over to the photo. As I squinted at the grainy snap of six rows of boys, I quickly picked out the image of my fifteen-year-old husband. Although monochrome, Frank's blond hair made him stand out from the crowd. Anyway, I'd gazed at this picture that many times I could probably point him out with my eyes closed. Standing, third row up, fourth from the left.

However, my focus shifted to the boy standing beside Frank. A nondescript lad sporting a side parting and a scowl.

David Bolton.

As far as I was aware, in a few days from now, David's body, sporting a nine-millimetre slug lodged between the eyes, would be discovered in a layby up near Fairfield Woods. According to Frank, in some previous life, David murdered Jemma Stone.

According to Douglas Hartland, Barbara was supposed to time-travel and prevent her husband's death, which would be the catalyst to stopping her granddaughter from becoming a terrorist, blowing up Ten Downing Street and Andrew Barrington Scott.

Jesus!

"Miss Hart, are you quite alright, my dear? I must say, you don't look yourself. There's an awful lot of nasty bugs going around, you know. I do hope you're not coming down with something," Mrs Trosh asked, grabbing my elbow and peering at me as if an in-depth study of the side of my face could diagnose whatever.

In that moment, a few things occurred to me, along with some Krypton-Factor-type questions. If my darling husband had been vaporised on the London Eye in 2015, Frank Stone would be a missing D-list celebrity.

Or would he?

Was I here, as in now, as in 1979, and in 2015?

If Frank hadn't made it, the Frank I would meet tonight would only know me as Jayne, his bitchy wife's friend.

Would he still fall in love with me? Would he still kiss me?

And what of David Bolton? Barbara Denton didn't time-travel, so do I now have to save Dave Bolton and, in turn, save Frank's son?

I swivelled around, grabbed the Yellow Pages, and flipped over a couple of leaves until I found the number I'd been searching for.

"Mrs Trosh, I urgently need to make a private call to a man I haven't seen for at least twelve hours or maybe thirty-six years. I can't decide which."

Unsurprisingly, based on the fact that the new me appeared to be in my twenties, thus making the thirty-six-years comment somewhat odd, Mrs Trosh dismissively shook her head.

"Please don't think me rude, but I've always said to our Mr Apsley that you're a strange girl. A very strange one that you are, my dear."

A week from today, Frank would visit the school to inform me he and Jemma were splitting up and that he did, in fact, love me. We'd ended up being caught snogging by thirty of my pupils, who'd barrelled into classroom seven at a somewhat awkward moment. The news of Frank and I spreadeagled across a desk tore through the school like a Californian wildfire, causing me to endure a rather awkward conversation with Mr Clark and Jason. That said, I recall Jason struggling to contain his laughter during that excruciatingly embarrassing moment when Mr Clark had asked me to recount my pre-class activities.

Ever since that hellish episode, it's fair to say Mrs Trosh and I had not enjoyed the closest of relationships due to what she considered my unacceptable behaviour with a married man.

For sure, the first time I'd experienced the 20th of September 1979, this conversation never took place and, come to think of it, I'd never before taken Alf to school.

Worryingly, history already appeared to be changing.

16

Ding Dong

I remember from the early days of my career, which rather ridiculously appeared to be repeating, us teachers would occasionally need to make a private call. That would involve either using the phones in the office with the dependable Mrs Trosh earwigging or sneaking into Mr Clark's, the headmaster's, office when he was either in class or attending some meeting at County Hall.

Today, Mr Clark was the latter, and although I dialled the number from the sanctuary of his office, I fully suspected Mrs Trosh to either have slapped her ear to the door or be peering through the keyhole. With this in mind, I turned, faced the windows, and prepared to speak in hushed tones.

After dialling the number, a process that took a bloody age as I watched the dial spin back around – also frustrated Frank's office number contained one eight and two nines, thus elongating the process even further – with sweaty palms, I waited for my call to be answered by Frank's receptionist whose name eluded me.

"Stone and Wilson."

"You're dead an' all," I mumbled, just at the point the receptionist answered with a far too enthusiastic sing-song, jaunty voice.

"I beg your pardon?" she stated, and not surprisingly, after receiving a death threat, her tone changed considerably.

With my finger still outstretched when pointing to a photograph of Roy Clark, I attempted to recover the situation. "Oh, I'm so sorry. I didn't mean you. I was pointing at someone else whilst waiting for the call to be answered."

"Oh, I see. Well, no, I don't, actually."

"No, I'm sure. I was suggesting someone else should be dead, not you. Of course, you're not dead because you answered the phone. Sorry, I was referring to a picture of a man who is dead. Well, actually, I don't think he is, but he definitely should be."

"Err ... sorry, madam, but this is Stone and Wilson Builders. As the name suggests, we're a building company. Sounds to me like you've got the wrong number. Perhaps try nine-nine-nine instead?"

I huffed before slapping my free palm onto my forehead, narrowly avoiding uttering Homer Simpson's favourite word.

"Sorry, can we start again?"

"Okay, sure. Stone and Wilson Builders, how can I help?" she sang again.

"Ha, yes, thank you. Would it be possible to speak to Frank Stone?"

"Frank?"

"Yes."

"I'll just check if he's free."

"He bloody better be," I muttered.

"Sorry?"

"Oh, no, ignore me. Sorry," I hissed, wincing at my babbling.

"Sorry, you do, or you don't want to speak with Mr Stone?"

"Yes, I do, and it's urgent!"

"O-kay," she slowly stated, emphasising both syllables. "Can I ask what this is referring to?"

"It's private."

"Private?"

"Yes, Christ, woman, it's bloody private, alright? All I want to do is speak to my ruddy husband."

"Oh! Sorry, Jemma, I didn't recognise your voice. Let me see if he's free."

"No!"

"Sorry, Jemma, I'm a bit confused. You do, or you don't want me to check? Which is it?"

"No. Yes. Augh!" I hopped up and down, annoyed at my stupidity. "I'm mean, yes, I do. But, I'm not Jemma."

"Sorry, you've lost me."

"Please, can I just speak to Frank?" I asked in a more measured tone whilst tipping my head back and closing my eyes in an attempt to stay calm.

"Okay, let me check if he's free. Who shall I say is calling?"

"Jayne Stone."

"Jayne Stone?"

I shot my head forward and burst open my eyes. "Oh, no, sorry, I mean Jayne Hart."

"Jayne Hart?"

"Yes, Jayne Hart," the utterance of my maiden name stinging, as if I'd just flung myself into a bed of nettles.

"Right, hold the line, please."

While waiting, I nodded to myself, agreeing with my late father, who used to call me Calamity.

"You weren't far off the mark," I mumbled, thinking about how my dearly departed Pops would laugh when I'd performed some impromptu mishap, which usually resulted in me upended and splayed out on the floor. I thought of yesterday's performance outside Harrods, or was that now in the future? Either way, it served to confirm I would never grow out of my 'calamity' status.

"Hello?"

"Yes, I'm still here."

"I'm sorry, but Frank ... err, Mr Stone is tied up with a client. I'd put you through to Mr Wilson, but he's also unavailable at the moment."

"Did you say who I was?"

"Yes, I informed him it was a private matter."

"And he said what?"

"As I've just said, he's busy with a client."

"Christ!"

"I can take a message if you like."

I sucked in a lungful, trying to work out after what had happened why my husband wouldn't instantly dump his client in favour of talking to his wife.

"Are you still there?"

"Yes, yes. Could you please ask him again for me? As I said, it's very urgent."

"I'm sorry—"

"It's Alison, isn't it?" I interrupted, thinking it might be better to build a rapport with the woman rather than continue to bark instructions.

"Yes ... err, how d'you know my name? Have we met?"

"No, no, I don't think we ever did," I vacantly muttered, my mind drifting off the reservation when attempting to remember what happened to her when Frank and Paul Wilson dissolved the company just at the point Frank and I became an item. Which, if history repeated, would start tonight with that kiss.

Something in the back of my mind suggested Alison emigrated to Australia with her rugby-playing boyfriend. But, to be fair, that could have been his secretary at his charity who, at some point in the mid-90s, also emigrated. There seemed to be a theme with Frank and his assistants shooting off to the other side of the world.

"Sorry, Mrs Hart, but—"

"It's Miss." I interrupted.

"Sorry, Miss —"

"Well, no, it's Mrs, actually."

"Pardon?"

"Yes, sorry, Alison, I can see how that could be confusing. I am Mrs, but not Hart ... although, I suppose I am a Miss now," I babbled, raising my left hand to look at my ringless finger.

"Look, I'm sorry, Mrs or Miss, but as I just told you, Mr Stone is busy, and Mr Wilson is ... well, that doesn't matter. Either way, he's also not available. Now, as I said, I can take a message and ask Mr Stone to call you if you like."

"No, I don't bloody like! Alison, tell Frank I'm on the phone, and I need to speak with him immediately ... please," I added after a pause when remembering I was trying to build a rapport and not give Alison a good reason to slam the receiver down and disconnect the call. That said, unlike most companies and public services in 2015, she hadn't rattled through a prepared speech about the non-tolerance of aggressive or abusive behaviour, something I was close to demonstrating.

"Alright, I'll try again. But, as I said, he is busy."

I tutted and shook my head as Alison presumably put me on hold, which, unlike the future, wasn't an annoying rendition of some panpipe music but just the hisses and crackles of a poorly connected line.

"Hello, Jayne ... it was Jayne, wasn't it?"

"Yes."

"Yes, sorry, I tried again, but he's not picking up this time."

"Augh!"

"I'm so sorry. Would you like me to pass on any message?"

Thinking on my feet and desperately not wanting the call to end without speaking with Frank, I changed tack.

"Actually, I could have a word with Paul ... err ... Mr Wilson, instead?" I thought if I could bypass Alison and get to Paul, he might be of a mind to interrupt Frank.

"I said earlier, Mr Wilson is also unavailable."

"Oh, is he with a client, too?"

"Err ... no, not exactly." She elongated the last word as if playing for time to either decide what to say or conjure up a lie.

"I don't understand. He is with a client, or he isn't?"

"Oh, well, I s'pose it won't hurt to tell you, seeing as you seem to know Frank. You do know Frank, personally, I mean?" she whispered.

"You could say."

That had to be the understatement of the frigging century. I'd been married to the man for thirty-five years, and we had four daughters together. History that I prayed with all my heart was going to repeat and, over the next seven years, my girls would be born again. Not in the biblical sense, but you get my drift. So, considering I regularly cut his toenails and had, on one occasion, daily dressed a weeping sore on his bottom, I think it's fair to say I knew Frank Stone personally.

"Okay," she whispered. "Paul, Mr Wilson, isn't working here at the moment. Frank and him have had a bit of a to-do, you could say. So, following a falling out, Paul is taking some time off. I shouldn't be telling you this, so please don't say you heard it from me."

"Oh, right."

"Yeah, so, I don't want to lie and say Paul is with a client, 'cos he ain't."

As the conversation nudged past five minutes, I detected Alison's reception voice starting to slip, her diction returning to what I presumed was her more usual timbre. Sensing Alison was becoming more comfortable chatting, I thought I would do a little digging, hoping to keep the conversation flowing, which might just mean my husband's meeting might come to a close whilst I was still on the line.

"I know this is an odd question, but is Frank alright?"

"Sorry?"

"I mean, does he seem himself?"

"Oh," she paused. "I'm not sure I should say, really."

"Of course. Look, I've known Frank and Jemma for years. I went to university with Jemma, so you could say I'm an old friend. I know Jemma and Frank have had their issues recently, and I was just wanting to check he was okay because I haven't spoken to him for a while."

"Oh."

"Yes, so I just wondered, as you see him every day, if you'd noticed anything different about him?"

When only silence filled the void after my question, I presumed Alison was weighing up what she should say. I imagined her looking around the reception, chewing her lip whilst checking Frank's office door was closed and deciding whether to spill the beans. That is, of course, assuming there were beans to spill. I just prayed Alison was the gossiping type.

"You know, it's funny you should say that. It's like this week Frank *has* changed."

"Changed?"

"Yeah."

"He's different?"

"That's what I said. He's changed."

"How exactly? And can you be specific on the actual day he changed? I'm assuming he's different today to how he was yesterday?"

"Well, I can't say that, but it's kinda spooky. Oh, but don't get me wrong, he's changed in a nice way. I mean, I never imagined him standing up for me and punching Paul's lights out like he did. I mean, who would have thought?"

As if I'd been punched myself, I rocked back on my heels. I couldn't quite remember exactly when, but around the time of the day of that kiss, Frank had punched his business partner. Due to that fracas and Paul Wilson's frankly misogynistic attitude, the business folded a few months later. That had been when Frank set up Stone Architects just after we returned from Benidorm. I needed to know if that incident had happened today.

"Oh, I see. Did that happen today?"

"No, a couple of days ago, but Frank has been different all week. Oh, sorry, Jayne, I'm gonna have to go. I've got a delivery coming in. Please don't say I told you about Paul. Seeya."

"Alison, Alison, please don't forget to tell Frank I phoned." I was too late; she'd already disconnected.

Yesterday, when that Hartland bloke was rattling on about his organisation and those claims about their ability to ping folk back through time via one of the Capital's premier tourist attractions, I hadn't been taking much notice. Of course, my concerns were why my husband agreed with what appeared at the time to be fanciful twaddle, coupled with trying to conjure up a plan regarding how we might escape The Hooded Claw's clutches.

I gently replaced the receiver whilst racking my brain, trying to recall the conversation that I hadn't taken much notice of.

"Think, Jayne, think," I muttered whilst peering through the windows of Roy's office to check Alf was behaving himself. When the discarded copy of yesterday's Daily Telegraph that lay abandoned on the windowsill caught my eye, the fog surrounding that conversation cleared. "It's not an exact science," I mumbled. Hartland had said something about how they can't guarantee travellers will arrive on the exact day they plan.

Frank, assuming he didn't vaporise in the pod on the Eye, could have landed a few days ago or be due to land in a couple of days from now.

"Shit," I hissed before lowering my head to peer at Alf.

Earlier, I'd cranked down the passenger window an inch so the poor, scruffy pooch didn't suffocate. If I wasn't very much mistaken, Alf appeared to be frantically jabbing his paw through the gap as if pointing at the main entrance.

"Oh, Jayne, get a grip. Dogs don't point."

"Oh, you're back early, Mr Clark," I heard Mrs Trosh announce, loud enough to alert me that the headmaster had returned.

Roy was a bit of a pillock. Nothing wrong with him per se, but just a stick in the mud, and he could be protective of his office space. Earlier, Mrs Trosh had forbidden me from using his office without the Headmaster's or Jason's express permission. However, because of the urgent nature of my call, I'd pushed past her. Despite her comment that I was a 'strange girl', as she'd put it, the woman still tried to throw me a lifeline.

I hopped around the desk and plonked on the chair opposite Roy's desk as if waiting to see him when the door burst open.

"Oh, Miss Hart. Well, hello," he crooned, allowing the 'hello' word to linger.

According to Jason, Roy Clarke had always had a thing about me. Which, considering he was a good fifteen years my senior, I'd always thought was somewhat creepy. I recall being quite relieved when he left the school in the mid-1980s.

Roy closed the door and stayed in position whilst smoothing his Brylcreemed hair with one hand, Lesley Phillips style, allowing a playful, boyish smirk to appear.

"Sorry, am I late for a meeting?" he asked, raising a suggestive eyebrow as I turned to face him. "Oh, Miss Hart, are you quite alright? You look like you've seen a ghost."

"I have, and rather a lot of them, I might add."

17

Reach for the Sky

"Sit still! I'm not going to tell you again. If you can't behave, you'll have to go back to the car. And don't give me that look. Just drink your beer and be a good boy for me."

"Should he be drinking beer?"

"Probably not."

"I don't think I've ever known a dog to drink a pint before?" Jenny, Jason's wife, raised an eyebrow before slugging back her gin and tonic.

"To be honest with you, there's lots of things I'm learning about Alf today. You could say it's been a day of discovery," I replied, whilst employing both hands to physically encourage Alf to stay under my chair and lap up his pint of Double Diamond that I'd earlier poured into a dish for him. Of course, I wasn't aware that particular beer to be Alf's preferred tipple. However, it had been the first pump I'd spotted on the bar when asked which beer, and the barman said it *works wonders.* Whatever that meant.

"Oh, that sounds interesting." Jenny re-raised that inquisitive eyebrow. "What's happened?" she enquired, before calling to Jason, who'd nipped up to the bar to grab another round.

"Darling, grab me a bag of smoky bacon, please." When Jason nodded back, Jenny turned to me. "Go on, you were saying?"

I groaned and huffed before cupping my chin in both palms. Where do I start? Explaining to Jenny that as of less than twenty-four hours ago I'd time-travelled, I presume would not be the best place. I mean, spouting that sort of statement, and she would rightly assume I'd lost it, wouldn't she? To be fair, I was starting to doubt my own sanity.

"Oh, I don't know, it's just been a bit of an odd day, what with Alf's antics and ... well, other stuff."

If ever there was an understatement to rival any other in history, I'd just uttered it. There's Captain Oates's *'I might be some time'* statement, Sir Douglas Bader's *'bad show'* comment when losing both legs in a plane crash, and Spike Milligan's laconic summation *'I told you I was ill'* epitaph carved on his gravestone. However, Jayne Stone's *'It's just been a bit of an odd day'* really had to trump those.

After escaping Roy's office unscathed, I'd vacantly bumbled through the afternoon lessons. Classes which were an easier affair than the morning's due to there being no requirement to don my riot shield and flak jacket because I was done with F Band students for the day.

Despite worrying if Frank was ghosting me, or he'd evaporated, or hadn't landed yet, or whatever crazy, bat shit thing might have occurred, during the last lesson of the day, my mind became distracted by a certain pupil.

Rose Wood, a charming girl who consistently achieved top grades – incidentally, based on the surname, I'd always wondered why her parents were of a mind to name her Rose, but that's by the by – and went on to read philosophy at Cambridge University.

Unfortunately, it seemed she became influenced more by Voltaire and anti-establishment radicalism than Confucius, resulting in the pretty girl from a well-heeled background slipping off the rails in the early to mid-1980s. Of course, I lost touch with her after she left school, as with all my students. Well, if you discount Cycle-Clip-Kevin, that is. However, Rose flunked out of her studies when becoming the lead singer in a band rather horribly named *The Rabid Bitches*.

Just to clarify, I'm not suggesting Voltaire promoted punk rock, but he was known for his radicalism.

Anyway, regarding the band's name, I'm sure Alf would have had something to say about that. Not that I believe he knew his mother, and I'm sure she didn't suffer from rabies. However, at this precise moment, and with some relief on my part, Alf was doing as he was told, as in staying positioned under my chair whilst noisily lapping up his beer.

I guess you could say *The Rabid Bitches* were a throwback to the mid-1970s punk movement, trying to make it in the '80s when most teenagers were into the *New Romantic* scene. Anyway, the band enjoyed modest success before disbanding in 1985. That's when Rose came back to my attention. An article in the Fairfield Chronicle reported the death of Rose and the band's drummer. I recall it being only a one-column report, buried in the middle pages, outlining that Rose Wood's body, formally a student at Eaton City of Fairfield School, had been discovered in a squat in London. The post-mortem stated her death was due to a heroin overdose.

As I'd watched Rose perform her experiments in that chemistry lesson, I couldn't help wondering if I should have a word with her. However, what would I say? Advising the pretty blonde girl, who wouldn't say boo to a goose, that within five or six years she would be lying dead in a squat in London really wasn't going to cut it. I imagine that sort of conversation would enrage her middle-class parents and result in me having to endure another meeting with the headmaster. So, rather than offer up another excuse for Ding-Dong-Roy to corner me in his study, I figured if I was here to stay in 1979, I had time to polish that conversation.

Anyway, after school, I'd attempted to drop Alf at Mother's house, which was now my home again, before meeting Jason and Jenny for a drink as planned.

However ... yep, you got it, Alf steadfastly refused to be left behind. So, I'd ended up taking him with me to the pub. When the barman very kindly offered to pour Alf a bowl of water, I'd jokingly stated I think he'd prefer a beer, to which Alf licked his chops and grinned at me.

Of course he did.

So, here I was in the Murderer's, enjoying a drink with Jenny and Jason, just as I had in my first life. The only difference this time, I had the beer-swilling Alf with me and my husband hadn't materialised. The first time around, Frank was having a beer with his friend Tobias before they argued and then Tobias stormed off in a huff. That's when I, along with the Apsleys, were leaving, and I spotted Frank sitting at the bar all by his lonesome. As they say, the rest is history. History that, rather worryingly, appeared not to be repeating.

Jenny nudged my arm. "Jayne, you alright? You're in a bit of a trance."

"Oh, sorry. Yes, I'm fine."

No, I wasn't.

"You were saying you've had a day of it. I hope nothing's wrong. Jason said he had to take your class's register this morning because you were late in ... I take it something's happened?"

You could say that.

"No, nothing. It's just been one of those, you know," I shrugged, glancing at the door and the clock behind the bar. A head oscillating routine I seemed to perform every few seconds as I willed my husband to arrive before the clock struck seven.

Although I'd lived the first half of my life without a mobile phone, I now wondered how the hell that could be possible. I considered it must have been hit-and-miss when trying to arrange a meet with someone. What if you got delayed? With no ability to call or text, I felt my frustration bubbling, causing me to become fidgety and annoyed.

Of course, despite Alf suggesting it was a bad idea, and leaving my school teaching responsibilities to one side, I should have feigned illness and scooted over to Frank's office as soon as I'd escaped Roy's office. However, if Frank was the original Frank and not my husband, what the hell would I have said? Also, in terms of history repeating, Frank and I were supposed to be in the pub tonight.

Alf burped. Whether that was the beer *working wonders* or him agreeing with my musings, who could tell? Let's face it, my father's matted mongrel appeared to have developed some disturbing qualities, so why not mind reading, too?

Jenny grabbed Jason's cigarettes and matches, lighting one and taking a long drag. "I know, I've given up," she grimaced whilst extinguishing the match with a wave of her hand before continuing. "Chris and Beth have been a right, damn handful today, so I just need one. God knows what the hell my children are putting my parents through right now," she chuckled. "Have you given up? I haven't seen you smoke this evening."

"Erm ... yes," I mumbled, keeping my eye on the door, my heart leaping each time it opened, and then sinking to my feet when the person entering wasn't my husband.

I gave up smoking in November 1979 when becoming pregnant with Sharon. So, the absence of a cigarette held between my fingers now, only a couple of months before I gave up, didn't seem too much of a change to history.

"Oh, good for you. Of course, I only occasionally smoke these days. I've suggested to Jason he should give up. You know, with the kids in the house," she paused to take a drag and blow a plume of smoke to the ceiling. "Jayne, you sure you're okay? You seem ... I dunno ... distant."

"Oh, Jenny, I'm sorry. I've got a lot on my mind, that's all."

"Okay, well, if you want to talk, you know where I am. You know anything you tell me, I won't let on to Jason if that's what's worrying you? Has something happened at school?"

"No, school's fine," I offered a tight smile but nothing more.

Only yesterday, I'd been slurping champagne and glugging down oysters with Jenny and two other friends as we enjoyed a girly lunch to celebrate Jenny's seventieth birthday. We were also toasting that Jenny had received the all-clear after a scare with breast cancer. So, with my knowledge of the future, as with Rose, perhaps I should warn her. That said, suggesting Jenny should stub out that cigarette appeared an easier conversation to start than the one I need to broach with Rose.

Along with everything else today, including conversing with a whole host of people who should be dead, seeing my close friend at the age of thirty-three when yesterday she was seventy was kinda weird. Although Jenny was still a radiant woman in her later years, I'd forgotten just how stunning the auburn-haired beauty was back in the day. As for my boss and good friend, well, it would be a stretch to call him handsome. I mean, come on, anyone with ears that big would struggle to grab a modelling contract unless Enid Blyton just happened to be searching for a new friend for Noddy. Not to be too uncharitable about it, let's just say that Jason was punching above his weight with Jenny.

Alf, seemingly satisfied now he'd slugged his pint, shifted around and slapped his front paws on the table, nudging his nose against my arm. As I shot a look at him, preparing to push him back under my chair, Jason moved away from the bar whilst precariously gripping our three drinks with the packet of smoky bacon crisps tightly clamped between his teeth. The gap caused by his movement revealed a man hoofing down handfuls of peanuts as he perched on a bar stool.

"Tobias Heaton," I muttered.

"Here we go," Jason cheerily announced as he placed the drinks down and handed the crisps to Jenny. "I take it your dog won't be requiring another pint," he confirmed whilst tickling Alf's ear.

"No ... he's driving," I mumbled while keeping my eyes on Tobias.

"That wouldn't surprise me," he chortled before grabbing his cigarettes and launching into some tale about a group of students getting up to no good behind the sports hall during lunch break. Notwithstanding my knowledge of said location being the unofficially designated making-out and smoking area, and whatever Jason was relaying would be either shocking, amusing or probably both when presuming F Band were involved, I zoned out of his story.

Although I vaguely heard Jenny tut and ask about what happened to the condom, my focus remained on Tobias, the clock, the entrance to the pub, and Alf, who, despite consuming far too much alcohol for a dog, appeared on high alert.

I sensed my father's beer-swilling pooch knew something was about to happen.

I was right.

Not that I meant to, but my gasp when the door swung open caused Jenny and Jason to halt mid-conversation and swivel around to look at the entrance before both turned their attention to my gaping mouth expression.

There he was, my blond, ocean-blue-eyed man. The thirty-year-old I'd fallen for the day I met him in 1976 when Jemma presented her new boyfriend.

"Jayne?"

I side-eyed Jenny but didn't offer a reply.

"Jayne, who's that? That bloke who just walked in?" Jason asked, grabbing my arm and offering it a shake to presumably break my trance.

Alf growled.

I shot a look at my pooch.

"Alf, are you telling me Frank doesn't know?"

"Jayne, what are you on about?" Jenny grabbed my hand, the same arm that Jason had hold of my elbow.

"Alf, answer me!"

Alf dipped his head, pinned his ears back, and licked his chops.

"Oh, you've got to be bloody joking?"

"Jayne, what on earth—"

"Alf, has Frank, you know, travelled with me, or is that the original Frank?"

While waiting for his doggy response, I spotted Jenny and Jason giving each other a worried look in my peripheral vision.

Fair enough.

With that doe-eye response, Alf peered up at me from his position on the low ground.

"Shit, sorry, you need yes or no questions. How remiss of me."

"Jayne, do you—"

I dismissively waved my free hand at Jenny to cut her off mid-sentence.

"Alf?"

He looked up at me.

"Alf, is that the original Frank? Y'know, the one before the Wheel escapade?"

Alf dipped his head, which I took as a no.

"Oh, thank God for that!" When translating Alf's actions, the relief was akin to when firemen rescued Clara after getting her head stuck in the park railings for six hours. Clara was what you call a problem child, but that's another story.

I hopped out of my chair, only for Jason's grip on my elbow to halt my getaway.

"Jayne, what's going on?"

"Sorry, you two, I'll be back in a moment. I need to talk to someone."

"Who? Who's that man," hissed Jenny.

"That is Frank Stone. My husband."

Unsurprisingly, Jenny and Jason again shot each other a worried look. Raised eyebrows everywhere, you could say. Okay, I shouldn't have said that, but he was my husband. I, and four unborn girls, needed Frank Stone to be back in my life. Thankfully, that seemed more likely after Alf had confirmed that the man chatting to Tobias Heaton wasn't the original Frank Stone, as in the one who existed before the clowns at the Correction Years Association pinged us back through time.

With Alf hot on my heels, I scooted towards the bar. The mixture of excitement and relief, in equal measure, almost sent me giddy as I approached my husband. That said, apart from intending to give him a bear hug, Frank Stone was about to receive a mouthful from his time-travelling wife after ghosting me earlier when I'd called his office.

"How dare you ignore me, Frank Stone," I muttered as I barrelled towards him.

To my surprise and dismay, when spotting my advance, my husband appeared shocked to see me.

18

Hounds of Love

And he was.

Frank, now sporting a similar expression he'd offered that time when barrelling through the park to discover me in a state of hysteria and six burly firemen wielding various implements from hacksaws to angle grinders and one firing up a scary-looking oxy-acetylene torch when attempting to free Clara's head from the railings, rocked back on his stool and defensively held his hands up as I prepared to hug and kiss him.

In that moment, after hot-footing towards him and muttering my displeasure, I'd decided to offer affection first, then follow up with tearing a strip off him for the earlier ghosting.

"Woah, blimey! Hi Jayne. Christ, you alright?" Frank rocked back on his stool as I entered his personal space.

"What the hell d'you mean? Am I alright?" I growled before taking a step backwards.

I thumped my hands on my hips, rocked my head from side to side, and bug-eyed him as he held that rabbit-in-headlights look. Although wanting to hug him, my husband's posture suggested that wouldn't be welcomed.

"Well?" I shrieked, throwing my hands in the air.

Frank, appearing somewhat terrified and still defensively holding his hands up to his chest, side-eyed Tobias.

"Hello Jayne, how are you? Haven't seen you in an age. You still teaching?" Tobias asked, before tipping his head back and expertly funnelling a stream of peanuts into his open mouth.

"All that salt is bad for your blood pressure. No skin off my nose, but I suspect with your health record you can ill afford to risk eating them in such vast quantities." I nodded at the dwindling bowl of peanuts. "I should go steady if I were you. What was it? I've lost count. Four or five heart attacks?"

Tobias, mid-chew, parted his lips and shot a quizzical look at Frank.

As the years rolled by, after the revelation that Tobias and Jemma had enjoyed a fling – a sordid one-night stand at a charity function whilst Frank and Tobias's wife Clare were in the ballroom – Frank and Tobias drifted apart to the point where they'd rarely spoken for the last twenty years. In fact, I think this meeting was the night that pretty much ended that friendship when Frank apparently accuses Tobias of having that affair with his then-wife, Jemma. That was when Tobias stormed out of the pub, leaving Frank at the bar impersonating Billy-No-Mates.

Now, and on the subject of history changing, this time, I'd presumably interjected before Frank could get to the punchline. But that was okay, wasn't it? History would have to change now that Frank and I had time-travelled. We were already an item with thirty-five years of history together. That flirting that happened the first time around, when I perched on that bar stool that Tobias still occupied, didn't need to happen this time. We would get married, and we would produce our family again.

Oh, sorry, back to salted peanuts and their super-high salt content. Well, news amongst certain circles, which Frank and I still had connections with, suggested that Tobias suffered from high blood pressure and had survived a string of heart attacks which first struck when in his late fifties. So, although at the wrong moment in time, my warning to Tobias was valid, if not a little premature.

Alf nudged my leg with his nose, an action I was fast learning he employed when suggesting we should have a chinwag. And, based on the fact that Tobias looked dumb-struck and my husband also seemed to have lost his tongue, I thought I might as well converse with him. At least Alf wasn't just gawping at me as if I'd grown a second head. I glanced down at my father's pooch.

"What?"

In what I can only describe as a human reaction, Alf slowly blinked and shook his head dismissively.

"Sorry?"

"Are you talking to a dog?" I heard Tobias mutter through his peanut mulch.

Alf peered up with those doe eyes, again shaking his head.

"Shit! Are you saying what I think you're saying?"

Alf licked his chops.

"Brilliant! Oh, that's just peachy!"

"Jayne, what's going on?" Frank asked, accompanied by a laugh that one might uncharitably employ when deriding someone less fortunate. Perhaps the village idiot or that nutter on the Tube who, through sod's law, always entered your carriage. I presume my husband was thinking that very thought about me.

"Right. Okay, Frank, I need a word."

"Jayne," Frank chuckled, raising an eyebrow at the peanut-chewing Tobias. "You alright? You seem, I dunno, a bit odd. And what's with the dog?"

"Alf?"

"Your dog's called Alf?"

"He is. Look, Frank, we—"

"Jemma never mentioned you owned a dog," my husband interrupted whilst attempting to pat Alf, which my four-legged friend rebuffed with a growl, causing Frank to whip his hand away.

"Don't think he likes you much," Tobias threw in as he scooped up another handful of heart attacks.

"Okay! Sorry, Tobias, but your catch-up with Frank is over." I picked up his half-drunk pint and held it up to him, nodding at the glass to suggest he should take it from me. "Slug the rest of that and do one," I thumbed over my shoulder to indicate the exit.

"I'm sorry—"

"You heard. Bugger off! I need to talk to Frank."

"Jayne, wha—"

"Hang on, I'll explain," I interrupted my husband whilst continuing to wave the glass in Tobias's face, encouraging the man to comply with my demands.

"I'm not going anywhere!"

"Yes you are." Again, I jiggled his glass at him. "Drink up and go. Otherwise, I might feel the need to ring your wife and mention last Friday evening."

That stopped the pompous pillock in his tracks. I'm pretty certain that Tobias thought his secret trip last week to see Jemma was precisely that, a secret. However, I knew differently, and with the benefit of knowing the future, I also knew Frank did, too. As mean as it was, I enjoyed watching the man squirm on his stool as he weighed up his options whilst shooting looks between Frank and me.

As I was discovering over the course of today, my long-forgotten memories of yesteryear were resurfacing at lightning speed. My brain appeared to be benefiting from a reboot, and the downloading upgrade continued reinstalling years of previously lost details. Semanticization and gistification, I'm led to believe some expert coined the phrase about how memories fade over time. A process that sieves out the chaff to only hold on to the salient points or the gist of an event. Whatever, but my mind appeared to be reversing that action, causing the memory of last Friday here in 1979 to become clear. An event that I would struggle to recall yesterday despite the enormity of what had happened.

Jemma and I were enjoying a drink together at The Maids Head Hotel. I'd nipped to the ladies, and when returning to our table, I'd spotted Jemma and Tobias embroiled in a heated exchange by the hotel foyer. Jemma had pleaded with me to keep schtum, even though it was pretty obvious something was afoot. Of course, when Frank and I got together a week later, and the news broke regarding their affair, all became clear.

"I have no idea what you're talking about?" Tobias announced, in that rather haughty way he always portrayed as he attempted to regain his composure.

"Err … what was that about Friday night?"

"Frank, please." I grabbed his arm to halt what appeared to be the precursor to accusing Tobias of having an affair with Jemma. The conversation that should have taken place before I muscled in.

"Tobias, I won't say this again. I suggest you leave."

"Who the hell d'you think you are? No woman, including my wife, I'll have you know, tells me what to do."

I can only assume, due to not warming to his tone, Alf possessed a rather dim view of Tobias. He demonstrated this by clamping his jaws around the flapping material at the bottom of Tobias's flared suit trousers and, whilst vigorously shaking his head, offered a guttural growl.

"Get that ruddy dog off me!"

"He'll let go when you go!" I jabbed a finger in his face, thinking Alf deserved another pint for his exploits.

Tobias grabbed his jacket and attempted to kick Alf before he hopped off his stool. However, despite consuming a pint of ale, which must have dulled his reactions, Alf's fleet of foot, or should I say paw, resulted in Tobias performing an air kick. I swear to God, I'm sure I spotted Alf snicker like Muttley when Tobias lost his balance and, embarrassingly, took a tumble.

"Jesus, mate, watch out!" called out a thickset man, his size suggesting he could win a best-of-three arm wrestling contest with Geoff Capes, as Tobias's prone body bashed into his legs, thus causing him to spill his beer. "Suggest you naff off before I make you."

"Well said," I threw in.

"Christ, what the hell—"

"Frank!" I spun around as my future husband slid from his stool, appearing to ready himself for a bar brawl when jumping to Tobias's defence. "Please, shove a sock in it and be quiet for a moment." I patted his hand, leaving my husband sporting that gormless look he could occasionally give off when super shocked.

"Hey, love, you need me to teach these two idiots some manners?"

"No. Very kind of you, but I'm fine. This man is just leaving." I wagged a finger at Tobias, who scrambled to his feet and dusted down his suit trousers.

"Alright, but I can throw him out if you like?"

Frank stepped forward, an action I detected Geoff Capes's lookalike clock in his peripheral vision. Now concerned this was about to go south, I slapped my hand on my husband's chest, effectively halting his advance. I guess if I were a man, Frank would have pushed me aside. Fortunately, in this situation, I wasn't.

"Tobias, I suggest you apologise." I gestured my head to the man with tree-trunk biceps and spilt beer.

"Me? I have no intention of apologising. I nudged the gorilla, that's all. And, it was your damn dog—"

"Hey, you mugging me off? Who the hell are you calling a gorilla?"

"Woah! Please, let's not let this get out of hand. We're sorry, okay?" I held my hands in a placating pose, hoping the big fella would leave it be. All I wanted was to talk to the man who would be my husband, but now I seemed to have taken on the role of peacekeeper attempting to prevent a bar brawl.

"Okay, love, seeing as you said it so nicely," he smirked. "Hey, anyone ever said you look like that Kate Bush?"

I groaned before rolling my eyes. "Now you come to mention it. Yes, once or twice, you could say."

In this era, it had been a constant. As sure as the sun would rise, and with the regularity of striking unions of the 1970s, some knob would say I looked like Kate Bush. Of course, those comments dissipated as the years rolled on when I gained a couple of pounds and Kate didn't. I guess now I'd reacquired my waif-like figure, I could expect those comments to resurface.

"Ha, yeah, you do." Whilst giving me the once over with his eyes, he tapped his mate's arm. Not something I'd experienced for many a good year, and considered rather unwelcome, I can tell you. "Hey, Jimbo, this bird looks just like Kate Bush. What d'you reckon?"

"Oh, yeah, she does," Jimbo announced, as he also gave the visual once up and down. "Can I buy you a drink, love?" Jimbo grinned, offering me a vision of his less-than-well-cared-for teeth.

"Very kind, but no, thank you. I'm married."

"Are you?" Frank asked, still looking confused.

"Alright, love, whatever. If you're gonna pull that one, at least wear a ring on your finger," Jimbo suggested when nodding to my ringless left hand. "You look a bit stuck-up for my liking, anyway."

"Excuse me?"

"I say, that was extremely rude," interjected Tobias, as he squared up to both men.

"Oh, crap," muttered Frank before pushing past me and slotting himself between Tobias and the two burly chaps.

"Oh, great!" I exclaimed. How the hell had we got to this stage? One thing I knew for sure, although a future D-List celeb, charity mogul, and successful entrepreneur, my husband had never been shy with his fists when the situation demanded. Unlike Tobias, who appeared to be backing away.

"Gents! This stops now, or I'll call the police."

Frank, Jimbo, and the Geoff Capes lookalike side-eyed the barman before nodding in agreement.

"I'm a solicitor, you know," blustered Tobias with his favoured pompous lilt. Presumably, now my husband had stepped into the affray, Tobias thought he would be safe from any punches and could offer this pointless information.

"Tobias, you should go." I gave him a shove to encourage him.

"Get off!" he blurted as he stumbled backwards. "You're not right in the head! Clare always said you were odd."

"Yes, well, to be honest with you, after today, she's probably right."

"And that dog's a damn nuisance." Alf growled, causing Tobias to hop back a pace before wagging his finger at Frank, who'd retaken his seat when Jimbo and his mate turned away to continue drinking. "Aren't you going to say something?"

"I think Jayne is right. You should go."

"Jesus." Tobias glanced down at the leg of his trousers where Alf had deposited slobbery dribble and teeth puncture marks on the material. "You need to get a muzzle for that thing!"

"Tobias," I sighed. "Look, I'm sorry, but please, just go."

"Frank, I have no idea what's going on with you two, but I'm not staying here to be growled at by some stinking mutt and abused by Jemma's friend. If you still want to catch up another day, then call me."

"What did you say?"

"Sorry?"

Frank hopped off his stall, stepped up to Tobias and narrowed his eyes, causing Tobias to flinch. "What ... did ... you ... just ... say?"

"Alright, Frank, what's the matter with you? All I said was call me."

"I knew it! I bloody knew it!" Frank announced, as he raised his fist.

"Frank, no!"

19

Call Me

"Please, no. Frank, don't," I hissed.

Still with his hand raised, Frank nodded. I presumed, in that moment, deciding not to thump Tobias but maintain his stance as if intending to do so. Apart from the man who appeared ready to self-defecate being a bit of a pillock, I had no idea what had caused Frank to lose his shit with him ... pun fully intended.

"You're as mad as that bitch!" Tobias nodded at me, again flinching when detecting Frank's fist move. Before Frank could react, Tobias spun on his heels and shot out of the pub.

"Frank?"

My husband opened his fist as he turned to me.

"Sorry, Jayne. It's something he said."

"What? What did he just say?"

"Oh, look, it doesn't matter. Leave it." Frank pushed past me to the bar, plucked up his pint and necked the half-pint in a couple of gulps, leaving me to collect my thoughts and glance at Alf for inspiration.

Although he couldn't have, because I'm not aware dogs are capable of such an expression, I thought Alf shrugged in response, which wasn't overly helpful.

"Right, sorry about all that," Frank announced before wiping his lips with the back of his hand. "I'd better get going. When Jemma gets back at the end of the week, I'll let her know I saw you."

"Frank, look, can we just talk for a moment? There's something ... well, it's—"

"What? Hey, Jemma's in Parliament until Friday, so give her a call at the weekend if you want to catch up. I tell you, since she's become the ruddy MP, I hardly ever see her."

"Frank—"

"Actually, I hope you don't mind me asking, but has Jemma said anything to you?"

"About what?"

Frank winced, presumably not wanting to suggest his gorgeous wife was playing away with Tobias.

The first time this evening took place, Frank didn't leave on his own. We'd enjoyed a drink and, without any doubt, flirted with each other. Concerned that history was changing, I grabbed the stool vacated by Tobias and gestured to Frank that he should sit.

"Frank, what did Tobias just say that got you so riled up?"

"You know something about Jemma and Tobias, don't you? Did Jemma come clean when you met up last Friday?"

"Err ... last Friday?"

"You and Jemma went for a drink at The Maids Head."

"Hang on, Frank, you're getting ahead of yourself. Tell me what Tobias just said."

"Alright," he nodded. "He said, call me."

"So?"

"Last week, a message was left on our answering machine. A man's voice just said, 'call me', huffed, and that was it. I had no idea who it was and thought it odd.

"Tobias?"

"Yeah. Hearing Tobias say those exact words just now, in pretty much the same tone, confirmed it was him. That message wasn't for me. I know it was for Jemma."

"Right," I huffed. "And that bothers you?"

Frank shot his head back and frowned. "Err ... just a bit. I mean, why would Tobias be calling my wife?"

"Yes, I see your point."

This conversation with my husband clearly demonstrated that he hadn't yet landed in 1979, probably still scooting through time to catch me up after that excursion on the Wheel. Well, that's the thought I had to cling to and try to ignore the nagging worry that Frank had evaporated as that nutter The Hooded Claw suggested can, on the odd occasion, happen.

Although I knew he would fall for me and stop loving his wife, I prayed *my* Frank would hurry up and get here so we could return to holding a 'normal' conversation. The pain etched on his face that suggested he was hurting at the thought of Jemma and Tobias together was ripping holes in me.

"Jayne, I'm sorry to ask, you know, what with you being friends with Jemma, but do you know something?"

"You mean about Tobias and Jemma—"

"Is everything alright here?"

I spun around to find Jason and Jenny. Jason looked as if he was about to step in if trouble was brewing. I thought that was very decent of him, confirming the good friend he was and remained throughout my life.

Jenny gently laid her hand on my arm. "Jayne, are you alright?" she whispered, shooting worried looks at my confused future husband.

"I'm fine." I nodded at them both, offering my best convincing smile. "Honestly, I'm fine. Couldn't be better," I chuckled.

Frank grabbed my arm. "Sorry, what were you going to say about Jemma?"

"Give me a minute, and I'll explain," I shot him a reply surreptitiously from the corner of my mouth before facing Jenny again. With that plastered-on grin, I attempted to convince her all was good, which, of course, it wasn't.

"Jason," Jenny frowned, shooting a look of concern at her husband. "I don't like this."

"Oh, Jenny, honestly, I'm okay. Are you going now?" I nodded at the exit to encourage them to leave.

"Jayne?"

"Give me a minute, Frank," I growled. "Just hang on, and I'll explain." Well, I'll give it a damn good go. That said, if this Frank had never time-travelled, I feared the conversation could be on the short side. As Alf had intimated earlier, I hoped this Frank had travelled once.

Alf shot me a doggy look and licked his chops, which I surmised was my amazing pooch performing that mind-reading trick he seemed to have mastered. Jenny and Jason exchanged looks before she answered.

"I'm afraid we'll have to save my mother from the kids, so we should get going, but only if you're sure you're okay. You said that this man's your—"

I shot my free hand up, palm outwards, to halt Jenny before she mentioned the 'husband' word.

"Jenny, I'm perfectly fine, honestly."

Jenny, laying her hand on my arm, leaned forward to whisper in my ear, leaving Frank and Jason to introduce themselves and shake hands.

"Jayne, what on earth is going on?" she hissed, shooting worried looks at Frank, presumably assessing his nutter status, and thus was it safe to leave me.

"Nothing's going on ... promise. I just need to talk to Frank."

"Frank?"

"Yes ... look, it's ... well, kinda complicated." An understatement which could easily rival the *'it's just been a bit of an odd day'* comment from earlier.

"Oh. I'm all ears."

"Jenny, can we leave it? I'll explain later." Although I wouldn't because informing Jenny that the man now chatting with her husband was hopefully a time-traveller, albeit, at this point, only the once, probably wouldn't be a sensible move if I valued our friendship. Jenny and Jason were a normal, well-balanced couple, so I figured that wasn't a subject I should broach.

"Alright, if you say so," Jenny huffed. "I'm just a bit worried because you don't seem yourself, that's all."

"I know. As I said, I've had a strange day. Frank's a friend, and I'm perfectly safe in his company."

"Really? He looked like he was about to punch that man."

She made a good point. However, although handy with his fists, a product of being raised on that God-awful Broxworth Estate, my Frank had never laid a finger on me.

There was that time in that club in Benidorm when some bloke's hand became overfamiliar with my bottom, but that's another story. Let's just say the chap spent the rest of his holiday drinking through a straw and leave it at that. Not that I condoned his actions, but my Frank was a punch-first-ask-questions-later type of guy in his youth, as his business partner had presumably discovered a couple of days ago.

"Look, Jenny, I need to talk to Frank about something. I'll give you a call tomorrow, just so you know I'm still alive, alright?"

"If you're sure. With all the reports about that Yorkshire Ripper, I just want to make sure he's not some crazed nutter like him."

"Oh, blimey, you sound like my mother," I chortled. "Frank Stone might be prepared to use his fists, but he's no Peter Sutcliffe, that I can assure you."

Jenny frowned.

I winced.

Alf shook his head.

An admonishing gesture that suggested my beer-swilling, mind-reading pooch couldn't believe what I'd just said.

"Who? I know that name. That rings a bell with me. Who is he?" Jenny knitted her brows as if trying to recall where she'd heard that name before.

Of course, unless she or Jason were also time-travellers from the future, which despite what had happened, I felt sure was unlikely, or whether she had relatives in Bradford who lived on the same street as Mr Sutcliffe and had mentioned their neighbour in passing, there was no way that she could know of the man.

"Never mind. All I'm saying is that I'm safe with Frank. I'm probably safer with him than any man."

Jenny chewed her lip, giving Frank the once over as if that could decide his serial killer status.

"O-kay," Jenny delivered in a tone borrowed from Alison as she slowly emphasised both syllables before continuing. "Odd that because I'm damn sure I know that Sutcliffe name from somewhere."

Maybe she did have relatives in Bradford.

"You call me tomorrow, you hear?" she wagged a finger at me before pulling me into a tight hug. "I need to know you're alright."

"Promise. Dyb-dyb, scouts' honour." When we released our embrace, I offered the three-finger salute, which I wasn't sure was a thing these days, not being a Girl Guide in my day, but Sharon and Helen had joined, and I was aware that was the salute used ten or so years from now.

"Right, are we fit?" Jason asked Jenny before turning back to face Frank and offering his hand. "Nice to meet you, Frank."

"Likewise. Shame you have to leave, but I understand you're in a hurry." Frank replied, accompanying his 'hurry' statement with a nod to the door, suggesting he wished they would go so he could probe me further about his bitchy wife.

"Jayne, you going to be okay?"

"Oh, not you as well?"

"We've done that, Jason. Jayne said she'll be fine."

"I will! Christ, you're both as bad as my mother." I shooed them with my hands. "Now, go on, you two. It was lovely to catch up." I nodded at Jason. "I'll see you in the morning, and I promise not to be late." When they'd left, I turned to Frank.

"You going to buy a lady a drink?"

"Sorry, Jayne, but what were you saying about Tobias and Jemma? Has Jemma said something to you?"

"Frank ... a drink?"

"Oh, sure. Err ... what'll it be, then?"

"My usual?"

"Which is?"

"You don't know, do you?" Although he clearly wouldn't, it was still disappointing to hear.

"No, sorry. What'll you have?"

"Wine. I'll have a white wine, please."

"Sure, but then you tell me what you know about Tobias and my wife?" He wagged a finger at me before turning to grab the barman's attention.

I nodded, then offered a shrug to Alf.

"This is going to be fun," I sarcastically mumbled.

Alf licked his chops and grinned.

"Yes, well, that's not overly helpful, is it?"

"D'you often talk to your dog?" Frank asked after ordering my drink.

"Alf is technically my father's dog."

"Oh, yeah, I remember. Sorry about your dad. When was that ... back in the mid-1970s? Err ... a couple of years ago, I mean."

Although in my head, my father died nearly forty years back, I just nodded and shrugged. However, the mid-1970s comment he'd thrown out before checking himself offered a glimmer of hope that this Frank had time-travelled at least once. Surely, in 1979, you would refer to 1977 as a couple of years ago, not the mid-1970s, wouldn't you? There appeared to be only one way to find out.

"There you go, one white wine. Now, d'you want to tell me what's going on?"

I puffed out my cheeks to ready myself to utter a ludicrous statement, knowing I was about to discover if my 1970s comment theory held any water. If Frank looked blankly at me, then this really was going to be one hell of an uphill struggle.

"Okay, if I said the London Eye, would that mean anything to you?"

"Sorry?" Frank blurted before slamming his pint on the bar and bug-eyeing me. "What did you just say?"

"The London Eye. The Millennium Wheel, a large Ferris Wheel on the Southbank near the London Aquarium and Waterloo Station."

"Bloody hell," he announced. "Bloody hell, no way!"

That was a good response. Frank had time-travelled at least once.

"Yes way … and your bloody hell comment is a bit of an understatement. While discussing the ridiculous, can you order half of Double Diamond as well, please?"

Alf licked his chops and grinned.

"Sorry, Alf, just a half. You're driving, remember?"

20

A Bold Bluff

"Double Diamond. Half of." I repeated when noticing Frank seemed to have plunged into some odd stupor, which I guess was fair enough. That said, whether his perplexed expression was due to me mentioning the London Eye or a reaction to me advising Alf that he could only have a half, who could tell? "Oh, and can you ask them to put his beer in a bowl because I think Alf has yet to master using his paws to grip a mug?"

Alf licked his chops and wiggled his bottom as he impatiently waited for his beer whilst his swishing tail frantically polished the antique floorboards within the eighteen-inch radius of his posterior.

"Frank, Alf's beer?" I repeated, tapping his knee before swishing my hair over my shoulder.

Frank gulped but seemed incapable of hauling himself from whatever tangent my London Eye comment had sent him off to.

"Excuse me ... yoo-hoo? You there," I waved at the barman who'd previously threatened to call the police. "Can I have half of Double Diamond, please?"

"Course, love."

"In a bowl, as opposed to a glass."

"In a bowl?"

"Yes, in a bowl."

"What kind of bowl?"

"Any." I nonchalantly shrugged. "To be honest, I'm not sure my dog is overly fussy."

"Your dog?"

"Yes, my dog."

"You want half of Double Diamond for your dog?"

"That's what I said."

"I'm not sure we serve dogs."

"He's not asking. I am."

He raised a finger to indicate I should hang on before he shouted to the barman who'd served me earlier.

"Robbo, do we serve dogs?"

"Only if they've had a rough day. Get it?" he chuckled, before impersonating a dog. "Ruff."

"Friggin' hilarious. Well?"

"Yeah, that's okay. The mutt had a pint earlier and seems to be behaving himself. Cash, mind, no credit. I don't fancy trying to catch him if he does a runner before paying."

The bemused barman offered a 'whatever' shrug before snatching up a bowl usually reserved for Tobias's high blood pressure peanuts.

"Looks like your dog's got half a bitter on its way."

"Marvellous, thank you," I replied, before bending forward and addressing Alf. "Your beer's on its way, Alfie-Boy."

Alf grinned before increasing the tail-swishing tempo a couple of notches, presumably now on the full-speed setting.

As I peered up at Frank, I swished my hair over my shoulder again and noticed his eyes follow that movement. Thirty-six years ago, to the hour when I'd last perched on this barstool, I'd performed that very same action. Frank had later said it was the sexiest thing he'd ever seen.

Now, hang on there. I wasn't performing an erotic pole-dancing routine dressed in a dental-floss bikini. Neither was I pouting as if about to offer a blow-job to a chocolate bar, but, nevertheless, back in the day, my seductive hair swirl had been enough to capture my husband's attention. So, seeing as we were 'back in the day', so to speak, with that in mind and an urgent need for my unborn girls' sake, I performed a couple more hair swishes. Each flick, trying to make them as titillating as possible whilst employing my best flirtatious pose.

"Frank?" I slowly batted my eyelids.

Christ, come on, man, I'm not usually the sort to 'perform' when wanting to grab a man's attention. God forbid. I was a take-it-or-leave-it kind of woman. This was me, like it or lump it. I dreaded what I might need to do next if this hair-swishing routine failed.

"Jayne, err …"

"Yes, Frank?" Another swish of hair to the other shoulder for good measure as I exaggeratedly tipped my head to one side again.

"Look, I shouldn't say this … but you're stunning."

"Good, now we're getting somewhere. I won't have to crack out the two-piece with the cheese-wire thong, thank God."

"Sorry?"

"Oh, ignore that." I batted my silly statement away with a wave of my hand before continuing with equally ridiculous and unnecessary details. After two glasses of wine and a hell of a day, Alf better be up for driving. "Look, my extensive wardrobe doesn't house a cheese-wire thong and never did, actually. Of course, I tried them, but boy, are they ruddy uncomfortable. It's like suffering an all-day wedgie. Now, don't get me wrong, I like to look good as much as the next woman. Sure, I do. I'm aware they're Marmite; some women swear by them, and others detest the bum-slicing garment, but they are most certainly not for me. Bridget Jones all the way, I can tell you. Well, to clarify, more so in recent years. Comfort over style, that's what I say."

Frank smirked.

"Yes, well, too much detail, I guess. Anyway, I'm glad you think I'm stunning. That's a damn good start because we have a shite-load of catching up to do."

Frank leaned forward and offered a conspiratorial sideways glance before lowering his head to whisper.

"Jayne, have you time-travelled?"

I copied his forward-leaning pose, thus placing my lips just a few centimetres from his.

"Yes!"

"Shit! How?" he hissed.

"Same way you did, I suspect. Via an early morning excursion on the London Eye."

"When?"

"Yesterday."

"No … what year."

"Oh, I see. 2015."

"2015?"

"Yes, 2015."

"Wow! Why?"

"What d'you mean why?"

"Well, I mean, why did the CYA need you to travel back in time? What's your mission?"

"I don't have a mission, as such. You see, I shouldn't have travelled. There was a bit of a mix-up—"

The barman cleared his throat, causing us both to pull away from our conspiratorial positions.

"There you go, one half of Double Diamond for his lordship down there." He nodded between us as he eyed up Alf. "Never served a beer to a dog before, I can tell you."

"Oh, thank you." I gingerly plucked up the bowl as Alf joyfully leapt up, placing his paws on my knees and panting in anticipation. "Hang on, Alf, hang on. I don't want slops of beer all over my legs."

"How much?" Frank inquired, pulling out a handful of change from his trouser pocket.

"Nah, you're alright, mate. On the house. It's not every day you get the chance to serve a dog."

"Oh, cheers."

"Here you go." I placed the bowl down and patted Alf's head as he tucked in, his tail swishing slowing as he concentrated on savouring his beer.

"I thought beer, well, alcohol, was poisonous to dogs?" the barman enquired when placing his elbows on the bar to gain purchase and haul himself up to grab a better view of the circus freak show. Namely, Alf, the beer-supping pooch. "You should get him on the telly. Y'know, *That's Life* or something like that."

"Oh, not you as well. Everyone's obsessed with *That's Life*. Anyway, I'm not sure Alfie-Boy is groomed enough for television. I think a slot next to the bearded-lady show or the six-legged donkey at the circus would be more his mark."

Alf took a break from slurping to shoot me a disapproving glower before returning to the task in hand. Or paw, I should say.

"Blimey! You see that? He's human, your dog. I reckon he heard you."

"Oh, well, I think Alf is half-human. Anthropomorphism, I think is the correct term."

"If you say so, love. Does he want a cigar, too? I've got King Edwards or Hamlet. Or is he more of a Woodbine or rollie kind of pooch?"

"Oh, I don't know. Shall I ask him?"

"What?"

"I'm joking! Alf doesn't smoke."

Well, he may do. After today's events, I wouldn't be surprised to witness my father's mongrel light up and blow a plume of smoke to the ceiling before uttering a satisfied sigh. Hmmm, maybe that was taking it too far.

"Right, course not. Here, he's like those paintings. Y'know, those pictures of dogs playing cards and—"

"Coolidge."

"Sorry?

"Cassius Coolidge. Or Kash Koolidge, as he liked to be known. He painted a whole series of them."

"Oh, is that the artist's name? I never knew. My old dad had a print of the one where the dogs are playing cards."

"*A Bold Bluff* or *A Friend in Need*? There are others, but I can't remember their names at the moment."

"You what, love?"

"Which painting? Coolidge painted many card-table scenes."

"Oh, the one where there's this Bulldog passing an ace with his paw."

"Ah, that's *A Friend in Need*. Like most of his work, that was painted way back during the turn of the last century."

"You know your art. You studied it or something? Gotta say I'm surprised they're that old. I would have said they were late Victorian, not back in the early eighteen hundreds."

"Oh … yes, I see what you mean." Bugger, this time travel malarky could drop one in a spot of bother if not too careful. "It's a pity your father didn't have an original. One sold not long ago for a cool half a mil."

The barman gave a low whistle. "Blimey."

Frank cleared his throat, clearly wanting this small talk to end so we could return to discussing more serious matters like time-travel.

"Anyway, thanks for Alf's beer. That's very kind, but I'm sure you have a long line of thirsty punters waiting for you."

Taking my hint, he shot Alf one last glance and turned to deal with the next in line, a man looking none too chuffed about the wait times.

"Jayne, shall we grab a table?"

"Yes, I think we'd better. Alf's nearly finished his drink, so let's decamp over to that window seat."

Now we were afforded some privacy, well, the packed pub aside, but at least we didn't have the barman interjecting into our conversation, I took Frank's hand in mine. Although a little taken aback by my forward approach, he didn't fight me.

"Frank, we have so much to talk about—"

"Jayne—"

"Hang on. You always interrupt me. Have done for years and you know it annoys me so."

Frank crinkled up his nose, causing deep trenches to form on his forehead as he presumably tried to understand my statement. Which, of course, he couldn't. This Frank, the once-only-time-travelling Frank, knew nothing of our future life together. I just prayed *my* Frank would hurry up and land from wherever he was.

"Okay, this is all nuts, but here goes." I paused and lowered my voice when spotting a thuggish-looking chap casually leaning against the wall sipping his beer, attempting to earwig our conversation. "You time-travelled in 2015 after the CYA and that rather obtuse man, Hartland—"

"The Hooded Claw—"

"The very same, plucked you from where you'd apparently been sleeping rough. Hartland said you needed to return to 1979 and save Jemma, who was apparently murdered that year."

"She was. And will be unless I can stop that from happening next Friday."

"Not in my lifetime."

"Sorry?"

"Frank, the version of 2015 I come from, Jemma is alive and well and being as bitchy as ever. The damn woman, God love her, is as alive as you and me."

I squeezed his hand, just an involuntary show of affection when spotting my husband's confused look, when clearly struggling to slot the pieces together.

"What d'you mean ... y'know, you said I've been interrupting you for years? What does that mean? For the last ten years or so, after I lost everything, I've been living on the streets. I haven't seen you for, well, decades, I think it could be."

"Okay, I'm just getting my head around this. It seems that next Friday you do save Jemma—"

"Who murdered her?"

"Frank, stop interrupting. Christ, man, I just told you to stop that."

"Sorry, go on."

I paused, realising that talking in this tone to the man I was essentially trying to woo wasn't a particularly good idea. Thirty-five years of marriage had provided a closeness where we didn't need to mind what we said to each other. The year I came from, we still loved one another, but, of course, by that time in our relationship we'd moved past that flirty stage that young love requires. Now, back at square one again, I needed to convince this thirty-year-old man that I was the woman for him. Young Jayne's mind needed to dominate and suppress the mind of the woman I'd become. Namely, a sixty-five-year-old living a privileged lifestyle who could sometimes be accused of being more focused on her grandchildren than her husband.

A point that I now realise and regret. Not that we weren't close, far from it. However, since the grandchildren arrived on the scene, I could now see that I may have shoved my husband a couple of rungs down the pecking order. That was another thing I could change.

"Frank, sorry, I didn't mean to bark at you."

"You and Alf swapped places? He's now the human, and you …" Frank paused, probably realising calling me a dog wasn't going to be acceptable, even though we both knew what he meant.

I snorted a laugh.

"Sorry, I didn't mean to say—"

I wiggled his hand and offered my best young Jayne smile. "I know. Look, I really don't know what on earth is going on with Alfie-Boy. All I can remember of him is that he was a lazy, scruffy mutt that, after my father died, wasn't too interested in anyone else."

Alf shot me a look.

"See, I'm sure he can understand what we're saying. It's as if he knows what's going on since I've time-travelled."

"That's mad."

"I know, but so is our situation."

"Yeah, fair point. I've been here a week, and I'm still convinced I'll wake up in 2015 sleeping under a heap of damp cardboard down on the Queen's Walk."

"Oh, Frank, how did that happen?"

"I don't know, it just did. A gradual descent to the bottom, I guess." He took a sip of beer before continuing. "After Jemma was murdered, my life went on the slide. I started drinking, and one thing led to another. So, by the time I was in my early fifties, I was roaming the streets with all hope lost."

I took a sip of wine to prepare myself for the next question.

The question.

"You love her?"

"Jemma?"

I nodded.

Frank hesitated.

Shit, if he loved her, I was as good as doomed.

21

Earth Angel

When Frank hesitated, a plethora of hideous scenarios played out in my mind. Okay, if Frank still loved Jemma, then that was bad. Life definingly bad, to put it somewhat mildly. However, all was not lost because as soon as *my* Frank landed, all would be good. He would know our future and would definitely not harbour those feelings for his current wife. Frank would know he loves *me*, and our girls will still be born.

All good.

However, what if *my* Frank was not coming to rescue me and had evaporated into the ether in some time-travel mist that never solidified? As Marty McFly experienced when his father shied away from kissing his mother at the school dance, if I had a photo of the girls, would their images now be fading and thus eradicating their existence? I offered a slight shudder as I detected the heavy boots of fate stamping upon my grave.

If *my* Frank is no longer, and I don't kiss this Frank, our first kiss which leads to the start of the rest of my life, then my darling girls are history … gone and never existed.

All very bad.

I mused I seemed to be the queen of understatements today.

"Frank ... do you still love Jemma?" I had to push him to answer whether the answer was what I wanted to hear or not.

"Oh, well ..."

When my future husband paused, I bit my lip and winced. As the seconds ticked by, whilst Frank conjured up his answer, I half expected to taste blood.

"That's a bit awkward," he grimaced. "You know ... what with you and Jemma—"

"It's okay to tell me," I interrupted before taking a sip of wine to bolster my fortitude or just increase my alcohol intake if his answer was to be unpalatable. "Look, Frank, I'm a time-traveller like you. Christ! What a statement," I chuckled. "But anyway, I won't tell Jemma what you said. Or might say, for that matter."

Frank huffed, released his hand from mine and scrubbed his palms over his face before holding my expectant stare.

This was it. Despite that 'stunning' compliment he'd earlier thrown my way, what he said next would determine my and our daughters' future. If Frank was still in love with Jemma, I was doomed to that life Hartland claimed I'd lived before Frank time-travelled the first time. Namely, a spinster, school governor, living with a clowder of moggies. Not that he said as much, but probably also a part-time librarian, a big cheese in the local knitting club, whilst putting my mathematical skills to good use as the treasurer of the local carpet-bowls association. Not that I have any problem with all three of those activities, per se, but they just weren't me. Well, the me who I thought I was.

"When Jemma died. After she was murdered, my life imploded. Jemma was ... is my life. She meant everything to me. I loved her, adored her ..." he paused and looked away, focusing on the other punters, much as Alf seemed to be doing from his position under the table.

Shit!

"But ... since I've returned to now, as in 1979, I'm not so sure. In fact, if I'm honest, I'm not even sure I like Jemma that much anymore. She just doesn't seem to be how I remember."

Phew!

Frank turned to face me again. "Is that so awful of me?"

"No, not at all." I exhaled, unaware I'd been holding my breath. "Best bloody news I've heard all day."

"Sorry?"

"Oh, no, don't worry, please just ignore me. I was just muttering to myself, that's all. You were saying?" I peered up at him, now feeling a smidge better about life despite always harbouring affection for cats. Also, if pushed on the subject, I didn't mind a spot of knitting.

"You said a moment ago ... that thing about us knowing each other for years. That comment about my constant interrupting."

"Frank ..." I paused and chewed my lip. Was this the time to tell him his future?

"Jayne?" He raised his palms expectantly.

"At the bar, you said I looked stunning."

"Ah, shit, sorry. I shouldn't have said that."

"Do you like me?"

"Course. I've always liked you. I said to Jemma when she was bitching about you that you're the nicest friend she's got."

"Bitching about me?"

"Oh," he winced. "Yeah, she's got that nasty way about her. Always has, but it seems more prevalent now I'm back."

"Jemma calls me Plain-Jayne, doesn't she?"

"Yeah, which is ridiculous, 'cos you're not," he scoffed before grabbing his pint to cover the blush that invaded his cheeks.

"I'm not plain? You don't think I am?"

"Course, you're not. Look, apologies for my earlier inappropriate comment, but I suppose I've always thought you were stun … err, good-looking. Beautiful, if you like."

I did like.

Notwithstanding his embarrassment regarding the 'beautiful' comment, made evident by his ruddy cheeks, which his raised glass failed to hide, Frank appeared compelled to continue and fill the now silent void.

"I just never realised how … err … lovely, beautiful, until tonight, I guess."

"Oh, okay. That's a relief."

"Is it?"

"Most definitely. Because otherwise, the next few decades are going to be very different to how my life has been, not to mention the girls."

Frank knitted his brows at that comment before taking a slug of beer.

"And you think I'm nice? *Nice*, not the most descriptive word in the English language."

"You are," he shrugged. "You're stunning and nice."

"Well, that's a start. You see, in my world, the one I travelled from, you and I have been married for thirty-five years. We have four daughters, three grandchildren, and throughout your life, you've treated me like a princess. However, Frank Stone, not once have you called me *nice*."

"Oh … wow, really?" Frank bug-eyed me. His pint glass paused an inch from his lips, where he held back from taking another sip.

I grabbed his free hand again, squeezing it tightly as if feeling the need to hang on to him.

"And Jemma?"

"You divorce her."

"Right. And you and me …" Frank paused to wave his pint glass between us. "You and me get married and have … how many children was it?"

"Four girls."

"Blimey."

"Yes, blimey. So, Frank Stone, is the thought of you and me so terrible?"

"No …" I detected a pause, perhaps a precursor to a 'but'.

"But what?"

"Nothing."

"Oh, I get it. I'm not a traffic stopper like Jemma. So you're thinking you must have settled for second best. Is that it?"

Notwithstanding my inner strength, something I'd developed over the years, just through the process of gaining wisdom as you age, I could feel my eyes watering. Despite those flattering, although slightly annoying, Kate Bush comments, I knew I wasn't a beauty in the same league as Jemma. She was the sort that made men drool and caused multiple vehicle pile-ups when she sashayed through town. Whereas I was probably more of what you might call an acquired taste.

"No ... not at all." I detected Frank squeeze my hand. "Look, I'm fast learning, now I'm back in 1979, during my first life I wasn't as happy as I thought I was. I'm not in love with Jemma anymore."

"Good! Because Sharon, Helen, Trudy, and Clara are fully expecting to be born again."

Frank repeated their names to himself as much as anything before turning to face me again.

"Do we have to call her Sharon?"

"Sharon Stone?"

"Yeah."

"Because of the actress?"

"Well, yeah."

"Funny thing is, you objected to her name, but I was insistent, so you relented. I pushed you on why you didn't want her to be called Sharon, but you were coy with your answers."

"Because I knew the future?"

"I'm assuming so. Of course, the actress wasn't famous when our Sharon was born, so her name meant nothing to me. Anyway, our Sharon is far more stunning than that actress, and Denzil dotes on her."

"Denzil?"

"Oh, blimey, you have so much to catch up on. Sharon is married to Denzil Warlow. An absolutely wonderful man. You're gonna really love him."

"Christ! Denzil Warlow, bloody hell."

"What?"

"I've already met him."

"Oh. How?"

"Black guy, six-feet-two, build like a brick-privy, wouldn't hurt a fly, and has clown feet."

"Clown feet?"

"Size thirteen feet, giant plates of meat, they are."

"Yes, that sounds like Sharon's Denzil. But how on earth—"

"He was a fellow rough sleeper."

"Oh, really? Well, not in my life. Denzil and Sharon met at university."

"How ... oh, time has—"

"Changed?"

"Yeah, my time-travelling flit on that Wheel must have changed the future. Some tiny thing I've done has caused Denzil's life to take a different path."

"I guess it must have because Denzil runs—"

"Jesus, Jayne, what else has happened?" he interrupted, appearing giddy with excitement at the prospect of hearing tales of the future. I guess, based on the rather pitiful existence he left behind, the clamour to know how his second life would pan out was to be expected. "Tell me," he hissed, wiggling my hand. "You know everything. What we did, where we went ... how my life has changed. Come on. So, we get married and have four girls—"

"Beautiful girls."

"I'm sure they are. But what else?"

"Oh, Frank, there's so much. Three-and-a-half decades' worth. Won't it just be easier if we wait for you to catch me up?"

"Err ... what?" he exclaimed, shooting his head back. "Sorry, what d'you mean, catch you up?"

"Well, I'm assuming, praying, you will land any day now, and all your memories of our life will come flooding back to you."

"I don't understand. I've already travelled."

"Clearly! As much as yesterday I thought my husband was going ga-ga in his old age, you have actually time-travelled. But, listen, Frank, this is my point. You time-travel again. You and me together. I woke up today in 1979, whereas I can only assume you are still making your way here. And taking your sweet time about it too, I might add."

"Oh ... shit."

"I know. Tell me about it."

"Oh bollocks." Frank slapped his hands on his cheeks, drawing the skin down as he allowed his palms to slide south.

"What?"

"Well ... did Hartland mention anything about evaporation?"

"Oh, no." I slowly shook my head back and forth as the terror ripped through me. Of course, earlier, I'd pondered this may have happened. However, due to it being too horrid to contemplate, I'd dismissed evaporation on the Wheel as a possibility. But now, just hearing Frank mention it made that terrifying thought even more viable. "No, no, no, please, for the love of God, no."

"I take it he did, then. Evaporating in time, failing to make it through?"

"Uh-huh, because of the mix-up, which I'll come to in a minute, I wasn't really listening, but yes, he did say something to that end." I grabbed his hands before they slipped off his cheeks, almost white-knuckle-gripping them before continuing. "Please don't tell me you think I made it through, but you didn't."

"Well, you're here, and I'm not."

"But you'll probably arrive tomorrow or the day after, won't you?"

"I guess we'll find out over the next few days."

Alf turned and nudged my leg, causing me to glance away from Frank and look through the gap between us and the table.

"What, Alf? You can't have any more beer. You're probably over the legal limit already."

Alf dipped his head and peered up at me with those doleful eyes. Either my pooch had the beginnings of a hangover, thus indicating it was time to go so he could curl up in his basket and sleep off his drinking session, or he knew something that neither Frank nor I knew, but we were about to find out.

"Shit! Alf, are you saying what I think you're saying?"

Part 3

22

2015

Goody Two Shoes

Hartland raised a finger to indicate he required silence before Whitman enlightened him regarding the prelim results following tonight's monumental cock-up. Or, as she just put it, '*his* failed mission that has resulted in a catalogue of issues'. Brave words from an employee, Hartland fumed.

Whilst taking a hearty drag on his cigarette, he eyed up the senior analyst. Due to being the one and only employee who appeared not to be terrified of him, he'd always found the woman quite intriguing. Also, apart from being a brilliant mathematician who'd secured a plethora of letters after her name after leaving Oxford, Hartland considered the twenty-something woman could easily provide stimulation of a different sort. Despite her dour dress sense, Hartland thought the slip of a lass could be regarded as rather easy on the eye.

He flicked his ash in the glass ashtray before rolling the lit end around to form a glowing point, smirking at the thought of Whitman dressed as a Bunny-Girl.

"Sir?" she inquired.

"I take it I'm going to require sustenance to hear what you have to say about *my* failed mission, as you so eloquently put it?" Hartland dropped the smirk in favour of one of his famous death stares as he addressed the analyst who stood before him.

Johnson tipped his head back to peer up at the heavens. That said, all he could see were the polystyrene ceiling tiles. Whitman, although brilliant, on the odd occasion, could be accused of not tempering her attitude to suit her audience. Throwing accusations at her team was perfectly fine, but directed at the Commander-in-Chief could, at the very best, be considered foolhardy. Although Hartland appeared calm, Johnson knew Whitman had lit his boss's dangerously short fuse.

"If you mean alcohol, sir, then, yes, I think that might be advisable in your case," Whitman replied, accompanied by an exaggerated eye roll.

Without being asked, Johnson snatched up a bottle of single malt from the top of the bank of filing cabinets that lined the wall behind his desk, which Hartland occupied. From his position behind his boss, so out of his eyeline, he attempted to catch Whitman's eye when concerned about his analyst's attitude. Clearing his throat and waving his hand were to no avail because Whitman and Hartland appeared locked in a game of who blinks first.

"Not for me," stated Whitman, maintaining her hold of Hartland's glower.

Johnson nodded in response and poured two fingers' worth into each glass before handing one to Hartland.

"You don't drink, and you don't smoke, do you, Whitman?" Hartland asked before swallowing his whisky in one gulp. He grimaced and raised his glass for a refill while holding his senior analyst with his trademark vampiric stare. "So, tell me, what do you do?"

"I work, sir. I'm a brilliant analyst. So much so that I'm probably the most competent this organisation has ever employed. And, sir, I have no intention of poisoning my brain with alcohol, nicotine, or any other drug, for that matter. All of the above mentioned are totally unnecessary."

"Admirable, I'm sure."

"Sir."

"So, tell me, Whitman, what do you do for fun? Hartland asked whilst nodding a thank you to Johnson, who handed him a refill.

"Fun, sir?"

"Yes, woman, fun. Pleasure, excitement, thrill-seeking, general merriment. I'm sure with your educated brain, you understand the meaning of the word, fun. How do you entertain yourself? I can't quite imagine you're into bungee jumping, presume you're not one for strutting your stuff at the local discotheque, and I doubt you're often seen at one of those dreadful karaoke bars. So, Whitman, what do you do to amuse yourself, woman?" Hartland leaned forward across Johnson's desk, using his cut-glass lowball tumbler as a pointer.

"I read, sir. When I'm not working, I read."

"Riveting, I'm sure. I bet you're a blast at a dinner party."

"I'm not wild about dinner parties, sir. So, for that reason, I don't attend any, sir."

"Somehow, that doesn't surprise me," he muttered. "So, would you like to know what I do for fun?"

"Sir?"

Hartland hammered his fist on the desk as he bolted out of his chair, causing Whitman to shudder. With an outstretched index finger, drilling the air in front of her face, he bellowed loud enough for Johnson's team to look up from their monitors and peer at the soundproof glass encasing his office.

"For fun, Whitman, I rip employees limb from limb who have the audacity to talk to me in such a way. It's the only blood sport that's still legal, and I'm bloody good at it. That's what I do for fun!"

Whitman stoically held her position, flicking her eyes at Johnson whilst Hartland held his intimidating pose.

Johnson spotted a few brave analysts in the open-plan office still gawping at the scene, all sporting open-mouthed poses as they became transfixed by the vision of Uncle Joe's rage.

"Yes, sir. I ... I understand, sir," each word warbling as she uttered them. Again, Whitman flicked her eyes to Johnson, who rotated his hand, indicating she needed to keep going. "If I've shown any insubordination, please accept my apologies, sir."

"Hmmm." Hartland allowed a smirk to form as he retook his seat. "You're not terrified of me, are you?"

"Sir?"

"Why is that?"

"I respect you as our Commander-in-Chief, sir."

"Yes, I get that, but I don't scare you shitless like I do every other bugger here, including Johnson." He spun in his chair and peered at his Data Director. "Isn't that so, Johnson? I scare the bejesus out of you?"

"You do, sir."

"Good!" he chuckled, before swivelling around in his chair and again waving his tumbler in the general direction of Whitman. "But not you. Hmmm?"

"Sir." Whitman waved the file, indicating she'd like to crack on with disseminating the preliminary results.

"Yes, let's get on with it," Hartland grumbled. "Headlines only. First up, the *Monteagle Fault*?"

"Complete and total failure, sir. Jolene Horsley still blows Number Ten to smithereens."

"Hmmm. Okay. The lovely Mrs Stone, the woman we shouldn't have pinged back through time?"

"Dead, sir."

"Oh ... and her family?"

"Four girls, all of which don't exist."

"Shame, but never mind. Poor old smelly Frank," he sniggered. "I always liked him ... had a bit of a soft spot for the poor bugger. But there you go. That's show business, as they say."

Whitman raised an eyebrow. Hearing the Commander-in-Chief held a soft spot for anyone was new news.

"Right, let's get to it. Category changes?"

"Oh, well, where do I start?"

Johnson cleared his throat to remind Whitman who she was addressing, which the senior analyst immediately picked up on when opening her file.

"Okay." Whitman jabbed her finger on the first page before making a point of looking directly at Hartland. "One Category One change," she paused for effect, noting both men's eyes pop before continuing. "On top of that, if that wasn't bad enough, we have five Category Fours, and that many category Nines and Tens you could write a novel the length of which could make Tolkien's entire works look like a flimsy pamphlet in comparison. And to think, these are only the prelim results. So, hold on to your hats because God knows how many there will be when we have the full report sometime later today, sir."

The Commander-in-Chief allowed his hooded eyelids to drop to half-mast as he attempted to control his breathing. Although never one to be accused of being a worrywart, handwringer type, the news that this failed mission had resulted in a Category One change caused bile to rise and burn his oesophagus, resulting in him wincing and immediately rummaging around in his suit jacket to locate his tablets and cigarettes.

"Go on," instructed Johnson, nodding to his senior analyst, who waited whilst Hartland swallowed a handful of pills with a whisky chaser before lighting another cigarette.

"The Category One?"

"Let's hear it," Johnson nodded.

"The day that Jolene Horsley and her band of reprobates in the terrorist organisation known as *FART* bomb Ten Downing Street, this time, the Prime Minister also just happens to have a distinguished guest visiting."

"Shit."

"I'm not going to like this, am I?" Hartland asked before taking a long pull on his cigarette.

"Not much, sir."

"Who?"

"The leader of the free world. None other than the newly elected President of the United States."

Johnson let out a low whistle.

"Jesus! Are you telling me he is also murdered?"

"She, sir. The first female President. From what my team has ascertained, no identifiable body parts will be discovered, only splatters of the woman's DNA scraped from the rubble. That special relationship our two countries have always enjoyed ... well, excluding Eisenhower's threat to bankrupt the pound and Obama cosying up to Chancellor Merkel, but it appears us allowing the US President to die on British soil will result in the cooling of relations and that special relationship no longer being special."

"My good God," Hartland stammered.

"Well, at least that Category One change is in the future, sir. Thank the Lord for small mercies."

"Agreed."

"Okay, so we send an eliminator to expunge Mrs Stone the day she landed in 1979. Presumably, that will resolve the issue? Whatever changes she's caused, and the ripple effects from them, will be extirpated."

"I'm afraid it's not quite that straightforward, sir."

Hartland and Johnson exchanged a look before the Data Director nodded to Whitman, suggesting she should continue.

"I've already run that scenario, and there are some issues. Basically, it will cause a double fold back on time and thus result in the same outcome. It's an unusual situation that has occurred on a few missions. We had that case in 1929 when we tried to stop Oswald Mosley from forming the British Union of Fascists."

When Hartland offered a frowned response, Whitman continued due to presuming the Commander-in-Chief had forgotten the case.

"I'm sure you remember, sir. The Change Agent we dispatched decided to go rogue and actively help Mosley. Of course, we despatched an eliminator, a rough-and-ready sort, who'd seen active service in the Boer War. Catchpole his name was if my memory serves me correctly. Anyway, Catchpole completed the necessary and eliminated our Change Agent via a wire garrotte around the neck, but that only served to strengthen Mosley's position when our time-travelling Change Agent received martyrdom status. So, as I say, a double fold back on time."

"Yes, but Mosley was imprisoned, and what we thought would happen, as in alliance with Mussolini, didn't. We're talking about the death of a US President, which is a touch more sensitive!"

"Douglas, what Whitman is saying is a double fold back, which means that eliminating the Change Agent doesn't expunge the alterations to future events they've caused. She's quite right. We've had a few examples of this situation in our history. I think our only option is to invoke a live protocol status."

"Sodding hell! You're suggesting our only option to stop this terrorist attack is to inform the 'Circus' just prior to the bombing taking place?"

Johnson nodded, knowing Hartland's 'Circus' comment alluded to MI6. For many years, the CYA had used John le Carré's term when referring to the British Secret Service.

"We've invoked live protocol status on many occasions in this sort of situation and been quite successful. If you recall, we provided the intel to MI6, which foiled that breakaway Republican terrorist organisation's plan at the Jubilee in '77. We'll just have to do the same with this one."

"Sodding hell," Hartland muttered before taking one last drag on his cigarette and forcibly stubbing it out in the ashtray. "That as well may be. And, yes, I have the right contacts at the 'Circus', but it comes with tremendous risk. One, the higher-ups in that damn place start nosing around to discover the source of the tipoff, which we all know can't be allowed to happen. And two, there's a very high possibility they'll cock it up, and we'll still have the same sodding outcome."

"I know, sir. Less than ideal, I agree."

"I'm assuming due to the changes Mrs Stone has caused, good old Frank is no longer a celebrity, doesn't run a charity and isn't a millionaire or a Knight of the Realm."

"Correct, sir." Whitman flipped over a page and quickly scanned the document before looking up. "It appears that Frank Stone is again a nobody. He's a vagrant living on the streets in Central London."

Hartland started to chuckle. "Oh, dear. Oh, that is funny. The man's gone full circle. Bloody hell, poor old smelly Frank."

"Yes, although that does actually cause us another problem, sir. In fact, early data suggests that due to Frank not travelling through time tonight, being the first person to ride in pod thirteen and walk back out in the same year they entered, may be the reason we're in this mess in the first place."

"Whitman, you're talking in riddles, woman. What are you blithering on about?"

"Sir, my blithering may well save your blushes."

23

1979

Endeavour

"Frank, what's the matter?" Alf and I halted when Frank checked his stride and turned around to peer back up the street, distracted by something or someone.

"I've seen that vintage car before," he vacantly muttered.

"Oh, which car? Vintage doesn't exactly narrow it down much. They all look like they've rolled off the Ark."

"The red one."

"Gotta say I'm not that chuffed about having my old Beetle back. The damn thing rattles and clangs like an old boiler." I shook his arm to break the odd trance he seemed to have fallen into. "Earth calling Frank. Hello, anyone in there?"

I followed his eyeline to see which of the four red cars parked along the street had captured his attention while continuing with my jabbering to fill the silent void.

"Of course, not that I drove it much but, after only a day back in that old VW, I've now realised I didn't appreciate the finer points of my Lexus." I wagged my finger at the two closest cars. "I mean, look at those two. That Hillman Imp is almost in mint condition. That would probably be worth a fortune back in 2015."

"Not the Imp. That red Jag parked about a hundred yards or so up there."

"The one that looks like Inspector Morse's?"

"Yeah, exactly." Frank turned from where he'd been staring back the way we'd come to face me before loosely taking my little finger in his hand. When I didn't pull away, he curled his fingers around mine. "You know, it's such a relief to be able to talk to another time-traveller. The last week has been utter hell—"

"Really? Being back in 1979 has got to be better than your existence as a rough sleeper. I must say, now I know that's how you lived, it explains an awful lot about you."

Frank screwed his face up and hunched his shoulders. "Well, no, utter hell is a bit over the top. I'm thirty and fit again—"

"Very fit, from where I'm standing."

"Oh, thanks," he grinned and straightened his spine. "You're not so bad yourself, you know."

"Thanks. I suppose that's better than *nice*."

"Stunning."

"Better."

"No, what I mean is being able to hold a normal conversation. Y'know, like both of us knowing that red Jag is similar to Inspector Morse's. No one else on the entire planet could know that."

"Yes, I see your point. Anyway, what about that car?"

"Well, I'm pretty damn sure that car followed me from work. Now it's parked up there, and the driver is looking directly at us."

"Oh, right. Err … Frank, should you be holding my hand?"

"We're married, aren't we?"

"Yes, no, err … kind of. At the moment, you're married to Jemma. What if that's someone who recognises you or knows Jemma?"

Despite those concerns and knowing what we were about to do when we reached my car, I wrapped my finger around his to tighten the hold. Many a year had come and gone since we'd held hands in such a way. Yes, we would stroll arm in arm, probably most days when walking our dogs along the beach. Two golden Labs, both with significantly more doggy appeal than Alf with his bedraggled form and beer breath. That said, Alf was turning out to be far better company. And, I might say, this finger-holding felt different to those post-lunch strolls along the bracing coast of wind-swept North Norfolk. Exciting, almost tingly, exhilarating, as opposed to cosy and comforting.

"Have I committed bigamy?"

"Hmmm. Probably not, because you're married to two different women in two different timelines. I think that's right. Christ, not easy this time-travel malarky, is it?"

"Yeah, you're right."

Reluctantly, I released my finger from his. "At the moment, as much as I hate the thought, you are married to Jemma and not me. So, I suppose holding hands with me in public might not be the best idea. Especially if the driver of that car knows you."

Frank nodded and pursed his lips.

"Anyway, I've got to somehow convince you to fall in love with me first."

"How long did it take me last time?"

"Not long." I forced my tongue into my cheek and raised my eyebrows.

"How long? Going by the smirk plastered across your face, I'm guessing it wasn't too difficult to achieve."

"I know that look in your eye, Frank Stone. That's your lustful look. The look you give when you're angling for an early night."

"Do we still do early nights when we're in our sixties?"

"We most certainly do. In recent years, there's been a little less frenetic energy. Our swinging from the chandelier days are firmly in the past, but with the help of a little blue pill, we still manage to trip the light fantastic quite regularly, I'll have you know."

Frank jiggled his eyebrow. "Blimey. The man I was in 2015 would have needed more than a blue pill to raise my you-know-what. In fact, I reckon raising the Titanic would be an easier feat."

"Frank, you haven't ... have you? Y'know, since you've been back—"

"What?"

"You and *her*. You and Jemma." I chewed my lip, grimacing as I awaited his answer.

"Ah ..." Frank winced.

"Oh ... well, I suppose you hadn't met me until this night," I mumbled.

"No ... sorry."

"You won't, y'know, again?"

"No! I promise you. It's only happened once. The first day after time-travelling." Frank took my hand and placed it on his chest. "I told you only a few minutes ago when back in the pub. A week has passed since that trip on the Wheel and, since being here again in 1979, I really don't know what I saw in Jemma—"

"She's ruddy gorgeous for a start! In fact, the woman is so damn frigging pretty she should carry a bloody government health warning. I mean, looking like she does, the sodding woman is probably to blame for most of the road traffic accidents in and around Fairfield. Christ, I should know. You're forgetting I've been friends with her since our university days. Every Saturday night when out on the town was the same. Five minutes after entering one of the pubs, I would be left sitting on my own whilst every man under thirty, and some older for that matter, swooped down and encircled her like a bevy of rutting stags vying for her attention."

Frank grinned, causing me to pull my hand away and thump both palms on my hips.

"What the hell are you grinning at?"

"I know, as far as you're concerned, we've been together for decades. But for me ... well, for me at the moment before *your* Frank lands and takes my place, that is, I'm just getting to know you—"

"Oh, good point." I interrupted. "My rant wasn't exactly a come-on, was it?"

Frank blew a raspberry.

"Sorry. I'm supposed to be wooing you, not going off on one about how utterly drop-dead gorgeous your wife is."

"No, you've got it wrong. Your rant was just that."

"A come on?"

"Yeah," he shrugged. "I found it ... sort of, y'know ..."

"What?"

"Nice."

I walloped his arm.

"Sexy."

"Right," I nodded. "Okay. I'll take that. You always had a way of defusing an argument with that cheeky grin you're now pulling."

"Cheeky grin?"

"Yes." I wagged a finger at his lips. "That cheeky grin."

"So, listen up, Jayne Hart—"

"Stone. I haven't been Jayne Hart since the 12th of May 1980."

"Oh, so that's when we get married?"

"It is."

"So ... by my calculations, that means Sharon was conceived on the wrong side of the blanket."

"There were no blankets. Benidorm is still quite warm, even in October. In about five weeks from now, to be precise."

"Really? I've never been abroad."

"I know, but we go on holiday very soon. Just one point to remember when we get out there. The bloke whose hand wanders where it shouldn't, namely my bottom, when we're strutting our stuff on the dance floor of a crummy disco. This time, can you please just have a stern word and not larrup him one?"

"Oh. What happened?"

"I imagine he spent the rest of his holiday having to drink through a straw, and we endured four hours at the local Spanish police station answering some awkward questions."

"Noted." Frank raised a finger and offered an affirming nod. "I'll do my best, but no promises."

"To be honest with you, although I don't condone the use of fists, I was flattered that his bottom-patting annoyed you enough to knock him out."

"Anyway, the future Mrs Stone, I presume, and I'm not surprised based on the way I feel right now, it doesn't take me long to fall in love with you? So, do I just say it, or what happens?"

"Well, when you walked me back to my car this very night, we kissed." I dropped my tone a couple of octaves before continuing. "And I mean kissed. Not a peck on the cheek. I'm talking tongues, tonsil licking, and a spot of bum groping."

"Yours or mine?"

"Mine. I had my arms around your neck."

Frank shot a quick glance at my posterior, applying that cheeky smirk before raising his eyebrows at me.

"Of course, we stopped before we got to the point of performing a lewd act in public, but only just, mind. I'm quite sure if you'd have had your way, you'd have taken me across the bonnet of my VW."

"And you didn't want to?"

"Didn't want to, what?"

"You know."

"Christ, course I did. But I was hardly going to have sex with the local MP's husband across the bonnet of my car in broad daylight, was I?"

"No, of course not. I hope I was a gentleman."

"Just," I smirked.

"And then what?"

"Then, a few days later ... I seem to remember it was at least four because my mind was performing somersaults for days, you showed up at the school during lunch break and told me you and Jemma were finished before declaring your undying love for me."

"I said that? That's a bit ... well, gushy, I suppose."

"No, I think you said something like you wanted me."

"Oh. Hang on, if we performed this tonsil tickling, face-sucking thing, why are you worried about holding hands?"

"Fair point." I shrugged before wrapping my finger around his again.

"A second ago, you said something about my rough sleeping explained a lot about me in the future. What did you mean?"

"Frank, we agreed."

"Okay," he nodded, resigned to the fact he would have to wait another day.

Earlier, before leaving the pub, we'd agreed rather than I try to precis thirty-five years of our life into one evening's conversation, we would wait until tomorrow to see if *my* Frank arrived. Then, if that transpired, all the knowledge of our future would be installed in Frank's brain when we met tomorrow.

Now, just to complicate things a smidge further, we'd spent the last ten minutes in the pub trying to deduce if that happened, whether *my* Frank would remember this conversation or the flirty one we'd enjoyed the first time around, or both. We'd concluded that it didn't matter because one evening of differing memories was far easier to cope with than me trying to bring Frank up to speed on the events of nearly four decades.

Of course, Frank was itching to know every minute detail. I mean, who wouldn't? I'm pretty certain that if the tables were turned, I would have resorted to any measures, including torture, to gain said information. However, we agreed it was the best plan and, as tomorrow was now only hours away, Frank thought he could hold out until the morning.

In the interest of not sending my husband off on a tangent, I'd held back with all the finer points of detail regarding how we'd come to be on the London Eye in the first place. I'd used the line that he was at the Wheel to offer consulting advice to a traveller who'd then done a runner. As I said earlier, the rest is history.

If *my* Frank failed to rematerialize tomorrow morning, I can honestly say I didn't much fancy broaching the subject of Jemma's murderer, namely his closest friend, the boy sporting the side-parting and scowl depicted in that school photo.

David Bolton.

As far as I was concerned, Jemma wasn't murdered; Dave Bolton suffered that fate. However, at this precise point in time, unless Frank intervenes as *my* Frank told me he did, then Jemma will be murdered, and Dave Bolton will be alive. That will mean Barbara's granddaughter will not become a terrorist, but Frank's son, Andrew, will not exist. Clearly, to ensure Andrew is born, Jemma must avoid being strangled. Frank achieved this last time he was here in 1979. So, presumably, the deed could be replicated this time. Of course, that still didn't resolve the issue of Andrew's death in that explosion in the future. And, according to that disagreeable man, Hartland, the only way that particular nasty event could be avoided was to ensure Dave Bolton didn't die.

My head hurt thinking about it.

I needed *my* Frank to hurry along and land in 1979 because, despite holding hands with this Frank, I was lonely.

I missed my husband.

I missed my girls.

24

And Now, From Norwich

"Frank, look at Alf." I nodded to where my odd dog had padded a few feet away from us, head and tail down, ears pricked and primed as they stood to attention. Despite what I assume could be classed in doggy terms as consuming a skinful in the pub, Alf appeared to be on high alert. "He's spotted something."

We shot each other a look and then back at Alf as he emitted a low growl, which intensified when the red Jag pulled away from the kerb and sped past. Frank had been right to be concerned because the driver made a point of glaring in our direction.

"I guess your beer-guzzling mutt didn't like the look of him. Either that or he's not keen on Jags."

"Alf, what is it? What's up, boy?" I asked when placing my palms on my thighs and performing a half squat to position my head at a similar level to his.

Alf twisted his head at me.

"Oh, sorry, Alfie-Boy, you need closed questions, don't you? I keep forgetting."

"Can he really understand you?"

"Oh, Lord knows. As I said, my memories of Alf are a lazy lump that couldn't be bothered to bark, let alone drink beer and hold a conversation."

"This is getting weirder by the minute."

"Tell me about it. Alf, you didn't like that nasty-looking man in the car. Is that right?"

Alf licked his chops.

"Ah, so you didn't."

"He didn't say anything."

Still holding my position, I peered up at Frank. "He licked his chops. I'm beginning to understand that action means yes."

"Nice butt, by the way."

I glanced back, noticing my stance had the effect of jutting my backside at him. "Oh, thanks. That *nice* word, again, I see."

Frank grinned.

"We're going to have to work on your compliments. You've always been pretty good in that department, but I don't recall you majoring in the word, *nice*."

"Right, I'll do my best."

"Good. Now, we need to find out why Alfie-Boy, here, didn't like the nasty man in the red Jag."

"Alf, is that man following me?" Frank asked, when bending forward to talk to my father's pooch.

Alf shot him a disparaging look before turning his head back to me with his tongue hanging out, alert, and like a contestant on *Sale of the Century*, eagerly awaiting the next question and maybe a break for a *flash sale* to grab a bargain. Hmmm, maybe not, but Alfie-Boy did appear ready to be quizzed. I presume the cheesy show popped into my mind due to the annoying earworm of the show's tune that my mother had rather annoyingly gifted after humming it during breakfast. *Joyful Pete*, I'd read a few years ago the composition was called. Named posthumously after the composer.

"What did that mean?" Frank jabbed a finger at Alf. "Does a sideways glance with his tongue flapping mean no?"

"No. I think he dips his head to say no. I really don't know what this look is for," I mumbled, straightening up my stance. "Perhaps he only wants to talk to me."

"Oh, charming."

Alf licked his chops.

"So far today, Alf has growled at me, you, and that man in the Jag. Could that mean he can detect people who've time-travelled?"

"What about Tobias?"

"Tobias?"

"Well, your mutt had a good go at him back in the pub," Frank chuckled.

"Oh, he did. But that was different. Alf didn't growl at him. He just chewed his trouser leg when Tobias was rude."

"Okay. So, let's assume, just for argument's sake, we go with the theory that Alf can detect time-travellers. Who's the bloke in the red ... shit!"

"What?"

"Shit, shit, shit!" Frank hissed, pushing the words out through clamped teeth as he vacantly gawped down the road where the red Jag had long disappeared.

"Frank?" I grabbed his hand and gave it a squeeze to haul his mind back to the here and now.

"Eliminator. That man could be an eliminator."

"Frank, you're not making any sense. What are you talking about?"

"Jayne, before you travelled, when I was apparently trying to convince you I've time-travelled, did I mention Hartland would despatch an eliminator to remove me if I caused unacceptable changes or exposed myself?"

"What, like a flasher in the park? Frank Stone, you're a lot of things, but willy-waver, you're not. Although there was that towel malfunction around the pool in Rhodes," I chortled.

"Jayne, this is serious."

"Sorry," I smirked.

"When did we go to Rhodes?"

"Oh, twenty years ago, at least. That incident was funny, though. The two old girls splayed out on the sun beds in front of us got an eyeful."

"Oh, right. No, I mean expose myself as a time-traveller."

"How?"

"Well, telling people I come from the future for a start."

"I take it you haven't?"

"Jesus, no! I think I'd be carted off to the bloody funny farm."

"Fair point. Okay, so what other reason would that horrid man send some eliminator?"

"Well, Hartland pretty much threatened me not to go on a lunatic-styled betting spree—"

"Oh, yes, of course. I hadn't thought about that," I mumbled before inspiration struck. "Oh, Frank, we could make a killing!"

"Jayne—"

"Now, as you know, I've never been into sport much ... well, no, you wouldn't know, but you'll know that in the future. Anyway, my dad was a horse-racing fanatic, and Mother and I always watch the Grand National. It's a tradition in our house. Rubstic won this year's race ..." I paused as I uttered the winning horse's name.

"Jayne, are you alright? You've turned a funny colour."

"Frank, how the hell do I know the name of the winning horse from 1979?"

"Because your younger brain is taking over. This has happened to me over the past week. Details I'd long forgotten just seem to come flooding back."

"Will I forget my life? Our life?"

"No. I can still recall my life on the streets in 2015 in hideous detail. None of that has gone, unfortunately."

"So, we keep both memories? Is that how it works?"

"It seems to be the case."

I counted out the horses on my fingers as I remembered the winners through the decade. *Lucius*, *Red Rum*, *Rag Trade*, *L' Escargot*, *Red Rum*, and again in 73, *Well-to-do*, *Specify* ... I can remember backwards, but I have no idea who won in 1980."

"*Ben Nevis*."

"Oh, I think you're right. Hey, just think, although it's yonks away, we could bet everything we've got on next year's race and set ourselves up nicely for the future. We never liked that dreadful flat we purchased, did we?"

"I don't know, do I? I haven't lived that life yet."

"Oh, course not. Well, we didn't. The toilet leaked, and there was a mould issue in the bedroom. I had to throw away a lovely black coat I bought from Kendall's because our wardrobe was smothered in mould spores."

"Sounds delightful."

"Oh, trust me, it wasn't. So, that's my point. We can buy a house with the winnings, not that crummy flat."

"We can't. As I just said, if we start making bets that only a time-traveller would know, the CYA will despatch an eliminator and have us expunged." Frank rubbed his hand over his face. "If they haven't put plans in place already, that is," he hissed.

"Bugger. Okay, but please, can we not buy that flat? We must be able to afford somewhere better this time."

"I'm sure we can," he chuckled. "Anything for the new Mrs Stone."

"Good. I'll hold you to it. Okay, where were we? Right, you haven't told anyone you've time-travelled, and neither have you placed any bets. So, what other reason can there be?"

"As far as I can remember from what he said, if my travelling back in time causes a change to history that's deemed unacceptable."

"Like what?"

"Hell, who knows?" Frank exasperatedly threw his arms up. "But I guess just by being here, I, and now you as well, are causing all sorts of changes to the past. I mean, in our first life, we weren't standing outside this Snob shop on this very day having this conversation, were we? And you reckon our Sharon is married to a man I knew as a fellow hobo."

"Christ, this is weird." I glanced in the window of the ladies' clothing store, momentarily wondering what had happened to the retailer whilst turning my nose up at the Crimplene blouse on the mannequin, which sported collars that could rival the wingspan of Concorde. Worryingly, I think I bought one just like it at around this time. I made a mental note not to repeat the purchase. "Anyway, how will we know if we've caused history to change to a level that supercilious git, Hartland, deems enough to require our elimination?"

"We won't, I guess." Frank raised a finger when, presumably, a light bulb in his brain pinged on. "I'm in the future. You and me are alive in the future, yes?"

"Yes, Frank, we've done this. Well, not in detail, but I've given you a run-through of the headlines."

"So, that means Hartland didn't despatch an eliminator to finish me off."

"Oh, I see your point."

"Shit!"

"What now?"

"Maybe that *was* an eliminator in that Jag, and he's come for you, not me."

"Why?" I shrilled. "I haven't done anything. Christ, I've only been here a few hours."

"You haven't told anyone?"

"What?"

"Time-travel!"

"No! And I haven't raided the housekeeping from Mother's battered old Rover biscuit tin and spent all day in the damn bookies, either."

"Alright, I'm sorry. But did I say anything about eliminators?"

"When?"

"Yesterday, before you travelled. When I was trying to tell you what happened to me. It was only yesterday that conversation must have taken place."

"Okay, let me think. Trouble is, because I was more concerned that you were embarking on some sort of geriatric breakdown, I've got to confess most of what you babbled on about I just let wash over me."

"Fair enough."

"Oh, hang on, the day Jemma ..." I allowed my voice to trail away when realising I would have to mention Dave Bolton if I continued. However, in the Old War Office yesterday, Frank mentioned something about an eliminator killing Dave.

"What about the day Jemma ... what were you going to say?"

"Frank, you think because Alfie-Boy growled at that bloke in the Jag, that means he's a time-traveller?"

"Yeah, that's what I said. But what about Jemma—"

"And that could mean he's one of these eliminators?"

"It's a possibility. Either that or Jemma's hired a private investigator to tail me."

"Why would she do that?"

"God knows? I'm pretty sure it's her who's up to something, not me."

I winced and chewed my lip.

"You know, don't you? Of course, you do."

"Frank, we said we'd wait until the morning."

"Jayne!"

"Okay, okay. But, listen, we can't stand here all night in the middle of town while I run through what I know or can recall you saying happened. Remember, I said I wasn't paying much attention to your conversation or babbling, more to the point." I grabbed his hand. "Come on, we need some privacy where we can talk without being spotted. Yours or mine?"

"Oh, right," he grinned. "You are forward, aren't you?"

I allowed my mouth to sag.

"Hey, no complaints from me," he chuckled.

"Frank!" I hissed, before shooting looks left and right, concerned who else might be spying on us. "As much as I quite fancy the idea, I'm not suggesting nookie!"

"Oh."

"I'm not sure what my mother would say when scooting back from bingo to find you and me romping around in bed. And I really don't think, even though Jemma is in London, you and me bouncing around in your marital bed is the done thing either. Besides, although the horse has bolted, so to speak, as in we have four daughters, I'd like you to woo me a little before we get to that point."

"Course."

"No, I'm saying let's talk in the car. Come on, my old banger's only up there."

With Alf leading the way, we scooted over to my car parked not fifty yards further up the street. As we drew close, Frank released his grip on my hand to nip around to the passenger side.

"Frank Stone, where d'you think you're going?"

Frank paused before shooting looks at the driver's door, then back to me. "I assumed you'd be driving."

"I will be unless Alfie-Boy is up for it."

"Really?"

"No, he's had far too much to drink." I mused whether I might also be over the legal limit when grabbing Frank's hand and pulling him close. "But you listen to me, Mr Stone. We both may have already caused untold changes to history, but our first kiss is not going to be expunged."

"Ah, I see. Can I grab your bottom again?"

"I absolutely insist that you do so."

25

Nowhere Man

"What are you doing right now? Where are you, Frank?" I mumbled, my chin cupped in my hands propped up by my elbows whilst leaning on the cold quarry-tiled windowsill as I peered out of the metal-framed window of my old bedroom. Although this being the witching hour, a time when most folk were asleep and burglars were at the business end of their night's work, I'd lay awake for some time thinking about my missing husband.

The man I'd met in that pub yesterday evening *was* the man I fell in love with the first time I lived and breathed in 1979.

"Christ," I hissed, dismissively shaking my head at my inner thoughts about the possibilities of time-travel.

However, that man who kissed me, just as he had the first time, wasn't my husband. Well, not yet. Whilst I'd traced my eyes across the swirly pattern of the Artex ceiling – this design I believed to be called 'circles', an attempt to rejuvenate and instil some of that Art déco design into the drab mid-century housing stock – whilst fighting to get comfortable under the heavy blankets and pink candlewick bedspread – cursing my mother for not modernising the bedding in favour of a continental quilt, something she steadfastly refused to do at any point in the future – I'd attempted to piece together what my husband, Hartland, and that Johnson chap had said about the finer points of time-travel, now scolding myself for not paying enough attention.

In my defence, at the time, it was reasonable to believe that the content of all three men's conversation couldn't be described as rational, more the deluded rants of the unfortunate souls better suited to being incarcerated in Bedlam.

Had time-travelling on the London Eye evaporated my husband? The unanswerable question, and one that would only come clear if *my* Frank arrived here in yesteryear. Understandably, that thought had flushed away any hope of being able to sleep, hence the reason I now surveyed the street through the window of my old bedroom with that dated candlewick bedspread wrapped around me. The room which had been my place of sanctuary for my first twenty-nine years.

I glanced around at the white dressing table with faux mahogany handles, where once positioned beside the 1970s relic stood my Dansette record player with those black splayed-out legs. A gift from my parents for my sixteenth birthday. Something they soon regretted when I repeatedly played Chris Farlowe's *Out of Time*. My first seven-inch single, which I'd purchased from Wheelan's Music Store on the High Street. I remember saving my six shillings and eightpence from my Saturday job at the local bakers.

Mary Wheelan, the music shopkeeper's daughter and one of my best friends from school, used to sneak me into the listening booths at the back of the store. After closing, we'd huddle together, giggling whilst listening to the latest songs on the hit parade.

Of course, Wheelan's, originally a sheet-music store before diversifying into selling instruments, gramophones and those shellac seventy-eights, soon fell by the wayside when WHSmith's, Menzies and Woolworths muscled the independent store from its premier position to the less salubrious side streets. Back in the days when nearly every shop sold LPs, including Boots the Chemist. Anyway, old man Wheelan finally threw in the towel when Andy's Records opened in the late '70s and hammered the final nail into the coffin lid of the hundred-year-old family business.

As with most of my school friends, Mary and I lost touch, only enjoying brief contact when discovering each other on *Friends Reunited* around the time of the millennium. I'd heard through the grapevine she'd spend most of the following ten years serving a sentence for manslaughter after pulverising her husband's head with his favoured seven-iron, bringing literal meaning to the term golfing widow.

So, along with persuading Jenny to kick the habit and avoid many a meeting with an oncologist, having a word in Rose Wood's shell-like about avoiding the music scene and the associated drug-taking that accompanied it, perhaps I should contact Mary and suggest marrying a man who preferred to fill his free time with a sedate game of crown-green bowls. I figured, even if said marriage wasn't a roaring success, it would be significantly more challenging to swing and bludgeon the man with a two-pound lump of lignum vitae, despite being one of the hardest woods known to man.

"Hmmm, maybe not."

In terms of being a prophet of doom, I faced my own catalogue of potential disasters. A week from today, if all this time-travel malarkey was to be believed, David Bolton would offer a lift to Jemma and then attempt to strangle her in Fairfield Woods. Now, I accept Jemma could be a top-drawer bitch and liked the sound of her own voice. And don't get me wrong, as much as I hated the thought of her and Frank under the same roof, wringing the woman's neck was a somewhat drastic way to get her to shove a sock in it.

'You've got to be frigging joking' were the words Frank had blurted earlier when I'd informed him what his best pal would do to his wife. And as for his response to the news about her dallying with Tobias and then Rupert, the latter becoming Jemma's future husband, well, let's just say that was a bit more choice. The air inside my VW Beetle had turned blue, and even Alfie-Boy appeared a little shocked by Frank's vulgarity.

After Frank had explained his mission in full, filling in the blanks of *my* Frank's account yesterday, I was a smidge surprised that The Hooded Claw and his team didn't know who had murdered Jemma. Still, I guess they couldn't be expected to know everything. Frank had been sent on an Agatha Christie-styled 'whodunnit' mission to prevent her murder, which would apparently mean Jemma would become the Foreign Secretary in a coalition government led by the Prime Minister Sir Vince Cable. This would prevent the United Kingdom from holding a referendum on their continued membership of the European Union and what the CYA claimed to be a catastrophe in the future, which Frank only knew to be called the *European Fault*.

There was the first problem. David Cameron is the Prime Minister, and it isn't a coalition government. Oh, okay, Mr Cameron was the Prime Minister yesterday, but I guess now it was Margaret Thatcher again ... well, sort of, somehow.

Also, Jemma stepped away from politics in 1983. So, I knew Frank had saved Jemma, but Frank was understandably confused as to why, if he saved her as I suggested he would, that alteration of history hadn't led to her continuing her political career and thus eventually becoming a senior member of the Cabinet.

Of course, *my* Frank knew the reason. However, because of my unwillingness to listen to my husband whilst incarcerated in the Old War Office, I needed him to get a lick on, land in 1979, and fill in the gaps for me and the Frank I kissed last night.

Due to Frank being a wee bit put out about the news regarding his promiscuous wife – I'd noted a distinct annoyance rather than him being upset, which, as you can imagine on my part, was somewhat a relief – along with trying to get his head around why on earth Dave would want to strangle the woman, we hadn't gotten around to me informing him it was Barbara Denton, née Bolton, who'd been the intended time-traveller who'd done a runner from pod thirteen of the Millennium Wheel. Nor the tricky subject that Dave must stay alive for the sake of his son, whom he had no idea would exist in the future.

As if caused by a gust of wind, a set of misbehaving door hinges, or a bored ghost wandering around the house, my bedroom door creaked open with the accompanying horror-movie-esque squeak. Fearing one of those burglars at the business end of their night's work had ventured into Mother's house, I spun around, causing the bedspread to drop and thus expose my top half. Instinctively, I flung my palms to my chest in an attempt to cover my modesty.

"Oh, it's you," I huffed, relieved a burglar, or a see-through version of my dead father, wasn't on the prowl. However, after the events of the last twenty-four hours, I considered even that was possible and probably more plausible. "Can't you sleep either?" I whispered.

Alf dipped his head, shooting me that doe-eyed look, his eyes appearing to emanate a garish, green glow as light from the streetlamp bounced back off his retinas.

"What's up, Alfie-boy? You can't sleep up here. You know Mother doesn't allow you upstairs."

Alf offered no response as I padded around the bed, parked my bottom on its edge, and wrapped that faded pink bedspread around my shoulders. I know Alf's only a dog, but his staring at my, albeit significantly younger, firmer in all the right places, body felt a little disconcerting. Anyway, I'd already deduced my father's pooch was half-human, so I felt the need to cover up.

Earlier, when rummaging around in my dresser, I'd hauled out a collection of nighties sporting either the St Michael or C&A label, none of which I would use as an oil rag, let alone wear. So, I'd slipped my newly discovered younger body between the sheets with my top half in its au naturale state.

Unsurprisingly, my search for nightwear had resulted in an extensive rummage through my wardrobe and a rake through my chest of drawers on a mission of discovery regarding fashions from yesteryear. There'd been quite a few 'OMG' moments when hauling out a fair number of dodgy-looking dresses from Richard Shops. A retailer I'd long forgotten about, now remembering the stores being swallowed up by Top Shop. And that resurfaced the hideous recollections when there seemed to be this preference in many high-street stores for communal changing rooms. An idea that could only have been conjured up by a man, which all retailers thankfully soon ditched.

Most women my age … well, the age I was yesterday, had some tale to recount about an unfortunate incident in one of those places. Mine being a fight with your classic 'little black dress', little being the operative word, when shopping in Etam. The tight-fitting garment had regrettably bunched around my shoulders and steadfastly refused to move, leaving me trussed up in what then transformed into a polyester black straitjacket when I'd heard the material rip at the seams.

Three women, all in varying stages of undress, none of whom I'd ever previously met, then came to my aid and attempted to manhandle me out of the damn thing. My overriding memory of the whole incident, once I'd wriggled free, was a thirty-something woman asking me if I was okay as she held her bra by her side and showed off her breasts. A chest, the likes of which any budding page-three photographer would have struggled to capture even with the latest wide-angle lens.

My earlier ferreting around in the outdated furniture of my childhood bedroom had confirmed that the hideous blouse I'd spotted in Snob's window had already been purchased. My previous twenty-nine-year-old self hadn't possessed an eye for style and gave some credence to Jemma's claim that I was, in fact, *Plain-Jayne*.

At this stage, just one day into my life re-run, I had no idea regarding the state of my bank balance. However, because I still lived at home and presumably earned a decent wage, the chequebook needed an outing on Saturday. Apart from a pair of jeans and a couple of passable t-shirts, nothing in my wardrobe passed the hanger-over-the-head test in the mirror. For sure, Brown Owl from the local Girl Guides will receive a bumper injection of stock for their jumble sale, or the local charity shop will think all their Christmases have come at once.

"Come on, Alf, what's up?" I whispered. "If you're some pervert dog who's padded his way up the stairs in the middle of the night on the off chance that you might catch me naked, and grab the opportunity to ogle me, then you can sod off back to your basket." I tightened the bedspread around my top half and crossed my legs, thankful I'd at least seen fit to wear a pair of knickers to bed.

Alf dipped his head, allowing his flews to droop, thus giving the appearance of a frown. I guess his expression demonstrated the level of disappointment regarding my accusation.

"Alright, I'm sorry. You're not a perv. I don't know what the hell has happened to you, but you're a good dog."

Alf shot his head up and licked his chops.

"Okay, have you come to discuss what we do tomorrow?"

Alf licked his chops.

"Good idea. So, I call Frank first thing and see if he's arrived from 2015, yes?"

Alf dipped his head.

"Err ... why the hell not? Frank and I agreed that I'll call him as soon as I get to school. Christ, he'd better be *my* Frank."

Alf didn't move.

"Oh, closed questions," I muttered, as my eyes searched the room whilst formulating my question in such a way that would allow Alf to answer. My eyes settled on the cover of an LP, the one laying on the top of a stack of maybe twenty or so others, all at slightly different angles to each other as if they'd been abandoned in a heap and not neatly stacked. I offered a rueful smile, thinking how Frank would absentmindedly straighten the pile, whereas I wouldn't normally notice. Frank was Mr Tidy, and I was little Miss Messy.

That LP, only just visible in the half-light, had been a particular favourite. Even though I'd not listened to it for decades, I could name the tracks in order, the length of each song to within a few seconds, and I'd back myself to recite the lyrics to a reasonable degree of accuracy.

Rubber Soul.

Track three – *You Won't See Me.*

Track four – *Nowhere Man.*

As the tears filled my eyes, causing a watery film to form and blur my vision, Alf nudged forward. He laid his jaw upon my knee, his dolorous expression confirming what I feared.

Whilst using the Candlewick bedspread to dull the noise and mop the tears, I sobbed, my whimpering causing my nose to run. My vision distorted to the point where everything in front of me, including Alf, morphed into a colourless, indistinguishable mass.

Alf hadn't padded upstairs on a pervy doggy prowl. He'd come up to tell me that my husband, *my* Frank, was a nowhere man. As I tried to catch my breath, I laid my hand on Alf's head before stroking him repeatedly. After wiping my eyes with the bedspread to clear my vision, and in a cracked voice, I asked the question that I really didn't think I could cope with the answer.

"Alf ... has, has *my* Frank gone?"

Alf, still with his head on my lap, licked his chops.

With my head bowed, buried in that bedspread, I howled.

26

The Mortiferous Doctor Bickleigh

"Frank. Frank. Frank, are you there?"

Nothing, no response, no bolt of lightning, or seminal momentous signals were received to suggest this was that kairotic moment in time, and he was now present and reporting for duty.

"Frank," he whispered, elongating the single syllable to suggest posing a question rather than just uttering his name.

Again, nothing.

"I know you're in there, Frank. Come on, out you come," he hissed with a creepy, almost Child-Catcher-esque lilt to his tone whilst jabbing an accusing finger at the mirror for extra effect.

Still nothing, no influx of new memories, or revelations about his future wife, four children, three grandchildren and what must be a truly idyllic existence. He was still him, the man who'd taken only the one time-travel excursion on London's premier tourist attraction, whether that be via a one-way single or a three-attraction-saver ticket.

Frank plodded out of the bathroom and, guided by the streetlamp's yellow sodium-vapour glow that diffused through the landing window, apathetically padded back to the bedroom. Clearly, uttering his name in a variety of different tones, from friendly coaxing or employing an outright fiendish Mephistophelian timbre directed at the bathroom mirror in an attempt to see if his older self had arrived during the night, could be regarded as a pointless exercise.

The Hooded Claw and his sidekick, Morehouse, had stated that he would know when he landed in 1979 when someone uttered his name. Well, yes, that had happened a week ago when Jemma whispered in his ear the morning after travelling on the London Eye.

Sweet nothings, which at the time had probably been the most erotic and alluring voice he'd ever encountered. Now, knowing he no longer loved his wife and the fact that she'd embarked on a shagathon through their friends, acquaintances and colleagues, he regarded that suggestive tone she'd used with derision.

However, whether or not he'd time-travelled again, calling his own name in an attempt to 'wake' himself wasn't going to work. First thing later this morning, he would have to find someone to say his name and see if the man whom Jayne had been married to for thirty-five years had arrived in yesteryear.

Now, that was a hell of a thought. Not only could he remember his new life before that point, but he would then also hold two sets of memories of the future. The one he held now, namely a failed businessman whose slow decline down to becoming a vagrant living on the streets of the nation's capital after the murder of his wife, and the life he was about to embark upon with his soon-to-be wife, Jayne.

Unsurprisingly, his brain was on one. As if he'd guzzled a crate's worth of those energy drinks – those brightly coloured cans sporting a picture of a bull on them he often discovered discarded in his preferred 'pitch' by the derelict toilet block on the South Bank – not that he'd ever purchased one, but following the revelations of the previous evening his brain struggled to cope as the mass of electronic pulses zipped back and forth resulting in being unable to focus on one thought and certainly not sleep.

With his arms folded, leaning on the windowsill, Frank surveyed the view of the street. Unlike his head, nothing much was doing. All quiet on the Western Front, as his long-departed father used to say. But then his old pops came from the *Greatest Generation,* which meant he'd lived through two world wars. Worn the t-shirt, eaten the pie and seen the movie, so to speak.

Despite the mess in his head, one thing was abundantly clear: last night, after just a few hours with Jayne, he'd fallen in love with the woman. Whatever would happen in the future with Jemma, Dave, Tobias, or his older self arriving from 2015 to take his place, that *Holly Golightly* woman he enjoyed a drink with would be part of his life. Frank nodded and afforded himself a smile when assessing that, based on the happenings of a few hours ago, the rest of his days appeared pretty rosy.

For sure, Jayne Hart had stolen his heart.

That was the easy bit. Very little brain power was required to understand what was in his heart.

"Dave," he muttered. "Why did you kill Jemma?"

Frank snorted a derisory chuckle, aimed at himself for speaking out loud as if expecting the ghostly see-through apparition of his reflection in the window would strike up a conversation like two mates chewing the cud whilst perched on a couple of bar stools.

And that, incidentally, just happened to be the very activity he and Dave should have enjoyed a week ago during his first evening after arriving back in 1979. But, no. Due to his old buddy's situation, as in being booted out of the marital home by Barbara after being caught dallying with a young girl at work, Dave had vented his frustration at Frank. Specifically, lose his shit about Jemma, and go off on one about what a stuck-up bitch she could be.

Frank raised an eyebrow at his reflection. Fair enough, Dave had made a valid point.

However, for the life of him, Frank couldn't see how Dave's dislike of Jemma could escalate to murder. According to Jayne, when recounting what his older self had said to her the night before she time-travelled, Dave would strangle his wife the following Friday evening. And on the subject of changed timelines and different histories, the world Jayne had travelled back from, The Hooded Claw had duly dispatched an eliminator to kill Dave and save Jemma.

The man in the red Jag?

"Good question."

If that was so, why had Hartland sent an eliminator to perform the task he'd already been pinged back in time to complete? Also, according to Jayne, two bodies were discovered in Fairfield Woods. Dave Bolton, and a man whose name eluded her, but she remembers older me saying the chap was ex-services. The two eliminators that Hartland had suggested might travel back and dispose of him if he were to cock up were both ex-military. So, that would indicate that the second body would be one of those chaps, suggesting both eliminators were dispatched. Question is, was Red-Jag-Man the other body, or the man who would kill Dave and the other chappie come a week from today?

"Christ, Frank, where the hell are you?" Frank wagged an accusing finger at his half-reflection. "You'd better get your arse in gear and hurry up and get here because I need to know what happens in the future, mate."

Of course, if he could grab another few hours of shut-eye, he might wake up as that Frank, the one Jayne knew and loved. Notwithstanding his desire for that to happen, Frank glanced at the bed and dismissively shook his head.

"No chance."

Accepting sleep was done for the night, Frank rubbed the goosebumps from his forearms before resting them back on the windowsill and refocusing on the dark vista of his and Jemma's front garden. Whilst churning his thoughts around, lobbing shovelfuls of complexities into his already full and labouring concrete-mixer brain, Frank conjured up an idea.

During the last few days, when embarking on his whodunnit mission, he dismissed the idea of somehow preventing Jemma from venturing out into town the night she was murdered. He'd figured that wouldn't obviate her death, just delay the inevitable. However, since Jayne had time-travelled, and following that conversation last night, she'd furnished him with additional information. Extra clues to the mystery, like throwing two sixes and thus reaching the required room in a real-life game of Cluedo. Therefore, affording him the opportunity to change tack.

Dave Bolton wasn't a serial killer. Serial chest fondler of women who weren't his wife, but not a killer. Not yet, anyway. After witnessing his fragile state last week, perhaps, in the heat of the moment, something had snapped in Dave's brain, leading him to strangle Jemma during a fit of rage. Maybe she'd said something catty, which she was more than capable of, and Dave just lost his shit?

"Hmmm," he muttered and nodded at his reflection. "What about afterwards?"

In the days and weeks following Jemma's disappearance and the discovery of her body ten days later, Dave's actions and demeanour were not that of a guilty man trying to cover his tracks. Nevertheless, Jayne was clear that Dave had murdered his wife. So, could that point to the fact that the deed was planned, malice aforethought, and not the spur-of-the-moment action of a desperate man?

"Christ," he mumbled, before being distracted by movement in his peripheral vision.

An urban fox hovered by the low wall that encircled the front of the property, seemingly frozen in time with one paw raised as if ready to take the next step, but presumably spooked enough to halt proceedings. Frank mused how rare a sighting this to be. The rise in the number of urban foxes in 2015 meant that even when bedded down under that heap of damp cardboard on the South Bank, he would often spot one of the night prowlers. Either trotting past or with its nose stuck in a discarded fast-food wrapper that sullied the appearance of the high-tourist area. This alert vixen, still holding position by the low wall, made eyes with Frank.

Rough sleeping afforded Frank oodles of free time, far too much, which he would fill with either people watching or reading discarded newspapers and magazines. He wasn't fussy, from *The Financial Times* to *Horse and Hound*, all the way down to a copy of the lads' mags, *Nuts, Zoo,* and the comic *Viz*.

Frank would read anything to while away the hours of boredom of street living.

He could recall an hour or two spent perusing the articles in *People's Friend* and a copy of *Double Glazing Monthly* from January 2012, the latter being the premier publication for all budding replacement window salesmen. Also, he'd thumbed through many dumped copies of *Betterware* catalogues and now classed himself as somewhat of an authority on kitchen storage solutions, must-have personal care products, and mobility aids.

Anyway, an article that was most definitely not nestled amongst the scantily clad pictures of pouting ladies in *Zoo* or *Nuts*, and probably in something like *Witches Weekly*, suggested that spotting a fox, a creature incorrectly associated with trickery and deception, was a sign that someone close to you may be dishonest and trying to manipulate the future.

Was that seemingly well-nourished vixen, still giving him the eye, a sign to confirm Jemma's and Tobias's duplicity? Like Alf, Jayne's dearly departed father's scraggy mutt, could this fox be conveying that those closest to him were not as they seemed?

Paul Wilson, Frank's business partner, had shown his true colours. The way he conducted himself suggested he wasn't a man he could remain in partnership with. Dave Bolton, his closest friend from way back, appeared to have changed beyond recognition. Fondling the young cash-office girl's chest aside, the man Frank knew would never strangle Jemma despite that infuriating 'I'm-better-than-you' attitude she'd habitually convey.

Time-travel, even just the once, appeared to have cleared Frank's vision and removed the cataracts that had previously clouded his perception of those he once held dearest.

Presumably satisfied that the man standing at the window had understood what she was trying to convey, the vixen nodded at Frank and trotted off, disappearing into the shadows in the blink of an eye. Whether the Frank who Jayne knew and loved showed up by the morning or not, tomorrow he would be taking to task his old school buddy, and previous best mate, Dave Bolton.

What the conversation starter would be, Frank had no idea. Perhaps … *'Hey Dave, how you doing, mate? Oh, just wanted to mention, could you see your way clear to not strangling my annoying wife?'*. Or, *'Dave, I'm a time-traveller from the future, and I know you're in a spot of bother at the moment with Babs, but I need to advise you not to venture out next Friday because, if you do, you'll become a murderer or the victim of an eliminator'* … neither sounded great.

When accepting that sleep was done for tonight, Frank grabbed his dressing gown and padded down to the kitchen to grab a coffee, notepad, and pen. With at least a couple of hours before dawn, he had time to improve on his first thoughts.

As he waited for the kettle to whistle, Frank allowed his thoughts to drift to Jayne. He suspected she would be fast asleep, dreaming about her husband's imminent arrival in 1979.

"Frank, my old mucker, you need to get a shift on. Look lively, old son, and get your arse back here."

27

Later that day

Jerusalem

Whilst keeping eyes on his target, Pinkie Sinclair absentmindedly picked at the wax paper wrapped around another *Pacer* mint-flavoured, chewy sweet. After his dirty nail caught and lifted the flap, he unwrapped the last in the packet of what he considered the long-ago-discontinued treat. Pinkie popped it in his mouth, scrunched up the wrapper, and pinged it through the two-inch gap of the driver's door window of his 1963 Mark 2 Jaguar.

When in his seventies in 2015, living in that council flat in Croydon, perhaps Pinkie wouldn't have littered the streets. The sixty-odd years of *Keep Britain Tidy* campaign had undoubtedly changed attitudes to littering, even shaming a man like Pinkie Sinclair into complying with *'Keep it, Bin it'*. Now, thirty-nine again, after spinning back through time via the London Eye just an hour after that tramp bloke Frank Stone travelled, Pinkie again couldn't give two shits about littering, just as he hadn't in his first life.

Okay, now back in the 1970s, The Wombles were still giving it large. The New Seekers, Harry Secombe and even ABBA had bashed out adverts about keeping our green and pleasant land just that, pleasant. However, this was 1979 again. So, along with smoking being perfectly acceptable, even encouraged, littering not seen as a capital offence, single-use plastic regarded as revolutionary, no social media, no politically correct police monitoring everything you said or thought, women's rights back in their box, and a nice ruckus at the footie on a Saturday afternoon with his 'football hooligan' mates, Pinkie felt right at home again.

The good old days.

2015 was not the era for Pinkie. For years, far too many in his opinion, he'd resided in his crappy, damp, tenth-floor council flat, scraping by on the meagre state pension. Despite successive governments banging on about the applied 'triple-lock' to protect pensioners, no bastard could live off a hundred and ten quid a week.

Following a career in the Royal Marines and more lucrative mercenary missions in far-flung places, as a man in his senior years in 2015, Pinkie rarely ventured out onto the no-go estate. A typical South London housing hellhole run by drug gangs peddling their product whilst waving their machetes around to intimidate and threaten anyone who didn't conform, which included a seventy-five-year-old ex-serviceman who'd fought for his country.

No, Pinkie didn't miss that life. A pitiful existence where it seemed every minority group of bleaters had some axe to grind. Women ruled the sodding world instead of being at home with their pinny on looking after their men, and you had to freeze your bollocks off in the pub car park when you fancied a smoke. Yada yada yada, the frigging list was endless when thinking about his shite life in 2015.

And on the subject of litter, well, even KFC had started their *Don't be a Tosser* anti-littering campaign, which just added to all the other poxy do-gooder campaigns that pushed the poor road sweeper to the dole queue.

"Frig sake," he chuckled. "Thank God I'm back in good old 1979."

After a couple more mint-infused chews, he swallowed the sweet. Pinkie grabbed his cigarettes before preparing to follow his target, who'd just entered the ticket office at Fairfield Station.

Of course, how the hell that lot at the CYA managed to ping folk back through time was anyone's guess. That said, he couldn't care less. His mission, which Pinkie was grateful to receive, was a simple one. Locate Frank Stone, and along with assisting in preventing his wife from being murdered, advise the man he must also persuade the woman to abort the pregnancy, thus ensuring the course of history alters to the path the CYA required. Apparently, assuming Frank succeeds, Jemma Stone should become some high-flying Cabinet Minister, which will cause a significant shift in European politics.

Pinky didn't care about that. As far as he was concerned, Jemma Stone appeared better suited to flash her jugs on *Page Three* than to be spouting a load of old shite whilst leaning against the Despatch Box. Anyway, if Frank failed, Pinkie's instructions were explicit and relatively straightforward. Eliminate Frank Stone with minimal fuss, and then he could crack on with living his life for the second time.

Since time-travelling back to his much-favoured era, Pinkie had set about his surveillance work. For sure, that bloke Stone wasn't cut out to be an investigator, so he thought he'd have a good ferret around and see if he could identify the man who would soon murder his wife, the local MP. For sure, if he could offer Frank the heads up on who would kill Jemma Stone, that would surely aid success and negate the need for Pinkie to exterminate Frank.

A win-win result. All good for everyone concerned and less messy.

Now, more than a week into his task, Pinkie had a few candidates who he thought were likely to be suspects for murder one. Paul Wilson, Frank Stone's business partner, the man he was following, being one of his top three.

As Pinkie grabbed the door lever, the passenger door opened and in slid a man holding a gun with a silencer attached, which the new arrival jabbed into Pinkie's ribs.

"Don't move. You so much as twitch, I'll kill you."

Pinkie swivelled his eyes down at the gun barrel, then back up at the man with his finger wrapped around the trigger. Pinkie, having served in Aden in the Arabian Peninsula, along with a few tours in Northern Ireland, could spot a military man from a mile off. They had a look, a smell about them, and vacant eyes that had seen far too much for any man to have experienced without affecting his well-being. The geezer, now perched on top of a few sweet wrappers on the passenger seat, like Pinkie himself, was one such individual.

"Waving a shooter around in broad daylight ... bit daft, ain't it?"

"Do I look concerned?"

"You're taking a risk. I eat twats like you for breakfast."

The man with the gun snorted a laugh, jabbing the barrel further into Pinkie's ribs before responding.

"I presume you're carrying?"

"Carrying?"

"A piece."

Pinkie huffed. "Glovebox."

Without taking his eyes off Pinkie, the man asking the questions flipped open the glovebox. He paused, waiting for the right moment before shooting a nanosecond glance to confirm Pinkie Sinclair's claim. As he expected, the ex-Royal Marine attempted to make his move.

"Don't be a dick," he growled, pushing the barrel under Pinkie's rib cage, causing the man to wince, before flipping the glovebox closed with the gun still inside.

"Can't blame a man for trying, can you?"

"Londonderry '74. You were there. I also know you pimped out your services in Libya in and around '82 and '83 when training Gaddafi's lot for a pretty price."

"As it's 1979, I'm assuming you've been sent by the CYA."

"And they say squaddies are thick," he chuckled.

"I'm no thick squaddie. It's Sergeant Sinclair of the Royal Marines to you."

"Staff Sergeant Collinson. Royal Engineers."

Although Collinson was a 'Sapper', Pinkie nodded, accepting he'd been outranked. Also, not being a thick squaddie, he quickly deduced the CYA had presumably dispatched Collinson via the London Eye to eliminate him for whatever reason. Maybe the mission had gone south.

Disappointing.

"So, what happens now? You stick a couple of slugs in me, leave me to bleed out here in my motor, and you get on with living your life again?"

"Maybe."

"Unless, of course, you get double-crossed, and the CYA sends someone to dispose of you, too."

"Maybe that as well."

"Why? What the frig have I done in the last ten days or so that requires my removal?"

"It's Bruce, isn't it? I know everyone calls you Pinkie, but your name is Bruce."

Pinkie nodded.

"I'm Richard. Richard Collinson."

"I'd shake your hand. But with that thing sticking in my ribs, I fear if I move you'll stick a couple in me."

"That depends."

"On what?"

"How you react to what I'm about to tell you."

"I'm all ears, pal. You mind if I smoke?"

"I do. Sorry, for the moment, I need you to stay still. Keep those hands on your lap where I can see them, and just listen."

Pinkie raised an eyebrow. He'd faced this sort of situation before. Usually, he would play for time, looking for an angle or the tiniest opportunity to gain the upper hand. However, the look in Collinson's eyes suggested he was ready for that kind of move. This was to be expected because the CYA only employed the crème de la crème. Collinson wasn't going to fall for any move, and Pinkie suspected he would happily pull that trigger.

"I was dispatched back to this year the day after you and Frank Stone. I dunno about you, mate, but I'd always thought their claims about time-travel to be a load of old bollocks."

"You're telling me," Pinkie nodded. "Y'know, my old mum, God rest her soul, always had this saying—"

"Oi, shut it and listen. Although the monthly retainer the CYA paid came in handy, I never thought I'd be in this situation. But, here's the thing—"

"Bleeding right, mate. A man can't live on the state pension. It's a bloody disgrace."

"D'you always interrupt? Even when there's a gun in your ribs?"

"Apologies. I was just saying the state pension is unacceptable, that's all."

"Couldn't agree more. But as I just said, shut your gob and listen. It seems we're both here in 1979. So, we ain't going to be collecting our pensions for a few more decades yet—"

"Looks that way, pal. You sure I can't smoke? If this is going to be some long, drawn-out shaggy-dog story, I could do with a fag." Pinkie raised his hand to reach into his jacket pocket.

"Uh-uh," Collinson shook his head. "Nice try, but the answer is still no," he grinned, applying pressure with the gun barrel to enforce his point.

"Fair enough. But if at the end of your tale you still fancy filling me with lead, d'you reckon I can have a smoke before you do? Y'know, condemned man's final request sort of thing."

"Jesus, Bruce. Stick a sock in it, will you?"

"A fag would be better."

"Just shut up. I've met guys like you before. Windbags who can't stop yakking."

"To be fair, you're not the first to accuse me of that. My old mum, God bless her, reckoned I had verbal—"

"Oi, shut it!" Collinson hissed.

"Diarrhoea."

Collinson huffed, annoyed this tosser seemed to want to have the last word. For a split second, he considered pulling the trigger. He could then finish his mission and crack on with his second life.

"You going to listen, or shall I just pull the trigger?"

"I'm sitting comfortably, ready and waiting. Is this going to be like a fairy tale or more of a Jackanory-type story with Bernard Cribbins? That said, I've always had a thing about Floella Benjamin. She floats my boat; that one does."

"You're getting on my tits."

"To be fair, you're not the first to say that. My old Captain used to say—"

"Oi, I'm losing patience, and my trigger finger is getting twitchy."

"You can get pills for that."

"You probably can. But, you gobby git, you can't get pills to cure being dead."

"Fair enough. I'm all ears, Sarge."

"The day I travelled on the wheel followed a coup d'état at the CYA. Some bird called Pitstop moved against Hartland and ousted him. Anyway, she considered this mission to be an embarrassment and so sent me to clean it up—"

"Dispose of me?"

"Spot on."

"I'm guessing something's happened. Otherwise, my seven pints of claret would already be staining the tan leather seats on my old motor."

"You suppose correctly. While you've been following the three or four geezers you have pegged as the potential murderer, I've been keeping tabs on Frank Stone."

"No flies on you."

"Last night, Frank and that little brunette—"

"The one with the cute arse who looks the spit of Kate Bush."

"That's her. I wouldn't mind."

"Me too."

"Anyway, last night, when in a boozer in Fairfield, there I was, minding my own business when supping a beer and earwigging Frank's and the little brunette's conversation. It seems that Kate Bush bird has also time-travelled."

"Do what? When? When the frig did she travel?"

"This is my point. She was trying to convince Frank that in the future he and her were married with a whole brood of kids. Four daughters, apparently. Would you believe they called the eldest Sharon?" he chuckled.

"Sorry, mate, you've bleedin' lost me back at the bit about Kate Bush time-travelling. So what if they called the kid Sharon?"

"Sharon Stone."

"Oh, yeah. The bird with no knickers."

"You got it."

"So, how come Frank don't know this, then?"

"Yeah, that had me brain hurting all night, that did. So, this is what I reckon. Frank Stone time-travelled the same night as you—"

"I know that bit."

"Yeah, I know. Shut up and listen, will you?"

"Jesus, grumpy one, ain't you? Bet you were a barrel of laughs in the Mess."

Collinson tutted. "With your mouth, I'm surprised you ever made it all the way to pensionable age."

"Funny you should say that …" Pinkie paused as Collinson forced the barrel another millimetre towards his heart. "Alright, Sarge. Relax. You were saying?"

"Frank time-travelled as we have. Whatever happens to the lovely Jemma Stone—"

"Now, on the subject of fit birds. Jesus, have you seen her? Frig me, I wouldn't crawl over her to get to you, that I can tell you." Pinkie let out a low whistle. "I mean, that Kate Bush bird ain't half bad, but that Jemma Stone … well, you don't need a wank mag to shoot your load when thinking about her, do you?"

"You finished?"

"Go on. All I'm saying is I wouldn't mind a spin around the sheets with that one. That Frank bloke can't half pull the fit birds."

"So, Jemma, dead or alive come next Friday, is irrelevant because Frank lives his life and marries this Kate Bush lookalike."

"Then years later, Kate Bush time-travels back before she and Frank get it together. As in now? Is that what you're suggesting?"

"Yup, that's what I reckon."

"But why?"

"That much, I don't know. But listen. If Frank has lived his life again, all the way up to 2015, marrying the Kate Bush bird, having four kids, and not living his life as some hobo on the streets ... then we don't know what is happening at the CYA at that point."

"Frigging hell, I can't get my head around this."

"Time-travel, mate. Kate Bush has lived that life with Frank. Frank, who, like us, travelled in 2015 the first time, doesn't know the life he's about to have."

"Okay, so why's his bird travelled back?"

"Who knows, but—"

The back door of the Jag opened before a thickset man sporting a buzz cut and a Glasgow smile slid onto the back seat. Collinson paused mid-sentence as his eyes were drawn to the barrel of James Bond's weapon of choice, which now filled his field of vision.

Pinkie could only hear the door open, whereas Collinson, in a twisted position in the passenger seat, had a nanosecond to make a decision. Namely, keep the gun in Pinkie's ribs or aim it at the new arrival.

That nanosecond of hesitation left him vulnerable.

"How you doing, gents? Let's say you place the gun down between the seats. Nice and easy, mind. We don't want any funny business, now do we? Then we can all have a nice wee chat. What d'you say? Or I could just blow both your brains across the dash of this lovely old vintage Jag. Your choice, gents. I ain't fussed either way."

28

The Winds of War

If anyone happened to be remotely interested enough to ask the question, I think today, the second time experiencing Friday the 21st of September 1979, had to be up there in the top two or three for my answer. In fact, Friday the 21st of September 1979 in my first life could probably sneak into the top ten.

So, what's the question?

Okay, list the ten worst days of your life. That's the question to which today was jostling for top position, along with the day my father unexpectedly died in 1977 and the harrowing fourteen hours spent by the telephone waiting to find out whether Helen, our second eldest, had survived an avalanche in Switzerland when on a school skiing trip in '96.

Of course, many others vied for a position in Jayne Stone's (née Hart) hit parade of *dies horribilis*. Mother's passing being particularly difficult. An upsetting day for the girls, losing their grandmother, but for me strangely welcome to at last witness the end of the hideous decline in her mental health. A wicked disease which had transformed my annoying mother into an inert vegetable incapable of wiping her own bottom. So, not to be too uncharitable about it, a blessed relief.

The hours before getting shitfaced on cheap Riesling when retiring to the greenhouse following a day of pure hell with four girls under the age of seven would be in the top twenty. Clara chundering over the Christmas tree on Christmas Eve in 2002 when pissed and high on Ecstasy following a two-day rave and a pub crawl had to figure there somewhere too.

Notwithstanding that lot, and many others to boot, your father's half-human mutt suggesting in the wee hours that your husband probably didn't time-travel but suffered evaporation, and then the same man a few hours later confirming he was still young Frank, pretty much had the effect of shooting today straight in at number one.

Okay, you still have your husband or future husband, I hear you scream. True, I do. And we still have all those years together in the future. However, the shared memories were gone. Only I knew our future. Whereas, for Frank, every day was a new day.

I mourned my husband, who was still very much alive.

Bizarre.

As far as Frank was concerned, we had a week before his current wife would be murdered. As far as I was concerned, we had a week before Dave Bolton had a date with a nine-millimetre slug that would enter his brain through a hole in his forehead. Only *my* Frank, the man now missing, knew what actually happened during those seven days in which he and Jemma would agree to split, and Dave Bolton and A N Other die in Fairfield woods.

The only thing I can remember about the up-and-coming few days was that awful date with Cycle-Clip-Kevin. Oh, and, of course, Frank's visit to the school a couple of days later to tell me he loved me and, a few days after, the news breaking regarding Dave Bolton's death.

History had already changed, so I would have to do the decent thing and inform Cycle-clip-Kevin that Saturday night's planned date with Alien and Pizzaland was a non-starter. Apart from the obvious, as in not being an experience I should repeat, the relief at the thought of not making a complete tit of myself again was palpable.

Just as I had this very same day in my first life, I left school at lunchtime to drive over to Frank's office. The difference this time, I didn't chicken out and return to school. Plus, I had an unkempt, matted mutt called Alf riding shotgun.

After feigning time-of-the-month problems, a surefire way to avoid probing questions from any man regarding the state of your health, I skived off afternoon lessons. Jason, the poor sod, picking up the planned double lesson with F-Band. An experience which had a way of rounding off each week and leaving you urgently feeling the need to dive headfirst into a vat of wine. At the very least, a lie down with a damp copy of the *Radio Times* on your head, acting as a cold compress.

With a killer smile and a set of gnashers that could be employed as a billboard poster for those teeth straightening and whitening companies of the future – or she could be dressed in a white coat starring in a TV commercial for toothpaste that claimed eight of ten cat-owning dentists swore by their product – Alison beamed her welcome when Alf and I entered the bang-average, dreary reception of Stone and Wilson Builders.

I was half tempted to rip the young girl a good 'un for lying yesterday when she claimed she'd informed Frank I was on the phone. Something Frank later claimed hadn't happened.

Apparently, Alison had stated I was some pushy woman who wouldn't take no for an answer.

To be fair, a label which had been levied at me on the odd occasion when my middle-aged tongue felt the need to offer someone the benefit of my wisdom. However, never an accusation thrown when at the age I am now. Of course, having an old head on young shoulders certainly offers advantages – Ding-Dong-Roy receiving short sharp shrift yesterday afternoon when cornered in his office being a case in point – but presumably, apart from Frank, I must seem different over the last couple of days to how most folk would expect young Jayne to behave. Luckily, Mother, lost in her own little world, wouldn't have spotted if I'd grown a second head.

Okay, back to Alison. Now, I say young girl, but we were of similar ages. Notwithstanding the blatantly bloody obvious that was plainly evident when looking in the mirror, I was still getting used to the idea of being in my twenties again. Meanwhile, in my brain, I was a confident middle-aged lady who could, as I just intimated, on the odd occasion, be accused of showing my brass neck too often. A product of wisdom and being super comfortable in my own skin during my latter years.

Hmmm.

Something to work on this time around, perhaps?

"Hello, Alison. We spoke on the phone yesterday. I have an appointment this afternoon with Frank."

The smile disappeared along with the dazzling teeth as she offered a frown. In fact, her change of demeanour dropped from pleasantly warm all the way down to outright frosty. So much so that even a passing snowman would regret not donning a pair of mittens and a woollen scarf. Also, I detected a wince forming before she turned up her nose when spotting Alf.

I sniffed the air.

Alison pulled a face.

"Alfie-boy, you haven't?"

Alf licked his chops and grinned.

"Oh, Alfie-boy, surely there can't be any gas left in you by now." I glanced up at Alison, who'd now pinched her nostrils together.

"Sorry about that. Alf likes Spam and luncheon meat with the odd pint of beer, but I'm not convinced they're good for his constitution. I had to drive with the window down all the way here, which probably explains why I look like I've been stuck in a wind tunnel all morning in preparation for auditioning to join the pop duo, Jedward." I tipped my head sideways and finger-combed my hair, attempting to reintroduce some style.

"Jedward?" she nasally enquired.

"Yes, you know, the sticky-up hair boys. They were on X Factor or Britain's Got Talent a few years ago. Christ, for the life of me, I can't remember any of their songs, but the girls thought they were good."

"Girls?"

"Oh."

That one word hauled me back to the present.

1979.

Death by a thousand cuts in the space of a microsecond as images of my four daughters appeared in my mind's eye. Whilst flinging my windswept locks over my shoulder, I took a deep breath and fought hard against the tears that doggedly battled for release.

"Sorry, you alright?" Alison asked when releasing her thumb and forefinger from her nose. "And what were you saying? Something about Jedward."

"Oh, forget that." With a waft of my hand, I batted away the remains of Alf's gasses and my stupid time-travel faux pas. "I'm fine," I sniffed and dabbed my nose with the tissue extracted from my cardigan sleeve. "Yes, so, as I was saying, I have an appointment with Frank."

"You and your dog?"

"Yes, I'm afraid so. Alf doesn't like to be left out. Also, if I shut him in the car for too long, the smell can be enough to knock you out."

"I can imagine."

"Oh, believe me, you can't."

Alison raised a finger, Columbo style. "Right, you're the lady I spoke to yesterday," she nodded and offered that killer smile again.

I'd been led to believe by *my* Frank that the poor girl had for many years been on the receiving end of Paul Wilson's lecherous advances. I presumed the despicable git had been mesmerised by that smile and many other attributes this girl had to offer. Despite Jemma's obvious beauty, she couldn't get away with calling this girl *Plain-Alison*. I stepped closer and shot a conspiratory look left and right before lowering my voice.

"I won't say anything to Frank about what you said, alright?"

Alison raised an eyebrow, presumably feigning she had no idea as to what I was referring to. I momentarily pondered that perhaps that teeth-whitening company would require Alison to crack out the tweezers and deal with her au-naturale brows. My girls would regard the full-brow Ali McGraw look with horror. Unperturbed by the hefty, raised caterpillars and noting I may have to tackle the unacceptable forest above my eyes, I bashed on.

"What you said about Paul. Your gossiping, remember?"

"Oh, yes." This time, the poor girl definitely winced. "Sorry about that."

"Don't worry," I chuckled. "Frank's told me all about Paul Wilson and his antics. Take my word. I know he'll get his comeuppance. The not-so-good ship Paul Wilson is heading for choppy waters. Come the millennium, the man will be pretty much destitute and feature prominently on the sex offenders register," I chortled, recalling the glee which oozed from *my* Frank when hearing how Paul's life had panned out.

"The what? And what's the millennium?"

"Oh … ehm. Never mind. I was just saying that you soon won't need to worry about that abominable letch Paul."

"Right. You know something I don't?"

"Quite a lot … like you wouldn't believe."

Alison shot those caterpillars up as she grabbed the phone before punching one button and waiting.

"Frank, I have your two o'clock here in reception. A Mrs …" she shot me a look when pausing.

"Sto-Hart. Miss," I stammered.

"A Miss Stohart … or was that Miss Smart?"

"Hart," I barked, unsure if Alison was trying to be clever or her memory was waning. I'm pretty sure I informed her my name on that call yesterday when she lied about telling Frank who I was.

Frank appeared at his office door, leaving his receptionist to jabber away to no one. He beckoned me to enter before turning to Alison, who'd started shouting into the receiver when no reply seemed forthcoming.

"Alison. It's okay, I'm here."

"Oh, I wondered why you didn't answer," she giggled when replacing the receiver in its cradle.

I leaned over her desk and patted her hand.

"Word to the wise, my dear. Make sure you and that rugby hunk husband of yours persuade your son and his girlfriend not to board a flight on Malaysia Airlines in March 2014."

"Do what?"

"Jayne!" hissed Frank.

"Just remember what I said. 2014, early March. Make sure your boy isn't on the manifest." I nodded to force home my point before heading for Frank's office and leaving the poor, perplexed woman to gaze absentmindedly into the middle distance.

Frank pushed the door to and swivelled around, narrowly avoiding trapping Alf's tail in the doorjamb as he snuck in.

"Jayne, what was all that about?"

"The Malaysian aeroplane, which disappeared last year. Well, 2014, if you see what I mean. You remember that, don't you?"

"Err … yeah, sort of. I read about it in one of the papers I fished out of the bin. Or it could have been in The Times, which some bloke used to give me each day."

I furrowed my brow, indicating I wasn't quite sure what he was babbling on about.

"I used to beg outside the entrance to Waterloo Tube Station. A woman who wore pink Micheal Kors trainers used to give me two quid every day, and a city gent type often handed me his paper when on his way home."

"Oh."

For a moment, I'd forgotten I wasn't in the company of *my* Frank, but the man who'd spent years sleeping rough and begging on the streets of London.

"I think because he used to see me completing The Times' crossword, he started handing me his copy each day when on his way home. I probably read about the crash in The Times, although I wouldn't be able to pinpoint the actual date of that disaster."

"You often complete The Times' crossword. You get quite excited if you manage to complete the thing."

"Ah, well, in the life I remember, I'm pretty sure I could successfully complete it most days. But why are you telling Alison about the future? Remember what I said about eliminators? They'll come after us if we expose ourselves as time-travellers."

"Sorry," I winced. "It's just that I remember you hearing through the grapevine from a friend of a friend who had a cousin living in Perth that Alison's son and girlfriend were amongst the two-hundred odd who vanished on that flight. Weren't there suggestions about dark forces at play, and some reports saying conspiracy theorists claimed the Illuminati were responsible for its disappearance?"

"The who?"

"Oh, I don't know. Illuminati, or some occult thingamajig whatever—"

"What on earth has a group of sixteenth-century Spanish heretics got to do with a missing plane?"

"Christ," I chortled. "I can see how you were so good at crosswords."

"Yes, well, there's a lot of free time to fill when you're homeless, jobless and hopeless."

"That must have been so awful." I grabbed his hands and pulled him towards me. "But listen up, Frank Stone. I promise you, your life will be a whole lot better this time."

"I'm gonna hold you to that because life on the streets is pretty tough. What Joe Public don't realise is that anyone is just a few ill-judged decisions and a dollop of rotten luck from losing everything and ending up living in cardboard city."

"I know. That's why, Mr Stone, you are such a wonderful man."

"Oh, because I lived on the streets?"

"Sort of. As I said, I have lots to tell you about our future life. You become the biggest force of change in tackling the causes of homelessness and help ... well, probably thousands of poor souls."

When on tiptoe, I placed my arms around his neck, allowing Frank to hold me in position with both hands cupping my bottom through the material of that regulation dowdy school skirt – another item soon to be gifted to Brown Owl – and kissed my husband with the gusto and passion as if I'd not seen him for decades. Which, technically, I hadn't. That said, the man whose face I preceded to suck, the man running his hands all over my bottom, wasn't my husband because, according to Alf, that man was missing in action, presumed dead.

"Sorry, Frank ..." Alison paused in the doorway, holding the door handle as she leaned in. Whilst still entwined in a lover's embrace, Frank and I shot a look at Alison. "Oh."

I allowed my heels to rest on the carpet-tiled floor and released my hands from the grip around Frank's neck. Frank offered a wince and then an exaggerated grimace before we both bowed our heads, akin to naughty schoolchildren when caught up to no good.

"Oh, sorry ... I didn't. Well, I wasn't ... you know," Alison paused to nod at me. "Sorry, I didn't mean to interrupt—"

"Alison, this isn't what it looks like."

Frank's receptionist shot both well-fed caterpillars up her forehead. I suspect reaching never-previously attained heights when indicating how ridiculous she considered Frank's blurted statement.

"Oh, well. Yes, alright. It was exactly what it looked like. Christ!"

"What about Jemma?"

"Shit! Alison, please, can you just pretend you haven't seen anything?"

"Course, Frank," she shrugged. "Anything for the boss. Look, I don't want to appear rude, but you know how I feel about Jemma." Alison offered me a tight smile before continuing. "Miss Smart here—"

"It's Hart. Miss Hart," I muttered when correcting her.

"Yes, okay, Miss Hart here seems okay, I suppose. If not a bit odd. Y'know, weirdo comments about 2014 and all that." She rocked her head from side to side whilst offering a nervous laugh. "A week ago, I'd have been jealous. But now I've met my new boyfriend, well, that doesn't matter anymore."

Once more, Frank's bubbly receptionist jiggled her head from side to side, causing her ponytail to swing to the rhythm of her almost sing-song voice. Frank and I exhaled with relief.

"Yeah, good on you, Frank. That catty wife of yours has never treated you right, in my opinion. Oh, sorry," she sang, emphasising both syllables when uttering that word, sorry. "That was rude. Mum says I should think before opening my mouth. Sorry, I didn't mean to be, well, y'know. I just want to see you happy. I like you, Frank, you know that."

Frank and I shot each other another look, he and I conveying the relief that we seemed to have got away with being caught … snogging for the want of a better word. Christ, how old was I?

Alison stepped forward to grab my elbow. "Oh, no, sorry, I didn't mean I like Frank like that. Not in that way … well, I did, but I've got a boyfriend, and so I don't any—"

"Alison!" barked Frank.

"Sorry, boss?"

"We're good?"

"We're good at what? Sorry, you've lost me? What d'you mean, we're good at what?"

Recognising that the term was probably an Americanism not popular in this era, confirmed by Alison's bemused expression, and no longer feeling like a naughty schoolgirl now Alison had indicated she was offering Frank and me the 'green light', I butted into their conversation.

"Frank was just asking if what's happened here can be kept on the Q.T.? Jemma will know about Frank and me very soon, but for the moment, we're just asking if you can keep schtum."

"Oh, yeah, sure. Blimey, everyone is talking funny today," Alison giggled before shooting a look towards reception.

"Everyone?" Frank quizzed, presumably clocking where Alison had indicated.

"Yeah. I came through to let you know that there's this bloke in reception, and he's demanding to speak to you." She lowered her head and dropped her voice to a whisper. "Right thuggish looking bloke, if you ask me."

"He's probably one of the contractors looking for Paul. Just tell him Paul's not available, take his number, and I'll give him a bell later."

"Oh, okay. I'll do my best to get rid of him," she sang before spinning on her heels and skipping to the door, where she grabbed the frame, leaned back, tapped her nose, and offered an impish grin. "Mum's the word for you and Miss Smart, you naughty boy, Frank Stone."

When the door closed, I turned to Frank and raised my eyebrows. "We're gonna have to tell Jemma very soon, I might suggest."

Frank pulled me close, allowing me to rest my head on his chest and throw my arms around his waist. Just how I had three-and-a-half decades in the future, two days ago, when in the bowels of The Old War Office.

"Oh, Frank," announced Alison as she swung open the door, smirking at our embrace. "I said everyone was talking gibberish today. This bloke said to mention the London Eye. He said you'd know what he meant."

29

Sergeants Three and The Tunnel of Love

"Hey, no skin off my nose. You either put the gun down, or I start spreading the lead."

Pinkie side-eyed Collinson, the non-verbal exchange enough for both old soldiers to agree they were in a tight spot. Although the new arrival had Collinson in his crosshairs, so to speak, Pinkie was abundantly aware it would only take a twitch of the wrist and a slight squeeze of the trigger to send a bullet through the back of the driver's seat and into his spine.

Collinson deliberately and carefully placed his weapon where indicated, keeping his palm open as he withdrew his hand to ensure no misunderstandings.

"Marvellous. You know it makes sense," the man in the back seat chuckled. "Reminds me of my brother, he does."

Collinson furrowed his brows at the odd statement. The man sporting the Glasgow smile retrieved Collinson's gun with his free hand before relaxing in the seat, pointing both guns forward in a ten-to-two formation. The Yosemite Sam pose, if you like, with a weapon pointing at the heads of both men.

"Del Boy. My brother, Ronnie. He's a spiv. Works the markets in Camden. And, before you get any ideas, I'm not a plonker like Rodders. Either of you as much as twitch in the wrong direction, and I won't hesitate."

"You're one of us, then?" Pinkie asked without turning around. "As far as I can remember, Del Boy and Rodney weren't around in 1979. Watched *George and Mildred* last night. Not exactly a side-splitter, I can tell you. Hey, you mind if I smoke?" Pinkie asked when reaching for his pocket.

"Oi, you think I'm some twat? No. Keep your hands where I can see them. Anyway, filthy habit."

Pinkie huffed. "Christ, you an' all. I'm getting withdrawal symptoms. Look, pal, don't pull the trigger if I start shaking with the DTs. I ain't gone this long without a smoke since being on a bleedin' plane. And even then, I had a crafty one in the toilet. Well, only a few puffs because I got rumbled by this overzealous nancy-boy air stewardess bloke. Anyway, he wore makeup. I mean, what's the damn world coming to when blokes start shopping the Boots' makeup counter as much as the lasses, eh? You know, back in 2015, when living in that crap hole of a flat in—"

"Jeeeesus, shove a sock in it, mate. You got verbal diarrhoea or something?"

"He does that," chimed in Collinson.

"It's enough to make your ears bleed."

"I love you too," Pinkie threw in with a smirk.

"Regimental Sergeant Major Harris to you, sergeant. So, if you're gonna address me at all, it'd better be, sir."

"Bollocks," muttered both men as their shoulders sagged and slumped in the front seats due to feeling deflated at being outranked.

"Course, I'm not as old as you two gits. And if you're wondering, yeah, I've killed before. Four of those Argie tossers at Goose Green, poor sods were only kids, and more than I can remember when leading a guerrilla force when doing an off-the-record, cash-in-hand job for this Colombian geezer in the early '70s. So, be clear, I ain't too fussed if I need to add two more twats to that list."

"Sir."

"Sir," echoed Collinson.

"And let me clarify something. The scar, my Glasgow smile, ain't anything to do with being a snitch. Some Columbian drug peasant got lucky with a swing of his machete moments before I relieved his neck from holding his bonce when cleaving the git's head off, alright?"

Both men positioned in the front seats nodded at the windscreen whilst side-eyeing each other.

"Okay. So, this is nice, isn't it? What d'you fellas fancy chatting about, then? The weather? The telly? Which I have to agree is total shite. Or shall we chew over the thought that I should just kill you both and save a lot of hot air?"

"Did you watch *George and Mildred,* too? Total bollocks, if you ask me. Then I had to watch some crap called *Rings on Their Fingers*. Comedy sitcom, apparently, although I have to say it lacked comedy. It was about as shite as *George and Mildred*. That said, it had that Diane Keen woman in it. I'd forgotten about her. Always had a bit of a thing about that bird, y'know." Pinkie turned in his seat to face Collinson, which in turn placed the Regimental Sergeant Major in his peripheral vision. "'Ere, d'you remember her in that Sweeney film? That lucky git, Regan, had her in that programme. Pity that wasn't on instead of having to watch the Ropers. That old Mildred bird ain't exactly easy on the eye."

"Why didn't you just turn it off, then?" fired in Collinson, followed up with a frustrated huff.

"Ah, I couldn't. See, I was relaxing on some tart's sofa and, whilst the lassie was seeing to my old chap, the telly was on. Difficult to change channels without a remote and some bird's head between your legs."

"I'm guessing this was a financial transaction and not because the woman was wooed by your charms?"

"You got it in one, sir." Pinkie turned his head and nodded at Harris. "Don't suppose you could see your way clear to lowering the shooters?"

"No."

"And I guess a smoke's still out of the question?"

"Correct."

"I'm not wild about the idea of dying before I have another smoke. Decent thing would be to allow a chap one last pleasure. Shame, y'know, that tart I hooked up with last night was up for a rerun later, and *Citizen Smith* is on tonight. Bleedin' classic, that one."

"Maybe I should just shoot you and save the Staff Sergeant's and my ears from having to listen to your incessant drivel."

"Good idea. Before you hopped in the back, I was just getting to that point," said Collinson.

"Hey, I'm just making conversation. Jesus, friggin' glad I didn't come across you two in the service. Wouldn't have exactly been Fun Boy Three, would it? Talking of which, I didn't mind them, you know. Although to be frank with you, I couldn't name any of their songs. Weren't they something to do with The Specials? Hey, d'you remember that song they did with Bananarama? Now, on the subject of lovely lasses, there's three girls who I could spend an evening or two with. Can't remember their names, but that's not imp—"

"Harris," Collinson interrupted Pinkie's flow. "For the love of God, do us all a favour and blow his bloody brains out."

"What? Oh, bloody charmin', that is. I'll have you know, Staff Sergeant Collinson of the poncy Royal Engineers, many an acquaintance has found my company stimulating and entertaining. Not everyone can be a miserable bastard like you. And another thing—" Pinkie halted when detecting the cold metal of a gun barrel against his neck. "Okay, sir. Fair do's. I have been known to run my mouth off on the odd occasion. I was saying earlier to the Staff Sergeant, here, my old Captain, right nasty bastard, he used to say—"

"Shut it!"

"Sir." Pinkie swivelled his eyes from the gun to look at Harris. "D'you reckon you could see your way clear to letting me have a smoke now?"

"Shut ... your ... gob!"

"Yes, sir."

Harris nuzzled the barrel of the gun in his left hand against Collinson's ear. "Don't even think about it."

"What?"

"Opening the glovebox. There can be only three places this dick with the big gob could have his gun stashed. Under the seat, but he ain't tried to grab it from there. In his jacket, where he claims his smokes are. Or in that glove compartment, which you keep eyeing up."

Collinson offered a slight nod.

"Right. Cards on the table because I'm getting bored. I'm here to remove you two from the picture. I think."

"Oh, well, frig me. That's all the thanks you get. Ten years I was on their retainer list. Ten years I stayed committed to the CYA. Now I get my chance, and both of you are sent to finish me off. Not exactly cricket, is it?"

Ignoring Pinkie's rant and keen to understand if he were to leave this vintage car alive, Collinson probed Harris. He hoped to get the man talking and thus expand on his earlier statement whilst hanging onto the thread of hope that because the Sergeant Major had revealed his mission, Harris planned not to follow through and complete it.

"Sir, if you're telling us this, does that mean you plan to go rogue?"

"Possibly. The way I see this, that lot at the ... what's it called?"

"CYA. Correction Years Association," Collinson replied, shooting a quizzical look at Pinkie. Either this Harris chap suffered from a failing memory, or he wasn't on the level and thus not who he claimed to be.

"That's it. So, hear me right. It appears to me that the CYA are far too keen on sending us eliminators to clean up their cock-ups and then sending someone else to remove us. You, Collinson, were dispatched to remove Mr Irritating here and save Jemma Stone in the process. However, unluckily for you, it appears the CYA also wants you removed. On that basis, this endless line of eliminators eliminating eliminators presumably means I can expect someone else to follow with a mission to remove me."

"Sir?" Pinkie interjected with a raised finger.

"What?"

"Your mission was to remove the Staff Sergeant here, not me?"

"Technically yes. You see, as I understand it, next week, Collinson will kill you. So, you'll already be dead. However, as complicated as all this is, I've time-travelled to a point before that happens. So, as I say, the CYA set a kill order for both of you."

"Why?" quizzed Collinson.

"I'm told the original mission, which involved Frank Stone saving his wife, has changed."

"What?" Pinkie shot his head around, stopping short when the gun barrel dug into his cheek. "They want that Stone bird to be murdered?"

"Shut your gob, pin your ears back, and listen. If you manage to do that, which going by your performance so far, I doubt, you might get lucky and get to watch *Citizen Smith* on the box later."

Pinkie and Collinson shot each other a look. Collinson's more of a plea for the other man to shut his mouth.

"Yes, sir. It would help if I could smoke. Sorta keep my mouth occupied, if you see what I mean."

"Shut it!"

"Take that as a negative, then, sir."

Harris jabbed the barrel further into Pinkie's skin.

"I'm all ears, sir. As God is my witness, I won't say another word on the subject."

"Frig sake, this is painful. The poor bastards under your command would probably consider being ripped apart by an IRA bomb as a blessed relief."

Pinkie opened his mouth to reply but thought better of it when considering that the RSM might not be too chuffed to hear his take on how he remembered his men would enjoy a bit of his barracks banter. Anyway, RSM Harris continued before Pinkie could conjure up a response.

"Right, I don't pretend to understand how moving through time works, but here goes. In 2015, you both travelled back with your missions. You," Harris nudged the gun into Pinkie's cheek, "were sent back to ensure Frank saved Jemma Stone, but also make sure the woman doesn't go through with her pregnancy. And you," Harris nudged the gun into the back of Collinson's neck, "were dispatched after Hartland was ousted and sent on a clean-up mission. Said mission was to ensure Jemma Stone avoided being murdered but was no longer required to abort her child. And, of course, dispose of Sergeant Sinclair at the same time."

"Bloody charming," muttered Pinkie.

Harris tutted before continuing. "So, next Friday, that's what happens. Staff Sergeant Collinson of the Royal Engineers, here, steps in to help Frank by way of killing David Bolton and you, the gobby Sergeant Sinclair of the Royal Marines."

"Who the frig is David Bolton?" Collinson blustered.

"Jesus! Was it him? Dave Bolton murdered the lovely Mrs Stone. Frank's mate did the deed?" Pinkie blurted when attempting to turn his head, which Harris forced back with the gun barrel.

"For someone who said he would zip it, you ain't half got a bad habit of opening your trap."

"Sir."

"Yes, David Bolton. Not Paul Wilson, the bloke you've been tailing today. Not that toff, Tobias Heaton, who's been knobbing the lovely Mrs Stone, and not anyone else on your list. Frank and Jemma split up, even though she gives birth to Frank's son."

"The kid is his? Not that Tobias bloke?"

"Correct. The kid is Frank's. Anyway, Frank goes on to marry another woman. A schoolteacher called Jayne Hart—"

"That Kate Bush bird."

"Spot on. She does, doesn't she? Could be the woman's double."

"I've always had a thing about Kate Bush—"

"Frig sake, Bruce. You seem to have a thing about God knows how many birds. Diane Keen, Floella Benjamin and Kate Bush." Collinson threw in.

"Floella Benjamin?" quizzed Harris. "The black bit of stuff on Playschool?"

"That's her."

"Fair play. I'm with you on that."

"Hey, the lovely lassie who kept me entertained through *George and Mildred* is an exotic wonder. She's Jamaican. And, listen to this, she's got a couple of flatmates if you're interested."

"You won't be seeing her again if you keep interrupting."

"Sir," Pinkie nodded. "My lips are sealed. Don't suppose, now we seem to be getting along much better, I could have that smoke?"

Harris sneered.

"No, guess not. Carry on, sir."

"Frank and his new wife live their lives right up to 2015 again. This time, Frank Stone is a successful businessman, not a tramp living on the streets. Also, although I'm a little sketchy on the details, Hartland, that senior bloke who was ousted, is back in full control at the CYA."

"What? You're joking?" blurted Collinson. "How the frig—"

"I don't know. But anyway, he just is. But here's the thing, not that I know why, but that lot requires Dave Bolton to stay alive. So, they planned to send someone back to make that happen. Then there's this big cock up which ends up with Frank's missus, that Kate Bush bird, travelling back to 1979, as in now, instead of the person they were supposed to be sending."

Pinkie and Collinson exchanged a glance. The conversation they were having before Harris jumped in the back seat, now becoming a little easier to understand.

"So, this is where I come in. Because of the monumental bollocks up, as in the Jayne Stone woman travelling by mistake, you two are regarded as two flies in the ointment who need swatting."

"Your mission is to kill us two and let history play out, which will presumably mean Dave Bolton doesn't die, irrespective of what happens to Jemma Stone?" Collinson asked.

"Technically, not my mission. But yes, mate, you've got it in one."

"What do you mean, technically not your mission?"

"I'm not at liberty to say at the moment."

"Sir?" Pinkie raised a finger.

"What now?" Harris, somewhat exasperated, replied with a roll of his eyes.

"I was just going to suggest that we shouldn't be too hasty. As my old mum used to say, act in haste and repent at your leisure. Which, I think, is sorta apt for this situation. Now, us three sergeants, we could perhaps come to some kind of arrangement. There's really no need for any unpleasantness or shooting. Hey, we could team up and ride together—"

"Are you for real? Is there something wrong with you? You just can't stop talking, can you?"

"He does that," mumbled Collinson.

"Hey, fellas, we're like the film."

"The Three Musketeers?" Collinson suggested, expecting any minute now that Harris would lose his shit and start shooting.

"No, not those nancy-boys with feathers in their hats. *Sergeants Three*. Always seen myself as a Frank Sinatra type, and I do a blinding version of *Fly Me to the Moon*. It's epic, if I say so myself." Pinkie jabbed his finger at Collinson. "I reckon you could be Dean Martin on the account of your iffy looks, and you ain't exactly easy on the eye. And Harris, being the RSM, could be Joey Bishop."

"What the bollocks are you on about?"

"Sorry, sir. The Western, you know, with Sammy Davis Jr. and all them."

"Sir, could you please kill him? If not, kill me instead?" mumbled Collinson, tipping his head back and praying his brains would be blown out and, therefore, not have to spend another second in the company of Sergeant Sinclair.

"Jesus." Harris slowly shook his head in disbelief. "How the hell did you survive in the Royal Marines?"

"My captain said my banter was good for morale, sir."

"Your captain must have been a dickhead."

"You're not wrong, sir. A few of the lads—"

"Bruce! Shut up!"

Pinkie raised an eyebrow and shrugged in response to Collinson's bark.

"Sir, I might regret saying this. But why haven't you just killed us both?"

"It's tempting now I've met you. Well, him," Harris nodded at the sulking Pinkie. "But the reason you're not dead yet is because I think we need to change the narrative."

"Stop the cycle of eliminators eliminating each other?"

"Yup, spot on. I kill you two, and I reckon there will be someone else following along behind to stick a slug in my head. We, gentlemen, if you agree, have an opportunity to break the cycle."

"Hey, fellas, far from me to be the sort to butt in, but I think that's a grand idea. Now, about these three lovely Jamaican lasses …"

30

Champion Boroughcastle Brigadier of Doune

Frank and I shot each other a look as we parted our embrace. His angst expression suggested we harboured similar thoughts. If someone had turned up mentioning the London Eye, then it was safe to assume that person to be a fellow time-traveller of the eliminator variety.

"Err ... boss. You okay?" Alison knitted her caterpillars to convey her bemusement regarding our lack of response.

"Frank," I hissed in desperation.

"Where is he? Is he still in reception?"

Alison stepped back into the corridor before returning and quietly closing the door behind her.

"Yes, boss. He's just sitting there with his arms folded. I gotta say, I don't like the look of him."

I took hold of my husband's hand as Frank bulged his eyes at his receptionist, encouraging her to expand on her reasoning.

"He's just got that look. Y'know," she shrugged. "Thuggish, football hooligan, type. Skinhead, they all look the same, don't they? Is he from the contractors for the groundworks on the car park job? They all look like they enjoy a good fight on the terraces on a Saturday afternoon."

"Probably not."

"Oh."

"Frank, what the hell do we do?" I hissed, unable to hide the desperation in my voice.

"I don't know. We could leave by the back exit and do a runner?"

"But he'll just find us again, either later today or tomorrow. We can't very well go on the run."

"Err ... boss, what's going on?"

Frank and I performed head tennis back and forth between each other and Alison. As our head oscillations increased, the poor girl appeared to pale. I guess her pasty hue could be attributed to her realisation that the situation wasn't favourable.

"Alison, can you stall him? Make him a cuppa and say I'm just finishing a meeting?"

"You wanna tell me what's going on? My boyfriend won't be too happy if I'm in some kind of danger."

"You're not. I promise."

"What then?"

I wiggled my husband's hand to gain his attention. "Frank, we don't know that for sure."

"Woah, hang on, what the hell is happening here? Who is he? You owe money or something? Is he a bailiff? If he's gonna get heavy, I ain't going back out there."

Whilst ignoring his receptionist, who now appeared to feel the need to slap on her angry face and thrash her ponytail back and forth to show her displeasure, Frank and I searched each other's eyes for answers.

"Jayne, he's not here to hurt Alison."

"We don't know what he's here to do, do we? What if—"

"It's you and me he's after, not Alison," Frank whispered his interruption.

"Yes, I get that, but what if he needs to make sure there are no witnesses?"

"Oh."

"Err ... Miss Smarty-Pants, what the hell d'you mean, no witnesses?" Alison shrieked.

"Keep your voice down," Frank hissed.

Although not overly enamoured with her 'Smarty-Pants' comment, I chose to ignore it and instead focus on Alf, who, commando style, crept up to the closed door with his nose to the floor as he sniffed through the gap at the bottom.

"Your dog. Is he like, vicious?"

"Alf? He's been known to chew the odd trouser leg or two."

"Can't we send him out to deal with the thug?"

"Frank," I jabbed a finger towards the door. "Look at Alf. He knows."

"Your dog knows what?"

"Alf. Alfie-Boy, is that Red-Jag-Man?" I hissed, ignoring Frank's receptionist.

"Jesus, you talking to a dog?"

Alf dipped his ears and lowered his head again.

"Oh bugger," I muttered.

"I can't remember. Does lowering his head mean no?"

I nodded and chewed my lip.

"Shit! Ask Alf if he's … you know, one of them."

"Boss, what are you two talking about?"

"Alison, just shove a sock in it for a moment. There's a good girl."

Presumably shocked by my rudeness – well, she had dished out that Smarty-Pants comment – Alison flapped her jaw but fortunately appeared too surprised to counter.

"Frank, I can't very well say that with Alison in the room, can I?"

"Well, ask Alf in a roundabout way, then."

"Alfie-Boy can only respond to closed questions, remember?"

Frank exasperatedly puffed out his cheeks and flapped his arms.

"Hang on, I know." I turned to Alf, placing my palms on my thighs. The stance I'd employed the previous evening when Frank had offered his opinion regarding my posterior. Somehow, I doubted a similar comment would be forthcoming today based on the situation being slightly more severe. "Alfie-Boy, is the nasty man in reception like the man in the red Jag?"

Alf licked his chops.

"Oh crap, there's two of them," Frank muttered.

"Why?" I asked when straightening my stance. "Why the hell would there be two of them?"

"I don't know, but I have a feeling we're about to find out."

"Jesus, Frank, what's the matter with you two? Is someone going to tell me what's going on here? 'Cos I ain't enjoying the vibes coming from your side of the room."

"Alison, that man is a private investigator." I squeezed Frank's hand, hoping he would read that action as a sign to come with me on my fanciful story that might throw her off the scent and buy us a little time. "Frank and I, obviously, are having an affair, and we think Jemma has cottoned on and employed a private investigator to tail us."

"Oh, right. Shit, that's bad."

"Yes, it is. I expect he's here to tell us we've been caught out. The games up, sort of thing."

"Oh. I always knew Jemma was a mean bitch."

Frank raised an eyebrow.

"Yes, well, despite your Smarty-Pants comment, I see you have the ability to judge character. You're not wrong regarding Jemma. I've known her for forty-odd years, and you're right, she's a super bitch."

"Forty?"

"Err, well, I mean four ... fourteen."

"Oh, right. Well, yeah, sorry to say that, but the truth is the woman's just a stuck-up cow. I never liked her, but I never said as much 'cos it wasn't my place."

"Alison, Frank and I need a moment before we see him. So d'you think you could do as Frank asks and stall him?"

In a hands-on-hips stance, Alison ran her bottom lip back and forth across her teeth, presumably weighing up my request. Whilst awaiting her reply, I addressed my father's mutt.

"Alfie-Boy, will Alison be okay with that man out there?"

Alf licked his chops.

"Good. And will you sit with her whilst Frank and I discuss our options? You know, offer Alison a bit of moral support?"

Alf offered that doleful look. Doe-eyed, as if I'd just suggested kennels for a year.

Alison took a break from lip and teeth grinding to peer down at Alf, then glanced up at me.

"Can your dog understand you? And can he actually reply?"

"Yes, I think he can," I vacantly nodded, half at her and half at myself, as I tried to accept that Alf seemed to have developed special powers.

"Wow. You should get him on *That's Life*."

I groaned.

Alison squatted on her haunches, putting her head at the same level as Alf's.

"So, Mr Doggy, Alf, whatever you're called. Will you sit by my side whilst my boss and Miss … err, Jayne have a quick chinwag about their situation? Make sure the nasty thug man doesn't do anything horrible to me?"

Alf shot me a look.

Just as I would have when receiving the same sort of look from one of my girls before they embarked on a tricky task, like scaling the climbing frame at the park, I nodded my encouragement.

Alf returned his attention to Alison and licked his chops.

"That means yes, he will."

"Oh, okay. No bottom burps, guffs, farts, though. You hear?" Alison held up a finger to his nose to enforce her demands.

Alf licked his chops.

"Okay, pleased to meet you, Mr Alf." Alison offered her hand, which Alf reciprocated with a raised paw.

I glanced at Frank, shaking my head in disbelief. But, then, the wherewithal, when considering the fact that we were time-travellers, a half-human dog with the ability to communicate and possess a half-decent command of the English language – a skill which could put most of F-Band to shame – could be classed as almost prolegomenon at the foundation level of ridiculousness.

Of course, there've been other amazing dogs throughout history. For starters, there's the original Lassie, a crossbred Collie that saved a sailor from the stricken Royal Navy battleship *Formidable* after being torpedoed off the Devon coast in 1915. And what about Bodger, that Bull Terrier who bravely helped his pals traverse the Canadian wilderness? Okay, that was a novel. Ah, but there's Slinky, the most loyal dog a man or toy cowboy could ever wish for, and he could actually talk. Okay, he was an animated cartoon. Anyway, I had a shabby-looking, beer-swilling mutt who could understand English, so what's odd about that?

Alison scooted out of Frank's office with Alf close on her heels, leaving Frank and me to mull over what we planned to do next. Apart from Frank's earlier suggestion of making a dash for it via the back exit, I feared our only option was to hold an audience with the man in reception and just pray he wasn't tooled up and preparing to blow our heads off. Maybe I'd watched too many Guy Richie films and unnecessarily escalated the situation out of proportion. However, whether I had or hadn't, the hooligan now being offered a mug of tea had to be a time-traveller.

"Frank, what the hell are we going to do?"

Frank puffed out his cheeks and shrugged. "We either make a run for it or risk that bloke waltzing in here waving a shooter around."

"Yes! I get that. Can't you come up with a better plan?"

"Like what?"

"Money? Bribery?"

"I can't see that working. If he's been sent by the CYA—"

"If!" I interrupted. "There's no if about it. Frank, the man said the London Eye. Unless that's some weirdly named pub you frequent or part of the Greenwich observatory I've never heard of, that must mean he's an eliminator."

"Yes, okay, okay. All I'm saying is we won't be able to bribe him with money, sexual favours, or plead to his better nature, for that matter, because I doubt the man has one." Frank jabbed his finger in the direction of reception. "The man Alison and Alf are keeping entertained is a trained assassin."

"Sexual favours? I hope you're not suggesting—"

"No, it's just a figure of speech, that's all."

"Well, that's as maybe, but *my* Frank would never suggest such a thing."

"Your Frank?"

"Yes, *my* husband, who we're waiting for to appear in your body." I heard my voice falter when remembering Alf had suggested that wasn't going to happen.

"I'm going to be your husband." Frank stabbed his index finger on his sternum.

"I know! But you're different from *my* husband."

"How so?"

"Oh, I don't know, you just are."

"No, come on. You can't just say that and then backtrack."

"I'm not backtracking."

"Yes, you are."

"No!" I stamped my foot, that action I'd copied from my granddaughter. "No, Frank Stone, I am not."

"You are! Come on, out with it. How am I different from *your* Frank? Mr bloody fantastic from the future."

"I never said you're fantastic. I think you're getting a bit ahead of yourself."

"Err ... hello! Only a moment ago, you said I was a fantastic man, something to do with the homeless."

"I said you are wonderful."

"Oh, right. You want a scalpel?"

"A scalpel?" I echoed.

"Yes!"

"Why on earth would I want a ruddy scalpel?"

"To split hairs!"

"Oh, well, if you're going to be childish about it—"

"Childish? What's the difference between fantastic and wonderful? I'm sorry, Jayne, but you said it. If Frank in the future is so damn great, how am I different?"

"Alright. For starters, *my* husband would not lewdly comment about my bottom in public."

"Sorry."

"You!" I jabbed my finger at him. "You said last night I had a nice arse."

"Well, you have. And, I might add, you're the one who insisted I have a good old grope of said posterior—"

"Excuse me!"

"You did! When we enjoyed a game of sucky face in the very same street that you now accuse me of lewdly commenting about your cute bottom."

"I never—"

"I hope this isn't an awkward moment …"

As the door swung open and the man interrupted our heated exchange, Frank and I swivelled our heads to be faced with an odd sight.

"Sorry, Boss. I tried to stop him." Alison stuck her head around the hefty-looking fella who sported a dog's jaw clamped to the front of his jeans. She benignly grinned, a facial expression that didn't fit the rather tight spot we found ourselves in.

"I don't suppose you could instruct this dog to remove his teeth from my tackle, could you? It's just that I think he's close to drawing blood. I've got a date lined up with this fit Jamaican lassie, and I could really do with all my bits remaining in full working order."

31

The Rise And Fall of Flingel Bunt

The thug with the buzz-cut hairstyle, sporting a long keloid scar on the left side of his face, giving the impression his hair was held onto his scalp by a singular shiny pink strap, held his hands up as a gesture to suggest he was still awaiting an answer to his question. Due to the shock of the man entering, the fact that Alf appeared to be swinging from his crotch, or a combination of both, a question that neither Frank nor I had responded to regarding whether we could see our way clear to instructing Alf to remove his teeth from this new arrival's privates.

Alison now offered a gritted teeth grimace following her apology for failing to stall the man.

A drooling Alf side-eyed me, presumably waiting for instructions.

As my future husband and I gawped back in shock, Alf held on tight, now gently swaying from side to side as he offered up a growl whilst all the time keeping those jaw muscles clamped around the man's crown jewels.

"Alison, thanks. That'll be all. We'll take it from here," Frank stated, not once taking his eyes off Alf.

"Oh, right. Will Alf be staying with you, then?"

"He will," I chimed in, keen for Alfie-Boy to hold on tight despite the difficulty of his position and the steady flow of doggy saliva that gave the impression Buzz-Cut-Man had wet himself. Which based on where Alf's teeth were positioned, I considered wouldn't be an overreaction.

That said, far be it for me to suggest I'm any kind of expert regarding men's private areas. Despite over the past thirty-odd years becoming intimately acquainted with Frank's, I wasn't well versed in male genitalia due to Frank being only my third lover.

The man, or lad, or perhaps fumbling buffoon being a more apt description, who'd popped my cherry in the back seat of his Austin A40 – and that's no mean feat, I can tell you – when parked in a dark corner of the car park at the back of the local discotheque, had been on the shy side and keen that I didn't ogle his manhood. There'd been none of that passionate panting on the back seat that Leonardo and Kate offered up. No, more of a tangling of stockings and Y-fronts and the occasional jab in the ribs as said idiot attempted to line up and cajole his thingy between my legs. Fair to say that the unilluminating experience, along with my second lover's wham-bam-thank-you-ma'am attitude to lovemaking, hadn't afforded me great insight into the nether regions of the male body.

Anyway, back to the thug and Alf. I suspected our eliminator would unequivocally be aware that one false move and the date he had lined up with that Jamaican lass may go south.

Alison disappeared down the corridor before Buzz-Cut-Man balled his fist, appearing ready to land one on Alf's hooter.

"Don't you dare hit my dog."

"Well, tell the bloody thing to get off me, then."

Frank nudged my arm and shrugged.

"What?"

"You might as well get Alf to stand down."

"I don't think so. Alfie-Boy has the situation under control. I don't see why we should concede ground at this point in proceedings."

"I know, but at the end of the day, he can't hang there, swinging off this chap's crotch forever, can he?"

"No, I see your point. But whilst Alfie-Boy is in position, that might buy us a bit more time."

"Yes, I get that, but the mutt can't hang there all day." Frank gesticulated with an outstretched finger at Alf as my pooch started to slip due to his clamped jaws supporting his weight.

"Err ... hello. You gonna get this thing off me?"

"Oh, alright," I belligerently spat. "Alf, stand down. Take a load off and come here."

Alf released his grip, dropped to the floor and padded to my side as instructed.

"Phew, thanks." Buzz-Cut-Man undid his jeans button and lowered the fly before gingerly pulling the material away to peek at the damage.

"Err, excuse me. What on earth d'you think you're doing?"

"Jesus, I can see teeth marks," he muttered, before delving his free hand into his underpants to rummage around with his presumably sore tackle.

"Sorry, but do you mind? I really don't want to watch you playing with yourself."

"Jesus, lady, I'm not playing with myself. Your damn dog has bitten me."

Alf growled.

"Good boy, Alf."

Alf licked his chops and grinned, seemingly delighted with the praise I'd afforded him.

"What d'you want? Why are you here?" Frank demanded. Despite our minor spat that this 'gentlemen' rudely interrupted, Frank flung his arm around me and pulled me close. I presumed it to be an act of protecting me rather than increasing the target area for Buzz-Cut-Man to aim at.

Whilst pulling a face of either pain or pleasure, it was difficult to distinguish between the two, the man before us, with his trouser fly at half-mast, rubbed vigorously at his genitals.

"Can you stop that, please?"

"Give us a sec. My bollocks are sore."

"Oh, charming."

"Well, it's alright for you. You didn't have a rabid dog with a set of sharp teeth clamped around them."

"I don't have any bollocks, thank you very much. And, I'll have you know, Alf is not rabid. I attest he's a smidge on the unkempt side, but he is not disease-ridden."

Alf nudged my leg. That telltale sign he wanted a chinwag.

"Sorry, Alfie-Boy, but you are lacking in the grooming department and, like it or not, your bottom puffs are quite unpleasant."

Alf nudged my leg again.

"Oh, sorry, you want to parley?"

Alf licked his chops.

"What is it, boy?"

With his nose to the floor, Alf scooted over to the man, who continued to give the impression he was masturbating. With his nose, Alf lifted the hem of Buzz-Cut-Man's right trouser leg to reveal a gun strapped into an ankle holster.

"Oi, get that mutt away from me," he shrieked, hopping back and, at last, refraining from his lewd act.

Frank and I exchanged a look. Although we expected the man to be carrying a weapon, actually seeing it didn't make it any easier to stomach. Frank tugged on my cardigan, encouraging me to step behind him. Notwithstanding his gallant efforts, I held my ground.

"No, Frank," I whispered. "We face this together."

"Jayne, for pity's sake, stand behind me."

Whilst buttoning his trousers, offering an odd shimmy to encourage his chewed bollocks to lie in a comfortable position, shake his trouser hem down to cover his no-longer concealed weapon, or both, Buzz-Cut-Man, for the first time in this encounter, offered a grin at our terrified expressions. The change in demeanour compressed his scar into a fiery crescent shape, which belied his grin.

"I take it you're what I know as an eliminator?"

"Um, yeah, I suppose so. Correct, Mr Stone. I am."

"Right. Great," Frank mumbled with sarcastic emphasis as he tightened his grip on my recently significantly shrunken waist. "So that means you're one of those two chaps who Hartland showed me a picture of before I travelled on the Wheel."

"No, Frank, I'm not. I'll explain. But first, what does a man have to do to get a cuppa around here? A biscuit wouldn't go amiss either."

"You want to enjoy tea and biscuits before you blow our brains out?"

"Fair question."

"Well?" I shrieked. "Are you going to kill us?"

"Hey, back up a couple of paces, lady." He held his palm up, traffic policeman style, causing me to flinch. "One thing at a time. Now let's—"

"Can you at least tell us why? If I'm going to die, I would appreciate knowing the reason that bloody man Hartland has ordered our execution."

"Hang on. Why have you been dispatched if you're not one of those two chaps? Were they sent but didn't make it through?" Frank threw at the man before he could answer my question.

"Make it through?"

"Yeah, evaporate on the Wheel."

"Evaporate on the Wheel?" he parroted.

"Yes! Evaporate. And why d'you keep repeating everything I say?"

"Oh, you mean like some travellers just disappear?" He fanned out his hands akin to a second-rate magician who'd just attempted to convince the audience that the playing card had disappeared in a puff of smoke and not through the sleight of hand.

"Yeah, that's what I'm saying. Did those two evaporate when travelling back on the Wheel?"

Frank's statement caused me to shudder. Alf and I exchanged a look, that act hammering home what my pooch had intimated last night when suggesting *my* Frank was now floating around the ether.

"Oh, I see. No, Collinson and Sinclair made it back to 1979 in one piece. I tell you, that Sinclair bloke is enough to drive a man nuts. The idiot's a regular motormouth and makes Speedy Gonzales appear like a mute in comparison. Mark my words, he ain't the sort you want to go for a drink with unless you're into listening to inane drivel for hours on end."

"Well, that's not likely because I'm assuming he's been sent to kill me."

"Yeah, he was."

"Was? As in, he isn't now?"

"Well, that's not strictly true. Bruce Sinclair was sent to ensure you save Jemma Stone, but also make sure that you persuade your wife to have an abortion."

Frank's jaw dropped. At this stage, I didn't know if he knew Jemma was pregnant with Andrew. Whether his reaction was due to Buzz-Cut-Man's suggestion that she was with child or at the thought that his unborn, which he knew about, had to be aborted, who could tell?

"Right, come on then, how about that cuppa? Oh, and a few biscuits, if you don't mind. I'm bleeding Hank Marvin." He rubbed his tummy as if to demonstrate his hunger. "Then, my friends, we can discuss business."

"Frank?" I nudged him with my hip to break his reverie. "Frank, shall I ask Alison to make tea?"

My future husband shot me a look.

"Tell you what, you two get comfortable and I'll get that cute lassie in reception to rustle up some refreshments." Buzz-Cut-Man swivelled around and yanked open the door. "Hey, love. How about a brew and some biscuits?" he bellowed.

"Jayne, what happens to Jemma's child?"

"Your child."

"Mine?"

"Uh-huh."

"I know she's pregnant because the police told me the pathologist discovered it when conducting her post-mortem."

"Well, in my life, the one where Jemma isn't strangled by Dave, she gives birth to a boy. Andrew. And he's definitely yours, despite her predilection for entertaining all sorts of men. Andrew *is* your son."

"He lives?"

"Yes. Rupert and Jemma raise him, but you, and me for that matter, regularly spend time with him. Weekends and holidays. Well, not now, as in 2015, because he's a grown man with two children of his own."

"My grandchildren?"

"Uh-huh. Prudence and Scott. Nice kids."

"Right." Frank scrubbed his palms up and down his face. "Christ, this is nuts—"

"Frank, I don't know whether he's come to kill us," I gesticulated to the open doorway that Buzz-Cut-Man had vacated when Alison hadn't answered his demands. "But I need to bring you up to speed on why you and me were in that pod when it all went belly-up and I ended up time-travelling."

"You said I was offering consultancy services to someone who was about to travel."

"You were. That someone, being Barbara Denton."

"Barbara Denton." Frank pulled a face after uttering the name. "Is that name supposed to mean something to me?"

"Barbara Denton used to be Babs Bolton."

"Oh, really?"

"Frank, that's not the half of it. This eliminator chap aside, we're standing in a deep puddle of doo-doo wearing wholly inappropriate footwear."

Frank glanced down at his brogues.

"Metaphorically speaking."

"Oh."

"Babs was supposed to be sent to ensure David Bolton doesn't die. Irrespective of what happens to Jemma."

"Shit!"

"Exactly. Your mission is out of date. As I said, we're knee deep in a puddle of doo-doo."

Part 4

32

2015

Rome's Ephialtes

Hartland wrestled his cigarette case from his jacket pocket whilst flaring his nostrils at Whitman in response to her insinuations and insubordination. Although not pawing at the ground with his feet or lowering imaginary horns, his inimitably indignant demeanour portrayed all that of an agitated bull full of attitude. Any savoir-faire he might usually employ was now evaporating following the shambolic calamities at the Wheel not twenty minutes ago. Also, Whitman's tone and attitude weren't helping.

However, as he lit his cigarette, he remained focused when doing his level best to avoid losing his shit, based on the fact their situation was so dire. All his efforts had to be directed at effecting an acceptable outcome and not, as he would like to, rip this smug, supercilious senior analyst to pieces.

After blowing a plume of smoke to the ceiling, Hartland allowed his hooded eyelids to drop to half-mast as he eyed Whitman, who remained stoically defiant to his intimidating glare, only allowing her eyes to shift momentarily when following the stream of smoke emanating from the senior man's nostrils.

"Get on with it, woman. What are you suggesting we do now, then? And what has smelly Frank got to do with our next move in resolving this utter shitstorm of a snafu we seem to have landed in?"

"We, sir? This shitstorm, as you call it, can I respectfully suggest, is due to the Transportation team's cock-up. We, the Data team, have caused no issues, what–so–ever!" Whitman separated the syllables to make her point whilst blushing, presumably realising she'd once again overstepped the mark. However, now building up a head of steam, she continued in her accusing tone. "I'm just putting it out there. Clarifying, if you like, that my team are entirely blameless regarding *your* organisation's foul-up."

"No, Whitman, I don't like. And just so you are abundantly clear, I can have you removed with a simple click of my fingers." Hartland raised his right hand and snapped his thumb and forefinger together to demonstrate, causing Whitman to wince. "You've been with us long enough to know what that entails. A similar fate that some of the idiots in the Transportation team are currently experiencing. I presume, despite your apparent boring existence, lack of party-going, associated dearth of friends, and aversion to dinner parties, elimination isn't something that floats your boat either?"

"No, sir."

"Thought not."

"My apologies, sir."

"Hmmm." Hartland drew on his cigarette as he exchanged a glance with Johnson. "I take it Whitman is worth retaining?"

"Sir? But, sir," blustered Whitman, her eyes bulging.

Akin to an overpaid prima-donna footballer when mocking the referee with their oscillating raised index finger, Hartland wagged a finger in Whitman's direction to halt her protests while peering up at his Data Director when awaiting his response.

"Whitman is the best we have, sir. Of course, no one in the organisation is immune from elimination—"

"Except me."

"Err ... yes, sir. I meant anyone but you, sir."

"Including yourself."

"Oh. Well, yes, technically, I suppose."

"Okay, so let's assume we put up with Whitman's foibles, as in the propensity to not know her place and that predilection for insubordination, you, Johnson, will be held accountable for her actions. Am I clear?"

"Crystal, sir."

Hartland swivelled around to face Whitman. "Now, I take it you like your boss?"

"Sir?"

"You like Johnson? I'm fast learning you're not that interested in people per se, but I take it you enjoy working for Johnson?"

"Yes, sir."

"Okay, so unless both of you fancy joining those poor fellows in the Transportation team who are currently undergoing the grisly process of elimination, I assume you will learn, and swiftly, I might suggest, the ability to toe the line. I imagine their fate has the effect of focusing the mind and tempering your behaviour."

"Yes, sir." Whitman side-eyed Johnson, who offered her an exasperated, pleading nonverbal response.

"Good. Now that's all cleared up. Let's hear your suggestion for sorting out this lamentable fiasco we *all* seem to be facing. And to be clear, I mean all."

Johnson offered an encouraging nod, indicating Whitman should continue, simultaneously crossing his fingers on the hand held behind his back when praying Whitman could temper her frustrations.

"Okay, as I see it, we have a few options open to us. Firstly, we do nothing and invoke live protocol status. Which I understand is less than ideal."

"Agreed. Next."

"Right, of course. I understand that option comes with, shall we say, difficulties?"

Hartland puffed on his cigarette but offered no reply.

"So …" Whitman cleared her throat, shifting her stance before continuing. "Another option … we could despatch an eliminator to dispose of Mrs Stone. As I stated, our preliminary data suggests that will not solve the issue, causing a double fold back on time, thus rendering the mission pointless. However, there are two considerations regarding this point. Firstly, our data is preludial, so the situation may change with more accurate intel at our disposal, which should become more apparent over the course of today. Secondly, if the intel doesn't change, at least that clears away any mess left festering in the past."

"Hmmm. I thought you mentioned earlier that Mrs Stone dies at some point, anyway. You said she doesn't exist in this time."

"Correct, sir. Data suggests Mrs Stone, who is, in fact, Miss Hart again, will die in a road traffic accident in …" she paused to consult her file. "Yes, here it is. 1980. What I have so far, it appears her dog—"

"Her dog?"

"Yes, sir, her dog somehow manages to get tangled up in the driver's footwell of her VW Beetle, resulting in Miss Hart losing control of the car and thus ploughing into the back of an articulated lorry. A Safeway Supermarket truck, the data suggests. Anyway, she's killed outright."

"And the dog?"

"Alf, the dog, escapes unhurt. Current location unknown."

"Well, unless the pooch is superhuman, I imagine by 2015, the damn thing is also six feet under."

"Yes. Sorry, sir. I meant in 1980, said mutt's location is unknown."

"I presume Miss Hart's premature demise explains why her family doesn't exist in the future, as in now?"

"Correct, sir."

"So why bother sending an eliminator when the woman is going to die in a few months?"

"Because, if our prelim data holds some inaccuracies, that will expunge the changes she causes." Whitman waved her hand across her file before continuing. "The plethora of Category Fours and Fives, not to mention the quite eye-watering amount of Category Tens. Also, with more accurate data, this action may resolve our main issue."

"The *Monteagle Fault* and the dismembering of the President of the United States?"

"Correct, sir."

"And if it doesn't? The double fold back on time still happens?"

"Correct, again, sir. That brings me to my third suggestion."

"Which is?"

"We have Frank Stone in the building, yes?"

"We do," chimed in Johnson. "He's currently ensconced in the containment suite after we apprehended him when he exited the Wheel."

"Well, okay, so I've run the numbers, and early data suggests that if we attempt to send Frank back, take the place of the man we've already dispatched when he was our original Change Agent for the failed attempt to stop the *European Fault*, that may well swing the game in your … err, our favour."

Hartland glanced up at Johnson whilst taking another hearty drag on his cigarette. "I imagine Frank is not in the best of moods?"

"No, sir. We've had no choice but to sedate him. After exiting the Eye and discovering his wife had disappeared back to 1979, he became somewhat hysterical."

"Yes," Hartland chuckled. "I imagine he did. I suspect Sir Frank Stone is fuming. So, Whitman, expand on your point. How will sending Frank back again help our cause?"

"Okay. I will need some time on this, an hour or two at max. Still, early data suggests that sending Frank back to 1979, replacing the Frank we sent before, might lead to him and Miss Hart again preventing Jemma's murder whilst also ensuring David Bolton isn't in Fairfield Woods in the first place."

"Which will mean the *Monteagle Fault* is sorted, and the UK will avoid becoming the pariah of the Western World when accused of failing to prevent the murder of the President of the United States?"

"Correct, sir."

Hartland glanced up at his Data Director. "What d'you think?"

"I think we give Whitman the time she needs; in the meantime, we prepare Frank."

Hartland nodded.

"When all is said and done, sir, we have nothing to lose. Suppose Frank fails or doesn't make it through. In that case, we despatch an eliminator to remove Miss Hart and the Frank we sent all those years ago. Also, dispose of Sinclair and Collinson, let Dave Bolton strangle Jemma Stone, and then invoke live protocol status in 2024 to prevent *FART* from blowing the Cabinet to smithereens."

"And the President of the United States, to boot."

"Yes, sir."

"I'd rather not involve the 'Circus' for the aforementioned reasons I stated earlier. Apart from the whole organisation being totally corrupt, their operatives are more *Johnny English* than *Bond*. I doubt any of those idiots could spot a terrorist if they waltzed up and introduced themselves as Tom Hardy wearing a mask whilst impersonating Darth Vader."

"Sir?" quizzed Whitman.

"Bane, in *The Dark Night Rises*. A part played by Tom Hardy."

"Oh."

"Get your head out of those books, grab yourself a bucket of popcorn and perhaps one of the good-looking lads in your team, and get yourself off to the cinema for a change. You never know, you might enjoy yourself."

"I doubt it, sir."

"Yes, you're probably right. Anyway, my point is, none of those buffoons at the 'Circus' are capable of identifying a pickpocket, let alone a bunch of amateurish terrorists who manage to pull off the most outlandish act of terror this country has ever witnessed. We need Frank, chipper, ready to go, and firing on all cylinders."

"One minor point, sir."

"What?"

"Regardless of this plan, we will still need to send an eliminator."

"Why? Surely, if Frank and his lovely wife pull it off, they can continue with their life."

"No, sir. As I said, I need some time on this, and I do have my team working on this as we speak," Whitman nodded towards her analysts as they beavered away at their screens. "But what I have so far suggests, if Frank is successful, as in he prevents Dave Bolton from dying, we will still need to liquidate him and Mrs Stone, along with Collinson and Sinclair."

"Why?"

"It's early days at the moment. However, there seems to be data filtering through, which suggests that if our original eliminator, Sinclair, stays alive, that slight change will cause a ripple effect. For some bizarre reason, it means Jolene Horsley will continue on her path of terror. So, I suggest we clean up the whole mess, remove both Collinson and Sinclair and dispose of Frank and Jayne at the same time. Clean away any debris, so to speak."

"Although I'm not one to champion the eradication of our travellers, I think Whitman makes a valid point, sir."

"Hmmm. Yes, I see. Are we saying if Dave Bolton lives, Sinclair also lives?"

"Yes, sir."

"And that has a negative effect on the operation?"

"Yes, sir."

"It's a fair point. Oh, but Mrs Stone dies when the dog—"

"Yes, but Frank is alive and living on the streets again. I think it would be cleaner to remove them all. We will need to dispose of Sinclair, so we might as well eliminate all traces of travellers in one fell swoop."

Hartland and Johnson shrugged.

"Fine, we send an eliminator to clear down the mess. Johnson, do we have a name that is capable and reliable?"

"Yes, I think we do. Bamford. He's ex Paras ... seen a lot of service over the years and has a good attitude about him."

"Excellent." Hartland clapped his hands together. "To quote John Hannibal Smith, I love it when a plan comes together," he chuckled.

"Oh, is that a quote from the commander of the Carthaginian Army, sir? When he led his elephants over the Alps during the Second Punic War before facing defeat at the hands of Scipio Africanus in what is now North Africa. I've read the works of Polybius and Livy extensively, but I don't recall that quote."

"Whitman."

"Yes, sir."

"You have copious amounts of data to crunch and algorithms to massage. However, when that's done, I really do suggest you get out more. This obsession with reading is making you a very dull girl."

"Yes, sir, I'll do my best, sir. Perhaps I might request to take some of the leave I'm owed? I could visit the British Library and perhaps take in a few museums. That would be fun."

"Christ, forget I even suggested it. Just get me the data and let's sort this ruddy catastrophe out once and for all. Frank Stone has a job to do before we obliterate him, along with that rather delicious wife of his."

33

1979

Here You Come Again

"Mind if I have the last one?"

After Alison had rustled up three mugs of tea and a plate of Garibaldi biscuits, Buzz-Cut-Man, who'd introduced himself as Kenny Harris, asked with his hand hovering above the near-empty plate of biscuits.

Based on the fact that neither Frank nor I had partaken, and Harris had scoffed the lot, I dismissively waved my hand to suggest he might as well help himself to the last one.

Harris slouched cross-legged in the chair opposite Frank's desk, savouring the refreshments. I perched my bottom on Frank's chair with my now somewhat stunned future husband standing by my side with his hand resting on my shoulder. If it wasn't such a dire situation, we would appear to be posing for a portrait. That said, our dolorous demeanours caused by the thought of what might come next, when Harris eventually made a grab for the shooter now clearly on display due to his raised trouser hem, probably would have made us prime candidates to sit for Pablo Picasso during his Blue Period.

Apart from Harris's munching, the only other break to the library-styled silence in the room came from underneath the desk, where Alf eagerly lapped up his tea served up in a plant pot saucer. Six sugar cubes, which I'm sure wouldn't be good for him, is what Alf had requested by way of six nudges to my leg when I asked the classic milk and sugar question.

"So, Mr Harris, can we get to the reason why you're here? I'm presuming, hoping, in fact, that you're not of a mind to kill Frank or me?"

Harris raised a finger to indicate he needed a moment to finish chewing, which he followed up with a slurp of tea loud and uncouth enough to rival Alf's performance.

"Ah, that's better. Bleedin' starving I was." He took another quaff of tea, swilling the hot liquid around his mouth to presumably rinse the mulched remnants of his biscuit feast from his teeth. "Okay, so let's get down to business."

I glanced up at Frank, who, despite appearing still locked securely in that catatonic state, which, following the news of Andrew and Babs, was fair enough, almost robotically extracted a packet of cigarettes from his pocket.

"Oh, if you don't mind. Please, could you not smoke? Suffered from a touch of childhood asthma that never really left me, I'm afraid. Sorry, I hate the smell of cigarettes, and I'm liable to break into a hacking coughing fit."

Due to having pegged Harris as a smoker, I raised a surprised eyebrow. Of course, there was no real science behind that thought, but he just seemed the type. That said, in 2015, most didn't partake, and that's where all three of us in this room had travelled from.

"Mr Harris. The reason you're here?" I quizzed, leaving Frank staring into the middle distance, still gripping his unopened packet of cigarettes. I laid my hand on top of his that remained resting on my shoulder, offering a comforting rub while waiting for Harris to respond.

"Yeah, course. Oh, has anyone ever told you that you're the spit of that Kate Bush?"

"Yes, once or twice," I groaned. "I suppose next you'll be suggesting that Alf should feature on *That's Life*."

"That's Life?"

"Yes, *That's Life*. You know, that satirical consumer affairs programme with Esther Rantzen."

"The bird with the teeth?"

"Well, if you mean the lady with an impressive set of gnashers that could rival Frank's secretary's, then yes."

"Oh, well, can't say I've seen it. It's called *That's Life*, you say?"

"Yes, but can we move on?"

"Right, so, me and the lads have had a wee chat about things—"

"Lads?"

"Yeah, the lads. So we were chatting, well, to be honest with you, Richard and I mulled over a few options while I held my hand over Sinclair's mouth to shut him up. I've never met a man with such verbal diarrhoea. Anyway—"

"Sorry, Mr Harris, who is Richard?"

"Oh, please call me Ken or Kenny, which most of my mates do. Richard is Collinson. As I said earlier, the CYA dispatched four eliminators. Technically, only three, but I'll come back to that point in a minute. So first up was Sinclair, the gobby git, whose mission involved helping Frank save his wife before ensuring Frank, here ..." he paused and waved his half-drunk mug of tea in my husband's direction before continuing. "Err ... persuades his wife to abort the child."

"But that didn't happen. Andrew Barrington Scott—"

"Correct." Kenny held his hand up, indicating he would like to continue without interruptions. I offered an acquiescent nod. Whether that decision would speed up the inevitable date with a bullet propelled through the barrel of his gun, who knew? "So, as I said, you are quite correct. The child wasn't aborted. That's because Richard Collinson followed Sinclair with a mission to save Jemma on humanitarian grounds and dispose of Sinclair at the same time. Clear away the mess if you like. You see, at that time, Hartland had been ousted, and this bird ... err, this woman, Pitstop—"

"Pitstop? As in Penelope?"

"Indeed, although I'm led to believe she wasn't the actual Penelope Pitstop as in the cartoon. And, of course, not to be confused with Lady Penelope Creighton-Ward, assisted by her butler Aloysius Nosey Parker and owned a modified pink Rolls-Royce, but she was, or is, called Penelope—"

"You know your Thunderbirds—"

"I do. I'm a huge fan. Anyway, she took over operations and instructed Collinson. Which, you and I both know, played out as they planned. Course, Frank ... this Frank, that is, is blissfully unaware of this new future," Kenny paused and knitted his brows as he glanced up at Frank. "Hey, is he alright? He don't look too good. I've seen lads with that look when facing the enemy. Used to be called shell shock, which now, or will be in the future, be known as PTSD."

Again, I rubbed my husband's hand, still maintaining eye contact with Kenny. "Frank just needs a moment to gather his thoughts. He's got rather a lot of updates regarding the future to come to terms with. Until yesterday, Frank believed he was a rough sleeper living near a toilet block on The Queen's Walk. Today, Frank's now aware that in the future, he'll become a successful entrepreneur with five children and as many grandchildren. Not something I imagine is too easy to cope with. Oh, and he's only just learnt that his best mate, Dave Bolton, in some other existence, strangled his bitchy wife, Jemma. Apparently."

"No, I guess you're right. Hey, does he know he's famous in the future? Come to think of it, didn't some society magazine do some feature on you both?"

"I hadn't got you pegged as a subscriber to *Hello!* or *OK!* magazines."

"Nah, but didn't *Saga* also run a feature?"

"Yes, they did. Good grief, are you telling me you read the *Saga* Magazine?"

"Hey lady, I was in my late sixties before I travelled. That Saga mag had some pretty nifty stuff in it for us oldies. I bought a decent pair of wide-fitting shoes with Velcro fastening from an ad in that publication. They worked a treat in sorting out my bunions."

"I'm sure."

"Course, I ain't got those issues no more, now that I'm thirty again, fit and raring to go." He rubbed his crotch and winced, presumably still feeling the effects of Alf's attention.

Talking of which, Alf continued to slurp his sugary tea from somewhere under the desk.

"You were saying. Collinson was dispatched via the Wheel after Sinclair."

"Yeah, sorry, we digress. Christ, I think that Sinclair bloke is rubbing off on me. So, Richard Collinson killed Dave Bolton and Sinclair before cracking on with his life. Which, of course, hasn't happened yet, this being before that event."

"And you?"

"Ah, yes, me. So, thirty-six years later, when in 2015 again, Hartland is back in full control and needs David Bolton to stay alive. Now, due to certain circumstances, which I'll come back to, I'm not aware of the reason that the Bolton bloke has to live. You see, all good operations are on a strictly need-to-know basis."

"To prevent a terrorist organisation from blowing up Ten Downing Street, killing the PM and most of the Cabinet, I'm led to believe." I glanced at Frank, who remained focused on whatever held his attention on the far wall of his office.

"Jesus, really? Is that what this is about? What terrorist organisation? When was this going to take place?"

"I don't know. As we both know, I wasn't supposed to travel through time. And *my* Frank, my husband back in 2015, is missing. So, this Frank," I patted his hand again. "This Frank, my future husband, doesn't know either."

"Yeah, sorry about that. That must be tough."

"Like you wouldn't believe."

"Well, I've dabbled in recent years. Not in such a way that I've actually been involved in terror on the front line, so to speak. But a few groups in various countries have pulled on my expertise."

"Oh, so you're a terrorist. Lovely!"

"Hey, lady. Sometimes, the only way to make things better is to take a stand."

"Killing people?"

"Not Joe Public, like those looney suicide bombers. But, yeah, some of these world leaders need sorting out. Are you telling me this terrorist lot in the future carry out an attack on our government, then?"

"So I'm led to believe. Yes, that's what Barbara Denton was supposed to prevent, but unfortunately—"

"You travelled instead of her."

"I did."

"Well, I can't say I'd be that bothered if some nut-crazed terrorist bombs Number Ten. They're all a load of lying, cheating gits." Kenny wagged a finger at me. "Now, hear me right, this era is far better. That Thatcher woman was, is, a revelation. Bloody Tories didn't know when they had a good thing, you know. Am I right, or am I right?"

"You don't happen to know a black cab driver in 2015 with a shock of platinum blonde hair, by any chance, do you?"

"Hmmm. Not that I can recall. Why d'you ask."

"No bother. Please, do continue."

"Oh, okay. Well, I'm a huge Maggie fan. Apart from Dolly, she's the best thing that ever happened to this country."

"Dolly?"

"Yeah, Dolly Parton."

"I think you'll find Dolly Parton is an American."

"Hell, yes, I know that. But she's toured the UK. I've seen her gigs hundreds of times and followed her all over the world, that I have."

"Whilst assisting terror organisations in blowing the great and the good to smithereens?"

"On the odd occasion, work and pleasure did just happen to coincide. That aside, I have a season ticket pass to Dollywood in Tennessee, and I've met her umpteen times. Now, hear me right, if you put Dolly and Thatcher together, you have the perfect woman. Balls of steel and a set of tits to die for."

"I'm sure."

"Pardon the tit comment. Lad talk, that's wholly inappropriate in your good company."

"Pardon granted. I'm partial to a bit of Dolly myself, but d'you think we can get back on track?"

Alf burped.

"Course."

"You were about to enlighten us about your involvement."

"Yeah. See, after you travelled—"

"By mistake. None of which is my fault, I might add."

"Yeah, true. But as I was saying, after you travelled that lot at the CYA needed to send another eliminator to clean down the whole mess."

"Mess?"

"Yeah. See, you shouldn't be here," Kenny paused and took a moment to think. "Well, what I mean is, you shouldn't be here in respect of being a time-traveller."

"Don't I bloody know it!"

"Course, you should be here as yourself, not your older self."

"I get it. Please move on."

"See, here's the thing, and hear me right. Because you travelled, and not that other bird ... err, woman, that Barbara Denton lass, that cock-up, apparently put the entire operation in a bit of a quandary."

Alf farted.

Seemingly unperturbed by my dog's flatulence, Kenny continued.

"The CYA placed a kill order. Basically, your good self, Frank, Collinson and Sinclair, to be eliminated. As I said, a clean-down operation to remove the mess, if you like."

"I don't like."

"No," he chuckled. "I imagine you wouldn't. I have to say, you're handling this far better than some of those Herculean Columbians and Argentinians, not to mention a couple of hard nuts in the IRA. Most of that lot shat themselves when faced with me."

"I can imagine."

"Jesus, what's that stink?"

"That's Alf. According to Jayne, he has a rather nasty flatulence problem," Frank chimed in, now hauled from his reverie by the smelling salts earlier puffed from Alf's backside.

"Ah, nice. I see you're back with us, Frank. Do you need a recap?"

"No, I'm fully up to speed. Does this mean you're not going to kill us, then?"

"That, my friend, depends. As Dolly says, I could be the *Dagger Through the Heart* or your *Unlikely Angel*."

34

Island Girl

"D'you think we should trust him? I mean, the git was sent to kill us both. That said, something stinks about his story. I'm not sure he's playing with a straight bat. And that lot can't play cricket, anyway. Don't you think he was a bit cagey about some of the details? It seemed to me half of what he was saying suggests the knob was making it up. Scottish, as well. Friggin' Jocks, do my head in. All that '*Och aye the noo*' bollocks. I mean, they made a right old mess of Wembley Stadium, didn't they? Sacred land that. What I'm saying is that place Bobby Moore lifted the Jules Rimet Trophy is part of our heritage. You can't have the Jocks running amok, can you now?"

"Harris ain't Scottish, you knob."

Pinkie paused at Collinson's statement, but only for a nanosecond.

"Y'know, I'm a bit miffed with that lot at the CYA. All those years on that retainer, and then what happens?" Pinkie glanced at Collinson, who remained facing away, gazing out of the passenger side window. "I'll tell you what happens. They send *you* to kill me. Friggin' charming! I mean, what sort of thanks is that? I'm in half a mind to bowl up to their fancy offices and give them a piece of my mind. Although, that said, I think I'll put that on hold on account that I'm looking forward to tonight. Don't want that bastard lot to spoil my thoughts about that lovely lassie who's gonna keep me warm later."

Pinkie nudged Collinson's arm.

"Hey, you wait until you see her two flatmates. Right crackers, they are. That song could have been written about them three. Crackers, I said. Alright, working girls, mind, but you wouldn't know it. Just ten quid for all night. Now, you can't say fairer than that, can you?"

"What song?"

"Do what?"

Collinson drew in his breath and sighed, still not turning to face Pinkie. "In the middle of that inane drivel that just poured out of your overactive gob, you said something about that song could have been written about them."

"Oh, yeah, that one by Elton John."

"Elton John?"

"Yeah."

"Which one?"

"Jeees, I can't remember."

"*Your Song*? *Crocodile Rock*? *I'm Still Standing*? *Don't Let the Sun Go Down on Me*? *Bennie*—"

"Frig, I don't know. That song about that tall, black chick. She was six foot five or something or other and had a tyre."

"A tyre?"

"Yeah. Now, don't get me wrong, but I've always liked a bit of Elton. Well, y'know, not in that way. I'm not like that, and I don't have a thing about him like the lovely Floella, if you get my drift. I don't swing a bat for the other side. That said, there was this bloke in my regiment who wasn't half pretty, but that's another story. Can get real lonely when you're in the jungle for months on end on some pointless mission."

"Don't flatter yourself. I doubt very much Elton would have given you a second look."

"Hey, I'm all man, me. That lassie last night wasn't complaining."

"And does this lassie you keep banging on about have a name?"

"Course. Everyone's got a name."

"And?"

"And what?"

Collinson turned to face Pinkie. "And what's her name, then?"

"Oh, well, you see, I was kinda distracted on account she was giving my old chap a good seeing to, so I might have forgotten to enquire."

Collinson tutted and turned away. "You're a real delight, you know that?"

"Hey, not my fault the lassie was a bit tied up and although a right cracker, she ain't the conversationalist sort."

"Shove a sock in it."

"Charming."

Since leaving the railway station and heading over to Frank's office, Collinson had been weighing up his options. Of course, Pinkie's gun still lay in the glove compartment, and it had crossed his mind to carry out his mission. Blow the gobshite git's head off, whack Harris, and then he would be free.

However, he couldn't deny that Harris had made a valid point. If he took that action, would the CYA send another eliminator to remove him? If that Penelope woman was gone and Hartland reinstated, there was a fair chance they would. He needed time to think and, now Sinclair had at last appeared to have tied a knot in his overactive tongue, Collinson attempted to collect his thoughts and formulate a plan.

"Did I mention I was married once? Well, not officially as in a jaunt up the aisle, but as good as." Pinkie glanced at Collinson, waiting for him to reply. When his new buddy appeared not to be forthcoming, he continued.

"Yeah, t'rrific lass. Well, she was, but she done a flit with some stuck-up Squadron Leader in the RAF. I mean, the RAF! Bunch of poofters zipping about the skies in their flying machines. That's not facing the enemy, is it? Oh, no, they're not knee-deep in shit in the trenches, are they? Whilst they ponce around in the air, us lot are taking flak, trying to avoid ringworm and the rats, not to mention trench foot. Suffered with my feet all my life. In fact, they're that bad, I'm a little surprised I got through my Special Forces training. Still, my old captain reckoned I was one of the best. He reckoned I was that good, he always made sure I was never near him. You know, him leading one set of lads and me the other. I could have been an officer. I was good enough, you know."

"Jesus."

"You ever thought about becoming an officer? No, probably not. Not in the poncy Royal Engineers. You lot are as bad as the RAF. Wielding your spanners, mucking about building pontoon bridges for us, proper soldiers, to hot-foot across and tackle the enemy. Well, apart from those Bomb Disposal boys.

Now, I have to hand it to them boys. Even though they're part of your lot, that's a hell of a job."

Pinkie paused. However, after a few seconds, when it appeared Collinson harboured no thoughts about joining in with the conversation, he felt compelled to fill the void.

"Hey, did I ever tell you about that lad who lost his head in Derry when trying to disarm a car bomb?"

"No! As we've only just met, that's damn unlikely, ain't it? Despite the fact for the last two hours you've drivelled on about total crap, I think I might remember some boring, pointless shite you regurgitated regarding your exploits in Northern Ireland."

"Fair play."

"Just shut the frig up."

"Well, I've kinda started the story now, so I'll just finish this little anecdote. Then I'll have a ciggy and take a breather. Now, was that in '73 or '74? Hmmm, nah, can't remember. But anyway, the silly sod popped the bonnet, and boom!" Pinkie threw his hands in the air before allowing them to slap down on the steering wheel. "Course, the blast resulted in decapitating the silly sod, causing his bonce to fly off."

"Decapitation tends to do that."

"You're not wrong, Staff Sergeant of the poncy Royal Engineers. It flew right across the playing fields, it did. Hit for six. Apparently, landed in some fella's greenhouse. Course, he wasn't too chuffed on account that the lad's head snapped a few of his prize tomato plants. Hey, you in to gardening? No, guess not. I only got me a shitty flat, but I'm partial to a few window boxes and a nice spread of geraniums—"

"Sergeant Sinclair. Shut your damn gob. Or help me, God, I will shut it for you. Permanently."

"I get it. You're a bit tetchy about the whole situation. That's understandable. We are, what you might say, in a bit of a tight spot."

"Jesus, man. What's the matter with you? Can't you stop? Are you ill or something? Is there a medical condition that makes you like this?" Collinson swivelled around in his seat and pushed his face towards Pinkie, holding up his hand and almost pinching his forefinger and thumb together. Pinkie shifted his head back and glanced at Collinson's fingers. "Can you imagine, for one tiny, minuscule nanosecond, what it's like having to listen to the torrent of crap that comes out of that stinking gob of yours?"

"Fair play. No. As I said, my old mum, God bless her soul, reckoned I could, on the odd occasion, allow my mouth to run away with itself. Also, my captain—"

"See?" interrupted Collinson. "That's my frigging point. All that was required from my question was a yes or no answer, but you had to conjure up a whole frigging sentence!"

"Sarge."

"I should just kill you, as I've been instructed."

"Ah, no, come on, Sarge, there's no need for any unpleasantness. Really, I thought we were getting on like a house on fire. Kindred spirits. The three amigos."

"Sergeants three."

"Exactly."

Collinson pulled away from Pinkie, flopping back in his seat before rubbing his palms over his face. As he halted that action mid-rub, through his splayed fingers, his eyes settled on the glovebox.

"No, Sergeant Sinclair, we're not getting along like a house on fire. Not to put too fine a point on it, but you're right royally pissing me off."

"Fair play. You know, you're not the first to say that to me. Down the local boozer, not that I frequented it much, but the landlord, nasty thug, used to say, 'Pinkie, shut it or I'll crown you'. I mean, not a pleasant thing to say to a lonely chap in his seventies just trying to enjoy half a pint and a chinwag—"

"Why do they call you Pinkie?"

Sinclair raised his right hand. "On account, I lost my little finger."

"Oh. How come?"

Pinkie shifted in his seat to face Collinson. "That's another story for another day, my friend."

Collinson detected a significant shift in Pinkie's tone. That one line, delivered with malice and undertones of threat, suggested Pinkie had also been running through options while allowing his gob to pour out that inane drivel for the last half hour. Plus, he considered it somewhat surprising that the man, who couldn't help himself when given the opportunity to run his mouth off, had chosen to hold back that particular story for another day. Throughout his service career, Collinson had experienced enough tricky situations to suggest he knew when to act.

However, whether due to being out of practice or being lulled into a false sense of security, this time, he was too slow.

Pinkie walloped his arm across Collinson's throat, effectively pinning the man into his seat, simultaneously flipping open the glovebox before snatching up his gun. Within a split second, Collinson felt the barrel embedded in his abdomen. The feral wildness in Pinkie's eyes suggested he wouldn't hesitate to pull the trigger.

"I guess that other day has arrived. Let me tell you a story. Now, are we sitting comfortably, Staff Sergeant Collinson of the poncy Royal Engineers?"

Collinson didn't move, not even a twitch of his facial muscles.

"Good. I lost my finger in a bar brawl some years back. This tosser bit it off, right knob he was too, so I forced my severed digit down his throat and gently persuaded the git to choke to his death. Too many idiots have underestimated me, all of whom have learnt the hard way and are now helping fertilise the planet. How many? I silently hear you ask. Well, Staff Sergeant, I've kinda lost count." Pinkie forced the barrel a few more millimetres into Collinson's gut when detecting the man attempt to shift his body. "Don't even think about it, tosser. Ever since we took a trip over here to this Stone bloke's office, you've been eyeing up that glovebox."

Collinson knew the angle of the gun would send the slug through his heart, probably rip a hole in his spinal cord and end up embedded in the seat. If he could knock Pinkie's hand, he would still take an excruciatingly painful shot to the lower intestines. But, and he considered it a bloody big but, if he got lucky and the slug missed his liver, he might survive. For sure, inaction was only going to lead to his imminent death.

"Now, despite what that RSM with the Glasgow smile reckons, we both know that us sort complete our missions. We obey orders without question or hesitation. You, Staff Sergeant Collinson of the poncy Royal Engineers, fully intend to do your duty and eliminate me as instructed. Whether that be this afternoon or this evening when that lassie has me in a compromising position whilst I take in a bit of *Citizen Smith* on the telly, who knows?"

"Perhaps we could come to some arrangement?" Collinson inched his left hand up, attempting to close in on Pinkie's gun hand. "Harris may have made a valid point, you know. As you said, we don't want to get too hasty."

"Oh, so now you want to be all friendly like. What happened to telling me to shove a sock in it? Changed your tune, haven't we, Staff Sergeant of the poncy Royal Engineers?"

Collinson whipped his left hand up and shifted his torso, simultaneously raising his right elbow to connect with Pinkie's jaw. Before Pinkie could react, he'd wrapped his left hand around the gun and twisted the business end away from its position of being firmly embedded in his stomach.

As both men tussled for control of the weapon, in the ensuing melee, a shot rang out.

35

Dead Men Are Dangerous

"You do like your Dolly songs, don't you?" I quipped, more through nervous energy rather than portraying any confidence in my quivering timbre.

"I do."

"Well, what's the state of play, then? You are, or you're not planning on killing me and Jayne?"

"Good question, Frank. I would like to try to avoid that scenario. However, that depends on what you two decide." Frank and I exchanged a glance as he paused. "See, me and the lads, as I said, were chatting. We think we should take control of the situation."

"Do you want to elaborate?" I asked, raising a quizzical eyebrow.

"Sure. The CYA has demanded that you two be expunged, along with Sinclair and Collinson—"

"Yes! You said as much."

"Okay, take it easy. You ain't half a feisty one."

"Excuse me!" I belligerently barked, feeling Frank curl his fingers on my shoulder, presumably encouraging me to temper my frustration. Fair point, the man still had our lives in his hands.

"I'm not sure whether I mentioned this, but I shouldn't be here either."

"Err ... I thought you'd come to exterminate everyone!" I threw my hands up, animatedly waving at nothing in particular but feeling the need to expel some pent-up energy and focus on trying not to cry. "That ruddy git, Hartland, sent you to kill us, did he not?"

"Not exactly. See, my best buddy in the Paras, John Bamford, who was held on a retainer with the CYA, was sent to clean up the mess. I just piggybacked a ride. Course, neither of us actually believed in this time-travel crap. So, when Jonny got the call, he came scooting around my gaff to see what I made of it all. As I'm sure you can imagine, the possibility that he was about to restart his life from the age of thirty-one had my mate almost frothing at the mouth. And that's despite him suspecting that travelling through time on the London Eye was a load of bollocks."

"Yes, I know that feeling," I muttered, my comment hardly halting Kenny's flow.

"Course, when he came around banging on my door to tell me about the CYA, I thought he must have had a heavy night on the sherbets. But when I realised my old mucker was as dry as an alchie at AA's annual dinner and dance, it got me thinking ... what if? So, like the good mate of nearly forty years that I am, I said I'd go with him to the Wheel and keep watch in case there's any funny business, like. Now, okay, he was a mate, and I'm not proud of what I've done. However, needs must, as someone once said. Utrinque Paratus—"

"Ready for anything," I muttered.

"Oh, you know our regiment's motto, then?"

"No, I'm a schoolteacher."

"Course," he chortled. "Is it Latin? I never really bothered to find out."

"So, you accompanied this Bamford bloke on the Wheel?" Frank threw in. Presumably, like me, keen to move Kenny along and not get into the finer points of the ancient Roman language.

"I did. Course, I wasn't supposed to."

"Where is this Bamford chap now, then? You've only mentioned the other two. And where are they?"

"Good question, Frank. Collinson and Sinclair are in the car park, waiting for me." Kenny gesticulated with an outstretched arm at the Venetian blinds, indicating the car park on the other side. "Unfortunately, it appears my old mate didn't make it."

"Evaporated?"

"I think that's the term. Course, I looked him up when I got here. To say the conversation was a tad on the strange side is an understatement. I made the mistake of mentioning the CYA, the Wheel, the future, and he had absolutely no idea what I was rabbiting on about. He reckoned I needed to see a medic, saying I'd finally lost my marbles."

"Yes, I can imagine. Where is he now, then?"

"That doesn't matter. John Bamford is the original man, not a time-traveller from the future. Course, he's still in the Paras, whereas I left in the winter of '78. Which, oddly, is now less than a year ago. Weird this time-travel, ain't it? Anyway, after his leave, Jonny will be returning to Northern Ireland, so he won't get in the way."

"And what do you mean by take control of the situation?"

Kenny shifted his posture, leaning forward and lowering his leg with the gun strapped to his ankle. Alf growled, causing the man opposite me to glance down and involuntarily cover his privates with his hand. Fair enough, once bitten, twice shy, as they say.

"I assume you both want to live?"

Frank and I didn't answer. A stupid question, if ever there was one, that didn't warrant answering. Unless you were hellbent on suicide, which neither of us gave the impression we were, it was plainly obvious we wanted to live. Anyway, for starters, we had four daughters in the pipeline waiting to be born.

"Yes, course you do," he chuckled. "Well, as it happens, so do I, as do those two out there," Kenny nodded at the blinds and rubbed his hands together. "So, we have to change the story. From the intel I gleaned from good old Jonny on the Wheel, David Bolton must stay alive—"

"And my wife, Jemma. Apparently, she's carrying my child."

"She is. However, I figure if we can manage to do what that Barbara Denton was sent to do in the first place, which, as I understand it from what Jonny was saying, is to keep David Bolton alive, then, whatever that action changes in the future, will be achieved. Now, Jonny stated part of his mission was to ensure Sinclair was removed from the picture—"

"Because he died with David Bolton in Fairfield Woods?" I interjected.

"I believe that's the case. Jonny was dispatched to ensure that happens. Also, tasked with bumping off Collinson and you two at the same time, just to keep things tidy."

"Tidy!"

"Turn of phrase. Please don't take it personally."

"Tidy is when you do a spot of hoovering, flick the duster around, and straighten the stack of magazines on the coffee table, not some assassin wielding a gun and sticking bullets in people's heads. Frank's and mine, not to put too fine a point on things."

"Alright. Christ, feisty or what?"

"Err ... do you mind? I won't be spoken to like that. Not by you, that's for certain."

"Jayne," hissed Frank.

Kenny held his hand aloft. "No offence meant. Now look, them two idiots out there think I'm working with them, and they don't know I'm not supposed to be here. However, I suggest we work as a team." He paused to wave his hand between the three of us while grinning, causing his scar to curl and shine. "We save your wife, Jemma Stone and, by association, your unborn son, then eliminate Sinclair. I obviously haven't broached that subject with Collinson as of yet, but I'll get him on my own and formulate a plan. Anyway, now I've met Sinclair, I really think the world is a far better place without the man. Then, and only then, we can all crack on with our lives."

My jaw dropped.

"What d'you say? Sounds like a plan, eh? I mean, if we get rid of Sinclair as my old mucker Jonny was supposed to, I really can't see the need for the CYA to send anyone else. David Bolton lives, Sinclair is dead, and all is good. And, according to you, the poxy government in the future will avoid being murdered at the hands of some terror organisation. Sounds like a winner to me."

"Mr Harris." Frank raised his free hand and pointed at the grinning man. "Are you actually suggesting we assist you in the act of murder?"

"I am. Hey, but don't worry. I'll be doing the actual killing."

"Oh, well, that's alright, then," Frank replied with more than a hint of sarcasm.

Akin to some of the more reticent students I taught, I tentatively raised my hand.

"Yes, Miss Hart."

"Why don't you do this without us? Why are you involving Frank and me?"

"Ah, good question. You see, I don't know all the facts. Jonny has always had a gob on him like the Blackwall Tunnel, so getting him to talk wasn't difficult, but time was limited. Now, I can rid the world of that gobshite Sinclair, but I'm not up to speed on David Bolton. As Jonny said, all operations are strictly on a need-to-know basis, and the info he had on that side of the operation was limited. I'll need your knowledge to ensure the David Bolton side of the operation is achieved."

"We ensure the CYA gets the result they want, and you think they will leave us alone?"

"Exactly. Simples, to quote a certain Russian meerkat."

"Frank! Sorry, boss, but there's something going on in the car park," Alison blustered as she barrelled through the door. "Two men in a motor are having some kind of fight. Shall I call the police?"

"Shit!" hissed Kenny, leaping from his seat before hot-footing towards the window and snapping down a run of metal slats of the Venetian blind to peer out to the car park.

Frank and I followed suit, all now standing in a line holding down the blind's slats. Never one to miss out, Alf hopped up on his hind legs and flopped his jaw on a few slats. The sound produced by his enthusiastic clamber to witness the events play out significantly out-trumped the human efforts and could easily rival any percussion ensemble. The clanging blind acting as the cymbals and his wagging tail thumping the desk behind mimicking the drum section.

"Boss?"

"What are we supposed to be looking at?"

I'd parked my VW Beetle next to Frank's Pontiac Firebird. I presumed the yellow Mini – the sort used in the *Italian Job* and not to be confused with the BMW-produced twenty-first-century version – to belong to Alison. The back window sticker, *'When I grow up I want to be a Rolls Royce'*, and the pink, fluffy steering-wheel cover didn't suggest it to be the car of choice of a roughneck-army-type-cum-trained assassin. That said, when aided by Professor Simon Peach's computer knowledge and the bankrolling support of Mr Bridger, Charlie Croker and his thieving gang tore up the streets of Turin in similar cars. So, when you have an iconic British actor and a '70s slapstick comedian not devoid of numerous double entendres, plus one of our most celebrated playwrights cast in the same movie, I guess anything was possible.

Perhaps three time-travelling mercenary killers were cruising around Fairfield in a yellow Mini? However, although I could only just spot the rear of the vehicle, the unmistakable shape of

Inspector Morse's car appeared to be parked on the other side near the reception entrance.

Kenny scooted out of Frank's office, leaving Frank, me, and Alfie-Boy peering through the blinds and Alison still waiting for an answer.

Whether the bang that followed Kenny's exit was caused by a car backfiring, something that happened in the movies, but I never really knew if that was actually a thing, kids were playing with fireworks or cap guns in the car park, or someone had discharged their weapon, the exchanged glances between the three of us and Alf's whimper suggested all was not well.

"What the hell was that?" Frank quizzed. "That sounded like gunfire."

"Boss, what's happening? I think I'd better call the police?"

"Sit down and shut up," Kenny's unequivocal, acerbic tone as he reappeared in the doorway caused Frank and me to swivel around, allowing the blinds to snap back into position.

Alison screamed.

I froze.

Frank sensibly followed my lead.

Alf, presuming he'd decided that caution was the better part of valour, to paraphrase Falstaff's quote in King Henry the Fourth Part One – can't you just tell I'm a schoolteacher, eh? – and assuming testicle chewing wasn't a safe activity to embark upon with a man waving a shooter, ducked under the desk and swished his tail under his bottom for safekeeping.

Kenny, holding a gun at arm's length, aimed at Alison's head, waited for a second whilst Alison finished her anguished cry.

"I said, sit down. No one's calling the police. We are all going to stay calm." By way of gesticulating with his gun, Kenny indicated we should join Alison on the other side of the desk. "So, hear me right. Unless any of you fancy a neat round hole in your foreheads, I suggest you stay calm and don't move."

Kenny, still with his pistol aimed in our direction, glanced back down the corridor towards the front entrance, presumably to take in the view of whatever was occurring in the car park. While holding that position, he swivelled his head back and forth to ensure the three of us complied with his request.

"Well?" Frank pushed him.

"Jesus," he muttered before turning to face Frank, his gun arm lowering.

"Did someone just shoot someone?" Alison asked before chewing her bottom lip. The gusto and fervour employed suggested blood would soon appear.

"Yup," Kenny huffed. "The trouble is, I don't know who shot who."

In my peripheral vision, through the bent blind slats, I spotted the Red Jag shoot out of the car park, kicking up gravel and dust in its wake.

"Looks like whoever fired the shot didn't want to hang around."

"What's the building opposite?"

"What does that matter?" Frank fired back.

"It matters because, despite one of those two idiots discharging their weapon in that car, gunshot can be heard from quite a distance."

"Oh ... I'm not sure. It used to be some lock-up storage place. It's been empty ... well, I can't say for how long because I've only been here a week, and my younger self can't quite remember."

"So there's no one there, then?"

"I doubt it."

"Boss, what d'you mean you've only been here a week?" Alison asked, her voice faltering as she flitted nervous glances between Frank and Kenny's lowered gun arm.

Frank grimaced at me. I just shrugged back. Although coming clean about time-travel to Alison wasn't part of the plan, at least it might offer a distraction.

"Boss?"

"Alison, you trust me, yeah?"

"Err ... sure, Boss, but—"

"Okay, so please, just run with me on this one."

"Run where? Frank, this bloke's got a gun, and I can't run anywhere in these heels."

"No, I mean, trust me."

"Oh, why didn't you just say that? Blimey, what's the matter with everyone today? And him, scar face with the gun, who the hell is he?" she shrieked.

"Lassie, calm yourself. Now, you remember that TV show *Callan?*"

"Callan?"

"Yeah, David Callan, played by Edward Woodwood on the telly. That's from this era, isn't it?" Kenny raised his hands in a questioning style at Frank and me. The fact that hand action also raised his gun caused us all to jump and Alfie-Boy to offer another whimper from his hidey-hole.

"Go with Bodie and Doyle or Steed and Gambit. They're slightly more on trend," Frank suggested.

"Oh, okay. I've only been back a couple of days, and it's difficult to remember what was on the telly in the '70s."

Alison knitted her caterpillars.

"So, lassie, think of me as the kind of bloke who sorts out problems, like on the telly shows Frank mentioned. I'm the good guy," he said, employing that scar-curling grin whilst tapping the gun on his chest.

"You pointed a gun at my head."

"Yeah, sorry about that, lass. Just had to make sure no one makes a mistake. The last thing I, Frank or Mrs Stone here need is police involvement."

"Why? And this is Miss Smart, Hart, not Mrs Stone."

"Yeah, I know. But she will be Mrs Stone, though."

"Boss?" Alison's caterpillars performed a triple salchow. "I don't understand. And why are we not calling the police?"

Kenny shot Frank a look.

"Alison … it's uh—"

"Complicated," I butted in.

"Complicated? Today, I discover you two are having an affair. Then this bloke turns up waving a gun around, and then there's this gunfight in the car park. Not to mention that everyone is talking funny, and your dog seems to be able to understand what you're saying. The world's gone nuts!"

"Yeah, I can see how that might seem that way," Kenny chuckled before raising an eyebrow at Frank and me. "Can your farting dog understand what we're saying, then?"

"I think he can."

"And who exactly were the two men fighting in the car park and shooting at each other?" Alison asked, not directing her question at anyone in particular, just throwing it out there.

"They, lassie, are the baddies. As I said, I'm the good guy."

Alf, commando style, crept out from the cover of my future husband's desk, turned his doe eyes up to me, dipped his head, and flattened his ears. Abhorrent flatulence, burping, and his unkempt way about him aside, Alf was fast becoming a vital asset in my new life. He appeared to know things that others didn't. That action suggested he wasn't altogether in agreement with the Dolly-loving Kenny.

Frank and I exchanged a knowing glance, suggesting to each other that perhaps Kenny wasn't on the right side of the equation.

36

Leatherface

"You! You, there. Are you the manager?" Susan Chalk, clutching her handbag and the carrier bag in her right hand, stepped sideways and blocked the man's advance. "I'm talking to you. At the very least, you should have the decency to respond. I tell you, politeness and good manners cost nothing. Nothing, d'you hear?"

The thirty-year-old downtrodden man, head bowed, traipsing towards the exit with his anorak folded over his arm, halted and took a step back from the advancing woman. Going by her bluster and bellicose stance along with all that sabre-rattling, well, a Freshcom's carrier bag, she appeared ready to vent her spleen.

This was all he needed. A shitty end to a shitty day, in a shitty week, of this shitty month. Not to put a too finer point on it, life was totally shite.

"Are you stupid? What's the matter with you?"

"No, madam. I've just finished work. If you require some assistance, then the staff in the kiosk will be more than happy to help you."

"I'm not queuing up there with all those filthy smokers! I want to speak to the manager. Who I presumed you to be." Susan waved her hand up and down, indicating his suit and smart shoes. "I take it you work here?" she sneered, flaring her nostrils as if faced with something even more unpleasant than the contents of her carrier bag.

With a hearty sigh, David fumbled in his pocket before showing the belligerent woman his name badge. A flimsy plastic item with his name Dymo-taped upon it.

Mr Bolton

Deputy Branch Manager

Freshcom's Supermarkets

"Yes, so you do work here, I see. Now, young man, where's the manager?"

"The manager is on his day off today."

"Day off! How can the manager have a day off? No wonder this damn shop is going to pot. My mother used to shop here, y'know. Well, not this awful self-service place, but back in the day when Freshcom used to be in the High Street and they provided proper counter service to its customers. A time, I might add, when this failing company that now thinks it's acceptable to palm off shoddy produce to customers …" she paused to animatedly wave the carrier bag and pull a gurning face. "Shoddy, rotten produce at extortionate prices, I might add …" Susan halted her rant, still holding the bag aloft. "Oh, you've made me lose my train of thought."

"Madam, you were—"

"And who on earth are you addressing as madam?" she shrilled, adding bug eyes to her repertoire of expressions of displeasure. "I don't run a house of ill repute. I am Mrs Chalk, not madam. D'you hear?"

"I'm sorry, I—"

"And that man there," she shot her right arm out to her left, indicating a shortish man in his sixties sporting a Bobby Charlton-styled comb-over. Said hairstyle, now standing erect and swaying rhythmically like an erotic dancer performing the rumba with the gentle breeze which flowed through the open front door. Clearly embarrassed by his wife's performance, with his hands clasped behind his back, the poor man gave the impression that he'd rather be pulling his fingernails out with a rusty pair of pliers than standing at the entrance of a supermarket. "That man is Mr Chalk, secretary of the Eaton Residents' Association, no less."

"Yes, Mrs Chalk."

"And, as I was saying, before you rudely interrupted me. Once upon a time, this company afforded customers courtesy and respect. Not any more, it seems."

Although Dave harboured thoughts of punching her square in the face and, when she was down, kicking her to death before gleefully jumping up and down on her prone body to ensure all two-hundred and six bones snapped at least once, he offered his best, deputy-branch-manager-how-can-I-be-of-assistance-madam smile.

Why had he chosen a career in a supermarket?

He pathologically detested customers.

So much so that with disturbing regularity he imagined running amok through the shop wielding a meat cleaver and cheese wire, indiscriminately hacking off customers' limbs before garrotting them.

Dave's obsession with horror films had grown since becoming mesmerised by Norman Bates's antics in *Psycho*, which he'd watched on his parents' rented television ten years ago. Although not gory, it seemed real compared to the somewhat tame vampire *Hammer House of Horror* films he was used to watching. Rather sadly, on his own at the back of the auditorium, he'd managed to grab a viewing of *The Texas Chainsaw Massacre* before the Board of Control banned it soon after its release in a few London theatres.

Although imagining himself enacting the deranged actions of the film's main character were private thoughts, on a number of occasions – and while we are on the subject, Dave thought far too many – Babs, his wife, had said that his anger and mood swings were frightening.

Anyway, whatever. A supermarket career. So, despite the above issues regarding wanting to gruesomely murder those 'customers who paid his wages', the salary was above average for a middle management role, and the pension was regarded as industry-leading. Bonuses and staff voucher schemes for discounted food helped with family finances. Not to mention the subsidised canteen facilities and the Staff Association discounted trips to Great Yarmouth each summer. Also, promotions were on the cards as long as you were prepared to knuckle down, work hard, and brown-nose senior management. And, not forgetting, lots of pretty till girls who looked up to him. Some even batted their eyelids. Alright, just one.

He probably shouldn't have added the last point to that list based on his current circumstances. Because that girl hadn't minded a fumble in the cash office, and they'd been caught in the act with his hands where they really shouldn't have been, Dave was now living back at his mother's and his wife flatly refused to allow access to see his daughter and was even threatening divorce proceedings.

Although living back in his teenage bedroom, still with shelves littered with Airfix models in various states of collapse, Plasticine moulded into indeterminate shapes and colours, tatty copies of *Famous Five* books intermingled with his school mathematical tables books that listed a plethora of calculations regarding cosines, his *Adventures for Boys* annuals, a heap of *Eagle* comics and a hardback copy of short stories about pirates, Mother had steadfastly sided with his wife.

Fair enough.

His father kept his head down, seemingly permanently engrossed in his newspaper.

Fair enough, too.

See, the trouble was, although feeling sorry for himself, that voice in his head repeatedly advised him that he was a complete idiot. Despite numerous attempts to counter that statement, Dave knew it to be an accurate and honest assessment of his character. The disdainful scowl Mrs Chalk afforded him is how his rational mind viewed himself.

A prat of the highest order.

"Well, what are you going to do about it?"

"About what, mad … err … Mrs Chalk?"

"This!" She thrust the bag to Dave's chest. "The rotten produce that your store believes is acceptable to display on your shelves. I tell you, I suspect the Corbyn family will be turning in their graves. I'm quite sure they couldn't have imagined it would come to this when they started the company all those years ago. My neighbour had to return rotten fish only yesterday, and now I'm here today. I purchased this for Mr Chalk's supper, and just look at it!"

Dave peeked into the bag, regretting said action and pulling his head away when assaulted by the stench.

"Exactly! Rotten meat. Unless I can receive satisfactory compensation and an apology, I will be contacting Trading Standards. Let's see what they have to say about it, shall we?"

"Be my guest." Dave offered the bag back to a stunned Mrs Chalk.

"Sorry?"

"I said if you want to go to Trading Standards, be my guest."

"You can't say—"

"Mrs Chalk, I'm happy to deal with your complaint, even though I've already finished for the day."

No, he wasn't. He wanted to kill the curmudgeonly cow. Strangle Mrs Chalk whilst revelling in the sound of her choking anguish. Perhaps force the husband to watch, as well. Presumably, going by the two minutes he'd already endured of her less-than-scintillating company, that act would be doing the husband a favour. Dave allowed a smirk to creep into his mind before continuing.

"However, I can't help you if you're throwing around threats of Trading Standards. Of course, that is your right, but I'm afraid I will have to end the conversation there. Although that chicken is clearly off—"

"Obviously! What about my husband's supper? I was planning coq au vin. It's his—"

"And if you would like me to assist you, then can we please stop throwing around threats regarding Trading Standards?"

"Oh. I demand a refund, at the very least. What about compensation? There's the cost of the petrol to get here? Mr Chalk drives a modern car, but four-star is still nearly a pound a gallon these days."

"I'm sure I can help with that."

"And what about the blancmange I had to throw? The stench in the fridge tainted Mr Chalk's favourite pudding."

"And the blancmange, Mrs Chalk."

"I had to throw the mushrooms in the bin, too."

"And the mushrooms. Is that it?" *"Anything else you'd like to try and rinse out of me, you haggard old battleaxe?"*

As Mrs Chalk thought for a moment, and based on the fact that she seemed calm, he assumed the second part of his earlier statement mustn't have been said out loud.

"Well, yes, I suppose so. I don't think you've apologised, though." She wagged an accusing finger, raising her eyebrow at him.

Dave beckoned over a supervisor before offering Mrs Chalk his best hate grin. "Please accept our sincere apologies, Mrs Chalk." After proffering a contemptuous lip curl at the woman, he turned to address the supervisor. "Lucy, please can you refund Mrs Chalk two whole pounds and fifty pence? And ask the boys in the meat room to get rid of this." Dave held out the stinking bag like one of his daughter's nappies.

"Oh, very kind. Thank you." Mrs Chalk flared her nostrils and offered a supercilious 'I've won' grin.

"You're welcome, Mrs Chalk. Good day to you." Dave pushed past, leaving the woman in Lucy's capable hands. "You poor bastard," he mumbled as he brushed past her husband, who appeared to be on the losing side when embroiled in a battle with the breeze when attempting to control his hair.

Dave afforded himself a smug grin regarding his performance when dealing with that woman and, although he was due back at work early in the morning, he decided copious amounts of beer in the local was in order. He just hoped Frank, his best mate, whom he'd argued with last week, wouldn't be there to sully his mood even further.

"Excuse me, sir."

Dave checked his stride and swivelled around to come face to face with a man of similar age, presumably another complainer. However, the cut of his jib didn't suggest he intended to raise a complaint regarding a ruined coq au vin supper.

"Sorry, can I help?" Jesus, how hard was it just to get out of work and away from sodding customers? If this bloke was about to launch into some boring protracted complaint about rancid meat, Dave feared he *would* strangle him.

"It's David Bolton, isn't it?"

"Sorry? Do I know you?"

"No, mate. I can't say I've ever had the pleasure. But knowing the type of bloke you are, I'd say I've dodged a bullet in that respect."

37

2015

Lady Chatterley

"Sorry, old chap, but a spot of bad news, I'm afraid. Can't be helped, as I'm sure you understand."

Frank, still feeling groggy from the effects of whatever these bastards had injected into him after exiting pod thirteen of the London Eye less than an hour ago, pulled at the restraints that clamped his wrists together behind his back.

"Frank, come on. Stop struggling. You're not going to wriggle free from a set of cable ties. Sit still, relax and let's talk options."

"You bastard."

Hartland pursed his lips and nodded before glancing up as Johnson entered the office and closed the door.

"I've been advised that Bamford travelled a few moments ago, sir. I've asked Whitman to join us as soon as she has any updates for us."

"No hitches? Bamford's clear on what is required?"

"He is, sir. He was late arriving because he nipped in to see a friend on the way, but he's gone now."

"A friend? He didn't? You don't—"

"No, sir. He just said he popped in to see a friend, nothing else."

"At half one in the morning?"

"Just a goodbye, I suspect. These chaps only get thirty minute's notice, so I presume he wanted to see an acquaintance before travelling."

"Hmmm."

"As I said, Bamford travelled via the Eye not ten minutes ago."

"I don't want any more foul-ups tonight."

"Sir, he's a reliable asset. Bamford won't have said anything he shouldn't. He's back in 1979, getting on with the task. Whitman will have preliminary data within a few minutes, and I'm sure everything will be just fine. Of course, we were a little light in personnel regarding the Transportation team due to Captain Pryor following through on his orders to eradicate those who failed us earlier."

"Hmmm. Had to be done, I'm afraid. Still, you say there were no hitches. Nothing to concern ourselves with?"

"No, sir."

"Good."

Both men nodded to each other, non-verbally confirming what they knew. Bamford had been sent to ensure Frank – that's the Frank still tied to the chair in front of the desk – along with his wife, Jayne, saved David Bolton. Then, the ex-Paras man would dispose of them, along with Sinclair and Collinson. Assuming the operation was already a success and thus consigned to the history of thirty-six years in the past, the Frank

Stone, who continued to fire death stares at Hartland, would already be dead. The poor chap would now be dumped in some unmarked shallow grave after Bamford put a nine-millimetre slug between his eyes.

Of course, Frank still lived and breathed while in the clutches of the CYA here in 2015. However, were they to let him go, which Hartland most certainly had no intention of doing, the poor man would instantly evaporate because he no longer existed.

A complex situation which mere mortals couldn't possibly understand or grasp the finer points of the time-bending skills at the CYA's disposal. As Commander-in-Chief, Hartland's job was to ensure no one ever did.

"Now, listen up, Frank. We don't have long. I suspect in a few minutes, Johnson's team will inform me that our operation is a complete success. However, that will quickly unravel if we don't send you back to 1979 again. You will be in pod thirteen, whizzing back to 1979 in a jiffy. That's the spot of bad news I mentioned."

"You sent my wife back there a bloody hour ago, you bastard."

"Yes," Hartland elongated that one syllable whilst rolling around the lit end of his cigarette in the glass ashtray, carefully forming a glowing point. "I'm sorry about that. Quite a disagreeable situation." He jabbed his cigarette towards Frank. "I can assure you heads have rolled for that unfortunate debacle." After taking a hearty drag on his cigarette, allowing a vampiric grin to form as the smoke drifted through his clenched teeth, Hartland continued with a chipper lilt to his tone. "Anyway, Frank. Never mind, eh? All's well that ends well," he chortled.

"What the frig d'you mean? All's well that ends well! My wife has been sent back to the bloody seventies and I'm still here."

"Yes, but you're also there in 1979 with your lovely wife. Come on, Frank, don't act the simpleton. Time-travel is at play. You're in both places at once. Don't you see?"

"Oh."

Frank bowed his head and closed his eyes in an attempt to defuzz his confuddled brain. Since the heartbreak of discovering his wife had disappeared, and he was still in 2015, Frank had spent most of the last half hour in a state of delirium. Apart from the obvious reason for his anguish, Frank's confused grasp of the situation had been aided and abetted by the actions of several operatives who'd pinned him to the floor of the pod before administering a tranquillizer. Then, about thirty minutes ago, he came to when locked in one of their containment suites.

"Frank, have you dozed off, old chap?"

Frank raised his head, slowly shaking it from side to side.

"Oh, no, look, he's awake," chuckled Hartland, raising an eyebrow at Johnson.

"Where is Jayne?"

"1979, my good fellow. I would imagine enjoying her newly discovered youthful body along with discovering her younger, fitter husband again. You, at the age of thirty. Quite a thing, eh? Your wife is a right bobby-dazzler, a real enchantress, you could say. I wouldn't mind betting she must have been quite something in her day."

Frank knitted his brows whilst glowering back at The Hooded Claw, who appeared to be enjoying himself.

"Well, you know," Hartland waved his cigarette in the air, an action he employed to suggest he wanted to bat away his earlier comment that Frank appeared to have misconstrued. "I'm not saying your lovely wife isn't quite something now, just that she will be in her twenties again if you see what I mean?"

"Where is she? Where is Jayne right now, as in 2015?"

"Oh, I see your point. Jayne's absolutely fine, my good man. Our preliminary data suggests that her life was pretty similar to her first, so there's no need to worry."

Johnson shot Hartland a look, an action that Frank picked up on.

"Something's happened, hasn't it? You're not being straight with me," Frank fired back, shooting looks between the two men, back and forth when spotting Johnson appear somewhat sheepish.

"Frank, come on, man. All is fine, as—"

"No! I saw that look Johnson just gave you. You're lying, you bastard."

Hartland aggressively attempted to stub out his cigarette, leaving the smouldering butt before turning to Johnson, who either felt a little hot and bothered due to the stuffy air in the glass-walled office or suffered from hot flushes when a bollocking loomed. When turning to face Frank, keeping him pinned to his chair with those piercing grey eyes, Hartland addressed his Data Director.

"Johnson, do you play cards?"

"Sir?"

"Cards. Playing cards. Diamonds, hearts, clubs, and spades. Most people understand what is meant by the term playing cards."

"Err—"

"So, you like the odd hand of canasta, a spot of bridge, a game of gin rummy with your grandmother, or cribbage at the local with the old boys whilst swigging down half a mild?"

"Err ... no, sir."

"No, thought not. I suggest you avoid poker. You'll lose the damn shirt on your back if you do!"

"Yes, sir. I'm dreadfully sorry, sir."

"You bastards—"

"You've already said that, Frank. Do you not have any other terms of endearment in your vocabulary that you could use to substitute for bastards? Change things up a bit, perhaps? Oh, but your wife *was* the schoolteacher, not you. Isn't that so?" Hartland allowed his famous death grin to form whilst his eyes belied the facial movement. A sickening smile which could turn a man to stone or, at the very least, cause him to piss himself.

Frank tugged at his restraints, grimacing as he felt the plastic cut into his wrists. "What's happened to Jayne? Tell me! What's happened? You ... you bastards!"

"Yes, that word again. Although, not totally inaccurate in my case. There's a bit of a dark secret in my family concerning my parentage. It's all hush-hush and somewhat embarrassing, really. My father liked to put it about, and Mother ... well, Mother, bless her, let's just say she enjoyed a close bond with the gardener—"

"Hartland, you ... you git—"

"Decent sort, you know. He and I apparently have similar hooded eyelids. The gardener, not my father, that is. Anyway, that's by the by."

Frank flared his nostrils, wriggling in an attempt to free himself.

"Alright, Frank, calm yourself, man. You'll do yourself an injury. Which must be avoided because you need to be in tip-top condition for your little excursion. Let's hope you actually travel this time." Hartland turned to Johnson. "Do we know why Frank didn't travel with his wife, yet?"

"No, I'm afraid not. I have a team working on that as we speak."

"Hmmm. It will be a sodding disaster if Frank remains on the Wheel or evaporates this time. We need him back in 1979."

"Screw you. Where's Jane?"

"Okay, I suppose it makes no odds now Johnson's all but given the game away. So, I'm sorry for this, old chap. I really am. I do like you, Frank, I always have, but your poor wife … oh," Hartland paused as he appeared lost in thought.

"What?" Frank hissed, the veins in his temples bulging. If he wasn't cable-tied to the chair, Frank considered he would have murdered Hartland by now.

"Well, actually, come to think of it, that lovely wife of yours isn't your wife."

"No, that can't be—"

"I'm afraid so. Sorry to be the bearer of bad news, but Jayne Hart died in an RTA in 1980. That's a road traffic accident. I do so detest acronyms, but that's the modern way. The proliferation of the damn stupid things seems quite the unstoppable force in today's society."

Frank hadn't heard the statement about acronyms; if he had, it hadn't registered. All the fight and pent-up anger fizzled away, dissipating into the ether, where it hooked up and entwined with the bluish smoke that steadily rose from the glass ashtray that held the middle ground between himself and The Hooded Claw.

"However, here's the good news …" The Commander-in-Chief paused to throw a look at Johnson, who nodded a response to indicate that he understood he needed to apply his best, non-existent, poker face before Hartland continued. "In a few minutes, you will be on the Wheel spinning your way back to 1979. So, after you sort out our little issue, you can ensure that rather delectable wife of yours avoids dying in said accident."

Whilst Frank rolled around Hartland's statement, a thirty-something woman sporting a florid complexion thrust open the door before grabbing the door frame to steady herself. Before stepping into the glass cube, she afforded herself a couple of deep breaths, either recovering from a particularly energetic Zumba session or in an attempt to calm herself before speaking.

"Come in, Whitman, why don't you? No need to knock," Hartland sarcastically growled.

"Oh, hell," muttered Johnson when clocking his senior analyst's anguish.

"You're a doom merchant, woman. D'you know that?" boomed Hartland. "Well, spit it out, woman."

"Sir. I just want to add a caveat to what I'm about to say. This is raw data, and I'll need a few more minutes to verify what my team has discovered."

Hartland and Johnson exchanged a look as Whitman took a deep breath again.

"Sir, it appears that Bamford didn't travel alone …"

"What the bloody hell do you mean, he didn't travel alone? You're telling me he took a sodding chaperone with him? His mother? Pet dog? The ruddy cleaning lady? Whitman, what the hell is going on?"

"Sir, it appears, due to the Transportation team being a little light with boots on the ground, so to speak, they couldn't man the platform. Basically, Bamford managed to sneak a friend into the pod who appears to have travelled with him."

Johnson hung his head.

Hartland bolted up from his chair, the force sending it scooting backwards on its castors, only coming to rest after its pinball-esque pinging off a few filing cabinets. The rage and pent-up anger that had earlier left Frank found a new home as it wormed its way into Hartland and caused the man to shake and turn a disturbing and presumably unhealthy shade of burgundy.

While the Commander-in-Chief's face raised the temperature in the room a degree or two, Johnson pushed Whitman for details.

"You'd better tell us what you have."

"Okay, so far, and as you know, this is all just from the first data run, but a man called Kenneth Harris travelled with Bamford. He is also ex-military—"

"One of ours?"

"No sir, not at all. He is on our list of potentials, the reserve list, if you like. However, as of yet, the HR team has not approached him about joining our retainer list. Data suggests the man to be untrustworthy, dangerous, a pathological liar, violent, unhinged, and generally what they call these days a real badass."

"Do we have any data on what this man—"

Johnson paused when the door nudged open and a hand shot through the gap, waving a single sheet of paper.

"Ma'am, you need to see this," squeaked a timid chap with his head bowed.

Whitman snatched the printed page from the man's grasp, allowing her colleague to scurry back to the sanctuary of his monitor screens and the perpetual rolling data they displayed.

"Well?"

"Oh ... my ... God."

"Whitman?" Johnson bulged his eyes at her.

"You're not going to believe what's happened."

38

1979

The Boop-Oop-a-Doop Girl

"Kenny, Mr Harris, whoever you are. My dog, Alfie-Boy, isn't convinced you're the good guy. I don't think you're being totally straight with us."

Kenny casually waved the gun around as he thought about my accusation, causing Alf to growl and the rest of us to make involuntary steps back and forth to keep out of the ever-changing line of fire. Without Kenny in the room, all three of us probably gave the appearance of performing an odd dance routine that could be some hybrid choreography combination of *Gangnam Style* and a Cossack dance similar to Boney M's *Rasputin*.

"Can you lot stand still?"

"Can you stop waving that gun around?" barked Frank in between a couple of exaggerated hops.

Kenny glanced down at the gun as if he'd forgotten it was in his hand.

"Mr Harris, please," I followed up, employing a similar tone to Frank.

"Alright. No funny business, though."

"No funny business," Frank confirmed with a nod and a placating hand gesture suggesting surrender.

"Err ... boss, d'you wanna tell me what the blue-blazes is going on?"

"Not really," Frank muttered, scrubbing his palms over his face.

"The short version, Alison, because I really don't think Frank and I have got the time or the will to bring you up to speed, a man was sent to kill Frank and me." I paused long enough to watch Alison's jaw drop; an unflattering look overused in cartoons and one Bob Hoskins perfected when spotting Jessica Rabbit on stage. However, as there was no Betty Boop around to close Alison's jaw for her, I left the poor woman in that state and continued. "So, the good news, that man is not here and probably will never be. Mr Harris here," I nodded at Kenny. "He's taken his place but is not planning on killing us." I turned to Kenny. "Correct?"

"Correct, love. I have no desire to kill you."

"Hmmm." I glanced down at Alf. "Alfie-Boy, you agree with Mr Harris's statement?"

Still holding his commando-styled crouched position, Alf peered up and licked his chops.

"Oh, good. That's a start. Why then, boy, did you not agree with Mr Harris's claim about being the good guy, then?"

Alf tipped his head sideways.

"Oh, closed questions. Sorry, I'll come back to that. But, Alfie-Boy, you'll need to explain yourself."

Alf licked his chops.

"So, Alison, as I was saying, this man, and Alf confirms, is not going to kill us."

"But—"

"Hang on, I'm still running through the short version of the story. The two men who were earlier fighting in the car park are potentially a whole different matter altogether. I believe one of them was here to save, help save, Jemma, and then maybe kill Frank if it all went pear-shaped. The other, I think, if I've got this right, was here to save Jemma and Frank but kill the first man and someone else, who must now stay alive. Otherwise, Frank's son will die in the future."

"Who? What? Sorry, what are you drivelling on about?"

"I'm not sure I should say. Unfortunately, I think I've probably already overstepped the mark." I shot a look at Frank, who confirmed with a slight shake of the head.

"And what d'you mean save Jemma? Save from what? Who?"

"Look, lassie, this is all a bit tricky. But here's the bottom line. Frank, Jayne, and I are time-travellers from the future—"

"Jesus, Kenny, you can't say that!"

Ignoring my future husband, Kenny continued. "See, there's this organisation that runs trips, excursions if you like, back to the past to sort stuff out. Kind of, somehow. Anyway, Mrs Stone and me weren't actually supposed to travel—"

"Frank?" Alison interrupted.

"Oh, well, that's done it!" I fired out, glowering at Kenny. "After that ridiculous monologue, I assume it's safe to say you weren't briefed? On account of the fact that you shouldn't have time-travelled, I take it you're blissfully unaware that part of the conditions of travelling is that you must never tell anyone you're a time-traveller." I raised my eyebrows at Kenny, who now shuffled his feet, appearing a smidge embarrassed. "Clearly not! Now, I suspect after that stupid comment and the inevitable fall-out when this girl tells the damn world, that ruddy man Hartland will probably send another eliminator to follow the plethora who've already been sent with a mission to exterminate us all!" My rising inflexion ended in a tone that could be classed as a hysterical shrill.

"Time-travel?" Alison blew a raspberry. "My God ... my grandad can tell some tall stories, but this—"

"Alison, look—"

"No. Sorry, boss, that's it," Alison interjected, forcing her interruption in with a raised palm. "I've had enough. I ain't hanging around here no longer. Whether I turn up for work on Monday, I can't say. But you've lost it." She wagged an accusing finger at Frank, who, with a flapping jaw, appeared to be searching for the appropriate response that wasn't forthcoming. "I have to say, you've been acting strange all week, and this is the final bloody straw. You just wait 'til I tell my boyfriend about all this—"

"No! You can't. You mustn't."

"Why? Why wouldn't I?"

"Because, if you do, that very act will put *your* life in danger."

"Oh, Jesus, Frank," Alison fired out her second raspberry before continuing in a distinctly disparaging tone, suggesting she wasn't of the mind to believe Kenny's claim of time-travel, which was fair enough. "You really have lost your sodding marbles." Alison jabbed her finger at Kenny when stepping towards the door. "And don't even think about waving that gun around. My boyfriend is six-foot-four, seventeen stone and built like a brick privy. Get in my way, and you'll have him to deal with."

"Alison," I pleadingly called out.

"As for you, Miss Smart, well, you're as bad as the rest of them. I knew there was something not quite right about you when you phoned yesterday."

"Alison. Two things. Please, these are very important."

"What?" she sighed, elongating the word in a similar fashion to how my teenage daughters would when suspecting they faced a lecture from either Frank or me. More often from me because Frank always liked to play the 'good cop' parenting role. "Don't tell me ... avoid the Daleks because they're coming to get me. Exterminate, exterminate," the last two words uttered in that familiar tone of one of those human-sized pepper pots with sink plunger arms that caused many a child to scurry behind the sofa on a Saturday evening.

"No, there are no Daleks or Cybermen," I paused momentarily, wondering if there might actually be, but quickly dismissed that thought and continued. "However, the absence of any Doctor Who monsters aside, please, say nothing about today to anyone. Frank's and my life will be in danger if you do. I beg you."

Alison huffed. "Alright, but only because I've always liked Frank. Well, I did before he turned into a nutter." She offered an exaggerated toothless grin as she jutted her chin forward.

"Thank you."

"Go on, let's hear it, then. What's the second thing?"

"Remember what I said earlier? That's also very important."

"Uh?" Alison scrunched up her nose and shook her head, causing her ponytail to swing. "What?"

"2014."

"Do what?"

"Malaysia Airlines, March 2014. Make sure your son isn't on the manifest."

"Frigging hell," she paused to offer her third raspberry. "Nutters! I'm off."

With her declaration delivered regarding our mental state, Alison spun on her heels and scooted back to reception. Before any of us had a chance to speak, that little yellow car, which aspired to become a Rolls Royce when it grew up, could be spotted through the bent blind slats wheel spinning from the car park in a similar fashion to how that red Jag had not fifteen minutes ago.

"Great! That went well. I think not."

Frank perched one bottom cheek on his desk, offering a heavy sigh and an apathetic nod to my assessment of the situation.

"Look, I don't know the rules about—"

"Oh, please. Just shut up. You waltz in here, waving around a gun, claiming you have this big master plan about how we wriggle free from the clutches of the CYA, and then you go spouting off about time-travel. I suggest you belt up and let Frank and me think about what the hell we do next."

"Oh, come on—"

"No, be quiet. Did you really think you could time-travel without authorisation and get away with it? That ruddy man, that git with that supercilious way about him, will probably have already pinged some mercenary back through time to hunt us all down, you idiot!"

"Hey, lady, if you're gonna be like that, I could just shoot you, you know."

"Be my guest. Either blow our brains out and save us the trouble of trying to crawl out of this stinking mess, or just shut up."

"Hang on," Frank paused and raised a finger at Kenny. "You said, your mate—"

"Jonny?"

"Yeah, him. You said the CYA sent him to clean down the entire operation?"

Kenny nodded.

"But actually, they pinged him back, or not as the case may be, to ensure future events go the way Hartland wanted. Which, if I remember correctly what you said earlier, he only needed to eliminate this Sinclair chap and ensure my mate, Dave, stays alive. Killing Jayne, me and this other eliminator were just to keep things neat."

"Tidy."

"Yeah, tidy."

"Frank, where are you going with this?" I asked, furrowing my brow, praying he was about to offer some pearl of wisdom which could significantly improve our situation.

"Well, what if that man—"

"Which one?" I interjected.

"Err …"

"Sinclair?" Kenny threw in.

"No, the other one."

"Collinson."

"That's him. If he's already killed Sinclair in the car park. Y'know, that gunshot we heard. Then the only requirement left is that Dave stays alive."

"Frank, we know that—"

"Jayne, hold up. You said, the night Dave was killed, I'd been for a drink with him earlier in the evening. Then, he somehow ends up dead in Fairfield Woods, along with Sinclair."

"In my world, yes. In your world, Dave strangles Jemma and gets away with it."

"So, next Friday, I go for a drink with Dave again, get him royally hammered, and Bob's your uncle. Dave, because he's three sheets to the wind, doesn't strangle Jemma. Basically, my old mate stays alive because Collinson won't be able to kill him in Fairfield Woods, and Sinclair is already dead."

"Oh. So the CYA have what they want and will leave us alone? Is that what you're suggesting?"

"Maybe."

"Sorry to piss on your parade, but what if it's the other way around?" Kenny chimed in.

"What d'you mean?"

"What if that gobby git, Sinclair, killed Collinson in the car park?"

"Oh."

"Frank, does that mean Sinclair is still tasked with eliminating the perpetrator of Jemma's murder? And still has a mission to ensure she aborts Andrew?"

"Probably. But, at this stage, Sinclair presumably doesn't know who will kill Jemma."

"Ah."

"What d'you mean, ah?" I barked at Kenny, detecting his tone suggested the man had screwed up again.

"Yeah, see, I may have inadvertently divulged that little tit-bit of information to both of them earlier today."

"Why?" I shrilled.

"Dunno, really. It kinda slipped out in conversation."

"Oh, frigging hell," Frank muttered. "Although thinking about it, we do have a week before that event. Jemma will be murdered next Friday."

"We might not, though."

"Sorry?"

"Well, you see, the fundamental part of how the military operates is down to all ranks following the orders of their superiors without question. It's a matter of discipline."

"So?"

"So, that means, if Sinclair is alive, and he knows David Bolton is the man who did, will … oh, I don't know, you know what I mean. Look, Dave Bolton is the killer in one of these timelines. So, now that gobshite bloke knows the killer is Dave Bolton, he'll follow orders and won't wait a week to do the deed."

Frank and I exchanged a look, both trying to grasp hold of the wavering thread of the conversation. With several timelines in play and a myriad of possibilities as to how the future could play out, that thread seemed harder to catch as the situation became more complicated when considering the three eliminators. All of whom were following a different set of orders.

"Look, to put it simply, Sinclair has his orders and will kill Dave Bolton at the first opportunity."

"Yes, because you told him, you utter imbecile."

"I accept that may have been a slight error of judgement on my part."

"Understatement, if I ever heard one."

"I'm sorry."

"Yes, well, sorry won't cut it, I'm afraid. I have no idea what the hell we do now." I raised my desperately-in-need-of-a-pluck eyebrows at Frank, hoping he would suggest a solution.

"Shit," hissed Frank.

"We're screwed then?" I threw in, helplessly flapping my arms as if to enforce my point.

"Maybe not." Kenny raised a finger, appearing to have just been hit with an idea.

"How come?"

"I think, just to keep things on track, Sinclair will ensure Dave Bolton dies at the same spot he did last time."

"Fairfield Woods."

"Reckon so."

"Alfie-Boy, what d'you think?" I placed my palms on my thighs and peered down at Alf as he stood and wagged his tail, presumably pleased to be included in the conversation. "Well, boy? What's your take on all this?"

Alf tipped his head sideways.

"Oh, um ... do you agree with Kenny? If Sinclair is alive, will he kill Dave at the first opportunity?"

Alf licked his chops.

"And he will commit said act up at Fairfield Woods?"

Alf confirmed with that affirmative gesture.

"Alf," Frank chipped in, pausing as he waited for my scruffy pooch to turn and face him. "What about Collinson? What if he's alive and not Sinclair?"

Apart from allowing his tongue to flap out the left side of his mouth, Alf made no telltale moves that could be construed as an answer.

"Alf?" I followed up, wondering if he would only answer me.

Alf flicked his eyes between us, appearing to roll his shoulders.

"Christ, did he just shrug?"

"I think he did," I muttered, trying to decipher what a doggy shoulder roll meant. I needed the doggy translation dictionary. A publication I doubted existed, even on Amazon, which didn't exist yet either. "Alf, are you saying you don't know?"

Alf liked that question, replying with a hearty lick of the chops.

"Oh."

"Bloody hell, is that how you communicate with him?"

"It is."

"But how does a dog know what's going to happen?"

"Well, I'm not sure he does. However, Mr Harris, to ensure Frank's son, Andrew, isn't murdered by Dave's granddaughter forty-odd years from now, we need to go on a teddy bears' picnic."

Kenny frowned.

"We need to get down to the woods today. Specifically, Fairfield Woods. If Sinclair is alive and Dave Bolton is now dead, we sure are facing some big surprises. Namely, a new eliminator on our tail."

39

For Your Eyes Only

Dave parted his lips, knitted his brow, and offered a slight shake of the head to convey he was still none the wiser to the identity of this new complainer. And, if he heard right, the bloke had said something about dodging bullets. An odd statement to make when presuming this chap required his assistance. Frustratingly, this new arrival seemed hell-bent on following up on Mrs Chalk's attempts to hinder his advance towards the pub.

"Sorry, what did you say?" Dave asked but kept walking, hoping this action would result in this bloke giving up and sodding off.

"I'll walk with you to your car. The brown Cortina is yours. Correct?"

"Err … how d'you …" Dave paused and checked his stride before the man waved the way forward, indicating they should continue.

"I still can't get my head around why in the '70s, car manufacturers conjured up such shit colours. No pun intended."

"Sorry, but who are you?" Dave repeated as the two men fell into step.

"I have to say, I don't think you were warming to that customer with the rotten chicken," he chuckled. "Fair play to you because I couldn't handle customers like that. I don't think I have the right temperament. My old mum, God bless her soul, reckoned I had a short fuse. To be fair, considering the amount of fellas who've struggled to warm to my charms when I've had me hands around their throats suggests the old girl was a pretty good judge of character."

Dave shot the man a look as he picked up his pace, concerning thoughts terrorising his mind as to who he might be. Placing the hands around the throat comment to one side, and although he didn't seem the sort, Dave wondered if this chap could be one of those head office auditors. That lot harboured similar looks to Mrs Chalk. The 'We're going to get you, Mr Manager' attitude as they ferreted through the files, making notes on their clipboards and disparagingly shaking their heads.

Or maybe this guy with the stupid, smug grin worked for solicitors specialising in family law. Frank's prissy, stuck-up wife, Jemma, used to be a solicitor before becoming even more up her own arse when becoming the local MP. Now, there's a woman he would willingly choke to death given half the chance.

Dave considered that maybe Babs had sought legal advice and this thug of a man was here to serve official papers upon him. That said, although Babs had threatened, he doubted she would actually divorce him. This thing, the incident in the cash office with that till girl, would eventually blow over. He just had to bide his time and pay his penance. Then he felt sure he would be back with Babs and little Sarah within a matter of a few weeks.

"Not been a bad day, again, has it?" the man asked, glancing up and squinting when the low early autumn sun caught his eyes. "I said, the weather seems to be holding up nice again."

"Sorry?"

"The weather. You don't seem to be much of a conversationalist, so I thought I'd mention the weather to get the ball rolling, so to speak. Always works as a conversation starter with us Brits. Course, the Yanks think we're just quaint. Y'know, obsessed with the rain, Shakespeare, tea and cakes with the Queen at Buck House with those silly sods wearing dead bears on their heads whilst standing to attention. Now, don't get me started on the Europeans. That lot are just grateful there's twenty-two miles of sea separating us and them."

"Right."

"Did I ever tell you about the time I stepped out with this cracking lassie when stationed near Dortmund? That's in Germany, by the way—"

"Sorry?"

"No, course not. I have a tendency to talk a lot. My old mum, God bless her soul, used to say—"

"Yes, yes, I've heard that. You have a short fuse. Well, not wanting to be rude, but so do I. Now, I'm sorry, but I must get going."

Dave halted at his car door and stabbed the key in the lock before turning to face this strange leech he'd acquired. Of course, supermarkets attracted all sorts of nutters, and he'd dealt with his fair share.

There was that tramp who burrowed his way onto the shelving in the toilet roll aisle, hoping to bed down for the night. That incident hit the local rag when a reporter was shopping and witnessed the fracas when Dave and a warehouseman manhandled the old git from the shelving. However, that wasn't half as weird as the woman dressed as a pantomime cow, mooing in the meat and poultry section whilst holding a séance and trying to contact dead relatives. The meat manager had inquired if that would be of the human or bovine variety and asked if she wanted to hold a pound of stewing steak to get a closer connection.

On a daily basis, strange folk entered supermarkets. However, although odd, Dave considered this chap didn't fit into the mooing or toilet-roll-sleeping categories.

When Dave yanked open the driver's door, the man snatched the keys from him with one hand and barbarously gripped his elbow with the other before placing his nose millimetres from his.

"Don't even think about it. You make a noise, scream, call for help, and you'll find yourself bleeding out across the tarmac," he hissed, digging his nails into the suit jacket material through to the skin, causing Dave to wince.

"What d'you want—"

"It's not what I want; it's what my employers want. That's the question you should be asking."

"Who—"

"All will come clear, David Bolton, Deputy Branch Manager of Freshcom's Supermarkets. Now, be a good lad and slip into the driver's seat while I nip around the other side."

"You—"

"David, you're not listening. Stop wriggling and asking questions. Do as I say, or you'll never see that pretty daughter of yours again."

"Oh, God, what have you done to Sarah—"

"Nothing. I'm not a monster. But I won't hesitate to turn your lights out. Now, this is becoming boring. So, as I said, get in the car and be a good lad for me."

Despite suspecting he must be on some show like Candid Camera or this bloke had got the wrong person, Dave complied with the instruction, allowing the man threatening him to close the driver's door. In those few seconds before his assailant hopped into the passenger seat, Dave focused on keeping control of his bowels.

"Right, lovely. This is cosy, eh?" The man chuckled as he settled into the passenger seat before shifting sideways to address the clearly petrified supermarket deputy manager. "Seat belt, lad. We're going for a little drive."

"Whe–where," Dave stammered.

"Fairfield Woods. There's a layby that truckers use." He held up the keys and jiggled them. "You'll need these."

"Why ... why are we going there?" Dave whimpered.

"Oh, simple, really. See, I'm a man of duty. Years in the service taught me that every good soldier must obey orders. That's how it works, see? And Fairfield Woods is where you're supposed to be." The man rocked his head from side to side before continuing. "Alright, alright, I accept that I'm a week early on account you should be there on the 28th, not the 21st. But, my friend, due to developments that have sprung up over the course of the day, I need to bring things forward a smidge. Expedite the situation if you see? Now, I'm of a mind that despite information received earlier today, and I can tell you, it's been a hell of a day, I was sent with a clear mission. As long as I fulfil that mission to the best of my ability, I can't be accused of leaving my post, so to speak. Navy term, my friend. Which will mean, just like today's weather, it will all turn out just dandy in the end. Well, for me, not you."

"I don't—"

"Start the engine, lad. We can't sit here gassing all day long, can we now? Also, there's a dead body in your boot that I'll need you to bury for me. See, now I've got you, there's no need for me to build up a sweat digging a hole to dump the miserable bastard in."

Dave's jaw sagged as he shifted around to glance at the back seats as if he possessed x-ray vision and could see into the luggage compartment.

"I popped it in there earlier, if you're wondering."

"How—"

"How did I get into the car? Easy, fella. In this era, it's a piece of piss. You wait twenty-odd years, then it ain't so straightforward as shoving a piece of bent wire through the window frame. Oh, no, those clever manufacturers ain't half made it damn tricky to pinch a motor."

"Wha—"

"Yeah, see, that Krooklock, which, if we're ever going to get moving, you'll need to remove, is ancient history, my friend. That's like something Fred Flintstone would use. Now, in the future, it's all sophistications such as alarms and immobilisers. Jesus, some top-end models even have GPS tracking installed. I wouldn't be surprised if they soon come up with that anti-theft device which Bond's Lotus Esprit had fitted. Such a waste. Although I can't imagine they actually blew that car up. Y'know, clever cinematography and all that. But, as I say, these days, a bent bit of wire and pop, you're in."

Despite the plethora of questions pinging around Dave's head, avoiding shitting his trousers seemed uppermost in his thoughts.

"Ah, I can see you're a bit flummoxed, lad. Now, to be honest with you, I'm not certain which Bond film that scene came from. Definitely Roger Moore, but that could be from the '80s, I guess."

Like the mooing woman, Dave deduced that this bloke, apart from potentially being dangerous, must be some loon. He'd mentioned the 1980s, which, considering that decade kicking off was still a few months into the future, all served to cement his suspicions. The loon had mentioned he was in the services, so perhaps a couple of stints in Northern Ireland had sent his mind all skew-whiff. Dave prayed that also accounted for the 'body in the boot' comment but thought it prudent to clarify.

"There's … there's a body in the boot?"

"Correct, David. You catch on fast. I can see how the great and the good in the higher echelons of food retailing considered you to be management potential."

"No, but—"

"That said, lad, I'm not sure what your bosses or the missus, for that matter, would say about that stash of mucky mags you've hidden under the boot lining. I had meself a quick flick through, as you do. It'd be rude not to, eh? Now, on the subject of rude, oh boy, that's not the sort of stuff you can pick up from the top shelf of WHSmith's, is it? Now, I'm a man of the world, and I've seen a few things in my time. Some of those seedy clubs in Germany had live shows that'd make even the most hardened of squaddies blush. But, I'll be honest with you, David, some of those images in your stash of mucky mags are damn right perverted."

Dave attempted to swallow, feeling his pulse race and thus becoming light-headed. He loosened his tie before gulping a few deep breaths. Whether this nutter had bundled a body in the boot of his car or not, he'd definitely found his secret stash. And he was quite correct when suggesting those magazines weren't the sort of thing Hugh Hefner would have produced, more the black-market-styled publication that would most certainly land him in a spot of bother with the authorities and absolutely result in divorce from Babs.

"Right, lad, are we going then, or you going to have a heart attack and save me the trouble? Gotta say, you're not looking too clever there."

Again, Dave's jaw sagged.

"Ah, the penny has dropped. Yes, David Bolton. I always follow orders. And, now I know, *you*, not that knob Paul Wilson, that toff Tobias Heaton, or any other bell-end I've been following will strangle Jemma Stone, I'm expediting the situation."

"Wha—"

"The days of dealing with those annoying, complaining customers and tugging your old chap when rifling through those mucky mags are over. Your time is well and truly up, fella."

40

The Love Bug

"Jesus, that smell again." Kenny – a man you might describe as a colossus who could easily rival the size Alison suggested her boyfriend to be, and the term 'refrigerator', as per that American football chap, being an apt description – more than filled the passenger seat of my VW, and cranked down the window as we hurtled towards Fairfield Woods. "Hear me right, that dog might be intelligent, but you need to conduct a deep dive into his diet. Whatever the mutt's eating, the end result is enough to make a man gag."

Alf, perched on the back seat beside Frank, snorted a response. From his reaction, I gathered that my pooch was royally unimpressed with Kenny's comment.

"I really think Alf's diet and resulting flatulence is the least of our worries," I spat back, flooring the accelerator after leaving the ring road and heading into open country.

I say floored, but coaxing my old banger up to a cruising speed of over sixty took time and patience, neither of which we had if we were to prevent Sinclair from killing Dave. Of course, we could be on a fool's errand. If Collinson was still alive, not Sinclair, he could also be hell-bent on killing Dave. Or, either one of them might be down the pub enjoying a tea-time beer, having decided one killing was enough for today. Perhaps they planned on murdering Frank's best mate later in the week or saving that task for the actual day this event was supposed to kick off. Namely, next Friday.

"The layby where Jemma was murdered is just around the next bend," Frank hollered from the back seat, attempting to be heard above the complaining engine. "I think you'd better slow down because we need to cruise past first and see if we can spot that red Jag."

Before leaving the office, Frank phoned the supermarket where Dave worked and then his parents' home where he temporarily billeted after Babs rightly booted him out. Due to his work informing Frank that Mr Bolton had left for the day and his father saying he wasn't home yet, suggesting we try the pub because he may have nipped in there for a swift one, our first port of call had been the White Bull Public House. When discovering Frank's murdering best mate hadn't dropped into that awful estate boozer, and really not wanting to bother Babs, we'd scooted out of town towards Fairfield Woods.

Frank made a good point because barrelling into the layby to be faced with an assassin waving a shooter around probably wasn't the best idea. I'd had my fill of being at the wrong end of a gun for today. And, although this Kenny chap was armed, I still harboured concerns about his intentions because Alf had indicated Kenny wasn't a man to be trusted.

As I lifted my foot from the dodgem-car-styled accelerator pedal, allowing the boxer engine to return to a more sedate rattle, we all peered left when trying to spot any vehicles in the layby. Unfortunately, the thick bushes that held on to their summer foliage blocked our sightline.

"Bugger," I muttered.

"Carry on a bit further." Frank thrust his hand forward between Kenny and me, pointing ahead. "Go past the entrance, do a u-ie and come back. We might get a better angle to see in."

Before I could follow Frank's instructions, Alf stuck his nose through the gap under Frank's outstretched hand and nudged my arm.

"What is it, Alfie-Boy?"

After offering me a canine grin, he shimmied backwards before placing his front right paw on the back window, pointing to the trees blocking our view.

"What's your dog up to?"

"Frank, what's he doing?" I asked when peering in the rearview mirror, just at the point when a Bedford Van approached from behind, the driver thumping his horn before taking evasive action to avoid rear-ending us. As the rusty crate cruised past, the driver offering a few more thumps to the horn just on the off chance I hadn't heard the first, or just being a dick, probably the latter, I spotted the passenger offer the finger gesture out of the side window.

"I think he's pointing," Frank replied.

"Alf or the knobhead in that van?"

"Oh, Alf."

"Alfie-Boy?" I turned the rear-view mirror to the left so I could see him. "Should I pull into the layby?"

"He's grinning, doing that thing with his tongue as if licking his lips," said Frank, which was helpful because Kenny's frame blocked my view.

"Right, nothing for it, then. We're going in. Kenny, get your gun at the ready," I barked, flattening the accelerator, waiting a second or two for the engine to rumble and kick the car forward.

"Yes, ma'am."

Based on the fact my old car sported an acceleration performance of nought to sixty somewhere north of twelve seconds, we didn't exactly fly out of the blocks. Only one miracle was in play – yes, my dog demonstrated a remarkable command of the English language – but my car had not gained the acceleration qualities of Herbie. Maybe the Love Bug's sense of humour when regularly refusing to start, but definitely not the speed.

However, after the old thing worked up a head of steam, I pulled down hard on the wheel and bounced the Beetle through the entrance to the layby. Alf and Frank ended up in a tangled mess behind me, and Kenny became far too close and personal.

Although a popular haunt for truckers to grab a pit stop, a brown Cortina appeared to be the only vehicle in situ in the hundred-yard pull-in area.

"That's Dave's car."

"David Bolton?"

"Yeah."

"I was correct then. Whichever one of those lads is alive, they're here to finish their mission."

As I drew close, I shot Frank a look. I presumed his old friend hadn't voluntarily taken a trip to the woods and thus suspected either Sinclair or Collinson had forced Dave to park the Cortina near the wooden picnic tables, all in a state of dilapidation that suggested that even teddy bears wouldn't deem them usable furniture for alfresco dining.

"Don't get too close," ordered Kenny, again waving around that gun, causing me to push my body against the driver's door.

"What now?" I asked, bringing the Beetle to a halt a good fifty yards behind the Cortina.

"Okay," Kenny slowly muttered, much to himself, before shifting in his seat to face me and thus placing the untangled Frank and Alf in his peripheral vision. "So, let's get this straight. If Sinclair is out of the picture and Dave Bolton stays alive, we're all good. The CYA will probably leave us alone?"

"Maybe. It's our only hope."

"Yeah, I agree." Kenny nodded to Frank.

"Although, in that scenario, I still have to stop my old mate murdering Jemma next Friday."

"True. But, as one of you said earlier, we have another week to sort that issue."

"True, we do."

"I know I asked you to get your gun at the ready, but d'you think you could point it somewhere other than at my chest."

"Oh, sorry." Kenny grinned before aiming the barrel at the passenger footwell.

"So, what's the plan, then?"

"Okay, because we think that scenario will resolve our problem. I suggest you wait here whilst I perform a spot of reconnaissance through the woods and see what's occurring."

"What if Sinclair or Collinson double back whilst you're in there? We'll be sitting ducks."

"Fair point. Alright, we'll all go." Kenny pointed the gun through the gap between the front seats. "But listen up, and hear me right, I'm not used to civilians tagging along. You follow my lead, and all keep quiet." He jabbed the gun at Alf. "That includes you, farter."

Alf widened his eyes before offering a dismissive shake of his head. An expression that suggested he held nothing but contempt for the man.

Twenty or so feet into the thick undergrowth, blanketed by the copse of trees that stretched out for a few hundred yards behind the layby, the late afternoon light faded, seemingly halving with each step we took. As demanded, Kenny took the lead. With an obedient Alf close by my side, I followed the man with the gun whilst Frank brought up the rear.

Although the passing traffic on the main road was still audible, each snapping twig and scraping of shoes through the undergrowth echoed off the trees, amplifying our presence to whichever of the two eliminators lurked ahead. The only one of the quartet who seemed capable of creeping along with any measure of stealth was the one with four legs.

Kenny held his left hand aloft, arm bent at the elbow, while keeping the gun held in his right, pointing to the ground. I'd seen enough war films to know that action commanded us to halt. Then he started waving his hand down. Another action I was familiar with. Frank and I followed Kenny's lead and lowered into a crouched position. Although I really didn't think he needed to, Alf followed suit when laying his belly on the bed of pine needles.

"Can you see anything?" Frank whispered in my ear.

"Shush," Kenny hissed.

I glanced around and rolled my eyes at Frank. "Who the hell does he think he is? Sodding Rambo? You watch. Any minute now, he'll be ripping his shirt off and tying a bandana on his head."

"Jesus, woman, shut it," Kenny hissed over his shoulder.

I have to say I was a smidge put out by his 'woman' and 'shut it' comments. The 'Jesus' part, although stated as blasphemy, didn't raise my heckles to quite the same level. However, on this occasion, based on the fact we were in a somewhat tricky situation, I thought I'd let it slide due to him being the one holding the gun.

Now, I'm no expert on firearms. In fact, discounting today, the only time I'd seen any sort of gun up close and personal was when shopping in a supermarket in Florida when we took the whole family for a three-week fly-drive so our grandchildren could meet Micky Mouse.

When on said trip, and whilst purchasing catering size packs of our preferred provisions from the supermarket – simply because that was the only size on offer, and I still struggle to understand why anyone would need a ten-kilo tub of peanut butter – Frank and I had been somewhat mesmerised by the array of firearms on offer in the display cabinet strategically placed between the gardening and health and beauty sections.

At the time, I'd presumed whoever designed the store layout may have been thinking customers wishing to purchase a gun may also require industrial-sized packs of ammonium nitrate and a few gallons of hydrogen peroxide to furnish their personal arsenal with bomb-making equipment and thus the store could capture some incremental sales.

In our crouched positions, apart from the distant traffic and the breeze rustling a few leaves, the wood took on a deathly hush as if the trees themselves recognised the pathos of the situation. That is until I heard the distinctive sound of a gun hammer being cocked. I'd always assumed that action was just for dramatic effect in the movies. You know, that moment when you realise the bad guy is there but just out of camera shot. However, and taking into account my limited knowledge of firearms, it appeared whoever had cocked the hammer on said gun was either doing it for a similar effect or had decided they *were* going to shoot.

"Harris, you miserable bastard."

41

Drat and Double Drat!

Kenny swivelled around to his right, raising his gun in the vague direction of the male voice.

"Gun down, fella. Easy, nice and slow, now. Throw it forward and stick your hands up nice and high for me."

During those few seconds of inertia after hearing the man's voice, Frank, Alf, and I held our breath as we waited for the inevitable gun battle to kick off. Although I considered there was a high possibility that I might self-defecate, Alf got in before me when offering particularly pungent flatulence to break the silence.

Fair enough. Who could blame him? We found ourselves in a pretty stressful situation, so blowing off was only natural. The fact we weren't confined to an enclosed space and the gentle breeze had picked up a knot or two appeared to be the only saving grace to avoid gagging.

In the act of desperation, and by no means did I consider my actions would assist in terms of avoiding being shot, I threw my arms around Frank's neck. Whilst Frank and I huddled together and Alf, seemingly totally unashamed by his farting performance, flattened himself further into the mat of pine needles, Kenny complied with the voice.

"Sinclair, you gobshite," Kenny muttered when a man appeared from behind a large oak not ten feet away.

"Regimental Sergeant Major of the poncy Parachute Regiment, no less. Delighted to remake your acquaintance. Y'know, I was only just saying to that Dave Bolton fella that I expected you to turn up at any moment. That said, a bit of a one-sided conversation on account that he's about as miserable as you are."

"Collinson?"

"Staff Sergeant of the poncy Royal Engineers is helping to fertilise the spring bulbs. I wouldn't mind betting there'll be a smashing spread of daffodils come Easter next year."

"Sinclair. Pinkie, old fella, we can work something out, I'm sure of it."

"Oh, you wanna be all nicey-nicey now, I see. What about all that earlier, threatening me with a gun if I didn't shove a sock in it? Changed your tune now, haven't we, you Scottish git?"

"Scottish?"

"Are you not? Well, bugger me sideways, there's a thing," he chuckled. "Funnily enough, that's what Collinson said before I shot him. To be honest with you, I've never been that good at languages. Did I tell you about my French teacher at school? Miss Dubois was her name. Not that I can remember many teachers from back then, but she was a right cracker, I can tell you. Anyway, she said I had this mental block towards languages and reckoned I was the worst schoolboy she'd ever had the misfortune of teaching. Course, I didn't mind so much on account I was afforded more one-to-one coaching. And, as I said, a cracker who sent my raging teenage hormones into a merry old spin." Sinclair glanced at me before continuing.

"Apologies, Miss Hart. Just boys' talk. I hope you can forgive the smut."

Although I didn't think I had much choice whether I minded or not, I offered a nodded response.

"Pinkie—"

"Hey, I know, Sarge, I talk too much. See, I can't help it. It's the way I am. My old mum, God bless—"

"Where's Dave?" blurted Frank, halting the incessant talker who appeared to be building himself up to launch into another long tale.

"Ah, the murdering, perverted David Bolton, no less. Well, pervert, yes. Murderer, no. Well, see, he would have been, but not this time. Because, on account of what the Regimental Sergeant Major of the poncy Parachute Regiment divulged earlier, I expedited my mission if you see what I mean?"

"Dave's dead? You've killed him?" Frank quizzed. Although *my* Frank, that man who'd disappeared, had told me, and in turn, I'd informed this Frank, that David had attempted to murder Jemma and then died at the hand of some bloke called Collinson, who, by all accounts, was now also dead, I detected the tremor in Frank's voice when asking for clarification.

"That's an affirmative. A good soldier follows orders. And, just for the record, I'm a good soldier. So, yeah, I'm afraid to inform you that Mr Bolton is no longer, and your good lady wife, Jemma Stone, need worry no more about being strangled. Now, fella, there is the slight problem regarding the second part of my mission. Namely, persuading you to have a word in your missus's shell-like and so persuade the current Mrs Stone to abort the child. However, and on account that the Sarge here has suggested there's been a few updates at the CYA since I travelled, I'm prepared to let that part of the mission slide."

"Jesus, you donkey, Sinclair," hissed Harris.

"Charming. You know, I really don't warm to you, Sarge. You're not really what I would call a people person."

"Killing Dave Bolton is as good as signing our death warrants. I told you earlier, the CYA want Bolton alive."

"I had my orders, Sarge."

"Those orders were expunged, you knob. Now they'll send another eliminator to rid us all."

"Are you going to kill us?" I asked, not recalling my brain thinking that thought before uttering the question. It seemed my voice now acted independently.

During that nanosecond of distraction, when Sinclair turned his attention to me, Kenny leapt towards his gun. I presume, in the few minutes when Sinclair had been running his mouth off, Kenny had been using that time to assess the location of his gun, which he'd earlier thrown, and whether he could reach it with one leap forward.

The sound of a single gunshot reverberated off the trees, making it seem as if we were under siege and taking shots from all angles. Frank and I held our hands over our ears, which was all reasonably pointless because the horse had bolted, so to speak. Alf, clearly not too enamoured by firearms, sensible dog, whimpered and buried his head in my lap.

"Eejit, as my great uncle Eugene used to say. Did I ever tell you about that time I went stag hunting with Eugene and my old dad? God rest his soul." Sinclair rammed his gun into the waistband of his jeans whilst raising his eyebrows at Frank and me as we remained cowering on the ground, still with our hands clamped to our ears. "I said ... oh, forget it. It wasn't that interesting, anyway. The landlord down my local boozer actually reckoned it was the most boring story he'd ever been subjected to. Rude some folk, don't you think?"

"Sorry?" I mumbled when allowing my hands to flop away from my ears. Not that I was apologising, but just that involuntary word we all say when you don't quite catch the thread of the conversation.

"I was saying how some folk are just damn rude."

"Is he ... you shot him? Is he dead?" Frank asked, daring to stand and help me up in the process.

"Harris? Well, I shot him straight between the eyes. I expect the back of his skull to be sporting a large hole where his brains fired out and splattered these fine-looking trees. So, if he's not, that miserable Regimental Sergeant Major of the poncy Parachute Regiment will have defied medical science."

"Frank." I shook his arm to gain his attention and thus drag his eyes away from Harris's lifeless form. "Dave's dead ... that means—"

"My son—"

I nodded, chewing my lip.

"Andrew ..."

"I'm sorry, Frank. But, yes, Andrew will die in that terror attack in the future."

"Holy crap."

"Hartland said that the only way to stop Bab's granddaughter from blowing up Ten Downing Street was to ensure Dave stayed alive. Then, for some reason, they claim Sarah's life path would change and her daughter, the terrorist, wouldn't be born."

"Christ, what the hell—"

"Frank, that's a long time in the future. Surely so much can change between now and then? We'll just have to find the right moment to tell Andrew and ensure he's not there that day."

"What about everyone else? I can't remember what you said, but—"

"Oh. Well, you told me—"

"Me?"

"No, I mean *my* Frank told me Hartland reckoned that every member of the government will be murdered."

"Err, excuse me for the interruption." Sinclair raised his hand and leaned forward. "And I can assure you, good people, that I'm not one for butting in on a private conversation, but would you like to enlighten me? Also, not to put a dampener on proceedings, we have three dead bodies in the woods here. Now, I can assure you that's not an ideal situation to be associated with if the local boys in blue fancy a late summer stroll in the great outdoors if you catch my drift."

"Mr Sinclair, I assume—"

"Pinkie, please. Let's drop the formalities now we're getting acquainted."

"Yes, well, as I was saying, I assume, no scrub that, hope being a more appropriate word, that due to you not waving your gun around, you do not intend to shoot either Frank or me?"

"You suppose correctly, Miss Hart. I've fulfilled my mission, and that's that. To be clear, I'm not like your old mate, purvy

Bolton. I don't go around murdering folk for the sake of it, you know."

"Good. I'm delighted to hear it. Although there does appear to be a large body count already."

"That is so, Miss Hart. Needs must."

"Okay, if you say so."

"I do so."

"Hmmm. However, because you've taken it upon yourself to kill David Bolton—"

"Hey, no need to thank me, Miss Hart. All part of the service."

"I wasn't going to thank you. Because Dave Bolton is dead, Frank's unborn son will now be murdered in the future, not to mention dead Kenny Harris's point," I paused to point at Kenny's body. "As that dead man suggested, a new eliminator will be on his way, if not already here, to finish us all off. So, thanking you for putting my life in even more danger than it already was is not something I was planning on doing. Capeesh?"

"Ah, I've never been particularly good at reading the moods of the fairer sex, but I'm getting vibes that you're not overly chuffed about the situation. Would I be surmising correctly?"

"Is he for real?"

"Frank, I have no idea, but it doesn't change the fact that we're standing in a whole heap of shit with the wrong shoes on."

"Hey, your dog. He don't bite, do he?" Sinclair backed up a pace, appearing terrified as Alf trotted over and nudged his nose around the man's trouser leg. "Did I ever tell that story about the Dobermann and this incident with the lady of the night when I was stationed out in Germany? Now, that was—"

"Alfie-Boy, what's up?" I interrupted the terrified assassin's inane drivel.

Alf performed an odd circling routine before settling his bottom on the ground and rubbing his nose affectionately against Sinclair's leg.

"Good dog. Nice doggy. Now, you really don't want to go biting Uncle Pinkie, do you now, boy?"

"Alf? What are you telling us?"

Alf tipped his head sideways.

"Sorry. Let me rephrase. Err …"

"Alf," Frank interjected as I paused. "Is Mr Sinclair the good guy?"

Alf licked his chops.

"Oh, well, Alfie-Boy, I really don't know what to say. Are you actually suggesting that the man who's just shot three people in Fairfield Woods is the good guy?" I threw in, a little shocked that Alf could regard a man who just casually blew Harris's brains across the woodland to be on the right side of the equation.

Again, Alf licked his chops.

"Now, would you look at that? See, me and dogs have never really seen eye to eye if you get my meaning. I don't mean that in terms of relative height difference, thus making direct eye contact at the same level, but as in temperament. My old mum, God bless her soul, she reckoned it all started during that incident when I was about twelve. See, there was this Jack

Russell, the neighbour's dog, nasty little bastard, I can tell you. So, one day …"

Leaving Pinkie to tell his story to Alf, Frank and I searched each other's eyes for answers. For sure, Dave Bolton dying couldn't be classed as good. However, since arriving in 1979 yesterday, Alf had been pretty bob-on with his assessment of the situation. Clearly, Alf had more to tell.

"Alf. Alf, listen to me," I barked. I know, I know, if you've got a dog, you don't need to bark yourself. However, I needed to raise my voice to break that mesmerised look my pooch had adopted when listening to the assassin recite his story about a vicious Jack Russell.

Alf turned and looked up at me.

"Alfie-Boy, you have more to tell, yes?"

Alf licked his chops and grinned before snickering like Muttley.

42

2015

Harry Paget Flashman

"Whitman, spit it out, woman." Hartland, after aggressively swiping his hand across Johnson's desk, his action sending a stack of Manila files and their contents across the room, a few sheets of paper still finding a resting place on the lino floor, glowered at the senior analyst. His rage, sparked by the news that an unauthorised member of the general public had travelled, still bubbling at the thought that this entire operation appeared to be morphing into nothing short of a total humiliation that would privately lay opprobrium at his door.

Whitman side-eyed Johnson before focusing on the incandescent Commander-in-Chief, the single sheet detailing more unpropitious information flapping as her hand shook in rhythm with the tremors that wracked her body.

"Speak, you stupid woman!" Rather uncouthly, globules of spit rained down on Johnson's desk to accompany Hartland's bluster before the man balled his fists and rested them on either side of the ashtray. Flaring his nostrils, the senior man in the room sported a look similar to an alpha male silverback gorilla, who'd missed his last two cognitive behaviour therapy sessions to manage his anger issues.

"The eliminator, Bamford. From the data we received on our first run, it appears that he didn't successfully travel, sir."

Hartland, still holding the gorilla pose, bowed his head.

Whitman faced Johnson and offered a grimace. "What now?" she mouthed.

Johnson shrugged.

"So I'm clear," Hartland spoke in a significantly calmer lilt. "Bamford evaporated on the Wheel. This other unauthorised traveller made it through. Some ex-military nut job, you say?"

"Yes, sir."

"As we stand, David Bolton is still dead after Collinson shot him along with Sinclair. Is that correct? Just like it happened when Frank was back in 1979." Hartland paused to nod at the man still cable-tied to the chair, mourning his wife. "So, Sinclair is dead, which we need to happen. But David Bolton is also dead, which mustn't happen. Is that correct?"

"I think that's the size of it, sir. I suggest we prepare another eliminator," Johnson replied.

"Sir?"

"What now, woman? If you're about to utter more bad news, so help me, God, I might just strangle you right where you stand." Hartland shot the senior analyst a death stare, suggesting he would carry out said threat.

Whitman offered a nervous laugh, only prevented from bolting from the office when Johnson laid an encouraging hand on her elbow and offered his best don't-worry-it-will-be-alright smile.

"Sir, you are correct. David Bolton is still dead. However, there appears to be conflicting data regarding the first two eliminators, Sinclair and Collinson."

Hartland glowered at her but offered no verbal response.

"Of course, I have my team beavering away on this, but the data coming through is … well, odd, I guess."

"Odd?"

"Yes, sir. Very odd."

"How so?"

"Okay, and please, sir, remember this is still preliminary—"

"Christ, woman, I know that. I'm fully bloody aware that the data is preliminary. I was running operations from this building when you were playing with Barbie dolls, had your hair in pigtails, skipping along in your black plimsolls and long white socks whilst swinging your satchel around."

"Tiny Tears, sir. Also, Sindy was more my generation, not Barbie. Anyway, my mother thought Tiny Tears was a more appropriate toy. However, I preferred playing with my brother's Action Man."

"I don't damn well care!"

Whitman jumped, Johnson shivered, and thirty-odd analysts, akin to a mob of meerkats when sensing a predator in close proximity, peered up momentarily from their screens to glance at the glass cube when Hartland offered his thoughts regarding which toys Whitman was partial to playing with back in the day.

When Uncle Joe shifted his glare to the few brave analysts still gawping at events, presumably all fearing for their boss, Whitman, Hartland bolted around the desk. After muscling

Whitman and Johnson out of the way, he yanked open the door to address the team.

"About an hour ago, I sentenced at least five men from our Transportation team to death. Unless you all want to join them, I suggest you get on with your bloody work."

The office, along with the glass cube, took on a funereal ambience. The hush only punctuated by the humming of computers and the steadily increasing keyboard tapping sounds as the analysts restarted their work, all now consumed with thoughts of execution.

"Sir?"

"What?" Hartland snarled before sending his foot through the wicker wastepaper basket, intending to launch said receptacle across the office, Pelé-curling-free-kick style. When the fragile wicker yielded to the force applied from his swinging Oxford Brogue, said basket became impaled on Hartland's foot, causing him to grab the side of the desk to regain his balance. "Get this bloody thing off my foot."

Johnson complied with his demand before setting the now defunct item back beside the desk.

"My team are doing their best, sir," Whitman bravely whispered.

"You're a bully. I met blokes just like you at school. Small-minded men who can only get their way with shouts and intimidation. You're an embarrassment."

"Shut up, Frank. Did I ask for your opinion? I've half a mind to have you removed. Permanently. There, that will shut you up."

"Be my guest. If what you say is correct, Jayne is gone and my girls don't exist, then I really have nothing to live for."

"Too bad, Frank Stone. Because you're going back to 1979 again to sort out this ruddy mess."

"Whatever. One day, one day—"

"What, Frank? Don't threaten me. You're forgetting that I have control over your life, whether you're here or back in 1979. Your fate is, and always will be, in my hands, you ungrateful git. Frank Stone, I control you."

"It's Sir Frank Stone to you."

"Not anymore, it's not. That title bestowed upon you by our Majesty no longer happened. Because your wife travelled, not Mrs Denton, history has changed, old boy. You are now just common as muck, Frank Stone."

Although Frank never used his title, he considered the Knighthood an honour. The title gave credence to his lifelong work supporting the need for change in society's attitudes towards homelessness. Despite what some idiot government ministers thought, homelessness wasn't a lifestyle choice. Frank shot looks at Johnson and Whitman, non-verbally asking for confirmation of the blustering bully's statement.

Whitman offered him a curt nod in reply.

"Right, you were saying. Preliminary data."

"Yes, sir." Whitman glanced at Johnson for encouragement before continuing. "It seems Collinson has disappeared. We can only assume he's dead and his demise took place many decades ago because we can find no trace of him after 1980. This is another Category Ten change to go with the myriad of others caused by Mrs Stone travelling instead of Mrs Denton. And, on the subject of Category Tens, Sinclair, who should be dead, appears to be alive and well, living in the Caribbean. Kingston in Jamaica, to be precise, with his wife and a whole host of children. More than enough to field a five-a-side team with substitutes to spare."

"Who the hell killed David Bolton, then?"

"We're working on that, sir."

"Sir," Johnson interrupted. "I suggest we send Frank now. Data still implies that sending Frank could change the outcome in our favour. Let's get Frank on the Wheel now while there's still time, and we can send another eliminator tomorrow night to clean up if you get my drift."

"Yes, yes. Let's get on with it. I'm still a little confused as to why David Bolton is dead. I thought Frank travelling was supposed to solve that."

"Sir," Whitman raised her hand. "It's difficult to see a clear picture because Frank is still here. As soon as he's dispatched, that may expedite the data and hopefully resolve the issue."

Hartland nodded, a gesture that Whitman took as confirmation that she would survive the night and not join the poor five souls in the Transportation team who apparently would miss breakfast later this morning and every other breakfast in the future.

"Frank, my good fellow. It's time to don your time-travelling boots once again."

"Bastard."

43

1979

Paint Your Wagon

"Frank, where the hell did you get to last night? I had to get a taxi back from the station. You said you were going to pick me up. I presume, as you decided to flop into the spare bed, you were out drinking with that idiot Dave or that lecherous prick you work with. You're not being fair. If you say you'll pick me up, then I expect you to pick me up. Frank, are you listening to me? I've had a long week in Parliament, and I think you should put me before drinking sessions with some of your stupid mates."

Jemma paused by the bedroom door, a towel wrapped around her, secured in her cleavage, with another wrapped turban-style around her head.

"Frank, did you hear me? Are you going to stay in bed all day? I'm off to the shops with Clare soon, but you'd better ring Dave's parents. They called earlier saying he's gone missing and wanted to know if you'd seen him. They said something about you were looking for him last night."

Jemma dramatically huffed before stomping back to the bathroom, leaving the dozing, fully clothed Frank splayed out with only the eiderdown partially wrapped around his body.

Frank pinged open his eyes.

"The man's a ruddy idiot," Jemma announced when reappearing at the bedroom door. "Hopefully, he's done everyone a favour and topped himself. Babs and that adorable little Sarah don't need him. I'm sure she could do better than being married to a silly supermarket manager. Frank, come on, get up. If you've got a stinking hangover, serves you damn right."

Jemma swivelled around, removed her turban towel, and stuck her nose in the air before scooting off to their bedroom. A few seconds later, Frank could hear her hairdryer blasting out that deafening sound which could rival Concord's Rolls-Royce engines on the logarithmic scale.

Although he didn't have a hangover per se, he had the mother of all headaches. Waking up after time-travelling is an experience that causes all travellers to run through a range of emotions during that nanosecond of realisation. However, for Frank, who'd now time-travelled twice, the shock of arriving in yesteryear in a much younger form was not so extraordinary. He'd gone through that range of emotions only a week ago, so this time, it wasn't such a momentous moment.

Frank Stone could now be classed as a seasoned time-traveller.

Placing his experience and skill in performing transtemporal travel to one side, as he lay on the spare bed, his mind fizzed as his discombobulated brain attempted to amalgamate three different experiences into one coherent memory. Thoughts of last night, when cable-tied to a chair in the headquarters of the

CYA, mingled with arguing with Tobias in the Murderer's Pub, along with remembering exiting Fairfield Woods with Jayne after Sinclair shot Dave.

For some bizarre reason, the memories of being cable-tied and arguing with Tobias seemed sharper and in focus. The other memory, the one with Jayne, lacked clarity. A fuzzing around the edges and out of focus.

Frank closed his eyes. Firstly, to avoid looking at Jemma, who he could partially see as she brushed her hair whilst perched at her dressing table, because, although not naked, it felt like he was cheating on Jayne just by looking at her. And secondly, to mull over his thoughts in the absence of any visual distractions.

Understanding how he remembered last night when arguing with The Hooded Claw before entering pod thirteen on the Wheel for the third time was easy to grasp. Arguing with Tobias, again, that was easy to remember because for the Frank who'd travelled just the once that experience was less than twenty-four hours ago. Also, for the Frank who'd now time-travelled twice, he could remember that argument from thirty-six years in the past due to it being the last time he'd seen his old friend. However, as soon as Jayne approached him in that pub, that's when his timeline split three ways, sending his poor thumping brain into a spin and notching up his headache to severe hangover status. He wouldn't mind so much if he'd enjoyed a skinful the night before, but he hadn't.

Frank, the once time-traveller, held distant memories of collecting Jemma from the train station. Frank, the twice time-traveller, had clear memories of being cable-tied to that chair.

All good. Well, in terms of memory, all good, but not in being tied to a chair or collecting his soon-to-be ex-wife from the train station.

However, there was this third, fuzzy around the edges, memory. Frank could only conclude when living that second life, the one where Jemma isn't murdered and Collinson kills Dave and Sinclair, that's when his timeline fractured. He, the once-only time-travelling Frank, had collected Jemma from the train station and, at the same time, witnessed Sinclair murder Harris in Fairfield Woods.

"Jesus," he muttered. His head pounded, and Jemma's 'jet-engine' hair dryer wasn't helping much.

Despite the cranial pain, Frank fought to remember the events after he and Jayne left the woods. Jayne—

Akin to one of those free-diving nutters – who deep dive down to ear-popping depths in the ocean without the safety of scuba equipment – coming up for air, Frank involuntary sucked in a lungful and pitched forward to a seated position.

"Jayne," he mumbled. According to that tyrannical bully, Hartland, Jayne would die sometime next year in an RTA. The Hooded Claw had mentioned a dog in the car with her. "Alfie-Boy."

After taking a few deep breaths, which did nothing to abate his head issue, Frank tried to rationalise the situation. Surely, just ensuring Alf never travelled in the car with Jayne and bingo, problem solved.

The plan he and Jayne conjured up last night involved Frank informing Jemma today that their marriage was over, and he and Jayne would make a go of it. Based on how Jayne said the future had panned out, they both thought they could do a pretty good job. Now Frank had travelled again, he also knew their future was pretty damn rosy.

Of course, this issue regarding Andrew, his unborn son, wasn't resolved. Frank knew – and at this point, he knew Jemma was fully aware she was pregnant – Andrew would be born next year and then die in the future when Babs's and Dave's granddaughter became a terrorist. As Jayne had said last night, they had many years to formulate a plan to save him and maybe stop the attack altogether. Perhaps an anonymous call to the authorities or something a smidge more sophisticated. But, anyway, they had time.

Now that he'd travelled again, after listening to that conversation between Hartland, Johnson, and that woman whose name eluded him, Frank knew Hartland was planning to despatch yet another eliminator. Of course, they'd sent him back to 1979 again with the sole task of saving David Bolton. Clearly, something had again gone awry with their timings because a few moments ago, when he was dozing, Jemma mooted something about Dave being missing when relaying a telephone conversation she'd held with Dave's parents. Although he couldn't be certain of today's date, he was surely too late to save Dave because Sinclair shot him along with Collinson and Harris last night.

On the subject of eliminators, after Sinclair made it quite clear he had no intention of killing either him or Jayne, the talkative assassin appeared happy to hang around and chat despite three dead bodies lying in the woods. In fact, he'd said that it would be nice to meet up again in the future. A reunion each year to mark the date, sort of thing. If Frank could recall the details correctly, Sinclair had, unbelievably and somewhat hilariously, suggested perhaps going for a slap-up meal with us and his new young lady he'd recently hooked up with. That was before he'd said something about finding a dog-friendly pub so Alfie-Boy could join them. Bizarrely, based on Sinclair's protracted fable about fear of dogs – specifically a certain vicious Jack Russell that terrified the brute of a man when twelve, the moral of the story remaining unclear – during that half-hour or so in the woods, Sinclair and Alf seemed to have formed some kind of bond.

Eventually, after reminding Sinclair about his earlier comment regarding the boys in blue, they'd managed to escape the man when he shot off after saying something about needing to see a man about a dog. Which apparently translated to meeting a young lady.

Okay, back on the subject of eliminators and away from doggie-diners. Collinson and Harris were dead. However, another eliminator was on his way. Frank scrubbed his palms over his face, letting his hand rest on his chin as he contemplated how he and Jayne could avoid that rather tricky issue. Hartland had said he controlled his life and always would. A statement that suggested Frank and Jayne would spend the rest of their lives looking over their shoulders, expecting an assassin wielding a book of travellers' cheques and a Baretta to show up.

"First things first," Frank muttered, his mumblings drowned out by Jemma's hairdryer. Frank nodded and took a deep breath, building himself up to enact the plan he and Jayne had hatched last night.

Jemma clicked off her hairdryer and padded back to the spare room. Still brushing her hair, she halted at the threshold to offer Frank, who remained in position on the bed, his arms wrapped around his raised knees, one of her famous disapproving glares.

"You're awake then, I see. Had a skinful, did we? Feeling like shit this morning, I wouldn't mind guessing. Did you hear what I said? That idiot … your stupid mate, Dave. He's gone missing. He probably threw himself off Beachy Head, now the wally's come to his senses and realised what he's done."

"You mean cheating on Babs."

"Yes! He deserves everything coming to him. Anyway, you don't seem that concerned. I know he's a class one prat, but his parents are worried sick. Don't you have anything to say?"

"I do, actually. You've been having an affair with Tobias, which I suspect was just a lust thing. The thrill of it all, I guess. You're also about to embark on an affair with Rupert Barrington Scott, who you *are* in love with. You can be a full-on throuple as far as I'm concerned because I couldn't give a shit who you want to shag next."

Jemma's jaw sagged.

"Also, you're nearly four weeks pregnant with our child. So, whilst we're laying cards on the table, I'm leaving you for Jayne Hart. Yes, that's *Plain Jayne,* as you call her. And, just to be clear, she isn't plain. She's beautiful … looks and personality, and I'm in love with her. In fact, I've been in love with Jayne for nearly forty years." Frank paused and held his hand out to indicate Jemma shouldn't interrupt him when in full flow. "I know, in your world, that can't be possible because I'm only thirty. However, I know I've loved Jayne for that long, so that's all that matters. Now, I accept you are beautiful too, but only on the outside, skin deep, and most definitely not on the inside. As Jayne often referred to you throughout our life, you're a super bitch. Right, I've said it. Close your mouth. You look like you're catching flies."

Whilst sporting the expression Frank had intimated, Jemma halted her hair-brushing routine with her head poised to one side.

"Oh, one more thing ... I want a divorce."

44

2015

Her Finest Hour

When ensconced in Johnson's office, Hartland stood with his nose almost touching the glass door, leaving just enough space to raise his right hand, thus enabling him to chain-smoke whilst penetratingly studying the twitchy analysts as they beavered away at their keyboards.

Frank Stone, although not in the best of moods, travelled via the Eye twelve minutes ago. Hartland rechecked his watch. Now it was thirteen. He shifted his focus to Whitman, the woman pacing along the line of analysts with her hands clasped behind her back.

"Come on," he hissed through the exhaled smoke that swirled in a heavy fog before escaping the glass cube through the minuscule gaps around the edges of the door. "We should know by now."

Whitman glanced towards Hartland as she completed yet another circuit of the desks, offering a slight shake of her head to indicate no meaningful data had arrived. As Hartland raised his cigarette to his lips, an analyst, a young, fresh-faced lad in his twenties, who Hartland didn't know nor wanted to know, perched in front of a bank of screens at the far end of the room, raised his hand and called out. Whitman shimmied through the desks, making a beeline for him.

Hartland drew on his cigarette, willing himself to stay calm.

Whitman, palms flat on the desk, stared at the printer as it chugged out the line of data, her head following the pattern of a printer's head as she read the words that the machine thrashed out.

From his position behind the door, Hartland could only watch the exchange as Whitman muscled the junior analyst out of his seat and thrashed her fingers across the keyboard, her expression suggesting she wasn't best pleased with the data received. Following thirty seconds of keyboard pummelling, Whitman pushed away from the desk and slowly shook her head in disbelief. The ousted analyst raised his palms in a 'see-I-told-you-so' gesture, which Whitman appeared to ignore.

After shooting a look in Hartland's direction, the expression offered appearing to be a mixture of fear and bewilderment in equal measure, Whitman tore off the printed page and marched towards the glass cube.

Dragon style, Hartland fired out a plume of smoke from both nostrils before turning on his heels to march towards Johnson's desk. After retrieving the chair from where it had earlier come to rest against the filing cabinets, he poured himself an unhealthy measure of whisky in preparation for whatever Whitman was about to divulge. For sure, if the senior analyst wasn't the bearer of good news, more heads would roll. Despite Johnson's, and hers for that matter, claim that she was the best of the best, Whitman's would be the first to topple.

Hartland slugged the sizable measure of single malt in one before rolling the liquid around his mouth. After swallowing, he toyed with the cut-glass tumbler, which he held aloft as if inspecting the item to assess its antique credentials.

"Cut-glass, the technique, can be traced all the way back to the Bronze Age. However, the modern process, as in glasses such as these, dates back to the eighteenth century …" Hartland paused to check he had Whitman's attention as she hovered gauchely in front of the desk. "A time when drawing and quartering was still a method of execution for treason." Hartland altered his sightline to bring the senior analyst into focus. "You read books, don't you, Whitman? It's what you do for fun. So, I presume you know that little interesting fact, eh? A damn effective deterrent if you ask me, and it wouldn't go amiss in the modern era. What d'you think? Terrorists, murderers, rapists, and perhaps analysts who fail their employers."

Whitman, choosing not to indulge in the Commander-in-Chief's intimidating game, glanced at the door as Johnson entered.

"Sorry about that, sir. That burrito I had for lunch seems to be causing all sorts of …" Johnson paused as he detected the atmosphere. Although odourless and tasteless, like the gents where he'd just vacated, it wasn't pleasant.

Hartland sported his well-developed death stare whilst Whitman shifted awkwardly, her complexion suggesting an acute iron deficiency in her diet.

"Whitman and I were discussing the merits of capital punishment."

"Oh, hell." Johnson turned to face Whitman. "What's happened? What's come through?" He checked his watch. "Twenty past the hour. We must have the first run by now?"

Whitman solemnly nodded before allowing a cheeky smirk to brighten that dour demeanour.

Hartland and Johnson exchanged a look.

"Sir," she cleared her throat and stood to attention. "I have some good news and some ... not-so-good news. Also, some data that's debatable if it's good or bad, so somewhere on the medial. I won't state the fact that this is preliminary data because we've already done that this morning. So, which would you like first?"

"Bad. Let's get the bad out of the way."

"Okay. First up, David Bolton is dead. Still dead. He died a week earlier than last time. The 21st of September, to be precise. Secondly, Sinclair is still alive. Still living in Jamaica, still with a large brood of children. Collinson is also still dead."

"Bollocks. I'm struggling to grasp how there can be any good news," Hartland hissed through clenched teeth.

"Ah, well, my team are triple checking, but from what I can see, the data is solid. The *Monteagle Fault* is resolved. Is no more. Is defunct. Also, nearly all category changes from earlier have been expunged. And Harris, the unauthorised traveller, cannot be traced, thus suggesting he is also dead."

"Sorry?" blustered Johnson before oscillating looks between Whitman and a suitably stunned Commander-in-Chief. The latter appeared paralysed in position and was only hauled from his odd stupor when the cut-glass tumbler slipped through his fingers and collided with the ashtray, sending spent butts across the desk.

"I can confirm, to ninety-eight-point-four-three per cent, rounding to three decimal places, that the *Monteagle Fault* is solved. It never happens."

"Bugger me," Hartland muttered, before raking through his jacket pocket, searching out his cigarettes.

"How? If Bolton is dead, how the hell has the *Fault* been corrected?" Johnson asked before grabbing the whisky bottle and a glass, his hand shaking as he poured.

The two men swapped the bottle and cigarettes without verbal exchange. Both, now with a large whisky in one hand and a cigarette in the other, studied Whitman as if the woman had morphed into some disturbing killer fungus multiplying at an alarming rate in a Petri dish.

"It's a complete mystery." Whitman raised her palms, a gesture borrowed from her analyst, who'd received the data.

Hartland gesticulated with his cigarette, stabbing the air between him and Whitman. "What was that percentage, again?"

Whitman glanced through the glass at her team, who stood by their monitors with their thumbs up. All grinning akin to a clowder of moggies with their paws in Devon's finest or, perhaps more aptly, a gang of condemned prisoners receiving an eleventh-hour reprieve from the gallows.

"It *was* ninety-eight-point-four-three. *Now*, it's one hundred per cent. A certainty. Sir, our mission is a complete success."

"My mission, Whitman. Mine. As you so eloquently informed me earlier, they are all *my* missions," Hartland chuckled whilst swinging his legs up and thumping the heels of his Oxford brogues on top of the desk. "Johnson, crack out the cigars. The good ones."

"Absolutely, sir."

"That's all, Whitman. You can let your team know they will all see the sunrise."

"Yes, sir."

"Oh, before you go. What was the middling info?"

"Sir?" Whitman halted and turned as she grabbed the door handle.

"You said there was bad, good, and data that fell somewhere in between."

"Medial. The term is usually used when describing the body. For example, the middle toe is located at the medial side of the foot. I just like the word … it's one of my personal favourites. Comes from the Latin phrase mediālis."

Hartland raised an eyebrow. "Drawing and quartering is always at my disposal, if I so wish, Whitman. You'll do well to remember that."

"Err … yes, sir. The medial data. Jayne Stone, née Hart, is alive and well, as are her four daughters and grandchildren. Her husband, Frank Stone, is again Sir Frank Stone. As you said, sir … *your* operation was a complete success."

Hartland's expression didn't change.

"Good morning to you, sir," she nodded to both men before skipping from the office to be greeted with a cacophony of raucous cheering.

45

2005

Never Gonna Give You Up

"Mr Denton? Miss Denton?"

Phillipa and Tom, after exiting the hotel with their overnight bags and mild-ish hangovers in tow, paused on the pavement side of the revolving doors when hearing their names being called.

The twins, now in their mid-twenties, after enjoying an evening with their parents in London to celebrate their father's birthday, and following an early breakfast, decided to head home and leave their parents to enjoy their day together. Barbara Denton had the day all planned out with an afternoon of shopping, which, rather bizarrely, her husband also enjoyed, followed by an early evening supper at The Ivy.

A day that should turn into a nightmare and become the catalyst that would lead to Barbara ending up potless and living in a B&B within less than ten years. To start with, Phillipa and Tom were soon about to die when suicide bombers detonate three bombs on the London Underground, followed up some years later when her husband made the credulous decision to invest in Bitcoin, resulting in the loss of their entire wealth and a heart attack which will kill Stephen.

Fortunately, the man calling their names would prevent any of those disasters, and the Denton family would be oblivious to what should have happened.

"Sorry, were you calling me?" Tom asked the man wearing a peaked cap and a pair of those mirror-effect sunglasses.

"Yes, sir. I take it you are Phillipa and Tom Denton?"

Philli, as she preferred to be called, frowned at her brother as Tom nodded in reply.

"Okay. I have a car waiting for you to take you back to Paddington Station."

"Oh, sorry, there must be some mistake. We didn't order a cab. We're going to jump on the Tube."

"Your parents organised it. I'm here to take you both as they asked. I've already been paid, so you might as well hop in." The driver, or more chauffeur, going by the suit and cap, pointed to the large black Mercedes parked not a few feet along the kerb.

"Really?" Tom quizzed, appearing a smidge surprised.

Sunglasses man stepped forward and whispered. "Your father, Stephen Denton, organised it. I normally chauffeur government ministers about, but he asked me to do him a favour and ferry you two back to the station to save you hauling your suitcases on the Tube."

"Oh, fab," grinned Philli.

"Shall I?" Sunglasses man pointed to their suitcases, gesturing to take them. "The car's open. Hop in, and I'll chuck your cases in the boot. I'll have you back to Paddington in a jiffy."

Although the journey on the London Underground would have probably been quicker, based on the fact the morning rush hour through Central London was pretty much gridlocked, the twins relaxed in the back seat, chatting about a barbeque party Tom and his girlfriend were planning for the weekend. Only when the driver pulled up outside the station did they again engage in a conversation with him as he settled their bags on the pavement after hauling them from the boot.

"Thanks very much." Tom thumbed out a tenner from his wallet to offer as a tip.

"Oh, no. I can assure you that really isn't necessary." The driver held up his palm to decline the offer before reaching into his jacket pocket to extract an envelope and hand it to Tom. "I wonder, could I ask a small favour of you? I was supposed to hand this to your father earlier, but I clean forgot. I know it's an imposition, but could you pass it on for me?"

Tom, and Philli by way of nudging her head by her brother's shoulder, read the front of the envelope, which stated their father's name, with the words urgent, private and confidential underlined beneath.

"Oh, okay. Sure."

"You won't forget?"

"No, that's fine," Tom tapped the envelope on his forehead. "Got a memory like an elephant, me."

"Thanks, I appreciate it. Enjoy your trip." The amenable chauffeur doffed his cap before scooting around to the driver's door and offering a wave.

"How odd," mumbled Philli, nodding thanks to her brother when he grabbed her case as well as his own.

"Yeah, I expect it's just something to do with his work."

"No, I mean Dad organising a car for us."

"Oh, yeah, it is a bit. Come on, let's grab a coffee. We've got at least twenty minutes before our train departs."

"Okay," Philli paused, turned and scanned the street. "Blimey, can you hear all those sirens? Something must have happened."

"It's London. There's always something happening."

"Hmmm. I hope Mum and Dad are okay."

"Course they are. Come on, I'm gonna need a Venti Americano to shift this hangover."

"Oh, excuse me. My fault. I was rushing. I do apologise … I'm a bit of a calamity, I'm afraid. It's a miracle if I can get through London without sustaining enough bruises to turn me black and blue."

Philli snorted a laugh as she and the forty-something woman performed that back-and-forth motion when trying to pass each other.

"Oh, sorry," the woman, who Philli realised was probably in her fifties but had pegged for some posh socialite going by the designer clothes, Hermès handbag, and figure that took time, money, and determination to achieve, stated as she stepped back. "Please, after you."

Philli offered a tight smile and joined her brother a few feet further along, who appeared to be gawping at the woman who trotted down the steps towards the Mercedes still parked at the entrance.

"Err, Tom. She's old enough to be your mother!"

"Oh," he replied with an exaggerated grin.

"Men! Christ, come on, you old letch."

"Hey, less of the old, if you don't mind," he sniggered as Philli linked arms with him before they strode towards the station concourse.

The woman sporting the Hermès bag opened the passenger door of the Mercedes before elegantly slipping onto the passenger seat.

~

"Where to, M'Lady," Sunglasses man asked.

"Really? Those sunglasses look ridiculous," I chortled. "You look like George Michael, who's about to bash out a rendition of *Bad Boys*. Talking of which, did you see that Tom giving me the once up and down?"

"The man's clearly got excellent taste."

"Hmmm." I playfully thumped his arm and smirked. "That hat isn't much better. You look like Johnny Morris or Blakey."

"I needed to have a credible disguise. I'm famous, you know."

"Minor celeb, my darling. D-list, at best."

"I quite enjoyed being a chauffeur for the day. Not a bad little job, you know."

"Hmmm. I'm sure. When you eventually retire, perhaps you can start a taxi firm, ferrying around all those day-trippers from Cromer back and forth along the coast."

"Oh, no. Perish the thought."

"Now, I take it all went as planned, Mr Stone?"

"Sir Frank Stone, if you don't mind?"

"Not yet. You have a couple more years before our Queen taps that sword on your shoulder. Then I will be Lady Stone."

"Yes, M'Lady," Frank stated in Parker's voice.

"That's better," I giggled. "So, all went as planned, then?"

"It did. Part one of Operation Save Barbara Denton is complete."

"And part two?"

"Tom—"

"The letch."

"The very same. He has the letter, and I'm sure he'll pass it on to his father."

"Okay, let's just hope Stephen heeds the warning and doesn't think it's written by some crank."

"Me, a crank?"

I shrugged, sticking my tongue into my cheek before offering my husband a whimsical smirk.

"Charming. You can go off people, you know?"

"You can't go off me. It's written in the future. We are together forever, to quote Mr Astley."

"Until 2015."

"Oh, don't mention that! I've lived the last sixty-odd years with you over two lives. Come 2015, I can't go through that again."

"Agreed. I'm never going near that Hartland bloke again."

"Yes, well, this time, I'm happy to just grow old together and avoid time-travel."

Frank took my hand in his, giving it a comforting squeeze.

"Frank?"

"Uh-huh."

"We won't get in trouble, will we? Y'know … for altering the future. We've always played by the rules 'til now."

"God, I hope not. But we agreed. We need to save Barbara."

"I feel awful about those people who will die today."

"I know." Frank checked his watch. "I think it's already happened. Those bombs went off during rush hour."

On that sombre note, Frank pulled away from the kerb, heading out of London to our Sheringham home.

"You think Alf was right about what he said?" I broke the silence after a few minutes.

"About Andrew?"

"Yes."

"I think he was. Alfie-Boy had the inside track to the future. He knew that the bombing of Ten Downing Street wouldn't happen."

"Why, though? What could have changed that stopped it? According to that supercilious git, Hartland, Dave Bolton had to stay alive. Christ, what would I give to slap that man?"

Frank side-eyed me and smirked. "I'd like to see you give that man a slap."

"Hmmm. But, as I said, you believe Alf?"

"I do."

After the incident in Fairfield Woods, and following intensive interrogation of my scruffy mutt, Alfie-Boy had been quite clear about Andrew's safety when employing those chop-licking and head-bowing routines, his yes and no gestures, confirming that the terror group led by Jolene Horsley wouldn't bomb the seat of our government.

Although we hadn't met her, Jolene was a five-year-old enjoying primary school, living with her mother, Sarah, and stepfather, Giles Horsley. Whether she would embark on a career of terrorism but just fail in her attempt to disrupt democracy, who knew?

Well, actually, Alfie-Boy knew, we think. In fact, my scruffy mutt had been adamant about changes to future events. That Saturday after the talkative Sinclair killed Dave – the day *my* Frank turned up, better late than never, although the relief was palpable on my part and not to mention the news that saved my life, as in Alf could never ride shotgun or join me on any road trips in the future – Alf had got into a bit of a tizzy before getting the right-old hump with our continued interrogation. After rolling his eyes at us, he'd trotted off in a huff to curl up in his basket.

The trouble was, Alf could indicate yes or no, confirming our daughters would be born, Andrew would be safe, the CYA had decided not to despatch another eliminator despite *my* Frank overhearing The Hooded Claw state he would, etcetera, etcetera. However, frustratingly, Alfie-Boy couldn't add any meat to the bones, no pun intended, regarding the whys to said events happening or not in the case of the bombing and the fourth eliminator being dispatched.

"D'you want to double-check? Ask him again?" Frank enquired as he glided the Mercedes to a halt at a set of traffic lights.

"Yes," I nodded. "It's been quite a while since we've seen him. Let's pay Alfie-Boy a visit and see what he's got to say for himself."

"Not much, I would imagine," Frank chuckled before performing a U-turn at the lights to head towards Fairfield.

"No, I know. But it will be nice. As I said, it's been ages since we've seen him. I do miss Alfie-Boy, y'know."

"Apart from his farting."

"Agreed, apart from his farts."

46

Blink of her Eye

"Hello Alfie-Boy, how you diddling?" I asked, my head resting on Frank's shoulder as we held each other close.

Alf didn't reply.

"Closed questions only, remember?"

"Oh, God, you'd think I would remember that, wouldn't you?"

"Ask him again."

"Alfie-Boy, are you alright? Are they treating you properly?"

"That's two questions. What if he has two different answers?"

"Oh."

"Alf, are you alright? I miss you."

"I miss you too, old buddy," Frank added.

"He didn't lick his chops."

"He might have. We just can't see."

After letting go of Frank's arm, I placed my palms on my thighs and peered down at the gravestone. The gold lettering was still bright and vibrant as had been my long-departed, desperately missed, beer-swilling, farting, scruffy mutt.

Wood is the traditional gift to mark a fifth wedding anniversary. Not that most people know that, but our neighbour, a retired carpenter, produced a rather splendid, ornate keepsake box as a gift for ours. A lovely gesture which, that morning, sadly, we found just the right use for. The marquetry inlay, stating *'Jayne and Frank – Special Keepsakes'*, seemed appropriate. Unfortunately for Frank and me, that day was sullied when we found Alf peacefully 'sleeping' when curled up in his basket. Fifteen years old, a miracle of the canine world, Alfie-Boy had departed for a better place. Canine heaven if such a place existed.

We were heartbroken, as was Sharon, who, at nearly five, couldn't understand the concept that Alfie-Boy wasn't going to wake any time soon despite her cuddling and pleading for him to do so.

Talking of our eldest, I still endured that epic labour. Despite suggesting Frank should perhaps come up with something better than uttering 'well done' when Sharon eventually popped her head out, he repeated history.

Men!

But I did love him.

It would be fair to say we followed the path of my first life, Frank's second, to the letter, with only a few notable exceptions. Frank didn't break the git's jaw who pinched my bottom in that seedy nightclub in Benidorm. That said, the terrified man was under no illusion of what would happen if he didn't leave the club immediately. Also, I swerved the kebab shop, thus negating the need to place my head in the toilet for a couple of days. You remember me mentioning that ill-fated school sports day when Helen bawled her eyes out and broke my heart? Well, she didn't this time. In fact, she banged on for weeks about how her brilliant mum, yours truly, came first in the parents' race, firmly consigning her comments about the Princess of Wales into another life. An existence that now didn't happen. Unfortunately, the day from hell that preceded the bottle of Riesling in the greenhouse repeated. It seemed a day my girls were hell-bent on ensuring their mother suffered.

The first time Alf died, when put down under Mother's instruction, the precise year I couldn't say, Alf was presumably cremated and his ashes tossed into the bin. This time, cremation was again our chosen method, but with his ashes in that keepsake box buried below the headstone. The simple inscription said it all.

Alfie-Boy

A special friend who we owe our lives to

Forever in our hearts

Although before we arrived at the pet cemetery in Fairfield, we knew Alf wasn't going to answer the question about Andrew's future, which he'd answered many times, usually accompanied by a roll of his eyes, visiting his final resting place was important. An event we always made a special effort and diarised on the calendar stuck to the fridge. Today was an extra, an inbetweenie if you like.

I leaned forward to transfer a kiss to my fingers and onto Alf's headstone before re-asking the question that Alf became so frustrated by.

"Alfie-Boy, I know this annoys you so, probably because we keep asking, but you're quite certain that bombing never happens and Andrew is safe in the future?" I turned to Frank and winced. "Silly, really, talking to a headstone."

"Hmmm, I think he just licked his chops like he did the million-odd times we've asked him before."

"I'm sure you're right, but I wish I knew why."

"I can probably shed some light on that for you, Mrs Stone, soon to be Lady Stone."

The hairs on my neck tingled as Frank and I swivelled around, stumbling back and grabbing each other's hands as the man who spoke approached.

Frank had always wanted to witness the action I took and, for many years, I'd dreamt of doing it. With fortitude dragged up from somewhere, despite what faced us, I slapped the man's cheek with such ferocity the echo boomeranged across the open space, bouncing off the gravestones of other beloved and missed pets.

Douglas Hartland rubbed his cheek and grinned.

"I suppose I deserved that. Mrs Stone, please accept my apologies for sending you through time. A wholly regrettable incident for which my team and I are truly sorry."

"Hmm, you bastard, I hate you," I spat, stamping my feet for good measure.

"Most do," he chortled. "Story of my life, I'm afraid. I was never the popular boy at school. My tedious wife detests me, feeling's mutual, and my employees are rightfully terrified of me."

"How come you're here?" Frank mumbled, a question to The Hooded Claw as much as a rhetorical one going by my husband's vacant expression.

"Yes, complicated, isn't it? However, how I move through time is not up for today's discussion."

Frank and I side-eyed each other. Like Frank, I feared our decision this morning to launch Operation Save Barbara Denton had already, and rather swiftly, caught up with us.

"Ah, you know, don't you?" he chuckled. "Correct. You have made the cardinal sin, as in tinkering with time."

"Sorry? But I have no idea—"

"Frank," Hartland interrupted, widened his arms and leaned back as if to suggest playing the innocent wasn't going to cut the mustard.

"What happens now?" Frank, now one pace closer to Hartland, aggressively jabbed a finger in his face. "As God's my witness, I'll kill you before you hurt Jayne or my family."

"Relax, my good man. I'm here to warn you, nothing more. I'll accept your little interference today because it has minimal bearing on the future. Stephen Denton, although sceptical, will believe your little note, so that pans out nicely for Barbara. Good sort, Stephen, you know. We're members of the same club."

"Oh."

"Now, you do seem obsessed with that question you keep boring poor Alf with."

"How d'you know my dog? Dead dog, I mean."

"First things first. The *Monteagle Fault* is satisfactorily resolved. The terror attack on Number Ten will not happen. Well, that specific one led by Jolene Horsley, that is. I'm sure there will be others that creep out of the woodwork as time drifts by. And threats like that will certainly increase as successive governments become more inept. The world is full of maniacs with some axe to grind, is it not, eh?"

"How come? You said Dave Bolton had to stay alive."

"Yes, well, funny how that one panned out in the end. A twist of fate, you could say. Now, you remember Kenny Harris?"

Frank and I nodded in unison. The image of his lifeless form whilst sprawled out in Fairfield Woods after the chatty Sinclair had fired a nine-millimetre slug between his eyes came spinning back into my mind.

"Yes, as I'm sure you're fully aware, Mr Harris was an unauthorised traveller, which I can assure you is not something that occurs too often. We pride ourselves at the CYA on delivering well-drilled, military-styled operations—"

I blew a rather uncouth raspberry.

As if to concur with my assessment of Hartland's statement, someone farted. It wasn't me, and Frank wasn't the sort. Also, although Hartland was many things, he didn't seem the sort either. I glanced at Alf's grave, raising my eyebrows.

"Surely not," I muttered.

"Mrs Stone, I accept there have been some minor difficulties on the odd, rare occasion."

I responded in a similar fashion before shooting a look at Alf's grave, half expecting to hear my dead dog blow off. I shook my head at the ridiculous thought.

"So, as I was saying. Mr Sinclair, in a rather fortunate twist of fate, when in those woods that evening back in '79, shot dead the man who would in the future make the explosive device that Jolene and her gang used to blow up Ten Downing Street."

Frank and I started catching flies.

"Yes, you see, Kenny Harris, an explosives expert, would, if alive, produce that infamous bomb. Now, because the man is no longer with us, and Jolene will fail to enlist an individual with the right skill set to produce a stable bomb, Barbara's granddaughter will take it upon herself to build the device. I presume she'll watch some YouTube training video that Al Qaeda or some other terrorist organisation will probably post in the future. Anyway, the woman will screw up, blow herself, her three co-conspirators, and some squalid back street public house in Islington to smithereens the day before she would have killed the PM, the Cabinet, the tea lady, two Cabinet secretaries, two footmen, and of course, Bubbles, the Chief Mouser to the Cabinet Office."

"Alf knew this about Kenny Harris the day he walked into Frank's office, didn't he?" I asked Frank, turning to glance quizzically at Alf's headstone.

When I turned around, Hartland was already a few yards away, sauntering along the path towards the car park. He turned and raised a finger Columbo style.

"Ah, how remiss of me," Hartland chuckled as he strode back towards us.

"What now?" I spat, thumping my palms on my hips. Despite now understanding what Frank and I had mulled over for the best part of a quarter of a century, I didn't fancy spending any more time in Hartland's company.

"Regarding meddling with time. As I said, I'm prepared to let your little Save Barbara Denton operation go without taking punitive action against you both. However, if you have plans to change Jolene's future, the consequences will be dire. Unfortunately, she must continue on her life path and blow herself, along with her co-conspirators, into unidentifiable lumps of flesh across a rather deplorable, squalid, undesirable part of our great capital."

"Why?" I asked, detecting Frank squeeze my hand, that act suggesting I should temper my anger. Not that we had such plans, but I felt the need to ask why this evil git desired poor Jolene to continue on her ill-chosen life path.

"Two reasons. Because if you intervene, I will have to have you eliminated, and secondly ..." he paused and grinned. "Because, Lady Stone, I say so."

"You are an evil, supercilious, rotten, totally despicable man!" For the second time, I slapped the man's cheek.

"I'm pretty sure Alfie-Boy would have licked his chops to concur with that statement," Frank chuckled when glancing back at Alf's grave.

I'm not what you would call the slapping type. Okay, I accept I'd delivered two hearty wallops within as many minutes. However, Frank was right. Alfie-Boy would have agreed with me. Anyway, the man deserved it. Whilst Hartland attempted to rub my finger marks off his glowing cheek, I turned my back to him and took hold of Frank's hand before addressing Alf's headstone.

"You agree, don't you, Alfie-Boy?"

The image of Alf licking his chops came to mind as we turned around, only to find ourselves alone. In the blink of an eye, The Hooded Claw, that evil Sylvester Sneekly, the villain of villains, had swished his metaphorical vampiric cloak and disappeared.

"Christ, Frank, where the hell did he go?"

"I think you just said it."

"Sorry?"

"Hell. Back where the man came from in the first place."

Whether caused by the gentle breeze which rustled the leaves of the giant oaks that encircled the graves on this glorious summer morning or due to some other unexplainable phenomenon that I didn't believe in, I sensed we weren't alone.

Now, despite the events of a quarter of a century ago regarding time-travel, I still deferred to my long-held belief in the sciences. Black and white, no grey areas or any of that claptrap about unexplained phenomena caused by those of the spirit persuasion. However, if I didn't know better, I would say I was experiencing some form of extrasensory perception.

As we stood with our backs to Alfie-Boy's final resting place and, despite my beliefs that suggested it wasn't possible, I detected a wheezy snicker emanating from somewhere close behind.

~

What's next?

Frank and Jayne will return in early 2025. As for Alfie-Boy, well, wait and see! My eleventh book, the fifth in the Jason Series, Borrowed Time, will be published in the summer of 2024. While you wait, perhaps check out my other books. There are three series … I hope you enjoy them.

Can you help?

I hope you enjoyed this book. Could I ask for a small favour? Can I invite you to leave a rating or review on Amazon? Just a few words will help other readers discover my books. Probably the best way to support authors you like, and I'll hugely appreciate it.

Free book for you

For more information and to sign up for updates about new releases, please drop onto my website, where you'll get instant access to your FREE eBook – Beyond his Time.

When you sign up, you get a no-spam promise from Adrian, and you can unsubscribe at any time.

You can also find my Facebook page and follow me on Amazon – or, hey, why not all three?

Adriancousins.co.uk

Facebook.com/Adrian Cousins Author

Author's note

I thought it only right to mention Pinkie's somewhat outdated attitudes. Unfortunately, the talkative fella came from an era when perhaps language wasn't so inclusive and, as he physically matured during his first life, those attitudes didn't.

However, I've heard on the grapevine that Femi, his lovely wife, recognising the man essentially had a good heart, managed to educate and drag Pinkie into the twenty-first century.

Now, he's a well-respected member of the Kingston community, where he can be found entertaining his plethora of friends with his tales and predictions of the future.

Also, despite his previous xenophobic tendencies, Pinkie and his new bestie, Hamish, can usually be found propping up one of the many bars in and around Beat Street.

Pinkie has forgiven Hamish for his compatriots' trashing of Wembley, and Hamish has likewise forgiven Pinkie's ancestors for Culloden.

Although we haven't eradicated racism, sexism, and misogynistic attitudes, thankfully, society has improved over the last forty years – let's hope education does finally rid the world of these abominations. So, to that end, I hope Pinkie's outdated attitude didn't offend you because that was not my intention.

Books by Adrian Cousins

The Jason Apsley Series

Jason Apsley's Second Chance

Ahead of his Time

Force of Time

Calling Time

Beyond his Time

<u>Deana – Demon or Diva Series</u>

<u>It's Payback Time</u>

<u>Death Becomes Them</u>

<u>Dead Goode</u>

<u>Deana – Demon or Diva Series Boxset</u>

<u>The Frank Stone Series</u>

<u>Eye of Time</u>

<u>Blink of her Eye</u>

Acknowledgements

Thank you to my Beta readers – your input and feedback is invaluable.

Adele Walpole

Brenda Bennett

Tracy Fisher

Patrick Walpole

And, of course, I'm so grateful to Sian Phillips, my editor, who makes everything come together.

Printed in Dunstable, United Kingdom